THE DRAGON SEA CHRONICLES
The Three Book Series

Brian Ference
Chris Turner

Copyright © 2018 by Cave Creek Publishing, LLC

All rights reserved. No part of this publication may be reproduced, distributed, or transmitted in any form or by any means, including photocopying, recording, or other electronic or mechanical methods, or by any information storage and retrieval system without the prior written permission of the publisher, except in the case of very brief quotations embodied in critical reviews and certain other noncommercial uses permitted by copyright law.

This is a work of fiction. Names, characters, businesses, places, events, and incidents either are the products of the author's imagination or used in a fictitious manner. Any resemblance to actual persons, living or dead, or actual events is purely coincidental.

ISBN: 9781791671297

TABLE OF CONTENTS

DRAGONCLAW DARE 1

THE RACE 1

FEASTING 14

SACRED ISLE 22

THE PIRATES 35

CAPTAIN SERLE 46

PIRATE COVE 53

TRAINING 67

A KISS 77

THE TRIALS 88

THE FIRE CORAL 99

DRAGON SEA: MAGE REBORN 110

THE SOARING CUTLASS 110

THE SEA SERPENT 119

KRATON 130

BOWELS OF THE VOLCANO 139

FREEDOM 151

AGRIPPA 161

A MAGE'S APPRENTICE 179

VALKYRIE	192
YOUNG SERPENT	207
CYRUS	218
THREE SISTERS' ISLES	230
JACE	241
THE DRAGON PENS	255
DRAGON BREAKING	271
WINGED COMBAT	282
BORMOTH	291
A MAGE'S PRISON	302
ESCAPE	321
ALLIANCE	329
THE CLUTCH	342
APPROACHING DOOM	362
EPILOGUE	372
DRAGON MAGE: UPRISING	378
A PIRATE RAID	378
CAPE SPEAR	387
REBIRTH	397
THE ROOKERY	410
ARCHITUTHIS	419

DENDROK	435
PACTS WITH THE WOLF	445
VALKYRIE ISLAND	459
SOLARICUS	473
THE COVE	493
DARKTHORN ISLE	512
A BOLD PLAN	525
SABOTAGE	533
DEADMAN'S HOLD	545
SKULLDUGGERY AT SEA	554
CURAKEE	567
SACRIFICE	577
A SEED IS SOWN	590
VISILEE	599
NAMELESS ISLE	610
NEW BEGINNINGS	620
EPILOGUE	626
SAMPLE CHAPTERS	628
THE WOLF OF DORIAN GRAY	631
THE CRIME SCENE	636
CURSE OF THE KRAKEN	640

I : LORE OF THE ANCIENTS 640

ABOUT THE AUTHORS 647

OTHER BOOKS 648

Map of the Dragon Sea

DRAGONCLAW DARE

Chapter 1.

THE RACE

The salt spray whipped across Darek's tanned arms as he pulled fast on the line, ducking the boom as it swung across the deck. His twenty-foot sloop tacked west into the wind during the race of his life. Two Dolphins' Rock was only a mile to starboard; the sleek hull knifed through the waves like a flying-fish dodging a barracuda. His eyes stayed glued to the twin grey rocks, shaped like dolphins poking up over the swells. The trials for the annual Dragonclaw race were in full swing.

The race was the most significant event in the entire Red Claw Islands. A colorful festival rich with cheer, days of feasting, and fat purses for the winners was high on Darek's list, now that he was of age. The event occupied the first few weeks of the Harvest Moon before the fall changeover. Open to all challengers, the event was relished by many, and anticipated by all.

Around Reeler's Reef Darek's craft sped. The sea was choppy this morning, the waves defiant and relentless. Purple clouds rode the eastern horizon in the region the islanders called the 'Serpent's Deep'. The conditions were challenging, but Darek was up for it.

The circuit looped past Mystery Isle, over to Two Dolphins' Rock and back to Cape Spear and the busy horseshoe-shaped harbor on Swordfish Island. The boats dodged each other and bucked the waves, each sailor set on finishing first. All of Cape Spear was about to see who the best competitors were.

Darek snatched a quick look back. The line of sailboats gaining on him was a surprise. He would have been well in the lead but for his two friends, Vinz and Grame. His other rivals, Clara and Bralig, were not far behind, their boats polished, lacquered, with whale hide covering their outer hulls. But Darek didn't care; he was too caught up in the thrill of the race.

Darek's fingers itched for the prize as he gripped the tiller. The ocean spray cooled the fire in his limbs as he glided over the swells, navigating like a seal. Sailing was his passion; it had been since he was a small boy. His skill at reading the winds was the envy of all his friends. Even his rivals respected his sailing skills.

A gray boat with lime green sails tried to turn too sharply and Darek heard a thin cry over the wind as the vessel tipped over, heeling in a breaking wave. The round-bottomed hull bellied up. Over it went, its sails dunking into the brine.

Darek winced. Tough break. His fate could have followed that of the sailor's. Some of the ships had no keels, and while sailing lighter and sometimes faster, they were disasters waiting to happen.

Darek edged behind Vinz's boat, with its blue sail and shiny silver cleats. He saw his friend's teeth flash, heard him bellow a roar above the sloshing waves, the blue spray stinging his eyes. Darek whooped with delight as he edged past Vinz and swept around the gleaming two dolphin-shaped rocks which blazed in the noonday sun.

Vinz shook a fist at him. Darek could only chuckle.

The judges, anchored a furlong away in their boats, took note of the competitors' maneuvers past the rocks. They had inspected each vessel and ensured the rules were obeyed. Any type of divergence from the rules was illegal—including the throwing of firebombs doused in oil, the sending out of smoke to obscure the turns, or any other trick that would give a sailor an advantage. This year's prize was a sleek, new runner craft and a place in Lared the chief's fleet. The runner-up would receive a similar boat built last year.

Rounding the Dolphin Rocks, Darek veered his boat downwind. The boom swung back and he quickly leaned to port. Shifting his sail with ease, he charted a path that would cut across the water in the shortest time possible. If the wind didn't change, this final leg would be a breeze. He'd have to sail by the lee for some of the time, but his mind was set on a glorious finish.

Only a few leagues remained to Cape Spear. The last part of the tryouts would be downwind and Darek looked for ways to sail with the tide. Grame caught up to the pack and he and Bralig were in close pursuit, searching for ways to edge him out. Bralig had caught a strong wind and his bow now slammed into Darek's stern, knocking him off course. Darek cursed, his boat spinning about, losing ground, but he trimmed his sails, recovered swiftly and surged ahead once more. Vinz and Grame looked on in amazement.

Of the fifty some odd boats, only a few would be selected for the final race. All of the qualifiers would receive high-quality fishing gear, rods and reels made by the finest craftsmen in the town, including master Dasio himself. Darek's family was poor. What he needed was that boat. The tackle gear was just a bonus. His father, Jace, hated sailing and had long given up hope that Darek could ever make a life for himself at sea. His mother had turned her back on him and Jace, taken up with Raithan, a captain of the rival Black Claw Clan. With a new sailboat, he could leave all this behind and go wherever he wanted. He could explore the uncharted places, the smaller isles, hunt for treasure or new tropical fish, dive in the lagoons. The possibilities made his heart soar with anticipation.

He flung the daydream from his mind. That distraction had cost him a beat, and now the other boats were gaining on him. The bold red and white sail of Clara's ship bellied to the wind. She had skill, and confidence. Of anybody, he wished her to qualify—not only for her good looks and her hourglass figure and gorgeous curls—but also because he respected her as a sailor. He wouldn't even mind seeing Vinz and Grame qualify, since he had essentially taught them everything they knew. He chose to interpret their ingratitude as that which might be expected from prideful students bent on surpassing their teacher.

The competitors weaved their way downwind, a mile parallel from the shore. All continued to look to either side for the next major wave to crest and surf. To maximize speed, boats often sailed by the lee where the airflow over the sail reversed from its usual direction and traveled to the luff of the sail.

His old rival, Bralig, was creeping up fast. That gull-eater! How could he get so much speed out of that boat?

Darek heard the harsh crack of palm wood on his hull. He turned. "Back off, you stupid oaf!"

An illegal maneuver, at the least, Bralig had deliberately rammed his stern in an attempt to unnerve him. But they had sailed past any judges and Bralig took another opportunity to bump his craft.

"I said, watch it!" Darek cried. He whipped back his slick, black hair and glared at his opponent.

Bralig's sneer lashed over the choppy spray. "What's the matter? Can't take it? Maybe I should rub your nose in the mud again."

Bitter memories from his boyhood hit Darek. Bralig, the bigger and meaner, had once terrorized Darek when they were fingerlings. Darek was easy prey then, but not now, with his budding frame and wiry leanness—and certainly not out on the sea.

Darek ground his teeth. "You asked for it."

He swung his boat in at a daring angle, trimming the sail for extra speed. The vessels just brushed each other. As Darek passed, he heard the grating of wood as his ship's keel lifted half out the water, raking across Bralig's rudder. A torturous scrape rose above the roar of the wind and Bralig tried to turn away, but instead, his sailboat spun about in circles, unable to steer itself.

Gaining vital seaway, Clara seized the moment and snuck in between Grame and Vinz, giving the two a cheeky high sign.

Bralig's curses rained down on the water like a passing squall.

Darek's chuckles ran short when the girl's ship outflanked his and whispered by, her sails rippling in a stiff new breeze. Codfish, she was good!

Vinz and Grame's boats closed the gap, both youths laughing at Bralig's floundering craft as Clara's sleek boat slipped by them all. Grame gave Darek the thumbs up as he cut through the wake of the leaders.

Darek shook his head in grim acceptance—a rueful smile crept in while he kept his eyes focused on the dark chop ahead. It would be a dash to the finish.

Darek crouched, pulled hard on the boom yards and angled his ship toward the sandy shore of Cape Spear and Old Town's harbor.

The crowd on the docks cheered as the first boats glided into the harbor. Clara had won by the smallest of margins, with Darek coming in a close second. Village punters ranged out in small skiffs to moor the incoming boats. The sodden sailors, stiff-legged and exhausted, stepped onto the dock, their brows and arms gleaming with spent energy. Darek's face could not hide his disappointment at his second-place finish. But he nodded in recognition of Clara's win as she sauntered between well-wishers. Hers was a clean win, unlike what Bralig had tried to do. Vinz and Grame hauled in soon after. Others brought up the rear and knew with glum certainty that they would not be part of the final race.

Wreaths were to be presented and rounds of grog to be quaffed, while cries of hangers-on echoed over the harbor, eager to curry favor with the victors. Darek looked on with waning interest.

His gaze traveled up the hills behind the public square to the stone houses with wooden roofs fanning up the slopes. Low clouds brewed, presaging rain. Darek hoped the foul weather would hold off, at least until after the feast.

Two of his closest friends, crowded around, pounding him on the back. "Way to go, Darek! You're like a golden starfish, finally climbed up all the way to the top of the reef."

"Even if only to be swept away by the tide," the other said.

"What does that even mean?" said the first with a mock grin, "But yeah, good show." He raised his pudgy hand. The second, gangly and fair-haired, stood in direct contrast to the first, who was short and lumpy, and even more so to Darek, who stood a half a head higher, pensive, lean, tall and muscular with a crop of long, black hair.

Darek nodded, inclined his head, but his eyes darted in rueful deference toward Clara.

The Red Claw Clan chief approached with a formal stride, a smile carved on his rugged face. His grey-gold curls shone with health and he reached out a firm, sea-worn hand.

"You've done well, Clara. Darek. Be proud. You've shown your mettle."

His wife, queen of the Red Claw Clan, dipped her head in respectful tribute. "You're to be contenders for next week's race. Both of you will go far in this world and 'tis an honor and joy to receive such talented people."

Darek bowed low. Clara curtsied.

The venerated judge affixed the ceremonial wreaths upon Clara's and Darek's heads. The middle-aged man muttered stern words and Darek reflected sourly on how he had lost ground because of Bralig's meddling.

Clara looked on with humble interest and leveled Darek a flirtatious challenge. Darek's blood quickened. She was not looking too shabby in her skin-tight leather garb with her sandy curls, trim waist, and beautiful face.

Vinz and Grame followed in their wake, somewhat less enthused, and accepted their honorable mentions in glum unison.

The damaged boats were soon towed in. One youth had overreached his competence and spun out on a rogue wave. These dinghies without keels were tippy and required expert control even on calm days. Bralig's face was rainbow-fish red and he scrambled out of the tow vessel and stormed up the dock, pointing an accusing finger at Darek. "Disqualify this mollusk! He wrecked my boat."

Darek laughed and shook his head. "You're mad, Bralig. You had the whole sea to yourself, and yet you came charging in at me like a bull shark. Way too close—that's against the rules. You've only yourself to blame." He shrugged off his rising anger, but his fists knotted, as a dozen old humiliations from the schoolyard came to mind. "Not my fault if you got in my way."

"That's eel-rot!" Bralig sputtered. "Your slag of a boat got in my way." He took a step forward and swung at Darek—who ducked the fist and moved in to retaliate.

"Enough already!" one of the judges ordered as all three judges hastened to pull them apart, then backed off, unwilling to risk offending Bralig or his influential family. Darek and Bralig glared at each other.

"Nothing we can do, Bralig. You should know better than to pass too close to another ship. There are witnesses. Darek was last seen clearly in the lead," said the lead judge, nodding toward Vinz and Grame.

Vinz and Grame each sported a sour face, but said nothing.

"They're his friends," objected Bralig with a furious gesture. "Of course they're going to agree with him." His snort landed on deaf ears. "Are you all oblivious?"

"There's always next year, Bralig," said the lead judge.

"Yeah, save it for next year, Bralig," piped up a baker's son, another past victim of Bralig's bullying. The young man ventured closer to stare Bralig down, emboldened by the crowd and the new muscle he had acquired in the past few years.

Bralig drew back. "Get away from me," he snarled. He pushed his way through the crowd and stomped off up the gravel path in a black mood, his teeth clenched and his heart seething.

"Poor old Bralig looks to have his nose out of joint," remarked Vinz.

"Yeah, seems as if Bralig's a sore loser," said Grame. "I don't know about you, but I feel no pity for the oaf."

"Just a stupid bully," mumbled Darek. "Got what he deserves."

Deep down, he knew Bralig had grown from a surly bully to a serious rival.

"Well, great race, Darek. I don't doubt you'll win the whole thing," said Grame.

Darek shrugged. "The winds were right and I got lucky."

The music and feasting continued into the afternoon and Darek tried his best to enjoy himself. But his mind was elsewhere. During a lull, Clara approached him. "Congratulations, Darek, that was smart sailing. You could have easily been scuppered by that hothead Bralig. I saw what you did to his boat." She stared at his tanned build.

Darek blinked, growing wary. "Why didn't you say anything to the judges about me banging into him?"

"Everyone wants that monkfish out of the race. He's just spoiled. The last person who needs to win this race and a prize is Bralig. He has everything he needs and more." She fixed Darek a sultry gaze—for a moment he did not know what to say.

He gave an awkward smile. "Glad we're on the same page, then. All of us are in the finals, so that's at least cause for celebration." He pointed to her new gear. "Guess you'll have your fill of snapper with those new rods."

"I hate the taste of fish."

"Uh, I forgot. Of course." *That was strange for an Islander.*

Clara's wet curls hung down around her shoulders, catching the golden glint of sunlight. Her aqua-blue eyes sparkled as she flung back a stray lock from her cheek with a glint of suggestive warmth that set Darek's pulse pounding.

"The race isn't for a few days," she remarked. "Maybe we can get together and clear the eastern reef of lionfish?"

"Yeah, I'd like that!—I mean alright, sure, whatever."

"Well, good, and if we don't see each other, let's just say—may the best *woman* win."

Darek opened his mouth to say something, but nothing came out. "Yes—the best man, I mean best lady—I mean—" He shook his head, flustered.

She winked at him, then swaggered over to a group of young bucks who had called her name. Darek could not help but stare at the poetic motion of her hips, and it had him swallowing hard.

He turned and met Bralig's eyes across the square. Bralig smiled at him and dragged his finger slowly across his neck like a knife.

Chapter 2.

FEASTING

Endless dishes of every imaginable kind of sea creature passed beneath Darek's nose. Smoked crab and steamed mackerel, oyster, yellowtail and squid, flash grilled and skewered on a stick. The aromas had Darek's stomach growling. Tables laden with chocolate-dipped oranges laced with stickypalm syrup held center stage. Darek ate like a starved wolf. When no one was looking, he, Vinz and others tucked as much salted filet and smoked kelp in their packs as they could to consume after.

The wine and music flowed as freely, with minstrels plucking stringed dotars and shaking decorative castanets. The twin towers off the main square hung with colorful red banners; the courtyard buzzed with excitement.

That evening was a celebration for Darek as he and his cronies toasted each other, wrestled, jested rudely and laughed at old jokes and tall tales of treasure-bitten sailors taken in by lusty sirens.

Under the protection of swaying stickypalms on the edge of the seaside forest, they did what most wild young men of their cast would do—drink and talk foolishly, long into the night. It was all in the spirit of fun; Nik, Fasouk, Vinz, Grame and Spunio, an all-boys' club—no girls allowed. Tradition demanded it. Darek preferred the company of some of the more delicate gender, particularly Clara, over the drunken quips of these knuckle-draggers who sat before him. The liquor in his blood slowed his thoughts, leaving him with a feeling of languor, somewhat wayward and uninhibited. His thoughts strayed again to Clara and how she would be a perfect companion. He remembered how her leathers had clung to her body as she had stood in front of him, dripping wet in the sunlight. He squirmed, a sense of lust stirring in his bones as he felt his blood rise.

He sighed and struggled to push the thought of her from his mind. No easy task.

"Eat up," said Spunio, "my aunt gutted and cleaned this fish earlier today, just for you, Darek!" He smoothed out his yellow peach fuzz then started in on a ribald song about a nice girl with a devilish streak, implying Darek's mother, with Vinz and Grame chiming in. The last two sat opposite each other, Grame half a head shorter with his thin sandy hair, and Vinz, long-faced and irascible with dark, shaggy curls. Darek lay back and exhaled, coddling a forced grin. His cup of ale gripped in hand, cut from a coconut. Nik sat off on the sidelines, his frame rake-thin and his skin tanned.

Fasouk, short and chubby, seemed uncomfortable with the whole scene, his lips working in nervous opposition.

"Come on, Fasouk," quipped Grame, "you're sitting a little too stiff on your log for a party. Have some more ale, ya priss."

Fasouk shook his head. "Stickypalm gives me the craps, Grame, you know it."

"Such a sap." They all laughed.

Spunio, rubbing his high forehead and what looked like a set of monkey ears, jabbed him in the ribs. "Come on, Fazbaby. A little stickypalm's good for the soul."

Fasouk still refused, shaking his head like a whipped hound. The others gave him a shove and piled on him, force-feeding him the ale, until he was half choking and spewing on the ground.

"Knock it off, you weasels," growled Darek. "He obviously doesn't like jungle juice."

"When did you get so righteous, Dairy boy?" grunted Vinz. He flicked back his dark hair.

"Since right now."

"Screw off, fishmonger, there's no room here for party poopers."

Darek felt his patience fall away. He lurched forward and pulled Vinz off Fasouk. "I told you to knock it off." Reaching down, he helped a grateful Fasouk clamber to his feet.

"You want to fight me, big man?" Vinz sneered. He advanced on Darek, his knuckles clenched white. Darek stood his ground, not intimidated by Vinz or any of the others. It was all bluster, this cock-of-the-walk posturing. He knew he could take Vinz, drunk or sober.

"Try it—or are you just a puffer-fish?" Darek saw the barracuda-gleam in Vinz's eyes. He frowned, puzzled. What game was he playing? There seemed to be a marked difference in Vinz lately. Something must be in the air. Tempers had been running short lately, what with Bralig's aggression and the recent spree of attacks by the Black Claw Clan and roving pirates.

Darek snatched a wedge of grog-battered shrimp from the tray to deflect his fired-up energy. He didn't take Vinz and Grame's aggression seriously, but it was sobering and distressing, to know it was part of his own nature too.

"Glub, glub, tuna fish. You're upset because you were bested by a girl."

Grame laughed. "Yeah, not so hot after you almost *won* that qualifying match?"

Darek stared. "Did she not outclass you too?"

Vinz sniffed while Grame shrugged.

"For the record, I could sail circles around any of you." Darek peered into Vinz's eyes whose pupils reflected the ruddy glare of the campfire's light.

"You think? You're an okay sailor, Darek, but not that hot. You've got quick moves and maybe a gut instinct to read the winds—I'll give you that—but I dare you to try sailing into Black Claw territory, across their sacred isles."

Darek defensively crossed his arms. "I've done it before."

"Ha, when? How will you steal a boat, or get past the Harbormaster or navigate the rocks, or the sea serpents?"

Darek's blood simmered. "Serpents! There are no serpents in this close." He could feel the stickypalm ale firing his blood and his arrogance. "We'll see, Vinz-o. I'll take you up on your stupid dare. I'll sail a ship past Devil's Whirlpool, past the lava flows, across Serpent's Teeth, through Pirates' Cove—anywhere you want. All you have to do is pay me a silver piece each for my efforts." His words came out in a gush.

A barely perceptible flush came to Vinz's cheeks. The baiter chugged back his cup of ale, wincing at the bitter taste of its aromatic kick. "I *dragon*-dare you, dolphin boy."

Darek's fists clenched. He gripped his fish skewer, itching to stab Vinz with it, oblivious to the danger in his inebriated state. "The sneaking part's easy. I can have a boat past Kark's eyes before he knows what's going on." He flourished his fish-greasy hand. "Plus, he'll probably be in a doze, as he always is in the wee hours."

"I say it's a dumb thing to do," said Nik. "Too risky, Darek. Don't listen to these two blowhards." He rubbed his temples with concern.

Darek only grew more sullen. He glimpsed the taunting mockery writ in both Vinz's and Grame's faces.

"You'll never make it," jeered Grame.

Spunio, ever the skeptic, cleared his throat. "How can we even prove he was out there? He could just spin around the islands sunning himself, and say he was out there."

"Not if he brings us back a piece of the wreck from Windbit Isle," said Grame. "That'll prove he was out there—in Black Claw territory."

Vinz smiled. "Yeah, a good test, Grame."

"Done," grunted Darek.

Nik's jaw dropped. "Are you out of your mind? Rumor has it that ship was chased by a sea monster and wrecked on the rocks. Something with three-foot fangs and a blue scaly hide. Only a few survivors lived to tell of it."

"Right," grunted Darek, "and others tell a tale of a drunken captain swept up on rocks in a sudden windstorm, spinning an extravagant yarn about serpents."

"As you say," laughed Vinz. "It's your life."

"Believe what you want," said Nik. "I still think it's a crazy idea."

Fasouk shifted his chunky body. He blinked his doe-brown eyes in uncertainty. "I side with Nik."

Darek mumbled his impatience. "I'll do whatever it takes to prove you sea snails wrong. I don't believe in spooks or monsters out there and it's nowhere near sea serpent territory. I've sailed those seas before. The Black Claws can't patrol that much ocean. I'm a better sailor than all of you put together." His bottom lip quivered, regret showing the instant the words left his mouth. But it was too late. He was too drunk to stop himself. He hated being this close to his friends when they knew just how to rile him up—especially when he was this incapacitated.

Nik just shook his head as Darek thrust out his chin and the others followed his unsteady progress down the seaside path.

In the dark before dawn, the whole group assembled at the moonlit wharf. The many sailboats bobbed in unseen currents, their canvases furled. The silhouettes of a few of the big sail-steamers loomed farther offshore. The dock lay empty with only candlelight gleaming from the window of the watchman's hut down the way. Kark, the only guard on duty and a glorified one at that, would have been exiled had he been caught napping. It was good timing. If Darek were caught, he could always blackmail Kark for sleeping on the job. If Kark were caught, the watchman could always plead there was little likelihood that any Black Claws would be foolish enough to put to port on a raid of Cape Spear—especially with scouts posted at each lighthouse a mile apart on either side of the harbor.

Darek hunched closer, a little unsteady on his feet, sizing up the craft he would borrow for the mission. A midsize boat, *Star-runner*, a fast sloop with an extendible keel, jib and mainsail bobbed halfway down in a sprawl of boats. Guiding her out would be the only difficulty, just a matter of getting her sails up. Stars pricked the heavens; only the rhythm of the waves striking the stone wall broke the silence.

"Any of you want to go with me?" asked Darek, wary of the many nervous and rueful faces around him. Only the shifting of feet and darting of eyes greeted him. He sighed. "Just as I thought. All that talk and no balls amongst the lot of you. All of you jellyfish, with no guts or tentacles." He licked his lips as he grumbled. "Well, you'll see!—When I come back after carving my initials and bringing a plaque from the shipwreck, you'll pay me the silvers."

"Quit squawking," said Vinz. "First you got to make it back. An unlikely event which makes us none the poorer. We'll even vote you club captain."

"Club captain, I second it," said Grame. He rubbed his hollow cheeks with a facetious smirk.

"I don't give a toss about being Captain of a kid's club," said Darek.

"Kids' club or not," growled Vinz. "The wager stands."

Chapter 3.

Sacred Isle

Darek threw off the lines and eased the boat into the dark bay. Heart pounding, he wondered if he would get caught by the authorities. *Star-runner* slipped through the satin waters. Only the sound of the waves slapping against her hull drifted across the swells, mixed with the creaking of masts from behind, but gradually those faded, then too the elfin lights winking from the harbor. Soon she was past the rocks and out into deeper water, and Darek knew he was safe.

His head spun in and out of dizziness; a slight ringing sounded in his ears. Stickypalm ale, unlike coconut mead, did not give half the crippling hangover, but by the look of Vinz who had quaffed twice as much as he, the partier would be having a tough time this morning.

Darek's lip curled in a shark-like smile. Served the fool right for being such a curmudgeon. Darek had second thoughts about this mission. Easy to plead an out and say he was drunk. But a part of him rebelled at such a course; there were too many awkward strings; namely, the embarrassment of knowing his friends had heard him and would needle him forever if he backed out now.

Darek shrugged and trained his eyes on the waters ahead. Red fangs of light glowered over the eastern horizon. Soon he would be away from Cape Spear and past the outer shoals and guardian reef. He trimmed the sails and headed straight into the rising sun. The sleepy harbor slipped by and the dark bulk of Swordfish Island receded to port like a reclining ogre.

The sea showed its tranquil beauty more than ever with the early morning sun. The waves lay burnished a copper-gold. Darek felt he could reach out and touch the entirety of the Dragon Sea. He inhaled breaths of salty ambiance without worry or care. Noisy gulls soared overhead, lured by his bright sails and the promise of fresh fish. Distant porpoises, blue backs long and sleek, leaped from crest to crest in tune with the sway of the sea. His boat glided over the gleaming surface like a dolphin. With a deft touch he trimmed the mainsail and close-hauled on a freshening breeze, gaining speed, east around Swordfish Isle then north toward the Black Claw Islands.

Freedom on the high seas... Nothing was quite like it. Darek's spirits soared as the ocean air sobered him up. Wind, sky and Dragon Sea merged into one. He wondered how there could be any conflicts in this world of perfection.

But there were. The Black Claw Clan was ever at odds with the Red Claws.

Darek gnawed his lip. His ship was small, harder to sight, so he was less concerned about arousing attention. He had sailed these waters many times before and had never been boarded or had a harpoon shot his way. He saw no reason to worry, especially with no ships on the horizon. But in these uncertain times that could change at any moment...

Darek clutched the teakwood tiller, guiding *Starrunner* closer to the northerly and he kept his eyes peeled for wandering sloops or a man-of-war, particularly those bearing black or yellow flags—the mark of the Black Claws or pirates.

The hours passed and the sun rose like a flaming apple, a bright ball of warmth massaging his skin and reddening his cheeks. Darek could spend his whole life on the water, riding the open sea, breathing the fresh air and feeling the spray of brine on his skin. Collecting coconuts and dates on the islands by day, lighting fires at night to cook a dozen varieties of fish caught in his nets.

But a frown curled his lip. Without friends or comfort, it was a lonely life. To miss out on the camaraderie, the joy of having someone like Clara, a shipmate, to curl up against besides a night fire—it was not the way to go. He thought of her body and his tensed with an instinctive thrill. He thrust the feeling off, forcing himself to concentrate on the task at hand—his duty was to show those squid-head friends of his what he was made of; nevertheless, he missed his family as it once was, and he missed Meira.

His eye caught the flash of a schooner riding to port, a Black Claw ship by the look of its dark sails, but he gave it a wide berth. His boat was much too small for the crew to detect. By late afternoon, he saw a blur of rock on the horizon.

Land ho! With a salty grin, Darek steered his craft toward the island's eastern end. Windbit Isle—he knew something about it—to some known as 'Sacred Isle', a stark place, harboring elf shrub, dead clams and fish bones that had washed up on shore. His solar bearings had been accurate; he was only off by a few degrees to the north. Others called it 'Serpent's Blood Isle', after the color of the sunset that stained the fang-shaped rocks ruddy copper.

The island loomed up, but as features formed in the late afternoon, Darek's eyes caught a blue-grey trace of steam. Smoke? It couldn't be. Windbit Isle was abandoned, a deserted blemish of rock.

With renewed caution, Darek tacked into the sandy cove around the far side of the rocky fangs that jutted from the seaside. This place was sheltered by a large outcropping of boulders. The wreck, the *Vissicur*, as he recalled, was closer to the east end of the island, beached on sand and rock in a half dozen feet of water.

He trimmed to half sails, slowing his speed while moving toward a stretch of beach. Whatever was the source of the smoke, it had disappeared behind rocks and trees. The water, placid and inviting, shimmered as a cove came into sight. The air was silent and still, but for a few persistent gulls.

He stared in awe at an emerging shape as the once-grand sail steamer, the *Vissicur*, revealed herself. Her primitive paddlewheels and boiler stacks marked her as one of the first of her kind.

Vissicur had deteriorated much in the years that had passed. On a heavy slant, she lay forgotten, her hull turned in with holes gouged by rocks in her side. When Jace, his father, had taken him out a few years back, he had seen only a vague form that looked like a boat. Her bleached rigging was spider-webbed with moss and her sails hung in tatters, masts poking up like rotting fish spines. Her timbers creaked to the waves, and there was a terrible, eerie majesty to her.

Darek wasted no time. He anchored his sloop and waded into the shallow water, sighing at the cool feel of it. He reached for her barnacled strakes, found some toe holds and lifted himself up onto the tilted deck. A shambles of broken planks and metal drums greeted him. Looters had scavenged here many a time. Only frayed ropes, rotten bales, wrenched-open, brass-bound trunks and odd bits of junk remained. Darek moved toward midships, working his way crab-like to the cookhouse on the crazy-tilted deck. Once inside, he snatched a broken copper pot and went forward to the bowsprit to carve off some of the letterheads from her once-proud wood. With his prize in hand, he suddenly longed to be out of this forsaken place.

The figurehead was a simple busty mermaid whose white, red and green paint had faded to the point where she now resembled a shapeless manatee.

A strange noise alerted him, like a bellow, distant, not like a whale, but more sinister—something he would rather not imagine.

He twisted about, straining to hear the call coming from the island, heart beating, holding his breath. The sound, unlike any he had heard before, did not come again.

He swam back to the sloop and deposited his trophies there. Perhaps the unlucky crew was protecting their final resting place? Looking around, he frowned. Nothing but wavering coconut trees and bare rock on Windbit's shore. A gull landed on the narrow sandy beach to his right. The beach seemed torn up from recent activity, as if a storm had ravaged it. On an impulse, Darek leaped from the ship and waded into shore. All the while, he wondered what had created that unsettling sound.

Seawater curled around his toes as he passed onto the sand. The rising surf lapped at his ankles, tinted rose-grey in the setting sun's rays. Amidst the vagrant breeze, the calls of pesky gulls warred for his attention, and Darek paused, stroking his chin, gazing at what looked like white whale bones not far from the wreck, picked clean by predators and feral seabirds. Well, some sea creature's bones, he guessed, but these pale ribs had extra joints and twisted knurls in them. He scowled in puzzlement over the dark mounds and unusual features etched in the sands.

Moving farther up the beach, Darek came upon a blackened fire pit ringed by rocks and several runestones—they were set in strange, pagan configurations. What would runestones be doing on a forsaken island? On a whim, Darek grabbed some of the small carved stones and swished them around in his cupped hands. They formed an ominous configuration, prompting him to blink in fascination. He saw skulls, fires, ruin, death, dragon teeth clawing human flesh, and his own hand in such destruction.

Shivering, he dropped the uncanny things as if they were sea-snakes. On the sand Darek saw what he thought was another skull formation in the random array of dropped stones. Was he hallucinating?

The place was cursed.

Another disturbing sound drifted from behind a sand dune—a low moan similar to what he had heard earlier. Darek stopped and cocked his head, training his ears like a hound.

He wanted to stay hidden but his curiosity got the better of him. His heart beat faster now and he pressed his feet toward the inland hill. An odd thrill pricked his bones—a peculiar premonition upon him. He footed his way up the low-shrubbed crest through the prickly grass.

Near the top he paused, looking down on his ship and the crab-shaped bay, weighing his options. He could make camp on the island and be back to Cape Spear by tomorrow. He did not relish the thought of sailing at night on such a small craft. Of course, he could drop anchor somewhere at sea, but even that was risky in unfamiliar waters. Darek sucked his bottom lip.

With a shrug, he made his way down the other side of the hill.

Another thin stretch of beach greeted him. He saw a flash of movement. A hooded figure?

He squinted, gasped to spy a black-robed man on the sand below, waving his arms wildly. Who was he? What was he gesturing at? The figure faced the other direction.

Something was moving in the water, an enormous, blue-black shape, idling restlessly by the shore. It looked like a *serpent*. A cold knot of dread snaked up Darek's spine, sending chills into his shoulders. Could it really be a sea serpent? With its strange, sinister oblong head and long, undulating green and black body, this could be nothing but.

The creature lifted its ugly head and gave another low rumble that shook the air.

The man raised an angry shout. The beast hesitated, then slipped back into the water that shimmered with an odd hue and was gone.

Darek blinked. He focused his eyes and saw another figure, a young man huddled beside a boulder. He seemed shackled or roped to the large boulder. His feet were on a tether.

The hooded figure advanced on the youth, shaking his head, evidently miffed that his monster had withdrawn. The prisoner cringed.

Darek's lips parted; his breath slowed.

Creeping closer, he saw the captive, a blond-bearded man, had matted hair and welts on his face and arms. He was bleeding from where he had tried to wrench himself free from the cord binding his left ankle. With only a ten-foot radius to move on the boulder, he might as well have been a hound tied in a yard. Another bedraggled figure lingered nearby with his head slumped in defeat. The prisoners' heels were bound together and tethered to an iron pin dug deep into the rock.

Darek shivered. These people were condemned to death—when the tide rose, the serpent would return. Darek shook his head. He made a two-fingered sign crossing his middle fingers to ward off the eerie thrall in the air.

Prompted by morbid curiosity, Darek edged closer on his hands and knees, using shrubs and rocks as cover. The figure's hood had slipped. Darek saw a strong back and broad shoulders with black hair and aquiline nose. But the face was cruel, with black eyes all too penetrating. Darek wondered at the depths of the man's depraved motives to be torturing these young men and flirting with serpents.

Something like the hissing of snakes rattled in his ears from the water. He crept behind the rocks, poked his head up.

The dark figure lifted his hands. In one, he gripped a staff with a hex-shaped stone at the end; in the other, an eerie lantern, lit by an unwholesome light, powered by unknown means, which did not seem to be a flame. An ancient cauldron, some black pot of corroded copper writ with ancient symbols boiled beside him over a wood-stoked fire pit, not dissimilar to the one he had passed earlier.

Should he know that man? He shook his head. He recognized something wiry and sinister about him. Darek's eyes shifted and wandered out to the cove. Two pillars of rock rose in the waters near the shore like fangs. Between these, the sea frothed and bubbled.

A thin green mist oozed from the boiling cauldron and sent questing fingers out to the sea. An accompanying parallel mist, like a mirror copy, curled from the water out at sea to greet it.

The figure spoke in an ancient language, *"Arnak! Tornik! Volkrek!"*

The coils of smoke opened like arms and the water between the rock fangs boiled faster; a sinister, repulsive shape lifted from below. Then the spell-caster spoke in the native tongue:

"Bring water and serpent to boil!

Thus comes beast and terror to roil!"

Darek loosed a gasp. It dawned on him what the figure was doing. *He was summoning serpents—a wizard then.* Rare were they among the islands. He had only known one—Agrippa.

Darek gazed in spellbound wonder as the green mist coiled in greater masses to condense into a tangible form. A wedge-shaped head with reptilian snout rose from the water, followed by a sinuous body. This was no apparition. Mist became a reality. The creature plunged shoreward with blue-black fins and huge flippers which it used to propel itself forward and grip the sand with a heart-stopping menace. From its tail coiled a poisonous barb that sent shivers down Darek's spine.

"Aha!" grunted the wizard in triumph. "My time has come! Arise, my pet! Arise, slave!"

Darek watched, transfixed and chilled. Dragons, serpents, sea monsters! It was like some kind of macabre dream.

Darek clutched his throat and ducked back in the shadows behind the rocks. He cursed himself for his folly of curiosity. If the mysterious figure discovered him...

Yet the scene was a source of eerie fascination for him, and he could not slink away.

The massive serpent slithered closer to the men chained to the rock in an unhurried fashion, as if it were drugged or under a spell. The thing's eyes, grim ovals, glowed like pale lanterns on a moonless night. The two prisoners wailed and thrashed, giving up on all hope.

From the wizard's lips burst an explosive sound, "*Agrikumph!*" The serpent broke out of its trance.

Lifting its head, the creature bared thigh-length teeth. Like a viper, it shot out and snatched the first prisoner in its razor-like teeth. His scream died quickly. The other young man who tried to scrabble away, tangled himself in his leg restraint and fell flat.

The serpent dragged the first victim out to sea, snapping the cord, dipping under the waves in a flowering foam of crimson bubbles. Darek's mouth sagged in dismay as he could do nothing to help.

Nearby, the wizard nodded and muttered a perfunctory sound. Darek's blood froze. A jolt of icy terror broke through his normal calm veneer.

This can't be happening! Am I in some dream?

THE DRAGON SEA CHRONICLES: THREE BOOK SERIES

A young man's life had been snatched away, like a child's toy. The black-garbed wizard had sacrificed one victim in cold blood and looked ready to repeat his handiwork. Darek swallowed the lump in his throat and crept back in the sand, jabbing his thigh against a crop of sea thorns.

Chapter 4.

THE PIRATES

The wizard prepared to murder his next victim. He moved toward the remaining man. Summoning his strength, power, incantations, whatever fiendish things were required to initiate the next rite as his face lit with bright-eyed anticipation. The prisoner scrambled about in near hysteria, uttering gibberish, pleading with the spellcaster to stop this barbaric sacrifice.

"Silence, mewling!" the wizard cried. Lifting a bony hand, he summoned the next creature from the sea in a similar manner as before, this time with yellow wisps of gas floating from the pot instead of green. The sea between the fangs of rock bubbled and frothed and another prehistoric head, crusted with green slime and amber barnacles floated above the surface, its eyes unblinking. This monster was more massive and toadlike and waddled onto the sand like a sprawling prehistoric beast.

Darek clawed back to flee. His breath caught in his chest, but he couldn't go far. A terrible feeling had risen in his heart that if he left that young man to die, he would condemn himself for life, a small-hearted coward running in fear.

He groped about him, his heart pounding with adrenaline and his fingers curled on a long-forgotten rusted spear.

Choosing his moment, he leaped up and the spear flew out of his hand. Both spellcaster and serpent were distracted, their eyes coveting the last human sacrifice.

The spear whizzed by the mage's ear and sank into the approaching serpent at the soft fleshy area near the base of its skull. The creature screamed in agony.

The wizard whirled about. "Who's there?"

Darek scrambled back in the shadows behind the rocks. He winced in horror, guessing the dark magician would discover him and blast him with magic.

The monster gave a ghastly bellow. It turned on the man, enraged. The startled magician blinked, frozen on the spot, then jerked his limbs to action, looking into the monster's ugly face which returned him only a bloodthirsty glare.

Too late.

The serpent snapped out of whatever spell it had been under and wrapped an angry tail around the man's waist. The mage was swept out into the cove as the serpent plunged into the misty water, coiling more slimy loops about his torso. Fine sprays of magic fire burst from the wizard's hand and sizzled water and serpent flesh. Steam rose from the turbid water as man and serpent battled in an epic struggle. Screams and curses mixed with reptilian grunts and the thrashing of water.

Darek wasted no time; he sent his feet skipping over the blood-speckled sand to free the quaking captive.

"Are you okay?" he gasped. "Hurry! We've got to get away from this demented place."

The figure nodded feebly. "A-Away from that madman."

Darek used his fishing knife to slash the cord that bound the man's ankle, then pulled him to his feet.

Up and over the brow of the hill they raced into the tangled wood. Darek caught a last glimpse of a black, bedraggled form as he thrashed and hurled echoing shrieks in the water below, muttering thaumaturgical words over the hiss of wind and spray. He shuddered and stumbled back down the other side of the hill toward the *Vissicur*. Oblivious to the rake of the shrubs, he felt his pulse surge.

The young prisoner was not much older than himself, Darek saw. His face paled in terror, but his long legs sped him to outpace Darek as they ran.

Whether the mysterious, black-caped conjuror escaped the sea monster's wrath, remained a mystery, so fast was Darek leaping with his ally over charred fire pits and exposed lichened rock. Whoever he was, the wizard had not yet mastered the serpents.

The two splashed into the water and dog-paddled toward the sloop. The young man lagged behind and in the struggle to keep up, his winded gasps made Darek think he would not make it. "Hurry, before that monster waddles after us," grunted Darek.

Paddling ahead, he gripped the rope ladder and hauled himself over the gunwales. He pulled in the anchor and swept his eyes out over the water. The prisoner at last reached the boat and Darek grabbed his wrists and pulled him in to lie half sprawled on the deck. With fumbling fingers, he raised the mainsail and the sloop moved out to sea, cutting through the gathering swells.

"Thank you for saving me," the young man gasped, his shivering arms draped over his chest.

Darek trimmed the jib to move them faster out to sea. "Only a coward with a stony heart could have left you to die. No one should fall prey to the jaws of that beast."

The young man stared at Darek with grateful amazement.

Darek wiped the salt water from his eyes and returned the stranger's gaze. "Who are you and how did you come to be in the grips of that madman?" The man lay half sprawled on the deck.

The youth croaked, "My name's Briad. My brother, father, and I—waylaid, doomed the moment we saw that passing ship. If you see a white crest and a black hull—flee! It belongs to that wizard. My pappy tried to protect us, run the accursed man through, but the wizard lifted his staff and sent my father pitching overboard to the sharks." He hung his head.

"I'm sorry." Darek realized with even more sinking horror, that it had been the young man's brother who had been eaten by the serpent.

Briad's eyes brimmed with tears. "That monster you saw on the beach—that abomination. It killed—it killed—"

"I know, your brother."

"T-The wizard enslaved my brother using some foul globe or prism. I was drugged on some herb. Next thing I knew, I was shackled and staring into the face of a beast of nightmare." Briad broke down in sorrow.

Darek shuddered as he recalled the various features of that gruesome sea monster. He looked back. The sacred isle was now a rounded wedge of green trees and bare grey rock, a dwindling spur on the horizon. His eyes caught a flicker of movement. A porpoise? He squinted against the cross-glare. Hellfire! Had the wizard survived that battle and set his serpents upon them?

Darek scrambled to trim the jib and pointed the bow closer to the wind. He steered in close-hauled to maximize speed against the freshening wind. The wind caught the sail, propelled the ship faster. *Star-runner* tilted against the slapping waves and her mast creaked against the strain. Darek urged her to greater speed. "Come on, old girl. Don't give out on me."

Another speck grew in size to port. What the—? Black Claw patrols? No, it couldn't be! There was only one other possibility.

A convoy of three-masted schooners with gaff-rigged masts loomed like a deadly plague. The lead ship rode with a black flag flying high on the mizzen, its spider-webbed rigging with ragged-edged sails flapping in the wind. A wave of distress swept through Darek's bones. Pirate cabals were known to rove these seas and he was not nearly close enough to civilization to seek help.

Bridling his anxiety, he looked for options.

He strove to get his ship as far away from the marauders as possible. Should they shoulder in and wind-block him... a tacking duel would be the result and he would lose. These ships were three-masted leviathans with massive sails and built for speed and power. Under no circumstances was capture an option. Only the gods knew what those savages would do to him. It was a long way back to Cape Spear, and there were no coastlines in sight. Only wind, sky and sea... and Windbit Isle, but no way would he be going back there. Nor could he, Darek thought with dismay, with a sea serpent threading closer.

Howler's Isle was five leagues distant. If he could beach *Star-runner* there, he'd have a chance of losing his pursuers on the island. To hide in some cave or foot it overland might work. Yes, he'd be stranded, and could die marooned on the island, but better having some extra moments of life to work out an escape plan.

Darek's dark hair whipped against his neck, wetted by the fine salt spray. He fixed his eyes on Briad. "Quick! Move to my side and balance our weight. We're going to need every ounce of speed possible."

Briad hopped to motion and sat a few feet from him on the teak gunwales. A loud screech cut through the air. Darek looked up in distress. High above, a sole sea dragon and its rider flew with authority, a lookout for the pirate ships. *How to escape this trap?*

Curse those bottom-feeder pirates! With all eyes trained on his ship, they must not have spotted the serpent yet. The lead schooner loomed larger every minute. He could make out bandana-bound figures on the decks, cutlasses gripped in hand, yanking on the canvas's yards. Six large harpoon guns hung mounted on her gunwales. Darek flinched.

A sinuous bulk with a slimy green wedged head floated to the surface next to his ship.

Darek jerked back with a gasp. The warted face rose out of the water, an ugly monstrosity larger than any sea serpent he'd spied thus far. A cross between a sea slug and a crayfish, with two pointy eyes on stalks. Darek swung the boat around and slid under the boom, switching to the other side of the boat as he gripped the tiller. "Here, move beside me!" he ordered Briad.

The sails luffed in the wind, losing their propulsion for an instant. The sea creature moved with the boat, as if with an evil grin carved on its crab-like face. *Star-runner* was doomed.

With a loud *clack*, a spring-powered harpoon launched at his ship. Another latched onto the hull. The hull shuddered, pulled along by the much larger craft.

"Kraton's Balls!" Darek cursed with fury. The serpent had vanished as quickly as it appeared. Perhaps it had plunged beneath the ship in preparation to attack it.

Darek could see the cruel, leering faces of the crew on board, their eager jeers anticipating their spoils. What could this motley lot want with two penniless sailors? The boat? Slaves? Or were they just hungry for blood?

The ophidian shape surfaced again and thrust toward the larger ship like a sea worm. It snagged the towropes as if to play with them. One snapped, then another. Shouts drifted from the men on board and as if on cue, the sea dragon with the red-and-gold horns bearing the pirate scout above swooped down to attack the serpent.

Darek looked back at the carnage and saw the serpent fighting the pirate ship's ropes. Harpoon towlines flew at random, hopelessly entangling one of the large masts. The creature bit into a section of the deck and took one of the pirates with it.

With a roar of rage, the serpent lifted its crusty, barnacled head and smashed into the hull like a battering ram and staved a hole in her side. Screams of anguish and terror filled the salt-sprayed air as doomed sailors pitched into the water and the beast snapped them up in its fanged jaws. A barnacled tail propelled it along like a viper of the deeps, some nightmare that would be for many their last memory.

Instead of helping, the other two schooners left them to their fate and tacked in on a beam reach to run down Darek's smaller craft. Within moments, a schooner had closed the distance on Darek's ship. As if attracted to the movement, the sea serpent left the sinking vessel to give chase.

The pirates were drawing the sea serpent right toward him!

In a panic, the pirate crew turned the ship and glanced *Star-runner* an echoing blow to the bow. Darek plunged into the chaotic water. Briad was thrown clear and disappeared into the frothing bubbles. Darek kicked as a white crest washed over his head.

Clinging to a piece of wooden wreckage, he choked down a mouthful of brine. The sea serpent swam toward him. He looked full on into the serpent's blazing white eye as it rose to half its full height. The creature scrutinized him from afar with a demonic gaze. Darek felt no fear. He was beyond that, armed with the knowledge that when his time came, he would die bravely. The serpent seemed to sense something of this and raised its repulsive head, its wide-fanged mouth rumbling in a hideous challenge. Darek's unblinking gaze met its own cold, beady eyes. For whatever reason he reached out with his mind and communicated with the beast, not sure how he'd done so. The beast's flippers rippled in answer, and yet it stayed its course, as if governed by a primitive impulse, or some power it saw in the boy. The beast did not attack.

Briad was nowhere in sight.

The captain of the companion ship seized on the creature's distraction and launched a full attack on it. He stood tall at the foredeck, a brawny man with arm raised in command and a curved sword gleaming in the other. He called out in a booming voice, directing the mates to veer the schooner in and sight harpoons on the beast's skull and scaly hide. Grim-bearded men released the pressure springs from the guns and iron bolts blasted into her hide, one catching in her eye.

With a grateful gasp, Darek paddled away from the blood and the terror.

Chapter 5.

Captain Serle

The creature thrashed and wriggled like a worm on a hook. In a last act of defiance, it bashed its scaly head against the forward strakes and the pirate schooner rocked in reply as the men of the crew cried in alarm. But the blow was not enough to sink her and she only took on a bit of water, though it scared some of the cocksureness out of the crew. The monster splayed hideously in its death throes and sank from sight. Darek watched, spellbound, paddling on his piece of driftwood, hoping to escape enemy notice. Other drowning men clambered to get on to his bit of sanctuary, but he elbowed them off, pushing away with his muscled legs.

The remaining schooner swept in to pick up the survivors in the bloody froth. Sailors lowered longboats into the chop. Bits of ship and men floated everywhere: masts, rigging, an arm, cracked planks and splintered oars. Gulls and other winged scavengers gathered and squabbled jealously over the feast.

A thick hand seized Darek by his long hair at the back of his neck just as more hands hauled him aboard. He cursed and struggled, though he'd hardly any energy left to fight.

Briad lay gasping on the sopping floor of that longboat like a beached mackerel, sucking air into his lungs.

"Aye, a scratcher and biter, this wee little one," croaked one of the six hardened rogues from the back of the boat, yellow teeth flashing in a sneer.

"Give him a bit of medicine, Alred. That'll teach the beggar."

A buffet to the crown lay Darek low. He found himself flat out on the sodden planks, shaking the stars out of his head.

The schooner, battered but alive with motion, anchored and set herself in irons. Rocking in the swells, she accepted survivors. The longboat bumped against her side and tarred ropes slapped down to draw men up. Darek, in his haze, saw the stark, black lettering under her gunwales: *The Persephone*.

Darek was thrust rudely onto the deck and wallowed in his bruises and aches. Briad slumped at his side. A medley of men with bearded faces and hairy fists wielded knives and other weapons and crowded in to leer at them. Rough deckhands prodded the two aft where the captain could get a look at Darek and the other survivors.

"A sorry mess. The serpent's dead," said the Harpoonmaster beside a keg of ale, muttering into his beard.

"Too bad we couldn't have got its filthy head and strung it on a spit," the captain growled, his black beady eyes narrowing thoughtfully on the captives. "Could have been a nice trophy, to roast over our fires for the spring feast." He spat a wad of phlegm on the deck.

"'Tis a dark and gloomy day, Serle. I see this as an ill portent."

"Quiet your tongue, Gibar. You'll jinx the seadogs. It only proves we're dauntless. We're men that can kill anything that swims. True lords of the sea. There've been more of these fiends every week. Vipers! Normally, they'd stick to the eastern deeps, not venture this far west."

"Dark magic is about, Serle," said the bosun who had joined the group with grumbles in his throat. "Demons come from the bowels of the sea. Like great Osun said of old, beasts be beasts, and the bane of our heritage."

The captain grimaced, his lips curling at the mention of 'beasts' and that ancient name. "Osun will protect us."

The schooner was still taking on water. A jagged crack in her ribs ran to midships on starboard.

The captain called down into the hold. "Man the pumps! Amest, have ten men down there with buckets! Where's your mend kit?"

"Here, Captain."

"Get a move on. Smear the sides with tar and board her up."

Darek's gaze swung from the sprawl of wreckage out in the swells to the savage pirate leader. The man had finely-rendered dragon tattoos running up his throat. His lean, muscled height gave him a sense of presence, despite a roguish and mirthful twinkle to his eyes, yet they were as cold as the depths of the Dragon Sea and as hard as an anchor. Most of these rogues sported ratty beards, some braided, others dangling with beads, but he had only a sandy mustache, oiled, and pointed at the ends.

While others helped the injured, the man in the crow's nest yelled down to the mates, "No other serpents, Cap'n. Nor ships—the water be clear."

"Very well, Halpar, haul it into Ridderwin."

"Aye, aye!"

Darek squatted on the deck and growled a curse under his breath. The noise caught the attention of the captain.

"This stripling must have been out for a joy ride on his daddy's boat. Cost him dearly—and me, too. Tow in his sloop. Seems as if it's the only collateral we have against our losses."

One of the brawny men who had drawn in Darek hissed a curse. "Poor Manx, the blighter, lost his ship and went down to the deeps. Reckon we lost nearly twenty men."

The captain chewed his lip while toying idly with the strange lettering on his cutlass. "Get the survivors cleaned up and these fingerlings in irons."

Five deckhands hauled Darek and Briad midships with no gentle handling and plunged them through a trap in the deck to the prison hold below. The door shut and darkness swept over them. Only the smell of moldy straw and rotten fish reached Darek's nose. A trickle of foul water oozed at his feet. "Well, at least we're alive," he groaned.

Briad shook his head. "I think I'd rather be dead."

* * *

Later that day, the two were brought up on deck again, into the setting sun's glare.

More grim faces swarmed around them; the pirates discussed their fate.

"These mangy rats caused us a lot of grief, Serle, and they should be put to death." The bosun fingered his cutlass and brought it close to Briad's neck. "This one's a mousy specimen, indeed." The haggard man shifted back, reconsidering his wish about being dead.

"Well, they're fisherboys—my guess. Look how soft this one is. The other's got a bit of meat on him."

Another Corsair snarled. "Aye, lost us a good ship and hearty men."

"Death's too good for 'em!"

"Better yet, hang them up by their balls!" snorted a rat-faced reaver.

"Hear, hear," cried others.

"I didn't ask you to attack my ship," cried a sneering Darek. "You got what you deserved. Hope you all die by serpents, or get mauled by monster squids."

The captain blinked at him, his gaze demanding silence. "A tetchy tongue you have." He squinted in surly amusement, as if wondering how one stripling and a wayward fisherboy could have survived a serpent attack. "I don't know how you did it, boy, but you're on my ship now. Only by my grace has your hide been spared. So you'd better keep a civil tongue in your head. Many of the lads wish to slit your throat."

There were many grumbles to this effect.

"Where are you from?"

"Swordfish Isle, Cape Spear," Darek replied in a sullen mutter. "What's it to you?"

"So, an islander? A soft Red Clan Islander?"

"A lie," snorted a red-bearded thug. "His friend's got a Black Claw slave mark on his wrist. See, here?" He pulled at Briad's right forearm to show the others. "A runaway!"

"No," croaked Briad. "A—A wizard branded me. Killed my father, set a serpent on us. My brother's been eaten alive!"

The pirates laughed. "And my mammy's the Queen of Nevermore... Wizards! There're no wizards about, laddie. No lies now. It'll go worse for you." The red-beard boxed his ears and tripped him to the ground with his foot.

Darek rose with an angry growl. "Leave him alone. He speaks the truth."

The captain rubbed his chin. "Perhaps he does, boy. We'll see. Helmsman! Guide *The Persephone* fair and true to the homelands. Darmestra'll be expecting us, and will have my balls if I'm not back with some choice spoils."

Chapter 6.

PIRATE COVE

For a day and a half, the wounded craft slogged through the swells, ever eastward toward Serpent's Deep. The seas were relatively peaceful this time of year, else it would not have boded well for *The Persephone* which was drawing in brine despite the crew's efforts.

Gulls cried symphonies as they swooped and dropped guano on the deck. Darek saw naught of other ships. The captain put him and Briad to work bailing water from the hold, then on deck, polishing the cleats, coiling ropes, swabbing the weather-worn planks, then gutting fish for the crew's dinner. Darek was grateful and preferred the work to huddling in miserable heaps in that filthy murk of a hold. Briad worked with a vacuous gaze, mute as a statue.

Ships bearing the yellow and black banners of the Free Band of pirates grew in number and the three-masted *Persephone* made her daunting last leg toward Devil's Lair. The pirate headquarters made its home on the northwest shores of the buccaneer isles and around the ring of Fang Rock and Crypter's Cove. Toadlike bulks of earth and rock topped with thick forest and bare grey crags loomed out of the blue-glinting sea. Two reavers sailed the battered *Starrunner* in the schooner's wake as her sails bellied to the winds.

Darek had never traveled this far east before; few Red Clan had—and fewer returned.

The schooner plowed through the sheltered waters of Dogdown Strait on half-sail. "Take her clear through," rumbled the captain at his helmsman.

Darek marveled at the ancient limestone towers guarding the narrow mouth to the pirate cove. The towers stood like sentinels, left over from a forgotten age. Impressive harpoon cannons pointed down between stone embrasures to skewer the crews of any invading ships.

Darek saw wooded shores from his crouched position at the windlass aft of the harpoons. He scrubbed the planks with renewed vigor, lest he incur Captain Serle's wrath. Treacherous shoals could rip out a hull's bottom here, Darek knew. He was surprised that Serle was not taking it slower through the narrow seaway with its dark shadows cast by the towers passing over the ship. The helmsman must know the waters very well.

"Hoy, make way, lads, to Ridderwin!"

The ship anchored in the long circle bay near the high wooden docks and the seamen piled into longboats and rowed them to shore. Looking up the beach and into the neighboring sea firs, Darek glimpsed blue smoke curling from primitive, thatched dwellings with low conic roofs and sides wrapped with hides. Oxen and brute beasts, much like aurochs, trod a muddy trail up into the low hills, hauling wood to the shore for ship-building and fuel. Banana and coconut trees swayed among the plumed stickypalms.

Other members of the pirate settlement pulled in the 'catch of the day' from the bay while enticing aromas arose from swordfish and clams sizzling on spits over open flames in the common yard. The smoke and cooked meat reminded Darek of his hunger.

Surly corsairs with tricorn hats, horned caps and shiny cutlasses shoved them up the seaside path, along a line of trees and beach. Briad sweated and panted behind him.

Down the bay stretched a shipyard of hijacked vessels. Masts teetered high—Black Clan, Red Clan, Blue Clan, even a Black Clan steamer that must have listed at sea and been towed across the Serpent's Deep for salvage.

Several island seamen sauntered out to greet the new arrivals.

"Crack open the kegs, Lygbryd," roared Serle, heaving himself forward to embrace his clansman. "What a day! I need some comfort."

"Aye, Chief." The horned-helmed islander thrust a whalebone cup of mead in his master's hands. "You look like hell."

Serle downed the mead in a single gulp. "Feel like it, too, Lygbryd. We lost a ship to those damn serpents out there. But we killed one of their number. Sent it on its way to the deeps." He wiped his mouth of the foam and thrust the empty cup in his retainer's hands. "What news?"

"The usual. Vestigix caught Marlot lifting coins from the treasury during one of our raids."

"Well, he knows the law," said Serle scowled. "The thief's hand comes off on the morrow. No man steals from me." He smacked his lips. "What else?"

Darek looked over at the stolen pirate vessels, nursing the ironic thought that Serle and his thugs were nothing but thieves themselves, scavenging ships and other islanders' valuables.

"Sala got in another catfight with your 'other half'. Near tore her eye out."

Serle grinned. "I like those squabbling wenches. Especially Darmestra. Feral. Just the way they should be. Well, let them fight over me. If anything of value is worth fighting over, it's me."

Laughter trickled from the group of men assembled before Serle.

Lygbryd motioned a hand. "Who're these pups, then, with the surly looks and the foul mutters?"

"They're a couple of codfish we picked up on that sloop—" he pointed to the slender, white-sailed craft being eased in by his men. "Varnor says we should kill them all for the mess they made of our boats."

Lygbryd nodded. "Varnor's wiser than most. I say we should kill them too. Less mouths to feed. Unless you plan to make them slaves."

"I've ruled they live, Lygbryd. They'll play in the games. Like minnows, let them sink or swim!"

Lygbryd grunted with a shrug. "Suit yourself, Serle. It matters little to me."

The wounded sailors were given over to the pirate women to attend to their injuries. Willowy figures coming out from brailwood yurts brought herbs and cloth bandages. Garish women indeed, thought Darek, ornamented in shells and shiny bracelets. They looked exotic enough, and not uncomely in their colorful, plaited bangs, thick, black curls and pleated sea-island clothing. Horsehair whips hung at their belts.

He saw their village ringed by several massive firepits. Copper and bronze spits still hung with last night's leftover meat: stag or auroch from what his eyes and nose could tell. The embers glowed and the charred meat and sweet-sour smell of stickypalm ale stirred his senses.

How his heart wished he could be a wizard and fly out of here! How he would curse those rogues and turn them into crabs! That would be a wizardly feat indeed. It almost made him laugh. If he weren't in such a dire circumstance, the situation would have been comical. He thought back to the black-garbed spellcaster on the beach of that stark, scrub island. A shiver passed through Darek's body. If that's what being a wizard was all about, he wanted no part of it.

His eyes strayed to the wicked-looking knives strapped at the nearby pirates' belts. If he could snatch one and make a break for it...

He scowled. Too risky. He'd be cut down before he could make it to the trees.

Bare-chested slaves moved in a towline alongside tusked oxen to the beat of whale-hide drums. Whips of horn-helmed slave-drivers slapped the men's gleaming thighs, pushing them to the maximum. Grunts and heaves filled the air. The slaves hauled barrows of copper-ore seaside; some dragged small, four-wheeled carts using chains.

Darek winced at the sight. Somehow, he intuited his destiny was to be that of backbreaking labor. That, or shipped to Fang Island to work in the copper mines. The threat of pirate enslavement kept Black and Red Claw nosers-about at bay, he reckoned.

Likewise, the pirate-slavers worked the horned, tusked beasts struggling under the weight of their loads hard. The raw copper ore mined from the nearby cliffs was as valued as nuggets of pure gold, as far as raw materials went. Down the slopes it was hauled for chipping and smelting to the refinery. Smoke billowed from twin stacks of the local smelter, a rectangular metal structure, tucked amid green trees off to the side.

The pirates were more industrious than he had ever imagined.

The path up which they were herded veered toward the animals' fenced-in pens: island aurochs and tuskoxen, large, shaggy beasts with down-sloping backs and massive hooves. White and yellow horns extended outward past their ears, tusks flanking snouts upturned like a boar's. When old, sick and weary, these beasts no longer served a viable purpose. Darek guessed the tough meat became a steady source of soup and stews, their hides thick coverings for the pirates' huts and leather for their backs and feet.

Sweating figures, mostly women, herded and fed the animals without fear, mingling within the built-in stalls. He was surprised to find pirates not just conducting mindless raids and slumming aboard their anchored ships, but investing in a mining industry and keeping livestock.

A tall, proud woman on an auroch rode straight toward them on the other side of the penned yard of tough wooden posts.

"Round up those strays," she yelled down in a husky voice to other women on foot or riding smaller mounts. "You too, Livis. Just because you're my daughter, doesn't give you any special treatment." She paused and frowned. "You're letting them get away, girl! Herd them in—like this." Her whip snapped on a headstrong auroch's back. She kneed the beast forward to shunt a group of the unruliest ones into the feeding stalls. "Only when they're young, can they be taught manners."

Serle stared with pride at his wife and daughter. "Well, good to see some grit around here."

Darmestra reared her mount, and it gave a low plaintive moan. Riding in closer, she made way for her daughter not far from her side.

"Took you long enough," she bellowed down at Serle, her surly gaze raking his grin with scorn. "What did you go and do with our boat? It looks near staved in."

"Had a little disagreement with a serpent is all. Lost Manx and the *Witherall*. Bad turn of luck."

"Bad turn of luck?" she snapped. "Is that all you can say?" She shook her head in displeasure. "Get a man to do a woman's job and what do you get?—incompetence." She laid leather whip on the hide of another recalcitrant beast. "Move, you feisty goat!"

Livis, her lustrous hair flying, struggled to control the disobedient beast she was managing, but seemed to be losing the battle.

Serle grunted at his wife's taunt, though warmed to his daughter's fruitless efforts. "The sea is a harsh place, woman."

With a typical ranch-hand swagger, Darmestra hopped off her mount, tossing the reins to an under-servant and scaled the fence.

She eyed Serle darkly, then cast Briad and Darek a sharp look and a dismissive shrug. "Only two? Poor pickings. Especially for the loss of a schooner, I'd think, and half the crew." She opened her mouth to say more but did not comment. Darek saw neither trust nor empathy in that expression. Only a scowl at the brunette Livis whose gaze settled on Darek and his tanned, sweat-glistening muscles with something more than interest.

"What are you ogling at? Get back to work," she hollered at Livis. "Clean out those pens. See that they don't foul their feed troughs. Won't become efficient haulers, these beasts, if we don't discipline them properly."

Serle nodded in agreement, deflecting the woman's 'poor pickings' comment.

"Let's see what they fetch at the auctions," exclaimed Darmestra.

"Ten silver for the young buck, I wager."

Her critical eyes swept from Darek out to the harbor where *Star-runner* was being anchored. "This boy must be noble-born to have a fancy ship like that."

"Quite possible," agreed Serle. "I figure we can get more silver out of him through trade or sale eventually, than having him chipping rocks for the rest of his days. This other—" he nudged a foot at Briad "—is up for grabs. The jackfish'll go through the trials, of course. Both of them, if they survive captivity."

Hreg, the red-bearded Harpoonmaster, looked to the bosun with a grunt. "We meet the cursed Red Claws at a gathering, next full moon, I remind you."

"Too late, too late!" cried Darmestra. "See that you get some silver back for the loss of our ship."

Serle smirked and saluted his wife, then he gave the orders to Hreg and four other rough seamen who hauled Briad and Darek toward a filthy pen a stone's throw away. It faced the woods and the trail of the sweating aurochs, but still was within earshot of the main encampment.

"Hurry up, get them holed up," said Hreg. "We've work to do on the ship."

Darek and Briad trudged with ill grace only to be thrown into a reeking sty among the swine and woodcocks rustling about. Darek stared with sour disfavor at a clucking woodhen that began pecking his leg. He shooed the bird away.

Hreg's son, a round-faced, sable-haired youth with a stocky build and sullen temperament, marched in and gave Darek a rough shove into a deep pile of dung in the pen.

Darek lurched to his feet, cursing. He flung off the brown reeking stuff. "What was that for?"

Hreg nodded with a laugh. "Looks like our little rich boy isn't too happy or so popular anymore without his fancy boat."

"Serves you right," grumbled the thickset teen. "That'll teach you for sending uncle Manx to the grave."

"I didn't 'send him' to the grave," rasped Darek in a low voice. "The serpent did. Did you not see, or are you blind? Blame yourselves for attacking my ship."

The youth edged forward, his eyes red and glaring. Every cell in his body seemed to be struggling with rage over the loss of an uncle dear to him.

Hreg moved in to grab his son's neck and haul him back. "Save it for the trials, boy! You'll get your chance at avenging Manx soon enough. Come on, Nax! We've got better things to do than scrapping." He locked up the pen. "Like catching some stags or curing some hides. Let's go."

On a signal from Briad, Darek bridled the insult on the tip of his tongue. He knew it would be useless to waste his breath. Bottling his frustration, Darek gripped the bars and rattled them with all his strength. To little effect. He jerked himself away—no use in venting anger at inanimate wood.

Others came to ogle them. With drawn breath, he and Briad accepted the abuse: curses, jeers, the pointing of fingers, the humiliating throwing of tomatoes and rotten fruits at their faces and limbs.

"Ya rotten slugs," cried a tough-looking youth dressed in whale hide. "You're crab bait once the trials are on." He hurled a rotten melon at them. Others joined in.

Darek wiped the foul fruit from his neck and saw that four other wretches occupied a pen in the near distance, resembling a large cage. Thick wooden slabs, like planks, lay overtop of the upright bars held together with tough cord made of hemp. A mix of old and young men: Black Clan slaves, he guessed, judging from their torn and ragged sea-dolphin hides sewn with shells and imitation sea pearls. Were they being vetted for their mettle while elders made a decision on who would be taken where?

Briad stirred, mumbling, "Well, we're done for now. I suppose I should be grateful for surviving the serpent, but slavery's a fate worse than death."

Darek said nothing. He stared across the yard out to the open sea.

"So what about you?" Briad muttered. "What were you doing on that isle?"

Darek gave a sullen mutter. He shifted his gaze to the dung heap in the center of the pen. Why did they separate the prisoners? He shook off the vagrant question. "I'm supposed to be in a boat race—tomorrow or the next day. I had a good chance of winning. But I took up a stupid dare from a hothead and braved the Black Claw waters. Now look at me—lord of the dung heap."

Briad sighed. "I could name any number of wrong choices I've made in my life."

"Like what?" muttered Darek sourly.

"Leaving the Cookmaster's fresh fish to burn while I snuck a kiss from his daughter. Got my hide whipped. The cook and my pappy—rest his soul—were they ever pissed—but you should have seen the Cookmaster's daughter!"

Darek's gloomy frown turned to a shadow of a grin. "Yeah, I know one girl I'd risk anything, for a kiss."

Darek saw the blood on the seaman's leg and took him aside. He plucked some fresh grass and moss that poked up just outside the pen's bars and smeared it on the young man's knee wound as a poultice. "Don't worry, Briad, we'll figure a way out of this mess."

"I admire your optimism. Thanks for the moss."

Faced with the strong bars and the knots of roving pirates, Darek was suddenly not so sure.

Despite the low ceiling, he paced the pen like a caged panther, shooing woodcocks away as he walked. What an insult it was to put slaves in with the animals and feed them the same slop! Surely a deliberate way to break their spirits.

The bars were doubled with hard brailwood and tied with stout bull gut, not to be ruptured, or cut without sharp-edged tool, Darek thought. Digging under the bars was not an option. Burrowing a mere three or four inches through woodcock dung revealed a floor laid of thick stone. Darek gave a sigh. He sat back on his haunches, muttering under his breath.

CHAPTER 7.

TRAINING

The next morning, Darek awoke to Serle and his men rattling the prison pen across the way. The thin, mustached thief caught a few days ago fought and cursed as they hauled him to the public square to meet his punishment.

It appeared the pirates had a custom whereby the accused would take on a clan champion, usually the chief, in a trial by the sword for his honor.

Serle looked down with distaste as he fingered his sword.

"What's wrong, Serle?" taunted Marlot. "You know the rules. If I defeat you, my crimes are wiped clean and I walk free."

"As rare an occurrence as that is," grunted someone from the crowd.

Several others laughed and nodded at this assertion. Serle moved in.

Darek perceived such a custom kept the chief's fighting skills sharp if he planned to survive daily challenges and enjoy the continued respect of the people. Marlot, for all his bluster, seemed uncomfortable with a blade in his hand, while Serle made his sword flow through the air like an extension of his arm. The faceoff would be brief. Marlot charged immediately, in a desperate attempt to take his opponent off guard.

Serle, backed up, steel-nerved, as Marlot rushed in like a billy-goat. The defender swung his sword in ham-handed haste, at first like a pickaxe, but Serle stepped back, giving ground, allowing the feverish man to exhaust himself. A crazed look showed in the whites of Marlot's eyes. On an ill-timed lunge, Marlot stepped in a shade too close and Serle twisted aside and back-jabbed the accused in the throat with the butt of his sword handle. Marlot made a gagging sound and fell to the ground. The match won, Serle chopped through the man's right hand, severing it.

Serle grimaced, never one to like spilling the blood of a kinsman, but the law was the law and he held his sword high to the cheers and jeers of those gathered. He looked on in stern forbearance. "Marlot was not without his honor, friends, and he served our clan with dignity despite his recent temptations. Osun has judged him. He will yet serve, despite the loss of a hand."

* * *

The days passed and Darek stumbled about the pen, feeling groggy and starting to despair. His sweat-doused face felt gaunt and his spirits sagged. No opportunity for escape had presented itself. When he and Briad were hauled out during the day to clean the auroch stalls or shuck clams by the shore, guards with sharp knives kept a close watch on them.

That breezy afternoon the girl from the auroch pens happened to stroll by, gathering wild leeks and savory herbs for the evening stew in a woven basket. She looked nervous, darting glances left and right before approaching. Her expression was not of contempt or disgust, but more of curiosity. She lingered and stared, and snatched glances when they weren't looking. Scuffing her feet, she looked down when they did, pretending to pick her plants. Darek decided to cast out a lure. After all, nothing to lose.

"You know, if you pick those yellow herbs over there with the flowering buds, the *menscus*, they'll give better flavor."

"Maybe, maybe not. How would you know?" she asked with a silky purr.

Darek made an easy gesture. "I'd know because my mother used to tell me." He beamed. "She was a wonderful cook, but she's gone now."

The girl's eyelids fluttered; her bright eyes expressed interest. She stepped closer and Darek looked her over from toe to crown and was not unimpressed by what he saw. Trim at waist and broad of hip, her fine, proud features were not unlike her mother's but prettier and devoid of the harshness of her father's long angular face. Lustrous brown curly hair coiled about her shoulders wrapped in leathers fitting snugly about a healthy figure. Tucked at her waist in a whalebone belt were both whip and hunting knife. She toyed with the whip's handle, as if in nervous energy and darted glances back to the figures in the glade and her father and his bondsmen at the pit.

Darek felt suddenly ashamed at being coated with unseemly dung.

"You don't look to be very well treated," she murmured. "Those cuts and scrapes could get infected with all that woodcock dung caked on them."

Briad snorted. "What do you care?" Though he smiled, warming to the girl's naive interest in them.

A figure stepped forth. *Nax.*

His thrust-out shoulder obstructed her view of the pen. "So good to see you, Livis." He ignored the prisoners as if they were on par with the pigs. "Looks as if we're both up for the upcoming fight."

She offered no reply. A cold cushion of distance had drawn itself about her and she jerked back instinctively.

The boy blundered on, nodding at the bouquet of flowers and herbs she had picked. "I was going to pick a mayflower or two for you, but I'm sorry to say it got crushed. Stupid Ulfe tripped me while I was on my way over. Called me a sissy for picking flowers. Not that I blame him." His half-leer did little to amuse the girl.

"Very nice of you, Nax, but I don't expect you to bring me flowers."

He scratched his head at that, trying to determine its cryptic meaning. "What are you peeking at these rats for? Bunch of grubs and slaves." He blocked her view again and put on that silly grin.

"Go away, Nax, and stop being so childish. I'll look where I want."

Darek could not help but laugh.

Nax whirled on him. "What are you laughing at, vermin? Keep your eyes on your dung pile, and off her," he grunted. "Or I'll poke them out." He turned his attention back to the maid who now smirked. "Oh, is it really so funny now?" He shot Darek a withering glare and chucked the wad of greasy fruit he had in his hand. Darek methodically wiped the yellow sticky fruit off his cheeks and throat. He could care less at this point. Briad's eyes turned away as if sensing trouble.

Livis stormed off, annoyed at the intrusion, but she cast Darek a look over her shoulder, mouthing words, *"I'll be back."*

A rough-necked man with a yellow beard and ale belly approached with three young helpers, carrying buckets of slop and dinner scraps for the pigs and two bowls of swill for the prisoners. He unlocked the chain twined around the bars, plopped the bowls down as if feeding a couple of stray hounds, then emptied the buckets in the swine troughs.

Darek curled his lip at the sludge.

"Eat up, boy," growled the brawny yellowbeard, who busied himself re-chaining the lock. "Think of it this way, you'll need it for what's ahead."

"I've got no interest in your rituals," scoffed Darek.

"Osun's hell, boy! You'll change your tune."

Briad winced at the man's tone and clutched Darek's arm as the man stalked off. "Don't make it worse for us, Darek," he hissed at him. "I'm worried enough about this ritual."

Darek grunted and shrugged off Briad's arm. He was beyond caring now. The sweat that beaded Briad's thin brow and his continued rasping breath signaled the onset of fever.

"Our only chance of escape is while the ritual's on," Darek emphasized.

"What are we supposed to do?" Briad asked.

Darek curled his lips. "I'll think of something." He looked to the open yard where Livis had slipped past the trees. His belly growled and he felt light-headed from hunger.

"You won't get any help from her," Briad grumbled.

Darek was not so sure. He caught a flash of dark hair and willowy figure strolling by the auroch pens in the yard. Ever since that first glance they shared, he felt Livis's eyes upon him.

"Not all these rogues are cutthroats..." he mused. His eyes stayed glued on the lissome figure.

"You think she'll go against her father? No chance."

Darek decided it was time he seduced the girl, either that or remain a pirate's slave for the rest of his life. She was his only way out of here.

Briad seemed to sense what he was thinking. "How are you going to convince her to free us?"

Darek was already visualizing himself on his sloop bobbing out in the gentle swells.

*　*　*

In the latter part of the day, Darek looked up from his drudgery to the clink of swords and the girl Livis sparring animatedly with her father. Both gripped gleaming swords and took up aggressive stances in the communal yard and did their best to try to penetrate each other's defenses.

Was he in a dream, or was it real? Darek did not know. The air was filled with the fumes of woodcock guano and his body so wracked with hunger that he wondered if he were hallucinating. He blinked and looked over at Briad whose hand rested on a sleeping piglet's back. The young man's pale, haggard figure looked in no better shape than his.

Darek rubbed his grubby chin and strained to hear what father and daughter were saying...

"Remember what I told you, Livvy, protect your flanks, lunge, then fall back to a protective stance. Like this!" The big, rangy pirate struck forth with sword extended and caught her blade on his.

She laughed. "I get it, Serle."

"Serle, is it now?"

"I'm too old to call you 'Pa'."

"I see." He glanced worriedly at his daughter's blossoming figure. "Well—I suppose I can accept that. "Are you set for the Water Trials, now? I see your mother's been pushing you hard with those damn tuskoxen. She's worse than an auroch herself, a harsher taskmaster than me." He reached over and felt Livis's biceps. "Woohoo! All your sword-training has been paying off, Livvy. I don't doubt you'll give big bad Beseny a run for her shells this year. That teen giant's got nothing on you in terms of speed."

A blush swept over Livis's rosy cheeks as she parried. She beamed in appreciation, despite her wish not to show it, liking the compliment, even if she knew her father was just buttering her up.

Her expression grew serious once more. "Those men," she began, "the new ones...I don't think you should treat them so roughly. The young one especially seems innocent, not of slave quality."

"What's this?" Serle raked his daughter a steely glance, lunging in hard. "And why do you care? They're just slaves, to work the grist mill as we command them."

Livis bit her lip. "It's not right. Starving them, treating them with such savagery. What did they do so wrong? The young one, for example, I mean." She gasped with the effort of parrying her father's last thrust.

"Young one? Rotten Red Claws," Serle grumbled. "You forget how those arrogant fools spat in our faces on our proposed alliance. The Black Claws think they're better than us, though they were pirates once themselves and the Blue Claws are nothing but cowards sticking to their crops and trade."

The fierceness of his attack surprised Livis and she barely leaped back in time.

"Sorry," he apologized. "I get carried away."

Wincing, she sprang left and Serle waved his hand. "It happened during the reign of Jnevr, my grandfather, long before your time." His flash of anger subsided as if the older man saw some premonition. "What do you see in that young dunghill cock anyway?" He shook off his mounting confusion and his expression grew hard again. "My edict stands. Forget about the young fool." His sword crashed against her blade, sliding off like polished glass. "He got caught in the wrong place at the wrong time. No mixing of Red Claw with pirate blood. You've plenty of suitors here. Nax's been making eyes at you, so make me a proud chief with lots of brats."

Livis cringed at the thought. "I don't want to have anything to do with that miserable slug!" Such was the intensity of her attack that her looping sword whistled by his ear and sheared off two of his wavy locks.

Serle stared in appreciation, but his face also twisted in annoyance. "You won't defy me now, girl! A woman's job is to strengthen the clan with in-clan blood."

"Women fight and even ride dragons in the other clans."

Serle could not restrain a laugh. "Always a fighter, like your mother."

She slapped at his sword, determined to pay him back for the bitter sting up her arm.

"Well, I promise I won't force you to wed someone you don't want."

"Thanks, Pa," she said, with a scornful grin, "I mean, *Serle*." But the older man could not help but notice the visible relief washing over his daughter's face.

THE DRAGON SEA CHRONICLES: THREE BOOK SERIES

Chapter 8.

A Kiss

Long into the night the pirates caroused and Darek caught glimpses of half-naked bodies dancing about the fire. Cups of arrack and ale foamed over at the edges, gripped in pirates' hands. Serle bellowed ribald songs from the corners of his mouth in drunken tribute and had a woman latched in each arm, tossing them both about in a lascivious manner. He was in his element.

Darek stirred in annoyance, struggling with several awkward emotions. A part of him could not condemn what he saw, or what a more primal part of him craved. His senses reeled. He felt drawn to the power, hungering to feel the warm skin of a woman under him. He shrugged off such thoughts. To escape this pigpen was his first priority.

He tore his attention back to the reavers. Many of the Ridderwin clan bore tattoos up and down their arms and shaved their heads with strips of hair running up the middle. Some wore braids, others were completely bald, while some even sported mullets with long hair trailing down their backs. In the orange flicker of the firelight, these cutthroats looked like underworld spirits of chaos. The tattoos gleamed like war paint on their bare arms and trunks. Dancers with tusked masks pranced around the fire, mouthing ancient words.

Serle, from what he had observed, entertained three wives who did not care for one another. Rarely had Darek heard such obscenities uttered by women. They were gypsies, these wild women of the north. Wearing bangles on their wrists and ankles and rings on their fingers and toes, they were fiery-eyed vixens, with curly hair and exotic airs who flaunted unfettered sexuality. He was surprised that Livis was so conservative by comparison.

A figure slipped out of the shadows. Slim, lithe, and like a fresh flower in bloom. Darek opened his mouth to speak, swept up in a thrill of anticipation and excitement. He pressed himself to the bars.

"Shh." Livis came close and put her finger to his lips. She smiled at him.

Bringing out of her pouch a packet of baked swordfish and mackerel wrapped in soft cloth, she passed it between the bars. Darek's and Briad's eyes widened in hunger. The home-baked smell intoxicated them and they ate ravenously, flashing grateful looks her way.

"I have no ale," she said in apology.

Darek shook his head. "You're a godsend, Livis. I thought you'd never come back."

"I said I would, didn't I?"

Darek's eyes darted from the girl's mesmerizing eyes and figure back to the closest bonfire. Nobody appeared to have followed her.

"I'd really like a knife like the one tucked in your belt," Darek whispered.

"Why?" she demanded with suspicion.

"So Briad and I can cut ourselves loose and steal back our boat when everyone's sleeping."

She snatched a wary glance back to the fire pit where her father and the other seamen continued to drink. "If my father catches—"

"Relax," said Darek in a reassuring tone. "I'll throw your bodkin in the sea. They'll never know it was you who helped us. Briad and I'll slip out like eels." Drunken roars and shouts of laughter drifted through the mist-laden trees, vying with the songs of the crickets. "This party's going to go on for a while yet," Darek murmured.

She cast him a doubtful look.

Briad sliced a finger across his throat. "Eel's the word," he muttered.

Livis gave a reluctant sigh. "Now that you say so..." Unhooking her gleaming blade from her belt, she passed it through the bars.

Darek snatched it with a croak of triumph. His heart flared with excitement at the prospect of escape. He felt his breath quicken. The weapon was cool in his palm; the knife had a whalebone handle with inlaid runes of quality and a keen edge. A fine piece.

"You're a star, Livis," he hissed in a low voice. "I swear to you that one day I'll repay you."

She shrugged. "Something I may never see come to pass. Promise it—with a kiss."

"A kiss?" Darek blinked. "Like right now?" A hot flush prickled his skin. He always thought he would have to promise a girl exotic gifts and woo her for several weeks to get this far.

"I'm waiting," she coaxed, moistening her lips.

He leaned closer, pressed himself to the bars, longing for the warmth of a woman's skin. Her face came close to his, her eyes slowly closing as she leaned in. Their lips touched and a rush of warmth filled Darek's body. Her mouth tasted slightly of wine and he was dazed by the intoxicating smell of the flowers in her hair.

Such a tender kiss in a dirty stinking place! A faint but wild tremor quickened his blood and he felt her stir in response.

"Well, if you're about done," grunted Briad in an impatient tone. "I'd love to get out of here before we find our necks in a noose..."

"Where will you go?" she asked breathlessly. "Never mind—I don't care, just take me with you." Her eyes twinkled like distant stars. "Father won't let me go into battle and he wants me to marry some sodheap like Nax and herd bullocks all day. When I'm near you, my heart beats for adventure and the freedom of the wind."

Darek's heart soared and he knew even as impossible as it might be, he wanted nothing more than to take her with him. He took her hand in his and smiled.

"What's going on here?" a voice stabbed out of the shadows.

Darek jerked around, only to recognize the gruff tone and pocked face of Nax, the same stocky youth who seemed to show up like a bad weed. He shouldn't have let down his guard against that bilge rat.

"Livis, is that you?" the bully called, squinting as he shuffled closer. "What in the name of three Osuns are you doing? Did I just see you give that sludge-licking slave a kiss?

Livis scowled. "Beat it, Nax. Go stalk some jellyfish."

Nax fists quivered as he looked at Darek. "How dare you put your hands on my wife-to-be!"

Livis clicked her tongue. "I'm not your 'wife-to-be'. I just came to check on these men's wounds."

"Aw, don't give me that crab-rot. I saw you sneak off with food for them."

She put her hand on her hips and sniffed. "What's it to you, Nack-head?"

His face turned beet red. He stepped forward and backhanded her across the mouth. She reeled back, wiping the blood from her lip.

Darek growled and pitched his full weight against the bars, rattling it with fury. "Leave her alone, you cretinous rodent!" His fingers clenched on the knife, ready to swipe it through the bars at Nax's midriff, then he remembered it was his ticket out of here, so he balled up a wad of dung and shot it at Nax's head instead.

The dung struck Nax full in the face and he grunted upon the impact. Wiping the mess from his eyes, he stared at Darek in disbelief. "You're dead, pig!"

Livis thrust herself between Nax and the bars. "These are my father's slaves. He'll have your eye if you kill them—"

"Shut up, you filthy whore."

Darek growled between his teeth. "Open this gate, Nax, and we'll see what you're made of."

Nax snorted, a low boar-like sound. "You'd like that, wouldn't you, pig? Oink, oink," he mimicked, like the swine from the sty. Darek was on the edge of throwing his knife through the bars, but desisted.

Livis was steaming mad. "Call me a whore, will you?"

Nax advanced on her again, but this time Livis was ready. She kicked him in the gut and he doubled over.

"Here, what's all this?" a voice boomed from the dark.

Nax recovered and flashed Livis a scathing glance. Hreg, Nax's father, lumbered in with heady grog on his breath. "What are you messing around with the prisoners for, boy? I told you to steer clear." He turned to glare at Livis. "And you, little miss good shoes, this is no place for a lady—hey, what's wrong with your mouth?"

She licked her bloody lip. "Nothing, Hreg. I just tripped over a root." Her eyes leveled Nax with a warning glance.

"My arse you did! Serle'll be furious to hear you've been skulking about the prisoner pens."

Darek plunged the knife deeper into his breeches, hoping it wouldn't be discovered. Briad stood frozen like a mannequin.

Hreg wrinkled his nose at the prisoners, pausing at the look of fire in Darek's eyes. Livis slunk disdainfully off into the shadows as Hreg faced his son.

"And you, you rotten mutt. Up to no good again? Wipe that stupid smile off your face."

"I was just—"

Hreg slapped Nax and grabbed him by the hair. "Fetch me some wine, boy! The night's still young." He hustled the glowering youth back to the campfire.

Darek's grin broadened as he watched the retreating figures. At least Nax got what he deserved. Now he had a knife. Neither Nax nor Livis would dare come back soon. Would have been nice to steal some more kisses from her, but there was no time. Hellfire, he liked her, perhaps more than Clara. Maybe in another lifetime...*No, better not go there. Time to escape.*

Too many pirates still loitered about the glade for him to saw through the stakes without notice. He gave a grunt of frustration. They'd have to wait for their chance. He and Briad slumped in exhaustion, their backs to the bars, listening to the pigs snuffle and the fowls cluck as echoing laughter drifted on the wind.

The party lasted well into dawn. Figures continued to mill about as Darek buried the blade in a dung heap to shield it from view.

Four pirates, haggard-eyed, black-circled from grog, opened the prison hatch as dawn's rosy fingers licked in. The seamen rough-hauled them out, leaving no time for Darek to retrieve the knife. "Up, you mackerels," grunted one. "Time for some action."

The jailers prodded them along with three other slaves up an overgrown path through the woods to a large glade breasting the hills. A few dozen drunken onlookers gathered before a long, crescent-shaped lagoon of greenish water.

Darek saw a grand maze of open walkways spanning the shallows. They interconnected in a curious crisscross of wooden-slatted gangplanks tied by hemp, which stretched over the lagoon. Some were supported by pylons about three feet above the water. Darek muttered his confusion. "What's this?"

A full-bearded sea dog with a missing eye seemed amused at Darek's curious stare. He chortled, "You'll find out soon enough."

Hreg gathered wooden staves from a nearby trunk and pushed them into Darek's and Briand's hands. "Good luck, flounders! You'll certainly need it." His guffaw wafted with the foul smell of grog.

Darek focused on Serle who now stepped up to address the gathering crowd with his hands held high.

"Citizens of Devil's Lair! Greetings. The trials are upon us and I would have your attention." The small crowd roared. "Our young seamen will prove their worth against the likes of these—" he gestured dramatically to the right where a group of men with their first set of whiskers stepped forth in light leather armor. Darek and Briad sported only threadbare, tattered garb. Darek saw Nax was among the competitors and stood watching him with an evil glare.

Serle called for quiet among the crowd. "The rules are simple. No deliberate killing or choking. If a competitor should call 'yield', then the other must grant a reprieve. Fail to do so and you will swim the fire-coral reef." He motioned to a narrow channel of water tinged red.

"If you are forced into the water, you'll be removed from the trials. Pacts and alliances are encouraged and expected. Observe the rules. The far end of the lagoon screened off with posts is off limits. Barring that, anything goes. Let the games begin!"

Darek muttered under his breath at the maze of crisscrossing pathways. "I wonder why we can't go over there?"

Briad shrugged, his face pale with anxiety. An unhealthy rattle sounded in his chest.

A slave nudged Darek in the ribs. "That's where the Nargale live."

Darek blinked. "Nargale?"

"Predators. Their sting is like the war manta, with a bite like a viper shark."

Darek's jaw hung slack. "Surely you joke?"

The slave shook his head, his grin as if an answer. "The pirates keep them for their amusements. In fights to the death. Lucky we aren't sparring over there."

"Lucky," Darek muttered. "I still don't get the maze concept."

"It's supposed to mimic deck-to-deck fights during a raid."

The start drum sounded. The contestants moved to the ramp over the waters, taking their places on the maze of walkways that spanned the serpentish waters.

Briad, no great swordsman, was to be pitted against the younger warriors, to the delighted jeers of the spectators. Their training staffs were made of polished sea fir boughs and would at least ward against serious injuries.

Darek hissed, "Don't worry, Briad, we'll watch each other's back. I used to spar the quarterstaff against both my friends, Vinz and Grame."

Briad nodded briefly, gripping his stave. A determined grimace framed his mouth, as if he knew he could count on Darek as an ally. "Likewise, I'll help you if I can..."

CHAPTER 9.

THE TRIALS

Darek was surprised to spy a figure with an eerily-familiar gait step up to join the other boys. Not so familiar perhaps—the contender had the faint semblance of Livis, dressed in full leathers, a horned helm pulled down around her face and hair clipped and dyed. *So her father didn't know she was competing?* Darek's eyes briefly caught hers. Her upraised brow expressed surprise that he was still a prisoner. Darek shook his head, in answer to her questioning gaze.

No sooner had the drum boomed than booted feet pounded the planks. Darek steadied himself on the swaying walkway and ducked a whistling strike that would have knocked him senseless. He plowed headfirst into an opponent, knocked the wind out of him and sent him spread-eagled to the planks. He kicked the weapon out of another's hand, then held the stave to his throat. "Yield?"

"Yield, I yield!" cried the boy.

Darek snarled and pushed his way forward, as did others. The defeated jumped into the water and swam back to shore. Briad was already suffering multiple hits and his muffled yells drifted to Darek's ears.

Nax jostled his way across the crowded pathway to get to Darek. There was nowhere to turn amid those hacking and jabbing staves. Dark bruises shone on Darek's left cheek under a black eye. Briad was no better off. The young man's breath rasped; his gaze was feverish. Darek lunged, hacked at another's legs, parried a high blow and nearly lost his weapon to the sting that shot up his arm. The end of a staff slapped into his stomach. A sharp pain arose. He doubled over, rolled beneath a cursing youth's boots, grabbed desperately at his ankle and upended him into the water.

Darek had been wrong to have taken that last turn and now was forced to backtrack. Nax had him cornered and charged with an impudent cry.

Livis, deep in battle with a blond-braided giant, turned about, distracted by the sound. A buffet landed on her helm. The tall youth's staff descended and struck low. He gave chase but tripped on an uprooted plank and lost his balance. Livis kicked him into the water and out of the competition.

She staggered through the broken wall, dazed from the hit. Darek fended off blow after blow from Nax.

Chance would have it that they were deep within the rear of the maze away from the shore, bordering the forbidden Nargale fish where Darek had unwittingly led them. The rope walkways swayed as fighters crossed them and their exertions threatened to topple the entire boardwalk into the lagoon.

Briad scrambled up behind Nax and struck hard, eliciting a sharp cry and a crack of bone. In a fury, Nax spun and knocked Briad back toward the barrier, smashing him through the protective housing that surrounded the forbidden waters. Briad nearly fell into the Nargale-infested water. Darek could see the fishes' cold blue-yellow eyes as they finned forth, whipping their flexible tails as they swam hungrily below. A peaked fin broke the surface and razor-sharp, white teeth showed above the water.

Sensing his friend's plight, Darek redoubled his attack on Nax. Darek hit Nax square in the jaw with a blow that sent a broken tooth into the water. The boy floundered with sputters and curses, and Darek took the opportunity to press his advantage and drag Nax over a slatted railing. Nax quickly recovered and crouched low in a defensive position.

Livis pulled Briad up, just as a fang-mouthed Nargale leaped below.

Briad gasped an incoherent thanks.

Darek peered around wild-eyed. Only a handful of contenders still remained on the boardwalks. Nax lurched forward, drunk for vengeance, swung with all his strength.

Darek's stave broke in two as Nax's weapon absorbed the impact. Darek cursed, and it fell into the Nargale water, surrounded by a flurry of bubbles as the creatures swarmed in with their wide grey mouths breaking the surface.

Nax gave a gleeful snort. He swung at Darek with deadly force while Livis threw herself at Nax, raining blows with her stave upon his back, fists, and feet.

Choking in anger, Nax struck back across her shoulders with his stave. She fell back, sprawled over the walkway's edge, her helm rolling free. Her long curls hung down to face the teeth of the leaping predators.

"Livis, no!" her mother screeched from the shore. Darmestra, faced with the sudden realization that her daughter had snuck into the competition, dug fingers into Serle's arm.

"Damn her," came Serle's curse. "Get up there! Now!" He yelled at several of his henchmen.

Pirates lurched up the ramp; Darmestra was in the lead, terrified that Livis's life was in danger.

Darek twisted under Nax's swing, in an effort to shield Livis with his back. Briad launched his own attack. Yet Briad's strikes did little but enrage Nax and earn him a sharp blow to the ribs. The pain doubled him over.

Nax stared, grim-eyed, rage thick in his throat. "I'll kill you."

"Yield, I yield," Darek gasped. But Nax laid into him again, windmilling his stave like a battle ax. Livis made a grab for Nax's weapon and pulled it from his hand. Nax twisted and pounced on Darek, straddled him, choking him with his bare hands.

Darek could feel his vision go dark and his breath wheeze out of his lungs. The brute intended to strangle the life out of him.

Like a disembodied spirit, Darek felt himself lift from his body. It was as if he traveled back through the ages where an instinctual memory burned in him like a beacon, whispering of survival. A sudden burst of energy coursed through his body; he visualized a ball of pulsing fire, that punched through the bully's thickset body. Nax's sweaty torso flew back, as if wrenched from behind by an invisible force.

What the—? Darek sucked air back in his lungs. He shook his dimming vision back to normal. The other pirates were nearly upon them. Darek dove on top of Nax and dug dirty nails into the boy's flesh, pressing his full weight on top of him. He bore both of them to the edge of the walkway.

Nax realized his danger and snatched a quick look below; he was inches away from an eager Nargale's mouth. He gave a high-pitched squeal of terror and squirmed like a worm under Darek's hold. Darek, straddling his chest, shoved his hands aside and pushed him down even lower. One swipe, two swipes of the bloodthirsty fish's teeth and Nax's life would be over.

The bloodlust in him fading, Darek thought he heard Livis calling his name. He didn't know what had come over him. With a grunt of effort, he hauled his enemy up onto the roped platforms and the two lay gasping on the planks. Hreg got there first and lifted Darek like a doll; in a mad dream Darek saw green water loom closer. But Darmestra snapped Hreg with her whip and ordered him to stand down.

With a vicious growl, Hreg stepped over his gaping son, rounded on Darmestra, his own sword gleaming in the sun's bright glare.

Darmestra caught the weapon with her whip, her grin wide and heavy. "Try it, Harpoonmaster."

Hreg seemed to realize whose wife he'd threatened and pulled back his weapon.

Serle spoke a dark word behind him. "Go ahead, Hreg, I'd like to see you try to dunk Darmestra. She's queen of the whip. Your son has already proven himself a fool. Let's not make his father one as well."

Hreg's bitter anger faded into shame as he let his sword arm fall.

Livis was carted away, while Hreg hauled Nax roughly to his feet. Two other seamen lifted Darek along with the dazed Briad and dragged them down the boardwalk to the shore.

*　*　*

In his private yurt, Serle interrogated his daughter with rough words. "What were you thinking sneaking into the fight and challenging Nax? He'll never marry you now."

"I've told you before—"

"What am I to do with a pig-headed daughter like you?"

"Why don't you let me join you on your raids?" she cried, her face pinched in pain.

Serle gave his head an angry shake. "It isn't our way. Already the more superstitious folk among us believe this Red Claw boy is a demon, some curse laid upon us that must be squashed. What if they're right? First Manx's death and our ship destroyed by serpents, now this. I won't add to it by having you killed sailing with us. As for the boy…"

A desperate look gleamed in Livis's eye. "But you saw, father… he saved me and his friend. He didn't even kill Nax when he had the chance. How can you call that a curse?"

"My hands are tied, Livvy, I cannot go up against the voice of the people."

Livis's face turned ashen. "You're a coward. What happened to the father I used to know? The one who defied rules and took on all challenges?"

Serle's lip formed into a curl of anger. "Don't press your luck, girl. From now on, you'll be confined to home."

"What? That's not fair!" she cried.

"Go!"

Livis shook her head in frustration and stormed out of the yurt, blinking back her tears.

Serle was afraid of what he had seen the boy do, both the violence and the restraint. He mumbled darkly to himself and wondered how the day had gone so sour.

Sometime later, Darmestra came to pay him a visit. "What did you say to her?"

Serle made only a gruff sound. "What she needed to hear."

"The girl's run off." She fidgeted with the seashells sewn on her cloak.

"What?" Serle demanded.

Putting an arm on his shoulder, she tried to calm her husband. "She'll come back. She always does."

Serle shook his head. "This time, I don't think so. I know her. She's taken with that slave boy. My daughter won't stand idly by and watch him be executed."

Livis's mother sighed. "I think you're right. I could sense the fire in her belly the first time those two laid eyes on each other."

Serle growled. "So be it, Darmestra. Livis'll have to understand the basic truth of things. Slaves have their place and no more. Like Osun who culls the fish."

"You spew this superstition about Osun as easily as that witch hunter, Jonse," she grumbled.

"Careful, woman. Your contempt for the old ways rankles and it'll go the worse for you before long. I have faith that Osun will guide us true and fair."

Darmestra's eyes flashed in sudden anger. "You're a fool Serle. You can no more control your fragile kingdom than you can Livis or me. She has come to realize it, and your daughter's old enough to choose her own life's course."

"Leave me be!" Serle threw his hands in the air. He hated being lectured, though he knew his wife was right. Denying it would change nothing.

* * *

Darek and Briad found themselves once again in their cell, this time with a guard posted. The tattooed man was one of Serle's and kept glancing Darek's way and making a sign of protection across his eye.

Briad winced in pain as he ran his fingers over the bruise forming on his ribs. "We should've tried to swim to *Star-runner* instead of staying to help Livis."

"How can you be so heartless?" chided Darek. "She saved your life."

"A lot of good it's done," muttered Briad, "I overheard one of the guards saying we're to be burned for witchcraft tomorrow—they would've done it by now but they wanted to wait for the one they call Jonse to come in on the morning tide."

Darek scowled. "We still have the knife."

"Great. One knife and two half-starved slaves covered in bruises against an island of pirates." Briad motioned to a table where a dark figure sat drinking slowly from a rum bottle. "You think Hreg over there is going to take his eyes off us after what you did to Nax?"

They might have been able to escape before, but it would be impossible while under the watchful eye of both a guard and the Harpoonmaster.

"Do you think he's dead?" Darek asked.

"Don't know," said Briad with a shrug, "you sure burned him up bad though."

They broke eye contact. It was best not to think of what had happened and Darek sank down hopelessly on his haunches and tried to ignore his wounds.

He must have dozed off, for shouts and commotion trickled to his senses. He blinked back confusion and stirred in bleary-eyed wonder. Men were scrambling about and someone was yelling "Fire!"

Darek shot to his feet. Early evening was upon them; a black swirl of smoke rose from the straw-roofed huts near the auroch pen. The terrified animals began to bellow, pushing against their pens as the smell of fire filled the air.

"Tend to the animals!" cried Darmestra, running toward them. A figure in dark clothing ducked into the shadows just as the gate abruptly swung open. The massive creatures began to stampede. Men, women, food carts, and wagons were swept aside by the charging sea of flesh. It was utter chaos—a perfect chance to escape!

CHAPTER *10.*

THE FIRE CORAL

Retrieving his hidden knife, Darek began to saw away at the lashings holding together the bars at the back of their cage. His fumbling grew to mounting frustration as the sun's dying glare provided little light by which to navigate. He had almost cut through one of the thick ropes when a face appeared on the other side of the bars. He jumped back in startlement, convinced that they had been caught and would be executed.

The pretty face smiled at them. "What do you think of my diversion?"

"Livis? Is that you?" asked Briad.

Her long brown hair was coiled in a tight braid and she wore a faded man's doublet and a pair of tight-fitting breeches. Darek grinned. Had she really set fire to her own people's buildings and turned loose the animals she had cared for most her life? This was a very determined young woman. Or, a very disenchanted one.

"Of course, it's me," she whispered with a wink. "Who else would save your sorry hide from the gallows?"

She produced another, larger knife and they quickly cut free two of the bars in tandem. It was enough for Darek and Briad to squeeze through.

Darek spared a glance toward the fire. The sun dipped low and stained the stickypalms a shade of deep red. Serle had organized a bucket brigade from the well. The water turned the black smoke to white. Soon they would have it under control.

"Quick," urged Livis, "we don't have much time."

They took off at a run and made it nearly halfway to the lagoon before a pirate noticed someone running away from the fire instead of toward it.

"The slaves are escaping!" hollered Hreg. "It's that witch-boy who started the fire! Drop those buckets and cut them down!"

A dozen strapping ruffians dropped their pails, drew their cutlasses, and gave chase. Livis might have made it to the dock on her own, but Briad and Darek slowed them down as they lurched up the sandy path, slowed to half speed by their injuries.

Darek snatched a glimpse back at the advancing figures. His heart sank in a premonition. "We're not going to make it. We're sunk. Leave us and go on alone."

"Forget that." Livis rushed back and lifted Briad's arm over her shoulders. Darting anxious glances left and right, she and Briad stumbled on to the sounds of crackling fire and mayhem behind them as their pursuers continued to gain ground. The pirates caught up to them just as they dipped toes in the waterline. The docks were too far away to make a run for it, but Darek was always a stronger swimmer than a runner, as most islanders were.

"Into the water!" he yelled. Ducking under the slice of a gleaming blade by the fastest of the pirates, he grappled with the man for a moment. Grabbing a handful of sand, Darek threw it into the man's eyes then kneed him in the gut, before turning to shallow dive into the water. He was determined to give Livis and Briad a head start.

The other pirates laughed at their sand-covered mate as he wiped his eyes clean. They kicked off their boots and dropped their swords in the sand. Short knives appeared in knuckled fists as they waded into the placid waves—each was an expert swimmer to a man.

Darek plowed his way through the gentle swells into deeper water, quickly catching up to Livis and Briad. Behind them, smoke curled from the ring of trees on the shore, echoing with the desperate cries of men and panicked animals. If they could make it across the strait, maybe they'd have a chance of escaping. Darek turned back to see the pirates were closing the distance. The glint of steel peeked between their clenched teeth as their powerful arms drove them closer. They would be on them in moments.

A sudden idea dawned on him. He motioned for his two companions to follow as he forged broad strokes toward the narrow channel of fire coral.

"Don't go into the fire coral!" Livis shrieked.

"We have no choice," grunted Darek. He knew from his own experience off the shoals of Cape Spear that a single brush against the fire coral could paralyze an unlucky swimmer with pain, leaving them burning for days as the poison worked its way out of the wound.

Kicking hard, Darek dove under the water like a dolphin, trying to stay in the center of the channel. The studded, bony limbs of the coral branched out toward his sides, like an alien tree. Already his eyes began to sting from the red-tinted poison in the water. If he could just make it through, he would reach his sloop docked on the other side. Seeing a clear path, Darek squeezed his eyes shut. He propelled himself forward as fast as he could. A few seconds later he cracked open an eye—just in time to avoid scraping against an oblong piece of coral that stuck out farther than the others.

Darek swam above it. The burning was getting worse, but he was almost through. With a last burst of speed, Darek pushed out into open water.

Briad screamed as a piece of coral scraped against his leg. Darek turned to see him barely staying afloat, swimming at the pace of a snail. The pirates would have caught him if they hadn't broken off to chase after Livis who was making speed in the other direction. The pursuers must have preferred a longer swim to braving the fire coral.

Darek turned back with a frustrated groan. He made his way into the darkening channel. Snatching at Briad's hair, he grabbed him just as he went under and dragged him upward—but not before the fire coral cut into his hand and struck at Briad's foot this time. By the time the two pulled themselves over the gunwales of *Star-runner*, the pirates had captured Livis. They dragged her toward shore, kicking and biting.

"Livis!" Darek howled in anguish, already feeling the loss.

"They won't hurt her. She's Serle's daughter," Briad cried. "If we don't leave now though, they'll kill us."

Darek gritted his teeth and cast off the lines. *I'll come back for you, Livis.*

Other ships came slicing after them, but Darek had a good lead by the time they had reached the higher swells.

Darkness fell on a moonless night as they approached the two guard towers on the outer reef.

"Finally, some luck," groaned Briad as he poured salt water on his swollen leg. The skin was inflamed where it had touched the fire coral. Darek slackened the sail, nursing his throbbing hand, as he approached the area he remembered peppered with submerged rocks. As luck would have it, they sailed closer under the nose of the harpoon guns, but the tower guards had dozed after chugging too much ale. No seamen would be crazy enough to navigate a ship through that treacherous channel in the dead of night...would they? Darek asked. Fortunately, he remembered where the rocks jutted up and he stayed well in the channel's middle.

But the slower speed cost them. The shouts of men and the creak of rigging soon accompanied them across the still water. The plish of a harpoon firing blindly had even Darek mumbling prayers. A dark, menacing shape loomed behind them.

Darek cursed as Briad wormed his way closer, clutching his arm. "They've sighted us. They'll kill us all!"

"Not if I can help it." Darek jammed the rudder hard to the left and he pulled Briad with him to the other side of the boat as he tacked across the bow of the incoming ship. He narrowly missed its sharp prow. A harpoon sliced inches from the starboard gunwales. There was more than a rock or two hidden in the shallow water.

Darek heard the harsh grating of wood on stone. He turned, his breath frozen. The lead ship had passed too close to the danger area and her side was now caught on a jagged rock.

A satisfied grin broke out on Darek's perspiring face. Angry shouts sprayed from the listing schooner and echoed across the dark waters. Lights went on in the tower as the guards finally realized what was happening.

Too late. *Star-runner* was out of range of the deadly harpoons.

Sailing through the darkness, Darek and Briad slept in shifts that night and set their heading by the stars. *Star-runner* lived up to her name. Darek tried to ignore the burning in his left hand as he formulated plans on how to rescue Livis. He was sure they had lost the other ships in pursuit and that they would turn around at first light...

How wrong he was.

The dawn revealed a set of sails approaching in the distance.

Darek's mouth sagged. He bet Serle himself was on that shadowy ship. He trimmed the sail and urged the sloop to greater speed. But no matter what he did, the brigade of pirate vessels behind them kept pace. A band of stars blazed above them like a trove of pearls. Darek could see dim silhouettes set against the darker water: wide-bellied hulls, thick at the waist, angling in on them like whale-sharks. If they could just make it back to the Red Claw Islands... the pirates might think twice and break off.

For half a day they sailed that way. Briad managed to snag a small grouper with a silver lure and line they'd found in a trunk below deck. The pair devoured it raw. With no fresh water their throats stayed parched.

The high peaks of Kratoke finally appeared before them, giving Darek hope that they might actually make it.

But a three-masted man-of-war appeared on the horizon, bearing down on them with speed. Darek sighed in frustration. Nowhere to hide from all these foes. He swung hard north but he could not outrun both it and the pirates. The man-of-war loomed in front of them like a great sea-hunting goliath. Darek struggled to turn *Star-runner* around, but the larger ship fired a harpoon across her bow as a warning.

Briad gave a miserable cry. He slumped to the deck in defeat. Darek, haggard-eyed and sullen, fingered his long knife with a sorrowful grunt. Cut off from his way home and now flanked from behind by the pirates, the young sailor had no choice but to fly a white flag of surrender.

* * *

Captain Raithan of the Black Claws scowled as his crewmen hauled the two prisoners aboard. He paused as he saw Darek's face, a gleam of recognition in his eye. The pirate vessels had fled as soon as his ship was joined by another flying the colors of the wizard Cyrus. At the presence no less, of a large dark shape that had surfaced near his ship. It could have been a whale, but looked like something more sinister still. With a flash of tail the creature had ducked under the waves and the ominous wizard, sole occupant of his ship, boarded Raithan's man-of-war, covered in a litany of scratches and bruises and in a very foul mood.

"Greetings, Apprentice Mage," said Raithan in a monotone, "how fortunate that you have arrived at this precise moment."

Cyrus smoothed back his oiled hair, his black robe swishing with sinister ease across the deck. Darek's blood turned to ice. Never would he forget that cruel, chiseled face.

"By my Master's grace. Tell me what you have found."

"We have a situation," grunted Raithan. "These two say they were captured by the Free Band Pirates near Windbit Isle. They have the scars to prove it. It seems that this is the *one* you spoke of who somehow managed to escape." He jerked a thumb at Darek who glowered, trussed up in a corner. "One of the pirate ships was attacked by a sea serpent, so my scouts say."

"Serpents, you say, this close to Windbit Isle?" Cyrus feigned an air of ignorance as he turned on Raithan. "That area is off limits, sacred and forbidden. If you were patrolling, then why weren't you there to put a stop to it?"

"My ships were nearby," Raithan growled, "but it is a vast ocean, isn't it?"

"Then how is it that these two *youths* managed to desecrate holy ground and escape, leaving you dependent on a mangy band of pirates to do your job?" Cyrus's scowl bordered on a sinister leer.

Raithan's jaw clenched in nervous reflex. An anxious hand strayed to his forehead. "I don't know."

Raithan looked at Darek with mixed emotions. It seemed, judging by his twitching brows and troubled stare, the captain was torn between conflicting interests. "What are we to do with this one?"

Cyrus glared at the boy like a snake sizing up its victim. "Punish him severely." The mage paused as if struck by a certain thought. "Work him to the bone but keep him alive. Death would be too easy."

"As you wish," replied Raithan. "And the other prisoner with fire coral rash on his leg?"

"Give him to me," said Cyrus with a smile that was missing two teeth. "I have need of a resilient slave."

Darek struggled against his bonds as Raithan's mates came to drag him to the foredeck. Where was the mysterious power that had flowed through his limbs and allowed him to throw Nax back in a heap?

Such force seemed to have abandoned him. The memories of diving in the lagoons at Cape Spear, sailing on the blue waves, the laughs of his friends seemed a thousand miles away. Would he ever see his friends again?

Dragon Sea: Mage Reborn

Chapter 1.

The Soaring Cutlass

A black-tipped fin cut through the water, surging through the waves as a shark might. Yet something much deadlier glided beneath the surface. Darek never could get used to the sight of a sea dragon swimming alongside the repurposed whaling vessel. The creature's purple snout and streamlined head emerged from the water, followed by a long, scaly neck. Plated shoulders and an armored body the size of a full-grown killer whale arced out of the water. The tapered shark skin harness lay exposed, secured as it was just behind the folded wings. The Sea Dragon Rider clung to the harness, taking a great gasp of air before diving back underwater in the hunt for the sea serpent, the finned tip of the tail vanishing with a final splash.

Darek blinked in amazement. Every child born on the Dragonclaw Islands learned to swim as soon as he or she could walk, but the Sea Dragon Riders made free diving an art form. The best could hold their breath for five minutes or more as their mount traveled through the water faster than the swiftest dolphin. Even then, a rider's body was put under incredible force clinging behind the contoured bulwark of the waterproof leather harness.

Darek wondered if his half-sister had ever achieved her dream of becoming one—or if she was still alive.

The crack of the Slavemaster's whip forced his thoughts back to the present. "I'll have no idleness on this ship!" Kern bellowed. "Leave off your patchwork for now and report to the boiler room. The Captain will want as much speed as we can muster for this hunt."

Darek, his biceps bronzed with soot, looked down at the canvas sail and long needle he now held motionless. *Stupid fool, you shouldn't have let yourself get distracted.* Instead of the light sewing work, he would once more be pressed into grueling labor. Life for a slave on a whaling vessel was harder and more dangerous than even working the mines.

The spotter atop the crow's nest squinted and extended his spyglass. He scanned the horizon. In the distance, three black spines shot through the water. "Serpent, off the port bow!" the man yelled down.

Barnabas the Bosun took up the signal, blowing his pipes three times to signal the target was in sight. The lanky man was growing nearsighted and slow in his old age, but he kept his pipes well-oiled and his lungs were still as strong as the day he had blown his first warning.

With a bang, the door to the captain's quarters flew open and out stepped the loose-garbed figure of Captain Raithan. As an expert in sea warfare, his uncanny skills had propelled the grizzly-bearded man to become one of the wealthiest hunters in the Black Claw Clan. He now owned more ships, sea dragons, and slaves than any other man—earning him a seat in the 'Clutch', the Dragonclaw Council that barely held back the clans from the brink of war.

"Bosun!" growled Captain Raithan, "turn us to port and bring us to hunting speed."

"Aye, Captain!" Barnabas saluted with a leathery fist. A long blast of his pipes quickly set the men into the rigging to unfurl the sails to their full size. Kern ducked below to the boiler room.

Out on the waves, a massive bottle-green shape surfaced and dipped into the waves. *Serpent!* Darek's breath rasped. The nerves in his back tingled from a patchwork of scars inflicted by the Slavemaster's lash and sent him hurrying below decks. An oppressive wall of heat rose in front of him as he descended the steps to the boiler room.

"So much for luck," he grumbled. He pulled a large scoop shovel off the rack on the wall and set to work on the mindless task. His dark hair and skin were further blackened after only a few minutes of scooping up the broken egg shells and tossing them into the furnace. Darek paused to wipe clean the three red lines tattooed on his muscular right arm—lines that covered the black mark of slavery below it. He hadn't been born into slavery and the mark of the Red Claw Clan was the only thing that still linked him to his sister.

"I will see you again one day, Meira," he whispered, "I swear it."

"Darek!" called Eloi, the head Fire-stoker. "Start feeding Henrietta." He was a free man, a fat engineer of sorts, tasked with oversight and operation of the two triple-furnace box boilers aboard the ship. Eloi had nicknamed the boiler on the port side 'Henrietta' after his wife. The starboard boiler carried the namesake of his daughter 'Wilhelmina'.

"Neither is ever full, no matter how much food you pour into 'em," he would often say with a laugh and a slap of his thigh. The joke always fell short with the slaves. A hunt could last for a full day or more before overtaking a sea serpent. Despite trading out in shifts, the slaves were often left with bleeding hands and aching backs, their arms numb and stained black from smoke and soot. Darek had thought to avoid the task when he drew the white straw of sail work from the Slavemaster's pouch.

The slaves increased their pace of shoveling as the ugly-faced Slavemaster appeared. He was a cruel overseer, pushing his charges close to the breaking point with some sort of misguided glee. Perhaps it was brought on by so few teeth in his mouth and so little stringy hair left atop his misshapen head.

"Hunting speed, you mongrels!" cried Kern as his whip struck as harshly as the man's words. "Form the line at each furnace and pray you don't fall behind." The men knew the threat to be real and quickened their pace, falling into line three men deep in front of each furnace. The Slavemaster gave a vindictive laugh at their expense. The goal was to have the next man step up and shovel in his fuel just as the last man deposited his with as little time in-between as possible.

Wilhelmina and Henrietta roared into life, the temperature in the room rising as the boilers shot steam out to propel the two side paddle wheels. The ship sliced forward through the water in response, gaining the speed that had earned her the name. Captain Raithan had spared no expense when having *The Soaring Cutlass* refitted.

She was the flagship serpent and slave hunter of the Black Claw Clan, a five-masted schooner with a dozen sails. Yet experience coupled with the two dragons swimming alongside her were no guarantee when it came to sea serpents. At five times the length of a sea dragon, a full-grown sea serpent was even longer than the ship itself. Their hides were just as well armored, but with teeth the size of an elephant's tusks and a mouth wide enough to swallow a man whole. Feared above all else, the serpents could cover the great distances of the endless ocean at a terrifying rate, attacking unsuspecting vessels at any moment. Normally they fed on whales, but had learned that sinking the ships would dislodge a group of tasty sailors. A regular ship would never be able to escape, let alone catch one in open water. Their numbers had to be culled to maintain trade routes.

Even if cannons were effective against the monsters of the deep, they were of limited use in curbing the reach of the Black Claw Clan's power. No ship could ever hope to bring one down through steam-propelled harpoons alone. Two or more sea dragons and their riders operating in concert with a skilled whaling vessel were the only thing that could make a kill like that.

The breakneck pace soon began to take its toll. Minutes stretched into hours. Darek's eighteen-year-old body was quick to heal, his muscles grown since his capture and hardened through labor. A little extra food now and again as a reward for performing more complicated tasks beyond the non-educated minds of the other slaves certainly didn't hurt. He tried to make up the time as the other slaves began to falter, until the Slavemaster's whip fell once again on their backs.

The signal for more speed came down. "Double-time!" screamed Kern, his mouth foaming with spit as he carved strokes into their hides. "Put your backs into it, you lazy barnacles!"

Shoveling as fast as he could, Darek ignored the burning in his arms. The massive boilers that powered the ship were stoked with the ground-up shells of sea dragon eggs mixed with coal. More like metal than eggshell, the fuel burned hotter and longer than anything else in this world. It only took a small amount mixed with regular fuel to spur the ship forward and match the speed of the swirling nightmare that was an adult sea serpent.

An older slave in his line collapsed from the heat. The Slavemaster started forward, scowling and muttering about murdering the 'useless fool'.

Darek gripped his shovel with one hand, grabbing the prone man's with his other. "He but needs a moment!" Darek cried. "I'll carry his load while he rests."

It seemed Kern would ignore the plea and kill the man, but then a sly smile appeared on the Slavemaster's face. "Very well, but you'll suffer twice as much for each minute you fall behind."

The older slave shook his head and tried to rise. "Rest," urged Darek. His muscles strained to do the work of two men. Each step between the furnace and the pile soon grew harder. Sweat poured off his body. *How long had it been since his last swallow of water?*

Gripping the handle of his whip tighter, the Slavemaster snarled at every moment that passed, yet Darek somehow managed to keep pace. He scowled as the older slave recovered enough to retake his place in line.

A runner appeared and reported directly to Eloi. The two men argued as Eloi gestured with both hands at the boilers, but the runner held firm and Eloi relented. A moment later the man came over.

"The—the Captain demands even more speed," said Eloi.

"We're at full speed," grunted Darek. He fell to his knees as the whip cut into his back, silencing him.

Eloi murmured an apology. "That's not technically true. If we preheat the feed water and close two of the furnace doors, it will increase the pressure and heat and produce more steam."

"You'll kill us all!" yelled Darek, heedless of the pain that followed.

"Quiet!" demanded Kern. "Get to it."

Darek's fists bunched into knots, but he stayed his temper, recalling the last time someone had defied the cruel brute's will. The Slavemaster had turned that defiant slave over to the Captain who had fed him to the sharks.

The slaves cringed back, wincing in horror as the other furnace doors were closed. The fueling continued. Three men stood alongside one another as three shovels at a time were thrown in. Soon the heat became unbearable. High pitched whistles sounded as steam began to escape from the joints in the piping. A moment later the main steam tube began to shake.

Captain Raithan's head appeared at the top of the stairs. He paused for a moment as he saw Darek, with something like regret. Then his eyes hardened. "More!" he called down. "Give me more speed and we have her!" A moment later he vanished above deck.

Eloi began wiping his already red face as he moved to turn off the blowdown and cut off the safety valve.

Darek's hand found his and prevented it from turning. "The boiler will explode," Darek cried. "I won't die this way."

A fury of blows rained down upon Darek. Before he could stop himself, Darek pushed Eloi back and turned, striking Kern in the face.

Kern staggered back, nose bloodied from the blow. "I'll have your life for that, slave!"

Gritting his teeth, Darek prepared himself for the worst. He might have avoided burning to death in an explosion, but would earn a slow and painful death instead.

A thunderous crack sounded and every man lost his footing as the ship lurched to the side. Darek smashed his shoulder against a wooden support beam, disoriented. The boiler momentarily lost pressure and flooded the room with steam. *What had happened*? Darek's ankles splashed in an inch of brine. Water streamed in from a breach on the port side. The ship was taking on water.

Chapter 2.

THE SEA SERPENT

Darek struggled to find his way to the steps. Water filled the room at an alarming rate, a portion of it filling the air with scalding steam. He bumped into two men and hauled them along with him. With a scream, the boiler re-pressurized and some of the steam receded. Darek saw he had saved Eloi and none other than the Slavemaster. The boiler room was nearly submerged, with no other movement from the doomed men below. There was still time to shove the Slavemaster back down to his death. A loud crack sounded above and the three rushed forward, bursting onto the deck.

The ship drifted in total chaos. Several bodies littered the area around them. The mizzenmast had cracked in half, burying the men beneath it in a landscape of sails. Flames ate at the lower deck, with several deckhands scurrying to douse the tongues of fire. The officer's cabin was crumpled—left in a mess of shredded timber—Captain Raithan was nowhere in sight.

A warbling rumble erupted from beyond the port railing. Darek's breath caught in his chest as the green, snake-like body of a sea serpent rose above the water. With glistening, diamond-shaped scales and a wedge-shaped head the color of moss, the creature was the largest of its kind that he had ever seen.

Wood exploded from the forecastle as a massive green tail slammed into the upper deck. An unlucky seaman was swept aside by one of the bristling, venomous black spikes at the tip. Clawing at his skin, the man lay writhing in agony as the poison liquefied him from the inside out. Darek shuddered. No other poison was as potent as sea serpent venom. Even sea dragons avoided it.

Two crew members ran for the port side harpoon, but the slavering jaws of the monster flashed to the quarterdeck, ripping them apart along with a huge section of the ship.

"Get down!" Darek threw the other two men behind a group of barrels. The ship rocked and the water roiled. Another crewman tried to make it below decks, but lost his footing and was tossed overboard.

The remaining crew tried to hide as the sea serpent lay waste to the top deck. Without warning, a purple sea dragon flew from the water with a reverberating cry. It bit into the thick neck of the sea serpent as its sharp claws slashed at the scales protecting the area.

The sea serpent bellowed, flinging its head about in an arc. Unrelenting, the sea dragon dug deep in serpent flesh with its long hind claws and refused to be thrown off. The rider not only remained on his mount, but struck out with a two-pronged spear in an attempt to skewer one of the sea serpent's eyes.

"Praise be to the Sea God!" cried Eloi. "Teach that sea slug a lesson!"

A second sea dragon burst out of the water, landing on the deck, with its rider directing his reluctant mount toward the poisonous tail of the sea serpent. If he could somehow pin the monster's main weapon to the deck of the ship, the sea serpent would be all but done for.

The Slavemaster's eyes bulged as the sea dragon dove to pin the tail just below the poisonous tip—too late—the tail swung upward just in time. The sea dragon twisted in midair to avoid the poisonous barbs. An impressive move, but one that dislodged its rider. The man smashed to the deck, cracking his head against the planks. The sea dragon, riderless, dodged swipes from the tail while positioning itself between the threat and the motionless form—it wouldn't move except at the command of the rider who trained him.

The sea serpent dove into the water, still trying to throw off the enemy sea dragon clinging to its neck.

"Maybe it'll go away?" whimpered Eloi.

"We're done for now," muttered the Slavemaster. "Better to sink and drown than be eaten alive in a hopeless swim across open water!"

Darek ran fleet-footed toward the downed rider. The sea dragon growled, warning him away with a set of razor-sharp teeth. Gray and orange stripes ran down the male dragon's horned crest. Larger than average in size, its scales shimmered with majesty in the sun.

"Easy," Darek said in a soothing voice. "I just want to check on your rider." He understood the need for haste and extended his hand to allow the creature to smell it.

"You're wasting your time," shouted the Slavemaster. "The dragon will never listen to you."

The sea serpent rose again from the water, intent on killing them all.

A tall, dark form fired the starboard harpoon. The curved spike bit into the back of the sea serpent, trailing a thick chain. Captain Raithan stood behind the weapon with a bloodied face but otherwise uninjured.

"Kraton take us!" moaned Eloi. "Now it'll never leave us alone."

The sea monster surfaced beside the ship once more, bleeding from where the harpoon had pierced it. The purple sea dragon still clamped down on its throat. The rider still hadn't given up and was stabbing again and again despite little effect. Smashing itself against the ship, the sea dragon's hold loosened and a hind leg slipped free. Darek knew in moments that the sea dragon with the purple snout would be flung off and devoured. The men left alive aboard would be next. Kraton! He had to do something…now!

The gray sea dragon, its keen eyes darting from the threat of the serpent back to his still unconscious rider, was oblivious of Darek as he inched closer toward the shark skin harness.

The tail of the sea serpent swung up near its own head. *Was it trying to knock off the sea dragon without hitting itself?* Strange behavior for a monster not known for its intelligence.

Darek grabbed the reins and jumped onto the back of the riderless sea dragon. "Attack!" he thrust a commanding finger toward the sea serpent. The sea dragon froze, then reared backward. Rather than attack, it shook and flung itself to the side, trying to buck Darek off. Darek slid down the dragon's hide and barely caught the head straps in time. When his fingers contacted the scaly skin, the creature calmed.

"That's it," Darek soothed. "We're friends. Just trying to help your rider—drinking buddies we are."

Pressing his fingers to the dragon's temple, he looked up at the sea serpent. The purple dragon now held on with only its jaws and foreclaws as the larger, snakelike head shot back and forth. "Save your rider and your friend," Darek whispered, then louder, "Fight!"

The sea dragon loped forward into a run. "Wait," Darek cried, regaining his seat.

He clung to the side of the harness, nearly slipping to his death as the sea dragon bounded off the broken mast and leapt over the railing. The serpent gave a thunderous roar as the gray sea dragon hit it in the chest, claws and teeth flashing. The dragon climbed the monster's scales, leaving a bloody trail and clamped down on the other side of the serpent's neck.

As the sea dragons cut into an artery, the serpent began to thrash as the dragons bled it dry. It sank lower in the crimson water, wriggling like a worm, then lay still. At last the sea dragons released their hold on the dead monster, their bloody teeth thrown wide and fearsome calls thrumming over the kill.

The remaining men aboard cheered. Darek dove into the water, too exhausted to do much more than cling to a floating barrel.

Eloi threw him a line and pulled him to the wreckage of the ship. "You must be blessed by the Sea God."

"The dragon did all the work," Darek said hoarsely. "Pray a ship comes to our aid before we sink completely."

The Slavemaster was still searching for his lost whip. "We're more likely to be found by another sea serpent than a ship."

* * *

They floated in aimless circles for what seemed like hours. The ship had taken on water, but it was well built and like a stubborn itch, refused to sink. The purple sea dragon and its rider circled the vessel, conducting a half-hearted patrol. The gray dragon remained by its still unconscious rider, unwilling to move from his side.

Darek sank into a dismal crouch amidships while Captain Raithan stared out at the desolate horizon. It seemed the man would go down with his ship. Then he stirred to action. Rushing to the upper deck, Raithan leaned out over the broken mast and lifted a hand to shield the sun from his face.

"Whirlpool to the port side!" he yelled.

Darek realized they had been moving faster, caught in the outer ring of the whirlpool's undertow. The hidden vortexes in the *Serpents' Deep* had led many ships to their doom. He could see the churning water in the distance—and it would mean death unless they could somehow break free.

THE DRAGON SEA CHRONICLES: THREE BOOK SERIES

"Hendrick!" Captain Raithan called to the Dragon Rider. "Tie on and see if you can pull us free of the current." He ran to the stern.

Hurrying to catch up, Darek and Eloi helped the captain tie off several lines to the mast and railings before throwing them into the water. Hendrick retrieved the lines and secured these to the back of his harness.

Hendrick called out an order with a quick pat to his mount. "Pull, Turso!—swim to starboard with all you have!"

The dragon struggled to free the vessel from the swirling currents. With repeated tail thrashes the creature inched forward, straining at the rope with all its might. Darek heard a loud whooshing like a fiendish waterfall. A shiver crawled up his spine. At first, it seemed fruitless and they continued to be drawn toward the churning waters. Turso bellowed a roar and his purple scales flashed as he clawed forward through the water.

"Put some muscle behind it. Bail water!" commanded the captain. Darek found a bucket, Eloi found another. While the survivors struggled to lighten the stern that lay low in the water, Eloi invoked every god and incantation he could think of.

The man's prayers must have worked, for their progress toward a watery death slowed, then stopped. In slow increments they reversed course and moved away from the whirlpool and back out into the open water. The men fell exhausted to the deck. Darek wondered if he would ever see land again.

They had nearly given up hope as the sun began to sink. In the last precious moments of daylight, Darek spotted a black sloop with a single mast approaching. The sail bore the white crest of Cyrus, Agrippa's young Apprentice Mage. Able-bodied sailors pulled the survivors aboard and deposited them on the deck like the day's catch. A ship medic prodded Captain Raithan, but he shrugged the man off, pointing to the still unconscious Dragon Rider. Darek stood in wordless suspicion behind Eloi and the Slavemaster. Aside from them, only the other Dragon Rider, the resourceful cook, and a strong-swimming midshipman from the crew had survived.

A sour-faced man wearing dark robes and a white crest appeared from the cargo hold of the rescue ship. "Thank the Sea God we found you in time," he said. He was in his mid-twenties, tall and thin, with the beginnings of a short black beard. "Agrippa will be pleased to learn of your victory. The serpents are hunting closer to the islands more than ever."

"That water snake almost had us," Captain Raithan replied, "smart he was, *too smart*—destroyed my favorite ship."

"They are mindless serpents," said Cyrus primly, "— merely lucky to fare so well against the famous Captain Raithan. You honor the Black Claw Clan with this victory."

Captain Raithan turned to watch his boat sink lower in the waves. "Honor will not cover the loss of my ship or the men who worked her."

"Let me see what my engineers can do to prevent her loss," said Cyrus, "there may yet be a way to salvage her."

A glimmer of excitement grew in the Captain's eyes. "I would be in your debt, Mage."

"Something we will discuss later," Cyrus said with a smile. "Ready the floats and tar patchwork!" he called to a team of engineers who hurried to obey.

"I've never seen a water snake turn and hit the side of a ship like that," murmured the cook.

The Slavemaster jerked himself forward. "Great Mage, he was summoned by this slave—cursed he is."

"You cur," growled Darek. "I saved your life—"

"Hold." Captain Raithan put up his hand. "These are serious accusations. What proof do you have?"

A gap-toothed leer appeared on the Slavemaster's face, then it vanished. "I heard him say he would 'kill us all' and a half minute later the sea serpent collided with the ship. You saw for yourself that the serpent was acting strangely—it was the slave controlling it!"

"But Darek saved us!" Eloi said as he stepped forward. "When the Dragon Rider fell, Darek jumped on the dragon's back and attacked the sea serpent. Why would he do that if he had summoned it?"

"A trick," bawled the Slavemaster, "to earn his freedom through sorcery. We should kill him now before he brings us another monster."

Captain Raithan glared daggers at the Slavemaster. "I won't have one of my slaves put to death for trying to save the ship," he roared.

"Silence," commanded Cyrus. He leveled a gaze at Darek. "Is it true you stole a sea dragon from its rider and rode it?"

"Choose your next words with care, Darek," said Raithan. "I promised your mother Thyphalyne I'd keep you alive, but this is out of my hands."

"Aren't you the kind one," Darek said sardonically.

"Answer the Mage," ordered the Slavemaster.

"Well..." began Darek, "I wouldn't call it riding—more like hanging on while it attacked the serpent—but I only did it because the Rider was knocked out and I certainly didn't summon any sea serpent!"

"Enough," grunted Cyrus, bristling with anger. A trace of surprise flickered in his expression. "The boy has admitted to riding another's sea dragon and stands accused of summoning. We all know the law. He must submit to the test and perform the Rebirth Ritual. Kraton awaits. Throw him into the volcano!"

THE DRAGON SEA CHRONICLES: THREE BOOK SERIES

Chapter 3.

KRATON

Three seamen dragged Darek cursing from his barren cell. His leather sea breeches were still ragged and bloody from the sea serpent attack. A group of villagers were waiting among the crowd, the same he had served with steadfast loyalty and who had taken him in as a pirate's slave. Darek spat. The ungrateful swine.

The chant came to his ears in a monotone, a terrible thrum, as from the mouths of a nameless enemy:

"In the blood of Kraton's fire,
Will ye rise and serve and never tire,
A mage reborn!"

The villagers cried an answering hail to the ancient sea chantey.

Bravix, head priest of the Black Claw Clan, shook his green-dyed dreadlocks and motioned to a gang of enforcers to follow his lead. They swung their flails, forcing Darek up the seaside path to the looming volcano behind the docks of Sparstoke. Many dragon ships bobbed in the rising waves. The crowd followed. From the summit came coils of gray smoke. Two days before, the same mountain was lifeless, a wolf-gray inert cone. Now it was brewing with wrath. Usually dormant, the spring equinox signaled the firebane's yearly eruption.

Kraton was a small, cylindrical cone, much like a grouper coming to the surface, its greedy gullet opened wide. The mountain shimmered the color of silt from the freshets that ran down its slopes to drain into the emerald sea. The clan members were too chicken-hearted to brave Kratoke, Darek thought, thrice its size, smoldering in the periphery like some fire dragon. That had been lucky for him. Had they endeavored to plunge him into that behemoth... He did not want to think about that.

A foul sulfur reek like rotten eggs wafted down from the mountain, riding wisps of fumes.

The priests had been predicting the triumphant return of Kraton for generations, but no one really knew when it was going to erupt. The coming of the volcano god would spill cinders and ash over the base of the mountain. These Black Claw people trusted the mountain far too much, thought Darek. They would all die, victims of their bloodthirsty deity. Daft superstitious bunch. It was their beliefs that had led him into slavery.

Being so long a slave, Darek could barely recall collecting bright seashells on the beach, chasing mischievous crustaceans as they scurried for their burrows, swimming at dusk in the warm lagoons, or spearfishing for tropical snapper. He had mastered holding his breath for four minutes, propelling his body down below the coral and the underwater castles. Strange thoughts flitted in his mind as he trudged onward. Like his first kiss in the crystal clear waters of Milgrun's lagoon, exploring the sea caves with a fisherman's daughter. The time when he had almost found real treasure—an old battered sea chest broken amongst the ribbed ruins of a pirate ship. Even if it was only a few misshapen coins lying by the skeleton of some old sea dog whose ship had run aground, his young heart looked upon it as the greatest find.

The memories swirled before him as the graveled zigzag path passed under their feet and took them to the summit.

As the sweat poured from his grimy skin, Darek could still feel the shame and terror of his capture two years ago. It would haunt him forever. Nor would he ever forget Vinz's dare that had spurred him to foolishness into braving enemy waters and the clutches of the pirates.

That scum of a glowworm Cyrus hadn't even bothered to make an appearance at this barbaric event. The cretin was too 'busy' to take time to see if he would die a painful death or become the next 'mage reborn'. Darek rasped an oath.

As the unforgiving group came to the top, Darek saw rickety, wooden scaffolding peeking out from behind veils of smoke. A crude mesh of timber planks greeted him, a makeshift ceremonial walkway that formed a gangplank out over the cone, like a diving platform.

The presiding priest, Bravix, nodded to the group. He lit his staff with flame, a *centure*, a magical staff that invoked the volcano God.

"Behold, slave. Mark your fate. Should you rise and survive, Kraton will bless you with his gift. If you do not, draw solace that you will have served the Black Claw Clan well. Try not to die too quickly."

A wild wave of resentment burned in Darek's heart. Venom seethed in his voice. "I will have revenge for this! My ghost will haunt these isles and one day cut down those who stand against me." His words were lost in the echo off the rocks.

"Silence, guttersnipe. Your blasphemous tongue irks."

"Such vindictiveness," agreed Bravix's attendant with a yawn.

"Enough. Goad this infidel forward. If he resists, prick him with steel." He turned to his head spearman. "Cut him loose! The slave will need all his resources when he faces our God."

On a nod, Bravix's spearman cut Darek's bonds and prodded the defenseless wretch along the gangplank.

Darek growled back. "Have it your way." He scuttled sideways, his eyes darting about in desperation for some means of escape.

There was none. Sharpened shell fencing ran the gamut of the sides, offering only a steep drop down into the smoking pit below.

"Get moving, guppy!" cried one of the larger clansmen. His black claw pendant lifted high. A jab in the upper thigh had Darek wincing. The strike drew blood which now trickled down his leg.

Bravix flicked the flaming staff in careless fashion. He pulled a dangling clump of matted hair from his prickly coiffure, and tossed it down into the inverted cone-shaped funnel below. With his upturned nose wrinkling, he uttered an incomprehensible prayer and signaled the underpriests to prod the prisoner the rest of the way.

With a defiant smirk, Darek turned, taking a running leap. Rather than give those arrogant oafs the satisfaction of goading him on against his will, he opened his arms wide and embraced the open air.

The wind whistled in his ears. The mournful cry of seagulls echoed in his mind, adding to the strange, hallucinatory madness as he fell. Darek slid and tumbled down into the volcano's mouth. His legs caught the inner slopes of pumice slanting down at a sharp angle, as the soft ash cushioned his fall and the smoke rose. He coughed and cried out as skin on his bare shins was torn away. He clawed for some passing rocks, but made only surface contact as he was buffeted sideways, funneled down a dark side shaft. Even if he did survive this murderous slide, he would be trapped in the volcano's gullet—unable to climb out. Only Cyrus had survived the dreaded Kraton years earlier—the mountain of doom.

Time stood still. He rolled and slid, wondering if the rumors were true, about the fabled mother dragon, whose breath drove the mountain to fiery wrath. Not that it mattered. He was doomed, and suddenly in free space, spinning...

With a splash, he landed in a deep, dark pool.

The water was warm. A muted roar came to his ears, a well of eternity smothering his senses.

Somewhere in his plunge down the chute, it seemed he had been directed away from the main conduit and tumbled into this secret pool.

His first impulse was to fight, to thrash like a netted fish. Instinct had him thrusting upward like a dolphin. He kicked to the surface, his lungs barely winded. Blinking in the dim light, he found himself in an enormous cavern. The bottle-green pool was only a small part of it. He sputtered to the shore, a strand of porous rock, feeling every inch of the stinging ache in his scraped limbs.

Crusty stalactites reared above him. Fat stalagmites rose to either side of him, stained sepia by the glimmer of fire from a distant side passage.

Where was he? Had he fallen into a deep pool below the sea?

Darek floundered several paces to halt before a dark hole in the wall. Could this be a way out? He peered down into the bottomless pit filled with a glimmer of red. Traces of fumes rose up the main shaft to seek the open air outside. The only escape seemed to be down into the volcano and out to the ocean.

A shudder ran through his body. He shook the dizziness out of his head. He glimpsed a shadowy opening to the side of the cavern.

A side entrance, an old lava tube? Darek had heard of the labyrinth of tunnels that existed in these near dormant volcanoes.

A hope grew in his heart, as did a lingering unease. The tunnel certainly was less steep than trying to crawl up the sheer sides.

He retraced his steps with renewed energy and swam through water, noting nothing more than a series of connected pools. The water was warm against his abraded skin, cleansed now of its blood, but stinging like the lash of a scourge. He kicked his way through the last mysterious waters and reached out quivering fingers to touch porous rock which felt hot to his touch, doubtless the source of the water's warmth.

Sprawled upon the shore, he forced himself to his feet and stumbled on toward the tunnel carved in the cavern's wall that he had spied earlier. A human skeleton lay in an undignified sprawl at his feet. He swayed, dripping water on the remains as vertigo struck. The arm bones lay twisted in grisly display. The blasted skull lay tipped down as if in servitude. Doubtless a sacrifice like himself who the Black Claw people had thrown into the pit. By no means must he share this fate.

Too many narrow escapes from death. His mind balked as it drifted to *The Soaring Cutlass* and the serpent battle. How had he managed to ride that out-of-control sea dragon and thwart the sea creature?

The lava tube rose on a steep slant. Darek knew the ascent up that shaft would be difficult, clutching at the rough rocks and pressing his toes into crevices to push himself up.

The rock around him shivered with a sudden blast of steam. Darek recoiled. He crouched on the balls of his feet, his eyes smarting from the sulfurous tang of the water. He squinted about in desperation. Smoke billowed from the conduit behind him. Tongues of flame now licked over the lip of the dark well, causing him to cough and gag.

No way to climb those slippery scree slopes which marked the tube. How could anybody, let alone any wizard, survive this hell? No new mages had been born in these lands for years. It was no wonder. How had Cyrus managed it? How did they expect anyone to survive?

The ground rumbled for a few seconds under his feet before falling silent. He had to move. Lungs filling with fumes, he felt nauseous. He didn't know when the mountain would blow.

With fingers fumbling in the murk, he looked about in wild despair. He was convinced he would become one of those desiccated corpses unless he took immediate action. It was either try or die.

Chapter 4.

Bowels of the Volcano

Squelching the panic welling in his gut, Darek sucked in a lungful of air, less sulfurous this time. He dove back into the water. Down through the murky pool he stroked his way as he had a thousand times on his adventures probing the sea floor.

The light started to fade from the water as he drew deeper into the plum-colored murk. The tunnel pitched at a sharp angle. Should he fail to find a source of air...

He did not want to think about that. Counting heartbeats, he noted two minutes had elapsed. It felt like an eternity passed in that haze of frenzied breast-stroking. A small spasm impinged on his lungs—lungs starting to burn.

The drowned tube arched up like a U. He kicked out with his feet, squelching a gasp. At last, his head broke the surface, his lungs near bursting. He found himself in a cavern similar to the last one.

Two pools lay at either side. One was just his size, the other slightly larger, shimmering a bottomless black that chilled his heart.

Darek's brain registered comprehension. During high tide, the sea water must flood the lower lava tubes.

He crawled out onto a flat section, his lungs heaving and his brain struggling for a plan of action. He squinted in the echoing chamber. Further down the cavern, he spied the tunnel that continued at a sharper angle above his head.

Rather than exploring underwater possibilities, his best hope for escape seemed through an external lava tube tunneling to the volcano's side. Rumbles and shakes and cracking rock made this hope seem distant. He realized he must have popped up in a pool at the same level as the last.

He could not distinguish much here in the dimness, except for fresh, smoldering embers at the cavern's far end. *Lava trickles?* They glinted like the fiendish eyes of a stingray, or a glass-eyed shark.

The sides of the chamber arched up toward the sky, glowing with green serpentine rock. Squinting, his eyes adjusting to the light, he registered new forms in the shadowy extremities. A series of dragon skeletons lay all along the periphery. Dozens of them were scattered about the perimeter like broken goliaths in various postures of decay and doom. Many were covered in hardened lava or yellow corrosion.

A necropolis? Darek thought such beasts were near immortal. What could have killed these majestic giants in a place hidden from the world?

Thrusting his head closer, he saw that the walls dripped with an uncanny luminescence, or a weird slimy coating which sent eerie chills down his spine.

His knees trembled. His skin, torn from his plummet down the volcano, tingled. Quivering with exhaustion, he padded closer to the dead dragons. Hefting a large broken jawbone, he grunted with the effort before letting it fall in a clatter of bones. He stooped to examine a large shape hovering in the shadows: a shape of fable, an ovoid egg, slightly greenish-gray and larger than a baby whale.

Another rumbling blast shook the chamber. Darek leaped aside as a stalactite crashed down, nearly impaling him.

Another rumble and Darek ducked as crimson flames licked in from the ceiling. He crashed against the enormous egg, cringing in terror. The breath caught in his throat only to erupt in a curse. The fire licked down the wall, heating his quivering skin.

The heat threatened to scorch his hands. Logic dictated he jump back in the water but a strange compulsion drew him closer to the dragon spawn. He embraced the egg, feeling its smooth coolness and its serpentine-white form as he steadied his breath. The egg seemed unaffected by the rising heat. How could that be?

Without warning, a jolt of energy tingled his flesh, as if the thing within had life. But how? The egg looked to be fossilized, possibly preserved for eons throughout the ravages of time. Darek closed his eyes. Again, a strange compulsion fell over him. He let his mind drift, allowing the inner reaches of his being to spider out and pass through the shell. Something stirred inside! He willed himself to connect with the being within in friendship and respect. To whatever was in the egg he bestowed his good will and his life force. But the stifling heat of the encroaching lava made him cough as the fire drew closer around them. If he was going to die in this accursed place, he would learn the secret of these dragon eggs.

Something dawned on him. All these dragons, now little more than moldered skeletons, had hatched and died, all but this lonely egg. They had roasted like ribs of meat on the spit above the unforgiving heat of the volcano.

How this egg had survived he did not know, but intuition told him that something still lived within. He felt a symbiotic connection with it, as if it were possible to communicate even through the rock-hard shell. A marvel which stretched his imagination.

The egg shivered and cracked.

Darek reeled back. Had it moved in response to the fire and his touch? His body surged with heat. Crouching, he gasped for air as if he were in the heart of the volcano itself.

The egg split and a slimy, sea dragon sprawled on the stone. Larger than seemed possible, it must have been curled up in a tight ball inside the egg. The newborn had wings and scaled flanks with silver speckles around the edges, like stardust. It licked instinctively at its glistening hide and oleaginous wings. Two silver eyes glared out from above a blunt snout. Four wings fluttered like a dragonfly's, though they were sturdier, like straps of old flexible leather. The wings labored without success in launching the thing off the crumbled ground as the creature took a small series of hops, grunting deep-seated rumbles from a wattled, bull-like throat. Its bloated belly waddled forth with the help of four lizardish legs.

Abandoning its attempt at flight, the dragon stared with hungry eyes and slavering jaws at Darek. It studied him, unblinking, yet with wary respect.

A gurgling at the cavern's far end had Darek turning. Lava had started to bubble from that side, spilling into the pool in a hot, sulfurous stream.

Darek coughed. The air was becoming unbreathable. More rocks fell and he whirled as red-hot smoking lava streamed down a rivulet and plunged, hissing into the nearest pool.

Darek crouched in panic. He stumbled forward, seeking clean air. The dragon advanced on him, eyes pulsing in the weird light. Its jaws opened, showing a line of jagged teeth.

Darek stepped back, knowing there was nowhere to run. He was trapped, faced with a newborn dragon bearing down on him.

Should he plunge himself into the pool? To brave the sinking lava stream would be a risk.

He trusted his intuition as he stared at the dragon. To show undue fear at this point was the wrong move and would only hasten his doom. He had heard of huge gyrfalcons that turned on their mother shortly after being hatched. But that thought was not helpful.

The dragon stopped, its powerful legs braced, snorting steam through its nostrils. It had no trouble breathing. Darek stood transfixed, as the beast now blinked at him in what appeared to be curiosity.

His gaze caught a trickle of watery light behind the dragon's saurian form. His ears registered a faint seaside roar. He leaped past the pools, toward the end of the cavern and behind the dragon from where the noise came. He could not see much, only an apple-sized hole that showed a cavern beyond the solid wall. Resting his ear next to the gap, he could hear the roar of the sea. The dragon backed away, studying him.

On a hunch, Darek snatched up the ancient jawbone and hacked at the opening. Bits of black rock fell at his feet.

With a grimace, he thrust his head through the opening, drawing in a fresh gulp of air.

A small amount of light filtered from the cavern's far side. Daylight? Darek sniffed, and thought to detect the faint salty tang of seaside air. His heart leaped with excitement. He looked down at the pool. Maybe that pool provided quick access to the cavern beyond?... filled with fresh air and salvation. But if the watery tunnel dead-ended or was blocked by fallen rock, what then?

The wary beast seemed to mimic his behavior and lumbered over to bash its head against the wall. It wanted to help, or at the very least live as well. But after a dozen strikes, the wall still held.

Darek fell back in frustration. "Hellfire! We'll suffocate here or be cooked by lava. Skewered by those falling rocks!" Another deep rumble shook the surrounding rock. More lava streamed from the fissure. Darek croaked in misery. The volcano Kraton was going to kill them.

He looked with doubt at the trembling surfaces of the pools at his feet. They would have to brave the sinking lava streams. Soon they would heat the water to unbearable levels. The question was, which pool to take? Left or right? The right showed promise, wider and able to fit both him and the dragon. But would it follow him? The left one, closest to the wall, was large enough only for him. Either could be a dead end. He risked drowning alone or in the foolish attempt to save the dragon.

The more he stewed, the more stalactites fell and he cried out in anguish, leaping closer toward the pool.

The dragon nudged its snout against him, spinning him out of his reverie. It lowered its neck.

Darek blinked, his lips peeled back. Could it be asking him...? No, his mind spun back to his pitiful attempt at riding the sea dragon on *The Soaring Cutlass*. He had commanded the beast and survived. This one looked capable of swimming. In three quick strides, he mounted the dragon and with an instinct for survival, wrapped his arms about its corded neck. He clung panting to its cool, scaly body and the rounded spine rippled behind him. The beast vaulted into the larger pool. Down it plunged, its leathery hide shooting forth like an arrow. Darek stared wild-eyed, his young heart aflutter, thinking himself in some fantastic dream.

The tunnel wound and the great dragon kicked outward with its powerful hind legs as it dog-clawed with its forelegs, plunging them ahead with speed. Dragon and human fled through the water, banging into the sides as Darek ducked, feeling the pressure in his ears and a scratchy rock scrape against his frayed leathered thighs. He resisted the urge to cry out. A plum-colored gloom fell over the tunnel, but some phosphorescence on the wall gave a precious trace of light.

Fire-fish with long tapered bodies finned out of the shadows. Fiercely territorial, they had red bands on their flanks and wicked white teeth. The predators attacked them from niches carved in the porous rock, disregarding all sense as they swarmed the larger creature in defense of their dens. They dug small fangs into the dragon's hide. One of the larger fish darted for its eye and sunk in its fangs, drawing out a clutch of white meat. The dragon jerked, spasming in pain and Darek felt the whole breadth of the creature's body quiver. It batted away the fish with a claw and shivered, but it did not let up on paddling.

Another bold fish bit into Darek's forearm, causing him to gurgle. It drew blood, and he stifled an urge to scream and draw water into his lungs. He shrugged off the offending marauder and clung desperately to the dragon's neck.

Up and over castles of rock, around curves, and past strange fluted formations the dragon swam, until it shot out of the water, to land with a thud on the crumbled shore.

Darek rolled off with a thump on the shale beach from a deeper cavern. He gulped fresh air into his heaving lungs.

Dragon and rider were in a cathedral-like grotto with pale light streaming down from its far end. Darek grunted in relief, for the light could only be daylight.

As he lay gasping on his back, the dragon's bulk loomed over him, dripping water and blood from its torn face. It was a female. He could tell by the slender tail fin.

Darek checked his wounds. Sucker marks peppered his shins and wrists exposed to the predators, but the wounds were not life-threatening. The scavenger fish, denizens in these seaside caves, grew much larger than their reef cousins—perhaps transformed from the lava that flowed forth during the spring equinox? Darek's head spun.

The dragon cocked its head, a mournful rumble in her throat. They had survived the god, but not before he had left his mark upon them. The young dragon was clearly blind in one eye, now dangling with flaps of skin from the silvery, iridescent skin. Darek cried out in shock. "Oh no, girl, your eye's cut!"

He reached out to see if there was anything to be done for it, but the dragon wouldn't let him near the wound. Tears formed in Darek's eyes. "You sacrificed your eye to save me. I won't forget that. I'll watch out for you from now on—I promise."

The dragon looked at him with one silver eye. *That's what I'll call you. Silver Eye.* He stroked her neck for several minutes until she relaxed.

With grim resolve, Darek stumbled ahead, skirting pools that led to the aqueous light he saw further in. Crashing waves and roaring surf were not far off. Silver Eye loped after him without question.

They pushed off from the shore and swam together out into the pale midday sun, Darek clinging to the dragon's neck, free at last from the mountain's oppression. He hoped they could make for the Clawreach Islands many leagues from the ominous volcano.

Behind him, Kraton stood like a wild blister. Wicked flames belched fumes and debris into the air. Darek wondered how the feckless villagers were faring.

He hoped they all died.

For what seemed like hours, Silver Eye thrust forelimbs and hind legs through the blue swells to bring them closer to a safe stretch of beach, far from the volcano. Disoriented by her damaged eye, the dragon paddled in jerky pulses, but managed to veer into shallow water. Meanwhile, Kraton continued to erupt in liquid flames, raging and rumbling thunderous booms.

Darek spotted a sheltered area up the headland. The dragon seemed to sense his destination and angled in that direction. They emerged slowly from the surf, awed and intimidated by the distant smoldering giant.

"Well, what do you say, Silver Eye? Shall we call it a day?" Darek tumbled off the dragon's back, slumping with exhaustion on the warm sand, feeling the weight of ages drain from his stiff limbs.

The tinkling movements of the dragon's scales chimed in tune with her low rumbles as she hopped up the beach. The surf lapped in a hypnotic rhythm, lulling Darek's brain into a trance as he crouched in a daze, letting the sun dry his skin. With a grunt, he shook off his reverie and staggered up the beach to lie in the sand-grass before a clutch of boulders by a low cliff.

No one would come for them here. They all would think he had died back in that infernal *firebane*.

Let them believe it! A vindictive sneer curled Darek's mouth and he fell into a much needed sleep.

Chapter 5.

Freedom

When he awoke, the early morning sun was peeking out between ragged clouds, casting a pleasant warmth on Darek's tanned face. The surf continued to play musical tones as he lay back and yawned. Silver Eye was out and about, clawing at mud pools farther down the beach. Land crabs the size of tortoises crawled across the sand searching for beached fish and other creatures from the sea. Darek stood, revitalized. He snapped off a branch from a piece of driftwood and wielded it like a wooden spear to skewer one of the slower crabs. Using sharp rocks for flint, he started a fire with the help of some dried driftwood. He hooked the meaty claws on a stick and toasted them, then munched ravenously.

Silver Eye had ventured closer and he wondered anew at this strange gift from Kraton. He tossed her some of the cooked meat, but she turned her nose away, more interested in stalking the live crabs. Darek watched as they tried in vain to scuttle away from the dragon before she crunched them in her teeth, shell and all.

"You're a quiet one, aren't you?" he mused. "Not like the other sea dragons I know. Like, chief Lared's dragon, Whalechaser. You're smarter. Your wings are larger than most sea dragons. Shall we try for a short flight?"

He put his hand on her back but she shied away, blinking her one eye at him. *Too soon maybe.*

Darek felt he could lie in the sun indulging in the ocean's bounty all day, but he had to keep moving. *Meira.* Was his sister still on the Red Claw Islands? What of Briad and Livis who had helped him escape Devil's Isle? He stared out toward the sea and marveled at its endless rolling swells. His eyes drifted past the breakers to specks of green that must have been the first outriders of the Red Claw lands, then he turned to young Silver Eye who had waded into the surf, busy gobbling up clams. He needed a ship. But without any hope of finding one, he would have to rely on the dragon—at least she could swim much faster than he. No way could he show himself anywhere on the island though. The Black Claw Clan would kill him on sight unless he had the power of a Mage, which he surely hadn't.

"Well, let's quit this miserable place, Silver Eye, and go home, shall we?"

The dragon appeared to grasp something of the words' meaning and made a guttural sound in her throat. She crouched and rolled in the sand like a pet hound and Darek climbed up on her back and patted her neck. "Atta girl! Think you can fly?"

With a peculiar squawk, the dragon hopped down the beach, gaining speed. With an ungainly leap, she launched herself airborne. Darek gasped as her juvenile wings pulsed with mad abandon and he felt a strange thrill in his heart. Up and up she flew, her four wings beating a fury out over the water and into the cloudy sky. Darek couldn't stop from smiling as they gained speed, the spray off the water diminishing as they lifted higher. He never understood why Meira had wanted to become a Dragon Rider—until now. The wind hit his face like a ship under full sail, but the entire sky was his domain.

"Woohoo!" What freedom to fly like a falcon, with a view over all of the Dragon Isles.

For hours he flew on Silver Eye over open water and now green foliage and countryside dipped beneath them like satin fields, a sea of undulating grass below. Up and over Whalehaunt Cape on the first of the Three Sisters' Isles, they passed where Markne's fish market shimmered below in the old town square. Over there, the twin lighthouses welcomed ships into port. Darek could see knots of people craning necks and eyes turning up to see an unfamiliar shape in the air. The silver-headed dragon carried its rider with an ease that was as natural as the wind.

The conical tops of the Caragon Volcanoes glinted from afar to the east. Curls and wreaths of cindery smoke rose from the two dominant volcanoes, Kraton and Kratoke, while the sparkling waters of the Barbasson stretched as far as the eye could see. Distant pocks of neighboring isles glinted on the horizon.

Darek noticed a strange bird tailing them, circling high above. He didn't think much of it, until Silver Eye deviated from her course in pursuit of a meal. He swatted her back to get her attention. "North, Silver Eye, head north! To Cape Spear and the heart of the Red Claw lands."

The familiar archipelago of Darek's birth began to loom below them now and he saw expanses of tree-crowned rock sheltering fertile plains. A small volcanic range swept several miles beyond that, rising like a row of broken teeth.

As Darek descended to his familiar waterside locale, he felt a wash of a thousand memories flood his being. *Where to next?* The beast upended him in Milgrun's lagoon, Darek's favorite haunt. The thrill of his coming home ground to a sudden halt.

Crawling to the shore, Darek blew out water from his nose. The dragon stared at him with an innocent look, but her talons tapped mischievously as she blinked in the bright light. *She had dumped him in on purpose.*

"Going to be ornery, are you? Not enough crab to your liking? Well, it's time to teach you some manners—"

A voice called from behind. "Ho-Dragon Rider. Hey, Darek. Is that you? No, impossible!"

Darek whirled about, his eyes rounding on a figure lurching out of the foliage, a fresh minnow trap in hand. "Fasouk?" Darek's old childhood friend was all grown up now. The faint brown beard and square-cut face did not hide the boyish grin and the freckles of youth he knew so well.

"Keep your voice down," grunted Darek. "I'm not supposed to be here, Fasouk—or even alive."

Fasouk flashed him a nervous grin, but Darek knew his friend could keep a secret.

"You're back from the dead," the newcomer remarked. "Margrir, our chief fisher-master, said you were long drowned—swallowed by a whale."

"Well, I'm here, am I not? Besides, no whale could ever hold me."

Fasouk laughed. "Where'd you go then? You been holed up in a giant clam shell?" He paused to blink with awe at Darek's young sea dragon. "Seems as if you have a friend." He peered at the gash on her face. "Poor thing. What happened to her eye?"

Darek held up a hand. "I don't have time to explain. Lingering here is risky enough." He flashed Fasouk an expectant glance. "Meira. Is she still around? Is she alive? Well?"

Fasouk scratched his stubbly chin. "On Whale Island, I think. Last I heard, she's pissed at Raithan for sending her away—and Cyrus for not accepting her as one of his apprentices, and, of course, you for dying."

Darek shook his head. Visible relief spouted out in an explosive gust. "That's Meira for you." He paused, cocking his head sideways. "Glad she's okay. I need to find her."

"Good luck," snorted Fasouk. "She's a Dragon Rider now, could be anywhere."

Darek's eyes darted to the sky. "It's getting too dark to fly." Not time enough to travel the many leagues without a moon. "Think you can spot me a place for the night?"

Fasouk looked up and pointed to the woods at the far end of the lagoon. "You can stay in our old fort. Remember the one we built together when we were kids?"

Darek gave a wry chuckle. "I remember it."

"Good. Then you know where to find it."

Remembering he had no tools, Darek wiped his brow with a sigh. "I just realized I need a knife of some sort—some flint and tinder too if you can spare it."

Fasouk waved a hand. "Sure thing, no problem." He rummaged in the pouch at his belt and tossed a knife with a hand-made leather sheath. "I want that back. I have to haul these minnows back to the docks before tomorrow morning or old Margrir will wring my neck. Meticulous bugger." He lifted the wire-meshed trap from the lagoon's edge. It teemed with a fresh catch. Fasouk dumped the squirming minnows in a canvas bag where he tied it with rawhide cord and replaced it with the empty one. "I'll come call on you at sunrise."

Darek saluted and watched him trudge up the seaside trail through the swaying trees. He disappeared in the sandy brow of the dune-like hill.

Turning to his dragon, he beckoned with his newfound knife for her to follow as he tackled the trail alongside the lagoon. The path was overgrown and narrowed from lack of use, obviously having seen no recent foot travelers. The lagoon swung out to meet the pale, tranquil sea. About halfway down, tall, plumed stickypalm with green parasols shaded the area from the hot sun. Their fruit were a delicacy, with their sweet pulp and juicy innards, worthy of a stop. Some had fallen like orange gourds. Mouth watering, Darek bent to sink his teeth in one, but Silver Eye snatched the fruit out of his hand before he could get his first bite. "You pig." Darek gathered up more fruit and turned his back on the dragon and ate until his stomach nearly burst.

The fruit gave him an idea. He notched a small hole in the top of an empty one, then cleaned it out. Filling it with water from the lagoon, he tied the gourd to his belt. With a whistle of satisfaction, he beckoned Silver Eye to follow him, then plunged through the undergrowth.

Organic odors permeated Darek's nostrils. He inhaled a lungful of fresh, earthy humus, beetlewort, decayed stickypalm, each scent bringing back a dozen memories.

A familiar thrum tinkled though the trees. He turned. The waterfall he knew from his youth sparkled in the sun as it tumbled over rocks and mossy earth. With a grateful cry, he shed his tattered clothes and waded out in the pool to wash the salt off his body. Silver Eye slurped mouthfuls of water while he cleaned up. She dove and played in the water, hunting for river trout to eat.

Donning his rags once more, Darek set off on the trail. He felt invigorated. The tree fort was lodged in a crook half way up an old stickypalm with three trunks. The fort looked in rough shape. Half of its roof sagged in from many accumulated layers of leaves. A thick coating of moss covered the sides.

He climbed the tree nevertheless, using the rotted footholds that were still nailed in the trunk. At the ramshackle door, he caught a whiff of rotted wood, but he inhaled deeply, reminded of summers spent building forts. This might not be the best place to bed down.

He climbed down the tree with a sigh and stretched his bulk out on the grass to wait out the night as the forest insects around him chittered their lively dusk-talk. The stars pricked the heavens and Silver Eye sprawled next to him, blinking with her good eye. The gentle murmur of waves lapped on the sand dulling his tremor of anxiety. The fort had rekindled more memories than he cared for. They ran deep, some of which he recalled with a wry smile. Kid stuff, pacts and dares: him, Fasouk, Vinz, Grame in the fort like a private clubhouse hunched under the candlelight plotting schemes. Lucky for Fasouk and others in the gang that they had not been drawn into the dare that led to his capture.

He had been juiced on stickypalm ale, not an excuse, it had only cost him what—two, three years of his life? When he caught up with the culprits...Vinz and Grame, things would not go so pleasantly for them. But that must wait for another day.

First he would seek out Meira. His sister was still alive, thank the gods! How he had worried about her. Not one word had he heard about her the whole time he had been enslaved on Raithan's ship. So much to contemplate.

There was still the issue of the dragon, and how he could keep her under wraps without the Black Claw Clan coming to look for him. He stroked the magnificent creature's shimmering scales gleaming under the moonlight. He could not help but glow with pride. Who else at his age had a live, loyal dragon as fine as this at their beck and call? Darek laughed out loud. Perhaps he would be the next Dragonmaster? The thought had him chuckling as he purred reassuring noises to her. He barely knew where his next meal was coming from, but he could likely count on Silver Eye to hunt him down some fish to eat.

Darek frowned. Truthfully, he was still unsure of where to start his search: Aster Island, Whale Island? Meira could be anywhere. His thoughts churned in an endless loop, until his head began to hurt and he gave up, pinching his eyes shut in exhaustion. With a yawn, Darek curled up to the scaly bulk beside him and fell fast asleep.

Chapter 6.

Agrippa

Darek awoke with a jolt before sunrise, the scent of spring flowers tickling his nostrils. Mist rose from the lagoon as he staggered over to wash his face and hands. Silver Eye was snapping playfully at colorful butterflies, not having much luck with her one eye, curious all the same at the magical mystery of her new world.

Darek stuffed as much fruit as he could in his pockets and washed down the rest with mouthfuls of water from his gourd. In refreshed spirits, he sought an open area breasting the trail where Silver Eye could lift her wings. Already he was on her back and moving in the glow of the sunrise, hoping to avoid Fasouk's prying questions.

Coppery light glimmered on the horizon as they took to the air. The rivers and hills passed below them, the air whistling in his ears. Silver Eye started to draw herself away from the strait and head back toward Cape Spear and the open sea to the north—the opposite direction from where he planned to seek out Meira.

Darek grabbed the dragon's neck and growled in a low voice. "Hey, where are you going?"

A dark shape suddenly whipped over his head. Darek's mouth opened in an 'O', as he saw a sleek winged mass head out to sea. His adopted dragon was hunting again and took chase. The sea eagle looked like the one he had spotted the previous day.

Silver Eye followed the predatory bird with tenacity. Darek swatted at her back scales, but it did no good. She plowed steadfast for the open sea.

"Come on," he pleaded, "turn around and I'll get you more clams and crabs than you could dream of."

The dragon flapped her wings and paid no heed. A low, piercing cry came to Darek's ear. Out to sea, dragon, eagle and flustered rider flew and Darek could do nothing about it.

But his dragon faltered after a time and plummeted many feet. Her wings were too young and weak for such a prolonged journey. She fell toward the sea, then splashed into the water.

Clinging to her neck, Darek sputtered water from his mouth. "Are you, crazy?"

His dragon did not respond, only doubled her speed and arrowed through the waves, swimming as if driven by some insatiable need.

Darek blinked out the salty tang of the water and scanned the horizon. The only place remotely in sight was a barren island of isolated grey slabs. Could this be Valkyrie Isle? The waves pounded at the feet of the volcanic-blasted rock.

Why here? Darek warred with the idea of ditching her, but he was too far out to swim back. He was a good swimmer, but not that good.

A chill tickled his spine.

The island loomed closer and Darek began to discern details: grey, lichen-streaked cliffs loomed out of the western face. To the south, a lower area of boulders spread among bits of sandy beach. On top, scraggly fir trees swayed in the wind and what looked like old towers.

Darek frowned. Silver Eye clambered out of the water onto a spare beach and dumped Darek, then she lumbered up after the eagle which perched on a tall dead tree. Darek gazed at the isle with curious wonder. It had been a long time since he had come here. Not much had changed—lots of gulls dumping guano on the rocks, with fierce cries competing against the roaring of the wind. The dragon knew where it was going.

With knees feeling strangely weak, Darek caught up with Silver Eye before she sprang again into the air. He clung to her sinewy neck as she swooped low over the stone battlements, a place he had not seen before.

He gasped. There stood two stone towers, battered and weather-crumbled, comprising what he thought looked like the end posts of an ancient gate to a ruined courtyard.

The dragon settled down amongst the rubble. Darek shook off his anxiety. He alighted from the beast with a thud, his gait not as springy as a few days ago.

An old man stood blinking, leaning on a walking stick: none other than Agrippa.

Darek grunted as a strident cry rang out against the wind. The massive eagle opened its razor-sharp beak to make a sound as low as a dragon's croak. The bird perched on the crenellations of the lowest watchtower, its white claws gripping the corroded stone.

This was Agrippa's eagle scout—that much Darek understood—without a doubt, the same bird that had spied them a day ago. It had reported the new dragon to Agrippa and now had come to fetch him and Silver Eye. In expert fashion had they been led here.

The old man ambled closer, his eyes twinkling in the bright sunshine. "So, you've found my secret isle," he said with a short chuckle. "How do you like it?"

"I don't." Darek rounded on him. "You made no efforts to save me from that foul volcano." His lips quivered in a snarl.

The old man snorted. "Nay, boy, I did not hear about your sentence in time. That wretched Cyrus saw to that. For some reason you were left there to find your destiny—as you have. 'Tis a miracle that you stand here before me." He shook his head with a baffled laugh. "It was spoken long ago to me in a dream. Still, I had almost given up hope."

"What do you mean?" demanded Darek. "Speak some sense."

Agrippa sighed. "A wandering mystic visited me long ago and told me a strange tale about a young slave who would change the face of the world and unlock the riddle of dragons. I didn't believe her then—this prophet of Elspior, being the hotheaded young man I was. Riddle of dragons, my eye. In my hubris, I thought it was me she was referring to. It took me many years to discover just how wrong I was."

"These riddles mean less to me than gull dung," complained Darek.

Rubbing the dragon tattoo on his wrist, Agrippa gave him a strange look. "I wish that were so..."

"Well, I survived the volcano," growled Darek. "I came out alive by my own ingenuity—and the guidance of this cunning young saurian here—Silver Eye." Darek motioned to his ally who squatted placidly on her hindquarters.

The old man followed the ex-slave's gaze. "Silver Eye, indeed." He scrutinized the dragon with some reflection. "The last of the elder ones, I think. I didn't believe there were any left, much less any ancient eggs." He laughed. "It takes a Mage—or what seems to be a budding one—to hatch a fossil like this one."

Darek grunted. "It was the heat from the lava that hatched her, not me." His eyes beetled to the three blue-grey towers on the low brow of the nearby mound. The ancient stone, crafted of chiseled blocks, seemed to arch toward each other. Broad weather-riven arches ran between the towers like spider webs. Darek imagined archers once stood here, defending a fort now long razed behind the non-existent gates and tumbled blocks, drowned in weeds and sorrow.

"As you say," replied Agrippa. The sea eagle still perched on its battlements and loosed a raucous cry, a massive bird armed with tusks on either side of its hard, yellow beak. It was definitely the same bird that had followed them yesterday. They were rare as golden clovers.

Poised next to Darek on the other side of the mound sat several windmills. Their long fans swept in rhythmic circles on the stiff sea breeze.

"I see you admiring my *windvanes*. They power my experiments below ground. Come! I will show you." The old man beckoned the wide-eyed youth with a gnarled forefinger, clutching his warped walking stick with the other hand. "You will see how they turn these great wheels which spark new creations in my tubs. I've been able to start fires with only dragon fat, and without the need for any flint and tinder."

Darek frowned, unimpressed. "What about Silver Eye?"

"No harm, the ancient youngling has nowhere to go." Silver Eye sat back on her haunches as if to wait. Agrippa smoothed back a lock of his wispy white hair and Darek noticed a strange seven-pointed star was carved on the back of his right wrist.

Despite his advanced age, Darek did not doubt the the mage was still master of dragons.

With spry step, the wizard trudged past the broken gate and into the ancient court, whose paving was broken and overrun by seagrasses and shrubs. A pile of rubble stood in the central aisle, weed-eaten and mossy, many of the blocks likely carried away by warring bands. An old stone hexagon lay off to the side, its standing stones towering over his head, carved in the likeness of animals.

"The stone configurations you see here were used by a tribe, the *Diori*, long ago," Agrippa declared. "I use this location because the ancient magic still holds a strong presence, though this is now a forsaken place. The *Diori* knew it well. They chose this location as their isle of 'sea rites'. Why they perished like so many others before them, I do not know. They were sea hunters and magicians, for I have discovered many a fishbone charm and primitive runestone strewn about amongst these blocks. Mostly a peaceful band—but somehow they rubbed an enemy the wrong way."

Darek inspected the huge megaliths that still stood with carven heads leering of old: of misshapen crows, immense ravens and mythical beasts of untold grandeur, some with tusks and fangs stemming from their beaks.

"The Diori were known to worship sea eagles," Agrippa remarked, "much like *Seavenger* here." He motioned proudly to his ally perched with dignity on a high stone projection. "Raised him from an eaglet. Trained him to obey my commands. He gives me word of what transpires on the high seas and the fragile islands."

"A good servant," observed Darek. "What did you say this place is called?"

"*Vyre*—I've seen inscriptions in the blocks, which resemble those in our language—or *Vkrye*, another translation. Which is why it is known as *Valkyrie Isle* to most. What you see of their stronghold here has been long razed. Now it is nothing but a pile of crumbled masonry. The watchtowers have withstood the test of time, but even they will disintegrate eventually."

Darek's expression dimmed upon seeing their precarious state.

"Each one of these stone statues is a God," Agrippa muttered to himself, answering Darek's unasked question. "The most powerful, these sea albatrosses and egrets with the larger heads, were ferocious hunters." He coughed out a warning, seeing Darek's dubious look. "Don't fool yourself. There is much of the world we don't know, Darek. We never will. Especially the ancient world. These eagles were as large as dragons at one time, and worshipped for good reason, the ancestors of the air dragons. They're rare these days. Seavenger here is a distant cousin."

"Where are the rest of your dragons?" Darek asked.

"Down by the beach, where they should be." Agrippa raised his stick. "I forbid them to wander up here, all except Cender, my first. He's lurking about somewhere. I keep a close watch on them and out of the sight and mind of all who I can. Cyrus's machinations run deep, and I don't doubt he's swaying the darker dragons, even the sea serpents right this minute. But enough of this serious talk."

Did he say sea serpents?

The old man hobbled with an effort, picking his way through the broken blocks to his laboratory with grunts and hushed murmurs.

Darek followed at a respectful distance, frowning, unable to squelch his rising unease.

In a cleared-out area, an iron gate stood with a stone staircase leading down into the earth—to some dim place below, Darek thought, judging from the size of the crude stairway lit by guttering torches that hung from the stone walls like eagle claws.

The windmills towered above them, casting pale, crooked shadows. Their wooden vanes beat the air as a stiff wind blew them like the sails of fleeing ships.

"Let me show you my latest invention," said Agrippa as he pulled a small copper lever protruding from the wall. A rumble followed by a great clanking sound came from below.

He tapped his walking stick twice on the ground and raised it into the air. The knotted wood doubled in length and a red amulet appeared on the tip. It lit up in flame, illuminating the chamber below. *Not a walking stick then—a mage's staff.*

"Come along," he beckoned and started down the stairs. Darek followed, pausing only once they reached the bottom to marvel at the enormous machinery revealed in the light of the glowing amulet. Steam boilers scorched black from use were connected with a patchwork of thin tubes. These connected to an opaque center column that appeared to be made from glass. The center column was surrounded by several massive canvas wings with large chunks of volcanic rocks and bits of dark iron coiled around them. A series of pulleys and wheels ran through it all.

"Those connect to the windmills above," Agrippa said, pointing to the copper piping that ran upward along the ceiling. "They can be used most days, but for this demonstration, we will use the steam from one of the boilers—if you wouldn't mind assisting?"

He gestured to a shovel and small pile of ground-up dragon eggshells.

Darek stared at him in disbelief. Memories of the blood, sweat and tears during the years of feeding the steaming boilers on Raithan's ship surfaced in a wild, angry rush. "You've got to be kidding?"

Agrippa was already turning small dials and making adjustments to the machine. "Huh? No, the boiler produces quite a bit more power."

Shaking his head, Darek gritted his teeth and fored himself to light the boiler and fuel it. He had the furnace roaring in no time as steam and heat began to fill the room. But his limbs shook with the effort and the memories only surfaced with more painful force.

"Excellent, excellent," murmured Agrippa. "Now, watch this."

With a grin, he pulled a series of levers and the canvas wings began to turn. As he began to spin a large valve, even more steam flowed through the pipes and the machine began to whir as it rotated faster and faster.

A thin line of red light flickered in the center of the glass column. It grew brighter as the sound of the spinning wings increased to a deafening roar. Wind buffeted Darek's face and it seemed as if the earthen ceiling might collapse. With a loud creak, one of the wooden wheels shattered, tearing a hole in the canvas below it as it crashed down into the equipment. One of the lines snagged in a pulley and a large gear stopped turning. The machine ground to a stop.

"It still needs some work," said Agrippa, "but what did you think?"

"Very impressive." Darek leveled him a stare, relieved to still be alive. "What does it do?"

"I call it Eel Light," said Agrippa. "It will have to be scaled down in size, of course, but one day this light will replace oil lamps and torches."

Darek's mouth curled in a doubtful grimace. "Why not just make more light-giving amulets like the one on your staff?"

Agrippa gave his head a shake. "Amulets like these and the kind Dragon Riders wear to control their mounts require a great deal of magic and organic material to make. We have become far too reliant on the slavery of dragons. What if we could no longer control them?"

Darek scratched his brow. "I thought you kept them under control. Why would that change?"

Agrippa's eyes grew very somber. "That's what you are here to prevent." He gave Darek a sly, if not troubled look. "Someday my laboratory and inventions could be of great use to a mage like yourself."

"I keep telling you," said Darek, "I'm not a mage."

"Why don't we find out." Agrippa winked. He dusted off a small chair and plopped down, crossing his arms over his chest with amusement. "See if you can summon Cender."

"Your dragon?" Darek asked.

Agrippa closed his eyes. "Precisely."

"But—" Darek began.

"—Just try it," replied Agrippa. "Reach out with your mind."

Was it actually possible? He calmed his breathing and closed his eyes. He let his thoughts drift. *This is ridiculous—and yet...* he felt the familiar presence of Silver Eye, down by the water. She seemed—bored. But he felt like he could summon her if he wished.

"A familiar dragon is the easiest to work with," whispered Agrippa. "Now search for another."

Darek exhaled a slow breath and turned his mind in a different direction. Several faint swirls of light began to appear, but they seemed fuzzy and far away. With eyes still closed, he turned and faced back up the staircase, past the arched portal and toward one of the watchtowers. There he discovered a burning ball of will.

"That's it," encouraged Agrippa, "now, summon him."

Darek focused on the blazing orb in his mind and with all his willpower summoned the creature. "Come!"

The dragon refused.

"Tell him you have fish," said Agrippa.

"What?" replied Darek, opening his eyes.

Agrippa smiled to himself. "Fish—he loves fish."

"All right, okay." Darek pinched his eyes shut and tried again. "Come—I have fish."

His thoughts reached out like a spider's thread, and he could feel the dragon's thoughts twining with his own. They were simple, feral, but powerful. Gone...The dragon's thoughts went back to its search of crabs on the beach with Silver Eye. He reached out again, biting his lip, this time with more force.

A crash sounded in the tower, followed by a rhythmic padding of feet as something descended the wide stone stairway. Moments later, a huge red dragon burst through the threshold, its girth scraped the walls as the creature bounded down the hallway toward the laboratory. Cender leaped down the steps, landing in front of Darek with an expectant look.

"Darek, meet Cender." Agrippa wiped his sweating face.

Darek lifted a tentative hand and let the dragon smell it. "Ah, hello, Cender."

The red dragon smelled his hand, then quickly looked at Darek's other hand. Finding nothing there, he gave a questioning rumble. Cender's predatory eye narrowed and he flashed his long teeth.

"Better give him the bucket of fish from under the workbench," warned Agrippa with a pointing finger.

Darek slid out a lead-lined box. Uncovering the top, he removed the bucket of fish inside and set it before the dragon.

Cender fell to the ground on all fours, happily sucking out fish and chewing them with a wet crunch. A massive claw shredded the metal bucket as he cleaned out the remaining scraps. Cender burped in appreciation.

"I think you've made a friend," laughed Agrippa.

"With friends like that," said Darek, "I might have been safer on a slave ship."

"He might be a bit aggressive," said Agrippa, "but he's like a loyal stallion and will fight to defend his own to the death."

Darek paled.

"What's wrong, boy?" asked Agrippa.

"Pretty soon the rumor of my survival will be out. The Black Claws will come looking for me."

"They all thought you dead, boy," Agrippa said, wiping his sweating face. "You're safe with me. They will know what it means to find you alive."

Darek shrugged. "But what am I going to do? I'm as notorious as a black eel in a flock of stingrays. Cyrus is going to kill me. You should have seen the look on his face when I stopped that sea serpent."

Agrippa tugged his chin. A thoughtful look crept in his eye. "I have long held doubts about Cyrus. He's a problem which must be dealt with sooner rather than later."

"I thought he was your apprentice? If what you say about me is true, how can there be three Dragon Mages?"

"Long before you were born, I came to these islands, a hollow-cheeked pilgrim on a journey of hope. Some called me 'exiled'. I called myself a lonely, broken man. At that time, there were no Dragon Riders. In the Islanders, I saw a simple, hard-working people, dedicated to tradition but superstitious." He turned to face the smoky mountain. "I tried to help them, but they betrayed me and sacrificed me to their blasted volcano God. But I survived, and in doing so, came into my powers and the ability to control dragons."

He turned to finger a map of the Dragonclaw Islands tacked to the wall. "It was a time of great progress. I forged the warring islands into a governing body. Peace reigned and we harnessed the dragons and their eggs to our will, building a civilization and creating many wondrous new inventions."

"What changed?" Darek asked.

"Eventually, I saw the need to find an heir who would continue my work, but I could find none with the same gift. Against my better judgment, I allowed the clans to resume the ritual sacrifices. I was shocked when Cyrus survived, and trained him as a promising student."

He sat down with a heavy thud, his lined face burnished copper in the glow of his amulet. "But he strayed to a dark path, for reasons I cannot ascertain to this day. At first I did not notice it, for I thought he was just wayward; a grimace of disgust here, a cruel comment or gesture to an innocent there. But his deviance grew to the point I became worried. I was blind and did nothing to stop it, electing fate to work itself out. Now he has become a menace."

"How did the dragons get here?" Darek said, staring at the silver-sheened creature who was now his friend.

Agrippa gave a knowing nod. "They were born of the volcano—perhaps the dragons are the root of the God's legend. No one knows what the significance of the legend is, or how it began or where it came from. It just is. It's as old as the volcanoes that pock these islands. The dragons and their eggs emerged from a time undreamed of, a time when dragons ruled the skies and serpents were but water snakes. Human and dragon weave a web in a never-ending struggle of symbiosis and domination through the ages." He leveled Darek a stare. "You, boy, have the gift to tame them and communicate with them—in more profound ways than I imagined. 'Tis a rare skill. I thought I was the only one who had such strong affinity."

He shook his head, as if to shrug off an impossibility. "I became fascinated by dragons when I first came to the Black Claw Islands years ago. I began work immediately to tame them. I almost lost my life, if not my arm, to old Cender, who is now my faithful ally." He winked at his dragon which sat off to the side, sniffing and staring down at Darek's impassive young female dragon with great interest.

"But that is a story for a rainy night and a roaring fire," said Agrippa. "You can sleep in the south tower. It isn't as sturdy as the other tower—sways a bit in the breeze—but Cender has already laid claim to the north one. Get your rest, boy. We begin your training at dawn."

Chapter 7.

A Mage's Apprentice

Darek awoke before dawn after a fitful night's rest. The south tower was drafty with several sections completely exposed to the elements. The rooms were damp and musky and Agrippa had neglected to provide him with a blanket as protection against the cold. He would have been warmer sleeping on the beach curled against Silver Eye's thick hide. As a slave, he had at least a clean section of floor to bed down on, but the south tower was ruled by a family of rats that had gone unchecked for generations. Too long had he had gone without a roof over his head to sleep again on the beach. Darek dug a small nest of his own among some moldy hay and settled in to wait for morning. The hours passed at a snail's pace as he drifted in and out of wakefulness.

Before the first ruddy rays kindled the swells, he was up and about. Wending his way down to the sandy beach, he heard only the sound of scampering rodents, skittering among the washed up stones. Agrippa must still be asleep. He reached the waterfront and found the area where he had last seen Silver Eye, empty. *Maybe she went for a swim.* In the first rays of dawn, he spied a silver shape gliding among the shallows, paddling toward a large school of Bluestripe snapper. A hindrance on land, Silver Eye's bulk and her long limbs became fluid and swift in the water. She was adjusting well to the loss of one eye. With a burst of speed, she shot through the water, surprising the school of fish. Talons and teeth produced a frothy red circle in the water as she gorged herself on the tender flesh.

Darek watched as the dragon surfaced, her keen eye spotting his slender figure on the shore. She arrowed through the water in his direction, using her thick tail and the wide membranes on her sides to swim and steer through the water like a dolphin.

Pounding out of the surf, Silver Eye ran to Darek's side and dipped her snout in a playful nudge to his ribs. *Had the dragon grown larger?* She opened her mouth and spat out two fish at his feet.

"For me?" Darek's face curled in a smile. "Thank you, girl."

He was doubtful that Agrippa would remember to feed him any sort of breakfast. Staring thoughtfully up the beach, he found a sharp rock and began scaling the fish. He shoved a stick through the gills then assembled a crude spit and hung the catch from it.

After gathering some wood, he turned to Silver Eye. "You wouldn't happen to breathe fire, would you?"

The dragon gave him a confused look. Darek spent the next few minutes searching among the short grass for a piece of flint.

Agrippa came up on him with surprise. Cender was at his heels, the creature's eyes locked on Silver Eye. As the pair approached, Cender gave a challenging growl.

"Be silent!" the mage commanded. "We are all friends here." He turned to Darek. "Glad to see you're an early riser. Looks as if you've done some fishing with your dragon. You could have helped yourself to the provisions in the larder, you know."

"The larder?" Darek frowned. "Right, I just wasn't sure if you had enough for the both of us."

Agrippa shook with laughter. "It's stocked well enough to feed a small army—with enough waxed cheeses and salted pork to last us a year." He crinkled his eyes and spat on the ground. "Thank you for your concern. I assure you, despite my humble appearance, I have more than enough. A boat brings me a fresh catch and every possible type of fruit each morning at the turn of the tide. An extravagance, I know, but nothing beats my pomegranate ceviche."

The old man turned to gaze at the cold fish. "Not every dragon is a fire breather." His mage's staff had returned to a common walking stick. He now pointed it at the dry wood that Darek had gathered. "Conjuring fire is a more advanced lesson—though I suspect you've done it once before. Cender, if you'd be so kind."

Darek sprang back and shielded his eyes as a burst of flame ignited the wood and charred the bottom half of his fish. Cender lifted his head with pride, basking in the attention as Agrippa patted him on the leg. Silver Eye gave curious inspection to the fire and its source.

"Great. That's one hot fire..." Darek spun the fish over to cook the raw top half.

Cender and Silver Eye moved off together, sniffing each other and nipping at each other's tails. The female dragon was smaller by half, but compared to the male she was lightning quick and much more agile on land. She had Cender on the retreat in no time.

"That's a special dragon you have," said Agrippa with a far-off look.

Darek agreed between mouthfuls of half-cooked, blackened fish. "Mmmm..." It had been nearly a full day since he had last eaten.

Agrippa had grown strangely quiet. He put his hand on Darek's shoulder just above the red lines that marked his heritage. "I'm sorry for how you were treated in the past. From now on you'll have regular meals and all the respect owed to a mage's apprentice."

Darek finished off the last bit of fish. "I appreciate that."

A wrinkled finger poked the black spot of slavery that sat below it. "Let's take care of this, shall we?"

Darek gasped as a wave of energy shivered up his arm. He looked down as the filthy circle faded and then vanished under a new layer of skin. *He was free.*

"Thank you," he croaked in wonder.

"No thanks is necessary," said Agrippa. "In a few years' time, you'll be skilled enough to return to the Red Claw Clan."

Darek's amazement faded. "A few years?" He jumped to his feet. "But I have to find Meira, now!"

Agrippa tapped a long fingernail three times on his cane. There were few who dared to contradict him. "Yes, I seem to recall something about your half-sister. Jace the Dragonmaster of the Red Claw Clan is your father, making your mother…"

"Thyphalyne, of the Black Claw Clan," provided Darek.

Agrippa scratched his beard. "Thyphalyne, Thyphalyne…I seem to recall Raithan the Shipmaster marrying a Thyphalyne of the Builders' Guild—ah, I see."

A fire burned behind Darek's eyes at the thought of that gull-eater Raithan. His mother had loved his father Jace at a young age and he had been born out of that adolescent passion. It was Kraton's cruel fate that the Master of the

Builder's Guild would die, leaving his family an unpayable debt. She had no choice but to marry Raithan or be faced with the ruin of her family. By marrying him, she could settle several contracts they owed to the Shipmaster—despite her son by Jace."

"Does my father still live?" asked Darek.

"He does," replied Agrippa, "though an accident took his arm and he no longer is as active. Jace barely kept up with his duties after you were sold into slavery. Relegated to instructing new recruits, he fell deep into his cups. For a while, he changed his name and went by the name 'Jarle', I believe."

"At least he had enough coin to buy grog," said Darek bitterly.

Agrippa turned to stare across the water in the direction of the Red Claw Islands. "Some men fare better astride a dragon than with the roll of the dice. Jace would have given anything to purchase your freedom. The guilt of it almost killed him. If it wasn't for Meira—"

"Meira is with Jace?" Darek's face lit with a rising hope.

Agrippa shook his head. "Not any longer. She lost track of him when he moved off island—to Manatee. Her fondness for the man is why Raithan sent her away."

Darek's eyes scanned the field for Silver Eye. He knew that trying to chase after the dragon would be pointless, but watching her was becoming a habit. The dragon was scratching her back against a small fir tree. A spry hare hopped by and she gave chase. Cender was nowhere about. Apparently he had taken offence at something and returned to his tower.

"I thought it was just over refusing to free me," said Darek.

"That too," replied Agrippa.

Darek's jaw hardened. "I have to get word to them."

Agrippa raised his hand and whistled. Seavenger gave an answering cry and streaked out of the ruins, landing on the mage's arm and beating its powerful wings with a fury. Darek wouldn't trust those sharp claws wrapped around his arm. Stroking the bird of prey's head, Agrippa soothed the animal to stillness.

"Seavenger will carry a message to your father, won't you?" cooed Agrippa to the sea eagle. "As for your sister, she rides a white dragon named Typhoon." He extended his other hand and summoned Silver Eye from across the field. She cut off pursuit of the hare and ran toward the mage with giddy excitement.

"We'll make it part of your training to summon her dragon, Typhoon, and your sister with it."

Darek struggled to follow everything that the old mage was saying. No easy task. He didn't dare anger Agrippa by pointing out his confusion, but the old man's thoughts seemed to jump erratically from one topic to the next, the past to the future. He wondered if advanced age and the stress of controlling the dragons spread across the three Dragonclaw Islands had taken its toll and addled the man's brain. Still, he seemed to be offering Darek a new way of life as his apprentice, free from the slavery of the Black Claws and with the possibility of finding Meira. Darek had no choice but to accept.

"When do we start?" he asked.

Agrippa laughed. "Good! Too long have I gone without the enthusiasm of a young mage."

The old man turned and put his hand on Silver Eye's neck. "Silver Eye—an apt name in her case. Do you know the importance of the name of a dragon?"

Darek shook his head. "I didn't think it mattered."

"That's your first mistake." Agrippa smiled. "So far you've communicated with dragons you were familiar with or that were close by. You've connected with them and given them a command. But what if you had never met a dragon and had no idea where it was?"

Darek thought for a moment. "I suppose we could call upon the dragon with a message?"

"Very good!" Agrippa rubbed his palms. "Only a mage or a Dragon Rider can name a dragon. It's part of the power that forges the connection between the two. If you want to summon a dragon, but don't know its name—" he flicked his gaze toward Silver Eye, "—then you can use the name of the rider."

With a slow nod, Darek closed his eyes and tried to sense where all the dragons on the island were at this moment.

"Not like that." Agrippa picked up a small pebble and hurled it into the surf. "You are a pebble in the entire Dragon Sea—it would take forever to find the right one."

"Then how do I find Typhoon?"

Agrippa grinned. "You must send out your location like a lighthouse. In this message, the dragon's name and that of her rider are the light from your beacon."

Darek gave a polite cough. *This was ridiculous.*

Seeming to ignore the interruption, Agrippa continued, "Instead of warning the ships away, you must pull *ALL* of the dragons toward you."

"All of them?" said Darek, "I don't think there's enough room on your island."

Agrippa rolled his eyes. "Dragons are naturally territorial. If you send out the name you want with enough force, the others will turn away."

Darek closed his eyes once again. "I'll give it a try."

I am here-Darek is here. Typhoon—Meira—come.

He opened an eye.

Agrippa nodded. "Again."

Darek here—Meira and Typhoon—I'm alive.

Tapping a long nail to his nose, Agrippa looked out at the water. He raised his walking stick and with a funny flick of eye, it transformed back into a magical staff. "We'd better send the message by water as well—*Caeli-Mare!*"

Darek gasped as a powerful gust of wind lifted him into the air and flung him past the shallows into deeper water.

Choking and spitting, he surfaced in shock. "What in Kraton's beard?"

"Try sending the message under water," called the mage, "a few laps around the island should do it. It'll help with the smell—you reek of rat droppings."

The mage's face was somber. Silver Eye seemed to be enjoying the show. Darek treaded water for a few seconds then smelled a strand of his long hair. It was beyond foul. *Cursed wizard and his drafty tower of rat dung.*

Ducking his head under the water, Darek swam at full speed. As he let his anger fade, his muscles loosened and his mind began to relax, his thoughts focused on the swim. He remembered races against his friends and a time when life was much simpler. Every few breaths he concentrated on the dragon and sent out his location. *Darek—Meira—Typhoon.*

By the end of his circuit, he was physically and mentally exhausted. He pulled himself from the water and made his way toward the stronghold's larder. An entire salted pig might stifle the gnawing hunger in his gut. Silver

Eye joined him as the beach gave way to a tall grass field on the east side of the island. He could just make out the crumbling north tower where he had slept last night. They had nearly reached the outer wall when Silver Eye gave a cry of warning and turned her eye skyward.

A white shape hurtled toward them in a spinning dive of wings and claws. Darek yelled and dove out of the way—narrowly avoiding serious injury as Typhoon pulled up short and landed beside him with a terrifying snarl. The female dragon was about the same size as Silver Eye, though longer and thinner, but with larger-spanning wings. A long scar ran down the dragon's side, a black trench marring otherwise perfect white scales. She had almost taken off his head. Darek jumped to his feet—only to find himself back on the ground as Meira leaped off and punched him square in the jaw. She looked around with wild anger, as if trying to make sense as to why her dragon had brought her here.

"You idiot!" she screamed at Darek. "They all might all be dead because of you!"

Rubbing his chin, Darek winced as he sat up.

"Who might be dead?" he cried.

Meira advanced on him again, but Silver Eye shot between the two, hissing and snarling. Typhoon met the challenge at once, spreading her wings wide and jumping behind Silver Eye—her claws would have carved out a bloody chunk of Silver Eye's haunches, had a voice not lanced out with authority.

"Stop!" commanded Agrippa, striding out from a rusted gate in the far wall.

Meira turned to face the mage. "Where am I? I have to go back! My Wing was under attack by pirates when Typhoon suddenly brought me here—I should have known it was a mage's doing."

"Peace, Meira," Agrippa said, raising his hand. "When I sensed Darek's success summoning you, I sent two other dragons to join the fight and ally with your company—your *Wing* is safe—the pirates are in full retreat."

"Darek's summoning?" she asked with a doubtful look at her brother.

"Nice to see you again too," Darek grumbled as he rose on shaky feet.

Typhoon inched toward Silver Eye, preparing to spring again.

Peace—Typhoon—she's family. The white dragon's head snapped in his direction, considering for a moment. Typhoon relaxed and trotted back to Meira's side.

"Did you just command my dragon?" Meira growled. Darek's face assumed an innocent look.

Her expression softened for a moment. "Glad you are safe, Darek. Where in Kraton have you been?" She shook her head in angry confusion. "Now, someone needs to tell me what in Kraton's balls is going on—this instant!"

Agrippa strode forward, motioning to Cender to keep his distance from the other dragons. "Darek is my new Apprentice. He has survived the Rebirth Ritual and been given power by Kraton."

"What the—? Little Darek, a dragon mage?"

"That's right."

"I'm not so little anymore," growled Darek.

"I see you've added some more muscles, and a cheeky leer, nothing but—"

"Your brother has changed quite a bit, Meira," said Agrippa. "Another reason why I've brought you both together. Each has a part to play in the upcoming storm. The Dragonclaw Islands are in peril. I've seen things in the sky, the air, the water, and the dragons. All signs herald doom."

Meira frowned, looking from the aged wizard to her sunburnt brother, broad-shouldered with the dark tangle streaming past his shoulders.

"I apologize for the way you were summoned here, but I needed a Dragon Rider, Meira. With your skill you can assist in the next phase of Darek's training."

Chapter 8.

VALKYRIE

Meira had refused at first to train Darek, providing a dozen reasons why she was too busy or ill-suited in the ways of a Dragon Rider to act as his nursemaid. But Agrippa was unyielding and she relented in the end.

After a brief meal of salted pork and much of Agrippa's savory pomegranate ceviche, Darek and Meira readied their dragons for the flight back to The Red Claw Islands. Both beasts were sluggish after gorging themselves on several baskets of fish from the larder.

Agrippa had been good enough to provide Darek with a spare riding harness. The ropes were thinner than Meira's, but the rig still proved an annoyance for Silver Eye. She had never worn a saddle for all of her brief life and she constantly tugged at the straps. Darek didn't see the need for it, preferring to ride bareback, but Meira insisted. It had taken five attempts to get the steel bit into Silver Eye's mouth without losing a finger. The dragon was still chewing on the metal viciously.

Ready to depart, the dragons flexed their wings and pawed the ground, restless to take to the air—but Meira took pains to explain the importance of proper harness care. On and on she droned for what seemed like hours.

"Remember to wash and oil it after every single ride." She pointed to the small grooves cut into the shark hide. "Always triple-check your bridle ties and make sure to re-tighten the belly cinch—dragons tend to hold their breath when you put it on and if you don't re-tighten it, the strap will be too loose."

"You've been over this three times already," complained Darek.

"A rider is only as good as—"

"—as their riding gear and the care they put into it," finished Darek. "I've heard Jace say that a thousand times, remember?"

"Well, you were always out sailing some dinghy," she scoffed. "I wasn't sure if you heard a word of it."

Darek gave a grudging smile. It was true. He had never shown any interest in continuing the family profession, always preferring the rolling deck of a ship to the bow-legged cramps of riding a dragon. He regretted now not paying more attention to his father's lessons.

"Mount up!" Meira called. She pulled herself up onto Typhoon's lowered wing and climbed up on her back. She swung into the saddle in one fluid motion.

Silver Eye provided no such assistance and blinked as Darek struggled to mount and get his feet in the proper place. Lengthening the stirrups was more difficult than Meira had made it look. Darek grabbed the reins, but the dragon tugged against them, shaking her scaled neck from side to side.

"It'll take a while for her to get used to it," said Meira. "Give the dragon her head for now."

Darek nodded. He loosened his grip and patted Silver Eye's neck. "Easy, girl."

Agrippa tugged at his beard. "I would go with you, Darek, but I must get that windmill drive fixed. I'm losing valuable power generation as it is while the winds are up. Meira, I suggest you take Darek to the north end of the island and begin his training."

Darek rolled his eyes. It felt as if he were still hiding beneath his mother's skirts. "What am I, three years old? How did I ever survive without Meira?"

Meira gave a hopeless sigh. "See what I have to put up with? If he's such a powerful dragon mage, why does he need rider training?"

"He needs to be able to think like a dragon," Agrippa said sternly, "and no one does that better than a Dragon

Rider. Show him the half rolls, the water skims, take him to the clutch. Teach him what it means to ride a dragon in battle—that kind of thing."

Meira nodded.

"When he has enough skill to circle the wind pillars and swim through the caves, he'll be ready. The eagle Seavenger, will show you the fastest way." He reached out and stroked Cender's head. Pressing his forehead to the dragon's, the two seemed to bid each other farewell. "If you don't mind, my dragon Cender will go with you. It's time he found a mate."

"As long as he stays away from Typhoon," warned Meira.

Agrippa laughed and turned to his faithful friend with a somewhat austere gaze, "Watch out for them, and see that they stay out of trouble. Send for me if trouble arises."

Cender tipped his iridescent orange-scaled snout, and shook his dark ears. His gleaming teeth flashed upon the mage in answer, as if he knew what he was saying.

"Take staves," advised Agrippa. "Every rider has a stave or a sword with him. Keep them handy at your side. Here—" he tossed Darek the wooden witchstick he kept strapped on Cender's flanks.

Meira grinned and took the lead. "Catch me if you can, Darek!"

Dragon and rider lifted off and Darek clicked his tongue, urging Silver Eye to the chase. An ungraceful take-off by any standard, first hopping on stubbly legs down the rubble-strewn courtyard wings outstretched, then a sudden flapping leap into the air. The juvenile dragon gained the air and soared overhead.

Meira looked back. "Don't fly too fast, you show-off! You're not used to that harness yet. You'll fall out."

Like kingfishers, the two darted across the cloud-filled sky while Cender and Seavenger took wing after.

Darek got a good view of Valkyrie Island and Agrippa's crumbling stronghold, a ruined scatter of battered towers and fallen masonry. Weeds and shrubs spread southward out to the ocean. Northward, rockier ground showed and more rugged, grey outcroppings among the greenish shrubs.

As they crossed the bay, Darek spotted a school of dolphins swimming below. Higher the riders flew, until the creatures faded to black spots in the water. They sailed among the clouds, buffeted by vagrant air currents. At last, Meira signaled they should descend. With a grunt of satisfaction, she landed on a windswept promontory overlooking the sea, on the very edge of Valkyrie Island. Looking eastward loomed Kraton and beyond it, Serpent's Deep. Darek noted specks of small islands and a few boats that weren't Red Claw fishing craft. He drew alongside her but landed at an awkward angle on a somewhat lower point. Cender touched claws down at a farther point and began snuffling around a small bush. Seavenger was content to circle high above.

Typhoon squatted and relieved herself in a massive spattering of steaming orange dung on a fallen slab of what was once a statue of the Sea King. Other slabs were strewn about, and pillars ringed the area with weeds and low prickly shrubs. The place was looking less spooky in the daylight than at dusk. Below lay a spired maze of rock pillars near a thin strip of beach down which the wind whistled with the crashing waves of the sea. The pillars, strange rock formations in themselves, continued on to a range of small islands where the kite-like shapes of wheeling pelicans soared.

"Why did we land here?" asked Darek.

"The old ruined fort." Meira pursed her lips. "Likely the first fortress of the Sea Kings' ancestors." Darek saw her shiver and dart eyes about in reflection. The place held an ancient feel to it, in much worse shape than Agrippa's abode, if such were possible. Even Darek could feel the ghosts of the past lingering here.

"It's peaceful here. I see why the old man wants to live on an island amidst only silent ruins," mused Meira.

"He has his dragons to keep him company," Darek said with a shrug. "Though you could never live here—not enough people to boss around." He smiled and saw Meira's lips twitch at the corners.

He kicked at the rubble. His eyes caught a yellow glint of a dull shape. He picked it up—an old coin. "Looks like gold."

"If it's new clothes you want, it won't help." She chuckled, with not much encouragement, eyeing the tatters her brother wore. "The pirates tried to trade them for real coin several years back." She waved a hand in front of her nose. "You smell like rotten fish."

Silver Eye began urinating down the stone king's nose. "I don't know how you can smell anything but dragon musk on that beast of yours."

"First lesson," she said, ignoring the comment and dismounting. "A dragon is a precious resource. He or she is to be treated with respect. The rider should always look out first to its safety—which means bathing occasionally so that the dragon can still scent danger."

Darek rolled his eyes. "I'll do my best. I already know how to ride, Meira. I don't need you to lecture me. Maybe skip to the juicier parts? Save us all some time."

"These are the juicy parts, codfish. Listen." She wiped away some black moss from the base of the Sea King's statue. Carvings of dragon claws wreathed the base.

Darek sighed and forced himself to pay attention.

"The Dragon Riders formed a guild long ago, more than two hundred years. Think of it as a long lineage of Red Claw tradition. We began riding the dragons while the Black

Claws were still cowering on their ships." She clicked her tongue with pride. "But the Black Claws caught on soon enough and it wasn't long before they trained their own riders and used their dragons to attack us. The Red Claws were more experienced and we beat them back and dominated the skies." She paused for effect. The history lesson had no impact on Darek, and she grumbled, wiping the hair from her eyes. "You never could appreciate a good story."

Darek yawned. For all her skill, Meira could sure be a bore. To her fortune she had good looks on her side, otherwise she'd be sunk. Something untamed lurked in her gangly limbs and fierce green eyes...her thick, curly hair trimmed short for practicality, or maybe to make her look more like a man. He laughed at that. He didn't appreciate her comments on his own appearance though. "You're never going to attract a man the way you act. Even a Dragon Rider doesn't have to be bossy all the time."

"What do you know?" Meira snapped with a harsh grunt. "I've got master Jemn making eyes at me all the time. The miller's son is a lot better built than you. It's not like anyone would want to take up with a codfish-smelling slave of your like."

Darek flinched at that and his eyes narrowed. She'd hit a nerve.

"Sorry," Meira shrugged, "I didn't mean it like that."

"There was a pirate girl I once cared for," Darek said with a tremor of grief. "She's gone now—daughter of a pirate chief on the eastern isles. Seems so long ago. Livis was her name." He gave a pained sigh with the recollection. "Then there was Clara—"

Meira frowned. "Clara? Of Cape Spear? Forget her, she's onto bigger fish. At least from what I've heard."

Darek's heart sank. He was unable to deflect the deep well of his emotions. The loss of both women had his long-held hopes evaporating.

Meira shook him out of his reverie. "Listen, lover-boy, we're here to train, not reminisce. Let's stay focused."

Darek agreed with a sigh.

"Let's talk about your harness." Meira motioned to the leather straps. "You managed it pretty well. You're sitting up straight more, not crouched down all the time."

Darek rubbed his legs. "I still don't like it. It chafes between my thighs." He shifted uncomfortably and arched his back, rubbing at the bruises forming there.

Meira forced a curt laugh. "Tough luck. The harness acts as a measure of protection against falling to your death."

"Would you get off the whole 'fall thing'," Darek cried with exasperation. "You're going to jinx me!" He still wasn't completely comfortable so high above the waves rather than on a ship.

"Nothing like practice to calm your fears. Now let's do just that."

With reluctance, he followed her into the sky. Meira steered her dragon over rocky fields of wild clover while Cender and Agrippa's all-observing eagle followed like a faithful pet.

Meira turned about. With a quick, sharp word to Typhoon, she came flying up underneath Silver Eye and nudged Darek's dragon in the belly.

"Hey, what was that for?" he cried.

The playful jab had Silver Eye squawking as Darek jerked back with surprise. Not expecting the jar, he lost his balance as his foot dislodged from the stirrup, and he began to slide sideways. He caught the thick leather harness in time with an outstretched hand.

"Just seeing if you're paying attention," Meira said with a grin. "See! I told you, that you could have fallen."

"I didn't though," corrected Darek.

"Only because of the harness." She circled her mount back over to the rock pillars by the seashore.

Darek put his full concentration on following Meira's fast lead. He maneuvered his dragon to fly alongside her with natural ease.

Meira looked back and sniffed. "You seem to have a knack for the easy stuff." Her face twisted in near envy of Darek's innate skill, perhaps because he hadn't spent years training like she had. She refused to let him know that. "You lack technique. You're sloppy."

"Who cares about technique?" scoffed Darek. "We can fly as fast as you can." He spurred Silver Eye on past her.

A husky growl rumbled in Meira's throat. "Until an unexpected gust of wind knocks you into a spin. You'll fall sooner or later and no one will be there to catch you."

"Silver Eye will catch me," Darek cried, patting his dragon.

"And if she takes a harpoon and falls out of the sky, what then?" she cried back at him.

Darek shuddered. Even the thought of that devastated him. He realized how attached he'd become to her. "I don't think she'd ever—"

"Hold your reins tighter," she commanded over the whistling wind. "Inbound incoming at forty-five degrees!" She angled in a sharp roll. Typhoon spun above and she swatted her stave across Darek's back.

"Hey, that hurt!"

Meira slowed Typhoon into a glide. "Do you think we're here to take in the scenery? The Red Claws use dragons to protect our islands. But they do more than that. They scout out whales for hunters and schools of fish for the boats. Who do you think delivers messages from isle to isle?" she shouted. "And then there's the pirates."

Darek copied his sister's moves, pulling back on the reins until Silver Eye slowed as well. He was starting to get used to the heights.

Darek knew all about pirates. He was about to yell something back at her but Meira steered Typhoon in again and thrust her stave at him. He parried as Silver Eye turned her to head to cover her blind side, but a second blow penetrated his defenses and he let out a squawk, feeling the hard edge of wood in his ribs. Darek cursed himself. Was he getting soft? He had trained with staffs on the beach with Vinz and Grame many times. He had always come out ahead. No, he was just not used to bouncing on the back of a dragon in flight while under attack. As much as he hated to admit Meira was right, he needed training in dragon combat.

On the next pass, he was better prepared and anticipated her feint, striking out with upraised staff to tap Meira on the shoulder. The move only irritated her and she swung her dragon behind him. "Lucky shot!"

"There's no such thing as luck, Meira, you should know that," Darek taunted.

Silver Eye appeared to be on board with the dodging and the dipping and easily bent to Darek's command, though she bared her teeth every time she was struck or Darek cried out.

Meira and Darek had been rivals since they were young. Meira, the older, usually had the edge, because of her speed and strength. But by the time Darek was in his preteens, he had grown strong enough to rub her nose in the dirt if he wanted.

Side by side they flew over the beach, jabbing and bantering while the sparkling waves passed underneath them. Meira criticized everything about Darek's posture, stance and technique. It should have made him angry, but he found himself glad to be with his sister once again. He laughed, feigning a sigh of boredom. "Shouldn't you be teaching me how to dive-bomb and roll? I've seen the Black Claw riders on Raithan's ship plummet from a hundred feet while baiting the sea-serpents."

"Those are advanced techniques," replied Meira. "Not for beginners. You're not ready. Plus, Agrippa would have my head."

"By Kraton's teeth, I'm ready. Watch!" He let up on the reins and eased Silver Eye forward so her nose dipped down into a dive. The air whistled in his ears as they picked up speed.

Meira looked on, not entertained, and dove down beside him. "Not like that! Here, watch! Agrippa, forgive me," she cursed.

She veered off and sent Typhoon looping around in a wide arc. Darek pulled up and watched the mesmerizing spins. Then she tore straight down in a near vertical dive. Closer and closer she came to the water, until finally they arched back up—kissing the water with a splash. Up she came, breathless, the fierce stance of a warrior, her dark hair whipping back, her green eyes gleaming.

"Wow, you danced on the water like a flying fish!" cried Darek. "Let me try."

"No, wait—" But he was already on the move.

Darek drew hard on Silver Eye's rein like Meira had. The dragon gave a low screech, reared up, legs splayed. Darek's world went topsy-turvy, near spinning himself upside down as he clung to Silver Eye's neck and harness. His heart pounded like a drum. Instead of dropping over the water, he banked toward a nearby island covered with trees. He barely missed the trees and shrubs below; Silver Eye's claws raked the top of a ragged sea fir before she pulled up with a breathless roar.

Darek wiped the sweat from his brow. "Well, that didn't go how I imagined it."

"It was also dangerous," said Meira.

Darek merely shrugged.

"Same old Darek, thinks he's too smart to listen to anyone else. Come on. This time, try and stay over the water. If you fall, at least you won't break your neck."

They practiced for nearly an hour by the shore at a place where the water was deep enough to cushion any fall. Darek wasn't as graceful as she was, but he managed to stay in his harness as Silver Eye twisted in a one hundred-and-eighty-degree roll. As the dragon's wings crested the water, he felt more alive than ever.

For most of the training, Cender had watched from a nearby beach, sunning himself and cooling off in the water. Darek looked on in surprise as the dragon opened his wings and took flight.

Meira dismissed it. "The old man probably summoned him. It's his dragon, after all."

Seavenger dove in and stole a fish from a group of gulls that screamed in outrage.

"Let's train somewhere else," said Meira. "It's noisy here."

"How can you hear anything over the wind?" called Darek.

"Come on!" She squeezed with both legs, urging Typhoon on, and shot out toward the wind pillars closest to the caves.

Darek vaulted after her, with a series of barrel rolls along the way.

"Showoff," Meira called. "All that fancy flying won't help you in a fight."

"I haven't even begun to 'show off', Meira. Come on Silver Eye!" With a youthful grin, Darek spurred his dragon toward the wind pillars at full speed. He was tired of playing it safe and now flew straight into the gaping mouth of a giant sea cave.

"Darek, wait!" Meira yelled.

But Darek had disappeared and Meira's shouts fell empty in the wind.

Chapter 9.

Young Serpent

The cave's blanket of darkness engulfed Darek and his dragon. The plink of dripping water echoed as it fell in cold pools and Darek felt as if he were in a vast, deep well. He saw phosphorescent mussels creeping on the walls. Who knew what dark things lived here? Shivers ran up his back, as he recalled his experience in the caves below Kraton and he wondered if he should have been so eager to enter this creepy place.

The cavern was high-ceilinged, and though it narrowed and curved like a horseshoe, bending back on itself, the dim light of the mussels grew brighter like that of sunlight. Eroded holes in the ceiling revealed Meira flying above.

She waved her hand with exasperation and shouted, "Get out of there, you urchin-brained fool."

Darek thought about ignoring her again, until a familiar rustle of wings and a deep cough had him flying out of the first opening that was large enough.

Agrippa reared up on Cender. "I see you two are more intent on playing cat and mouse than training," he quipped, confronting Darek and Meira who hovered above the top of the cave, surprised by his arrival.

The old mage and his dragon leveled out close to Silver Eye. "Let's see what you've learned. Charge me!" He spun in the air right in front of Silver Eye. Darek spurred her forward on a frontal attack, but Cender cupped his wings, caught an air current and drifted backward and below them, rising to attack from behind.

Agrippa's walking stick doubled in length and he smacked Darek on the back of his head then Silver Eye on her tail. Darek rolled his dragon to the side, but the old mage anticipated the move and matched it perfectly before streaking alongside them and scoring another hit on Darek's shoulder and across Silver Eye's flank.

Realizing he was outmatched, Darek raised two fingers in surrender. He floated down to the ground.

"Your balance is off," said Agrippa. "You're more like a stork on one leg. Too busy fighting like a man—you need to fight like a dragon."

Darek spurred Silver Eye airborne in a spurt of anger and struck back. The old man moved, quick as an adder, his staff lifting in a blur of motion. He deflected the blow, almost flinging Darek's stave out of his hands.

Darek gasped. "How'd you do that?"

"Don't look at me like a moonfish, boy, strike me!"

Darek hesitated.

"Come on! I'm not a straw man."

Darek grunted. He angled in close. With an agile movement too fast to follow, Agrippa ducked under Darek's whooshing strike and wheeled Cender in to slap him square in the back across the shoulders, near knocking him off the dragon and the breath from his lungs.

"Ow, that smarts!"

"And why shouldn't it? In a real fight you'd be dead right now."

Darek growled. He wasn't beaten yet. After recovering his breath, he urged Silver Eye into a dive. Cender followed and Derek willed Silver Eye to turn backward, preparing to strike at Cender's head. With a smile, Agrippa halted his pursuit.

"Very pretty, young Dragon Rider, but what good is it if I simply do not follow?" The old man glided down and his staff turned into a spear that batted the stave out of Darek's grip. It spun out of his hand into the water below.

"That's cheating!" called Darek and he rubbed his bruised wrist.

Agrippa grunted out a somber sound. "Nothing is off limits between mages." He gave his head a mirthful shake. "I saw you earlier, Darek. Meira's right, you are a showoff and you ride your dragon like a horse."

Darek frowned, adjusting his stance and patting Silver Eye on the crown. "That's okay, girl, we'll get him next time."

Agrippa wagged a finger in Meira's direction. "I hope I haven't misplaced my trust in you, young lady."

Meira inclined her head in haughty manner.

"Let's move farther out to the sea," he said, ignoring her dark look. "The air currents are different over water." He spurred on Cender and flew westward in the direction of the Red Claw Islands. Meira and Darek followed with some sheepishness despite their excitement. The wooded Swordfish Isle of their birth showed as a tiny speck on the far horizon.

Seavenger flew after, soaring high above them, keeping up their pace.

"There are smaller islands out here," Agrippa called over the hissing wind. "Not on any map, but perfect for our training as they supply some patches of earth to land on should we feel the need. The sea is a dangerous place. Sudden winds, whirlpools, serpents, and other creatures..."

Darek saw a dark blot on the horizon, a small ship maybe? But he couldn't make it out. Only a small movement caught his eye, like a glimmer of reflected light off water.

Agrippa motioned to a small island below, nothing more than a few bare rocks and some ancient, wind-scarred trees.

"See that petrified sea fir over there on that rocky beach?"

"Yeah, so?" said Darek. "A lone tree, bent over like an old man."

"When it was still alive, it was like a willow, surviving for centuries by bending but not breaking. So must a Dragon Rider meld with his mount, as free as the wind, as liquid as a waterfall, yet ready to snap back in times of danger. Even the bending was not enough to prevent that tree's inevitable decay."

Darek reflected on the mage's words. There was something wise about them.

"And you, Meira," Agrippa said, somewhat more sternly. "You ride well, but you're too concerned with control. You must learn to let go and give Typhoon her lead. She is fighting against your reins. You have all the technique down but something is missing."

Meira's lip quivered, not one to take criticism too graciously. She frowned as if recognizing the truth in his words, but her nose lifted in defiance.

Darek grinned, happy to hear his sister chastised. "I never knew there were so many small islands," he said, pointing his stave below.

Agrippa sucked in a breath of air. "'Tis said that the sea god Mercifer formed them from his own tears, each a once proud star pulled into the sea. The salty flood of his grief is what formed the Dragon Sea."

Meira sniffed in derision. "It's a wives' tale used to fascinate old maids and scare kids on dark nights."

"Perhaps, but there is truth to most legends," Agrippa called back. "Keep practicing, you two. I'll be back in a while. Seavenger seems to have found something on that island that has spiked his interest."

Watching the wizard fly off, Meira and Darek did some more maneuvers, as Agrippa had instructed them. Darek suffered several more cracks to his pride.

Kraton! She was good, but even he could see that Meira was holding herself back.

Before long, Darek could feel a shiver coming over Silver Eye. Looking back at her tail, he saw a yellow spray streaming behind her. He snatched a glance northward. The old man had disappeared from sight. With an impudent grin, he urged his mount forth in a high roll over Meira's head, letting the discharge sprinkle her clothing.

Meira sputtered and shook out her arms, quivering in rage and disgust. She wiped the warm, musky liquid from her jerkin. "Wait till I catch you!"

Darek could not help but double over in laughter. He put distance between them, flying low and completely missing the dull umber shape that surfaced in the water below.

An enormous snout with a wedged head rose from the waves. Massive jaws snapped with serrated yellow teeth below them, prompting Silver Eye to panic and streak upward like a waterspout. Darek slipped out of his harness and plummeted backward—plunging toward the slavering fangs below. His arms and legs pinwheeled. He cried, "Kraton's gods! Aiee!—"

Reaching out to summon Silver Eye, he twisted in midair wild-eyed, but his dragon was nowhere in sight. Darek gurgled out in despair. Meira flew in like a storm; Typhoon loosed a whistling screech as she bashed snout-first into the side of the sea serpent's skull. Darek crashed into the water. He surfaced a moment later to see the poisonous barbs of the sea serpent's tail pass close by his face. The grotesque spurs swiped at Typhoon and forced the defiant dragon back.

Powerful wings thumped at the air. Darek felt a pair of claws hook onto the tattered clothing around his shoulders. They lifted him gently out of the water. *Silver Eye!*

Several cries swirled about his head: Meira's, the dragons', Agrippa's...

The old mage, uttering a cryptic incantation, held his wizard's staff aloft as he stood on Cender's back. The dragon's orange-red hide glistened in the sunlight, but his teeth bared at the larger menace. The serpent was enormous. It still looked to be a juvenile by the stunted barbs on its tail—not fully formed, but jets of water sprayed between its fangs, and the hungry fledging turned its fish-green eyes toward its human prey.

The monster coiled in the water, then struck with curved fangs.

Cender darted to the side as Agrippa called out a fell curse. *"Agrak! Kronak!"* He smote his hazelwood staff on the monster's crown. Flesh sizzled as the wood connected above the nose and between the eyes. With a withering roar, the serpent retreated under the chaotic waves, a fiery burn etched across its scales.

Agrippa hovered over the area of the submerged beast, looking every which way, a wild look in his eyes. "Meira! Darek! Are you okay?"

Darek grabbed hold of Silver Eye's leg, pulling himself slowly up her haunches and onto her back. He shook his head, watching as the barbed tail vanished in a foam of bubbles. "One of those hideous serpents!" he sputtered. "Kraton...It came out of nowhere..."

"Serpentem Vectem Dominum," Agrippa muttered the strange words under his breath. "Evil follows us like a black shadow." He eased Cender in closer to settle in the water beside the two.

Meira gazed with anguish at a shallow gash along Typhoon's side.

"Both of you must fly back to Valkyrie Island," Agrippa hissed. "Something is very wrong here."

Silver Eye gave a fluting chirrup and brought Darek abreast of Meira. "Easy girl. It wasn't your fault I fell." In answer, she gave a rattling purr, and turned to blink at him with her one good eye.

Meira whipped back her brown hair, her green eyes flashing in restless frustration. "Why go back? What was that serpent doing so close to the bay?"

Agrippa glanced back at the water below. "Many things are amiss lately. More attacks from the sea serpents and the sea dragons appear edgier of late…"

He glanced less sharply at Darek's bedraggled form. "Well, off with the two of you. Porpoise's teeth, but you're looking like a sorry bunch! I'd say you've had enough training for one day."

"If you call getting attacked and nearly killed 'enough', then I'd have to agree," grunted Darek. "Why'd you send us out here, Agrippa, if you knew it was so dangerous?"

The old man sighed. "I have precious little time to coddle apprentices. The whole fate of the Dragon Sea rests in the balance. I knew you would test each other—but I didn't expect a serpent attack." He frowned, stroking his beard with a fitful hand. He pondered with a distant look in his eye, muttering words so abstract they couldn't understand them.

"I fear we will have to speed up your training." He cast an anxious glance at the sky and over to the place where the feral young serpent had almost consumed the two. "A young serpent wouldn't venture so close to the hunting grounds of the sea dragons. Not on its own." He wrinkled his nose. "If I'd only trusted my instincts—I could have taken care of this problem much earlier."

"What problem?" demanded Meira. She tugged at her harness, as if that nervous reaction would relieve her mounting stress.

The old Mage waved it off. "'Tisn't important. All will be revealed later. For now, listen to me with both ears and follow my instructions."

"I've had enough of your riddles, old man," cried Meira. "First you summon me here, then you team me up with my insufferable brother who I'd given up for dead, only to nearly get eaten by a monster serp—"

"Be silent!" Agrippa boomed. "Be grateful you're alive."

She cowed back, seeing the look of smoldering power on his face. Clamping her jaw in a sullen quiver, she bowed her head.

Darek blinked in surprise. *Meira did care that he was alive.*

That was when the black ship appeared...Just a small shape, but something significant. Its billowing sails moved across the crests of swells like a ghostly mirage, a thing not of this world. It bent on a northerly tack toward the Black Claw Islands.

Agrippa fell silent, his jaw clicking with repressed rage. "I should have known..." Not far distant, Darek could distinguish several bobbing shapes nearby that looked like large whales, moving in sync with the craft.

The mage's fierce gaze penetrated Darek and Meira. "Leave now."

"But—" began Darek.

"Do as I say!" Darek had never heard the old man speak so vehemently. Agrippa heeled Cender toward the ship with Seavenger, his trusty eagle, arrowing after him.

Darek turned to Meira in awkward silence.

His sister waved a dismissive hand. "Give the old man some time to cool down, then we follow."

"Is it wise to disobey him?" Darek's eyes swam with doubt.

"We need to find out what's going on," said Meira.

Not two minutes passed before they tightened their harnesses and flew after the receding mage. Darek felt a sinking pit in his stomach. He knew there would be grave consequences for disobeying his master.

Chapter 10.

Cyrus

Agrippa hovered above the waves on his snorting mount, a healthy distance from the black sloop. He positioned himself in front of the sun so that he wouldn't be seen readily. His former apprentice stood tall at the helm in black draping robes, white satin sash and white gloves. Seven serpents swam in a protective horseshoe around his ship with their massive, deformed fins and frog-like faces in plain view. Agrippa's expression was one of stony wrath and it grew more intense on sight of his enemy.

Hiding would do no good. It was time to face his old pupil. Amplifying his voice over the waves and wind, he called down from his perch. "Cyrus, release those beasts! They are an abomination upon the waters and a danger to the Dragon Sea."

Cyrus whirled about, staring, shielding his eyes from the sun as he located the source of the voice.

He used his own magic to project his response over the distance. "I've waited too long for you to hand over your power, Agrippa. You're living in the past. These creatures are stronger than any dragons. Look at their faces, their razor teeth. With fins powerful enough to swim for leagues, they can lay waste to your sea dragons."

"Not true, Cyrus," Agrippa called out. "The sea serpents know only death and destruction. It appears that you have chosen the same."

"These beasts will make me Emperor of the Dragon Sea! There is nothing you can do to stop me." Cyrus cackled, a sinister grimace distorted his face. He stepped forward, extending both arms out to encompass his glorious serpents. "The tribal chiefs are weak. Their broken pacts and jealous squabbles have held us back for too long. I will rule these islands with an iron fist and build a glorious new world."

Agrippa ground his teeth. This upstart's magic was strong and his knowledge extensive. Agrippa's teaching had seen to that. Could he defeat him? He reined Cender down to get a better look at the sloop's hull, wary of the serpents whose heads reared as high as Cyrus's black mast. The deck was bare of ornaments and the smirking mage stood in his voluminous black garb alone. His attention was divided between sailing the ship with his magic and controlling the serpents.

"You err, Cyrus. There are strong men and women on these islands. They seek only to feed their families, but you would loose monsters on them."

Agrippa circled the boat in a slow arc. "I've warned you before, our control over them is not absolute. They will turn on you eventually. The serpents, unlike the dragons, will always bite the hand that feeds them. None has ever succeeded in ruling them."

"That is because no one has had the knowledge. None has ever been as powerful as me," said Cyrus with a mocking lilt. "Even you."

Agrippa scoffed. "I thought you were wise enough to understand the truth. I see not. I have overestimated you."

"Overestimate all you want, Agrippa. I'll continue to raise my serpents and forge a new destiny for the islands. One chance I give you, to choose exile instead of death. You can live out the rest of your life on a faraway shore."

"Cocky to the end, aren't you, Cyrus?" said Agrippa. With sudden anger rising in his throat, he raised his glowing staff. "But I think you have miscalculated."

Cyrus looked to his line of serpents. "You are hopelessly outnumbered."

Two shapes burst over the crow's nest of Cyrus's sloop, their wings fluttering in fury above the undulating serpents.

Agrippa turned with a startled grunt as two familiar dragons flew in.

Typhoon and Silver Eye bared their teeth and snapped at their bits while Meira and Darek struggled to restrain them.

Agrippa flew Cender toward the two. "I told you not to come here! Now that you have disobeyed me, we must join together and fight."

"Three?" laughed Cyrus. "Is that all you can muster against my seven serpents?" His eyes grew dark. "This one," he leveled a finger at Darek, "should have been fed to my serpents long ago."

Darek's heart beat fiercely and he glared back at the dark mage with deep-seated animosity, knowing that at last he had his chance for revenge.

"I sent my youngest serpent to destroy you both. Now you will know my full power..." The mage raised a bony hand and summoned a ray of light from the runestones he clenched. His eyes glowed, like a smoldering balefire.

"Stop! You cannot do this, Cyrus!" yelled Agrippa.

"Watch me—and die!" The ray shot out like a lightning flare and skimmed off Agrippa's staff. It deflected toward Typhoon and Meira pulled her dragon back with a gasp of surprise.

A choked cry rang in Darek's throat. Something snapped in him. He bid Silver Eye forward, over the tops of

Cyrus's masts and she dodged a serpent's tail and tore through Cyrus's foresail with her claws.

Cyrus gave back a bellow of fury. He shot another blast of magic just behind Silver Eye's tail.

"Get back!" shouted Agrippa at Darek.

Darek did not hear. He was drunk with vengeance and thought only of the last two wretched years of his life spent in slavery. The dragon wobbled but stabilized and flew around Cyrus, dodging his repeated attacks. Agrippa swooped low with his staff raised, smiting the lead serpent at Cyrus's stern. His staff swung and spewed out a spout of flame at a second hideous serpent at his side. The creature, engulfed in fire, reared back, screaming in pain.

Meira spurred Typhoon forward, her teeth gouging bloody furrows into a brown sea serpent near the bow. The barbed tail shot out in reflex, but Typhoon was a dancer upon the wind, deftly dodging each thrust and bite and striking at the creature's exposed belly. She would have dealt significant damage had not the serpent submerged below the water and disappeared from sight.

Cyrus had already summoned his other serpents. Another massive head, blue in color, rose dripping from the water to menace Agrippa. Then a smaller one snapped its fangs at Typhoon from behind.

The old mage flew into the heat of the battle, twisting Cender past the blue-headed serpent's fangs. While gliding over its back, he whipped down bombs of fire. Cender's yellow-glinting teeth snapped, ripping out a chunk of the writhing serpent, while Agrippa's magic staff leveled fire at the poisonous tail. A plume of white flame melted the barbs off, leaving sizzled holes in the scales and sending the scorched serpent thrashing below the waves. Only five sea serpents remained.

Two exploded through the water toward Cender, one jabbing with its snout and sending the dragon spinning out of control. A third caught hold of Cender's left wing, unseating Agrippa and sending him into the ocean below. Cender roared fire from his mouth, charring the sea serpent to death. The creature fell, but not before a barbed spike punctured the dragon's chest. Cender fell from the air into the waiting black mouth of the larger serpent. The dragon died in a grisly crunch of bone and flesh.

Agrippa, treading water and still clutching his staff, gave a roar of anguish. He sent shivers of blue fire zapping about the creature's jaws. The massive black sea serpent shrugged the wounds off, turning on the old mage with a hiss, intending to swallow him whole.

"Agar Ka Ma!" Agrippa's explosive white fire rippled from the end of his staff and tore into the creature's gullet. The old conjuror shut his eyes against the painful glare, praying for vengeance.

The serpent's jaws split wide in a shower of blood and shredded bone that slammed the mage beneath the rolling sea.

Upon another spray of fire, Silver Eye reeled back and Cyrus turned his attention from Darek to two of the three remaining sea serpents plunging below the water. One soon surfaced, flinging its head from side to side. Agrippa clung to its large horn, his staff buried in the creature's maw. With a wave of Cyrus's hand, the serpent smashed the sputtering mage onto the deck of the ship.

Agrippa conjured some magic to shield himself from the impact but was still flung hard before Cyrus's feet like a freshly-caught tuna.

Agrippa slowly rose to his knees, his eyes as cold as death. "You'll pay for killing Cender," he gasped.

Before he could fully collect his wits, Cyrus lifted a runestone from which sprayed a blast of magic. The ray fanned out in the shape of glowing yellow prism, encircling the aged sorcerer. He cried out, trapped within a translucent prison.

Cyrus inclined his head with satisfaction and his former master floated two feet off the deck. A delighted smile played about his gloating mouth. "You may beg for your life."

The old man's roars went unheeded. Cyrus lifted a hand, bringing Agrippa closer. "What did you say?"

Darek flew to Meira's aid, maneuvering his dragon around the serpent's coiled mass. It retreated to join the other two in a protective arc around the ship while the mage's remaining three serpents swayed their heads like cobras, sharp teeth splayed in challenge.

Agrippa sent a stream of magical syllables from his lips. *"Agar Fugis Se Turl!"* The incantation was as ancient as time, incomprehensible to the ear. Concentrated power surged forth in the form of a translucent bubble that squeezed through the magical membrane of Cyrus's conjured prism.

The bubble expanded, throwing Cyrus back. The dark mage whirled before he struck his solar plexus against the ship's rail.

The serpents, distracted by the cry of their master, wavered, and Darek swooped and Silver Eye's claws raked the eye of the nearest serpent. Meira drove Typhoon through the knot of serpents, seeking to put an end to Cyrus.

Cyrus rolled away, rattling his eerie runestones and loosing another lethal ray of power. The beam caught Typhoon's back left claw and shore it off. The dragon gave an anguished screech. She veered out of control, whipping Meira back and forth. Meira clung to her scaly hide with a fierce doggedness that made Darek proud. He cried out as she bounced off the ship's mast, barely staying in the air.

Seavenger dove in, digging his beak and claws into a serpent that had turned to gobble Meira and her dragon whole. But flames rose from Cyrus's runestones and the eagle squawked back, fluttering in pain, as its wings were singed.

Agrippa's weak voice rumbled through the magical mesh. "Fly away! Doom is upon you. I will hold him at bay. Go!" He struck at Cyrus with a grey flame that threw the young mage back again.

In a surge of frustration, Cyrus regained his feet, his black garb smoking with the heat of Agrippa's magic. Shaking the daze from his head, he clapped his palms together with a wordless curse, as a powerful gust of wind rose. It buffeted Agrippa to his knees.

The mage gasped in agony. "Seek out Jace! Continue your training."

In an awesome display of power, Agrippa summoned a huge wave of water which smashed upon the ship, dragging Cyrus, the three serpents, and the old mage deep below the surface.

"No!" Darek cried out in grief, seeing his mentor struck down. He was about to dive below the waves when two of the sea serpents surfaced. Cyrus rode on one of their backs, but there was no sign of Agrippa.

Meira flew close on Typhoon. "Let's get out of here! The old man gave us a chance for escape. Don't let his sacrifice be in vain."

Tears of anger sprang in Darek's eyes. Every fiber of his being prayed that Agrippa was still alive. He hated to leave the old man behind, but Cyrus raised his staff to wield another blast and Darek turned Silver Eye up into the air again. Upon Cyrus's cursing words, the two last serpents coiled in a protective ring, their poisonous tails thrashing in defiance. It would be suicide to try to get through that. If he were a mage, he needed to learn to use his power and return with a sea dragon army to defeat Cyrus. "Fly, Silver Eye, Fly!" he cried and drove his mount on with new speed.

Back to Valkyrie Island Darek flew with Meira, both licking their wounds. Darek was raw and aching from the battle while Silver Eye, her scaly hide scratched and torn, blinked her good eye, which was now spidered with bloody veins. Greenish-black blood oozed from her wounds where Cyrus's serpents' fangs had raked her. Meira said little, sporting a wide gash on her forehead and her left upper jerkin torn and crimson stain on her arm underneath. Typhoon guarded a smoking black patch above the left ribs and her back leg with missing claw twitched at every beat of those powerful wings.

It had been a costly battle and Darek's heart felt like lead. He still could not believe that the old mage was gone…

Silver Eye landed with a thud before the ruined courtyard on Valkyrie Island, her thick claws crunching rubble. Meira's dragon landed nearby, breath wet and raspy from her wounds and shorn hind claw. Darek felt a hollowness in his gut as the afternoon light waned under the shadow of Agrippa's weathered tower. The mage's absence was deeply felt and a grayness hung heavy on the air.

"Where's Seavenger?" he muttered.

A flutter of wings came from behind and Meira pointed a finger. "There."

Darek saw a dark shape flitter out of the sky and land with a thunk in the scattered rubble. The bird's beak was parted, feathers singed. How had he even managed to fly back here?

Darek hissed out a breath. He gazed upon a sea eagle a shadow of his former self. Dismounting, he bent to caress the blackened feathers at the ruff of Seavenger's neck. The eagle had taken a painful blast from Cyrus's magic.

Meira went to fetch some healing herbs. "He'll live." She stepped away from the nearby bush. "Though I doubt he'll soon forget who is responsible."

"We'll have our revenge," Darek croaked. He looked out to the sea. "The old mage—"

"He's gone, Darek, forget him. Even if he somehow survived, that wretch Cyrus will never release him."

Darek hung his head, realizing as much. "What now?"

"We fly to the Three Sisters," she replied with a grim tone. "Seek out Jace on Manatee Island—honor Agrippa's command."

Darek gave a grave sigh. "I'll go fetch food then from the tower . What about Seavenger?" He considered the pitiful state of the bird. "We can't just leave the poor thing here."

"Can you take him on your dragon, if I make some sort of basket to carry him?"

Darek shrugged. "Anything's possible. I'm worried about Agrippa's dragons, though. What about them?"

Meira scanned the island and spotted several dragons dozing or fishing in the water. "They'll have to fend for themselves. Unless you can bring them with us."

Darek firmed his lip. "It might be safer if they stay here for now, but I swear I'll come back for them." His heart thudded in sync with the creaking of Agrippa's windmills. "I'll avenge Agrippa one way or the other for all he's done for us."

Chapter 11.

Three Sisters' Isles

Darek and Meira flew south over the deep blue waters around the eastern edge of Swordfish Isle, then on for nearly an hour to Manatee Island. The day was growing old by the time they glimpsed the first stretch of coast.

Darek scanned the sky. No dragons flew overhead. Jace's dragon school could not be that close. The shore loomed ahead, a raw sandy color with a touch of green from the sea firs. Gradually, features and buildings took shape: brick walls and wooden roofs indicating market stalls with figures moving about. Murle Town, in the old island tongue, was named for the fast, dangerous riptides and whirlpools off the beach, Siren's Kiss, just past the shoals. Darek veered his dragon away from the bustle of the town and beckoned Meira to follow him. Better to keep a low profile.

Seavenger shivered in the basket lashed to the back of Silver Eye's harness. The bird's head lay slumped, his beak tucked in his feathers, and his eyes nearly closed. The eagle needed immediate attention.

Darek and Meira landed in a glade surrounded by sea lavender, about half a mile from Murle. Darek stretched his aching back and looked about with hopeful interest. It seemed like a secluded spot here, safe from prying eyes.

"We should take Seavenger to see the dragon medicus," suggested Meira.

Darek nodded. "Let's leave the dragons here to rest and we'll get them later."

They cut through the bush and followed a dirt road that led into town. Wagons and foot traffic passed them by with hardly a second look: carters, millers, sea traders, some farmers and shipbuilders, of many ages and temperaments.

The harbor spread to their right. Bright sunshine sparkled off the protected bay. It had been years since Darek had visited any of Three Sisters' Isles, the last time on some business with Jace. Though he could remember little of the middle island, Sprawlee, he recalled eating red snapper as the gulls soared about the dockyards, looking for scraps of food. Those were tender years that filled him with nostalgia.

Murle had fallen onto hard times since he had last seen it, with stray hounds rooting through the refuse, and the dock posts of the seedy wharf showing rot beneath a layer of thick barnacles. The familiar smell of tar and grease assaulted Darek's nostrils. It made him wonder why Jace had chosen this town. This was the sort of place one went to avoid being found.

Among the market stalls, Meira searched out a female vendor whose limp brown hair and deep green eyes seemed at odds with her lively gestures. Her shelves lay stocked with various resins and fish products—oils and balms, from what Darek guessed. Meira selected several healing ointments; she also asked after Jace's whereabouts, expressing interest in a trainer of dragons.

"Jace? You must mean Jarle," the vendor said. "Runs the riding school on the other side of the bay. He's the only one-armed dragon trainer I know." She clucked her tongue at that and wrinkled her pink, sunburnt nose. "A bit of a lonely man, Jarle. You're not one of those queer Dragon Riders, are you?" She shook her head, shuddering in distaste. "Those pesky dragons are a menace. Their feces alone would fill this stall to the rafters."

Meira smirked, unable to hide her amusement. "I've heard that one before, ma'am. But thanks for your concern."

The vendor dismissed the remark with a shrug.

A portly man with sharp eyes and a short, crusty beard was loitering nearby. He happened to overhear the pair's conversation and stepped forward in two strides. "I can help you, friends," he said with a genial smile. "Name's Barbar. I run a ferry service over to Dunspur the other side of the bay.

I just came over to grab some crab kebabs. Grinny's are to die for. Highly recommended."

Meira looked on, staring in silence. Her mouth began to water at the deep-fried crab in his hand. "We've got our own transport, thanks."

"Well, unless you're dolphins, you're not getting across that bay. Or maybe you'll sprout wings?"

Darek studied the man's sun-browned face, his small eyes and high forehead. His sleeveless jerkin and bare feet pegged him as one of the island folk, though his black curly hair was wrapped in a plain sash.

"Something like that," laughed Meira, turning away.

The man scanned their garb, gesturing at their riding boots and the small whip at Meira's side. "Oh, I see—dragons, is it? Well, I know where you can purchase some hatchlings and healing herbs. I can take you to Brewer's Forest to see them if you want. They're the finest stock."

Meira paused, squinting at him sideways. "I thought the Dragonmaster claimed all hatchlings?"

"Anything can be had for the right price," Barbar replied.

Meira's eyes narrowed. "My brother here, does he get a special price too?"

"Of course." Seeing her skeptical look, the man put a hand to his mouth in shock. "I'm not a smuggler, just an honest citizen, trying to feed his family. Let's say, half a silver shell each to take you there?"

"My eye," she snorted. "I paid a quarter of that price not three moons ago."

Barbar smiled. "Half a silver shell then for both?"

Darek sighed. "We might as well."

"Oh, and I suppose you'll be the one paying?" Meira produced a purse at Darek's shrug and handed a half silver shell over with a huff.

"A bargain, then. Come, my boat's not far," he said.

He hustled them toward his lubberly, flat-bottomed barge berthed before the boardwalk on the way to the shipping docks. "I like the look of you two—I don't mind giving you the special rate. Always looking to help out newcomers."

Darek studied the man's vessel. A rusty stack and boiler rose mid-ship. The hull could use a good scouring and was badly in need of paint but was otherwise seaworthy. The ferryman obviously needed the business. Darek felt sorry for him, as nobody else looked to be waiting for passage.

They boarded with caution. While Darek inspected the deck—the old rotten coils of rope, the spilled tar and fish heads and smell—Meira stood aside, her arms folded over her chest.

The man, pleased at his slick catch of customers, cast off the lines and nodded to Darek before putting out into the bay. He appeared to go out of his way to make them comfortable. "Hope you don't mind the fish heads. I do a bit of trawling on the side. Sit. I'll bring your refreshments to the foredeck." He retreated to the small stern cabin and brought back a tray with two clear glasses of liquor with squeezed lemon. "Lemon Zarang," he explained, "with a touch of arrack for spice. Local specialty."

Meira glanced at the cup with suspicion, perhaps catching something in the ferryman's leer. "None for me, thanks."

Darek sat back on a cushioned bench near the bow and chugged back his arrack in less time than it took a snapping turtle to blink.

The boatman laughed. He hoisted a cup himself, eyeing the sword and knife at Meira's belt. "Suit yourself."

Few boats were plying the bay, mostly dories and small skiffs, giving an area of white churning froth wide berth. Darek pointed to some activity out in the water. A swishing motion roiled a stone's throw away.

"Dangerous tidal pools and harpies' rocks abound," Barbar explained. "Don't worry, we'll steer clear and dock at a safer location. There!" He lifted a sun-browned hand.

Darek's eyes followed the man's gesture and he nodded with a mariner's understanding. He had some experience with treacherous rocks.

Meira inclined her head. She gestured to the other docks straight across. "That mooring looks safe enough."

"A common mistake, made by the untrained eye." The ferryman laughed. "I've sailed these waters all my life. Just sit back and enjoy the ride."

Meira shot up and bared her knife, glaring at the boatman. "I'd like to use the main dock, like the other boats are."

"Meira," whispered Darek. "He's only trying—"

"To what?" she demanded, stepping forward. "Take us to a secluded spot so he can rob us?"

Holding the knife high, she began patting down Barbar's brown tunic. The man tried to spin away, but as he did, two objects dropped to the ground—a twisted knife and a strange star-shaped object, some sort of hurling weapon. "What's this?"

"You wouldn't deny an honest businessman the means to defend his livelihood, would you?" He glowered at her, his expression turning dark.

Meira threw her knife to the deck where it quivered upright, narrowly missing Barbar's foot. "You wouldn't want to deny me the right of defending myself from a thief after my coin."

He stared at her like an owl of prey. His brows narrowed as if he realized she might not be an easy mark after all.

Darek cast his sister a look of surprise. Either she had good instincts or was completely paranoid.

The ferryman's face clouded. "Pull a knife on me, will you?" His front yellow teeth gleamed in the sunlight as if weighing his chances to take them both. "That'll cost you extra. Give me all your coin and we'll call it even."

Darek drew his blade and Barbar's face quickly changed back to a smile.

"Fighters, are you?" The ferryman sneered. He gave a high-pitched whistle and three men dressed in tatters scrambled up from below. They carried dirks and cutlasses in their ham fists and wore evil leers.

Meira drew her sword and hopped back to take a defensive stance.

"Let's not make this harder than it needs to be," the ferryman growled.

One of the brawny brutes stuck out a dirty hand. "Well, lookee at this missus." He had a patch over his left eye and stood barelegged to the knees. "She'll make a good bride for tonight." The second lowlife made a grab for Meira's wrist but she slashed and twisted aside. He pulled his arm away oozing with a small line of blood.

"Feisty! We do like feisty, don't we, Pox?" cooed the scarred bandit with one eye.

"Aye, we do, Reji," replied the tallest of the thieves.

The third man was well muscled, but just waved his cutlass and smiled with a blank, gap-toothed grin.

Darek glared at the thugs and cursed himself for being so gullible. He put himself in between the foremost thug and Meira, glancing toward the shore as the ferry continued to float farther away.

Pox turned to size up Darek. "Where'd you get this puff fish anyway, Barbar? Thinks he can take on three of us?" The thug gave a mocking grin. "We should sink a gaff iron in him and throw him overboard."

"Why don't we sell them to the mines?" Reji asked. "Vex here lost his tongue in the mines. Maybe he could borrow one of yours." The silent man nodded and waggled the pink stub in his mouth.

The thieves laughed.

Darek, spitting with fury, reached out with his mind.

Silver Eye...Typhoon...Come! Hurry!

"He looks as if he's making his last prayer, doesn't he, his lips working like a bandsaw?" said Pox. "Let's hurry him along, shall we?"

Meira leaped into action. Snatching at a coil of rope, she flung it at Barbar's head. The man stumbled back and she rolled forward, scooping up her knife.

Reji swung his dirk, but Meira easily dodged and carved a deep gash into the man's forearm.

Vex moved in, stabbing with his cutlass—only to have Darek catch it with his blade. Pox tried to gut him, but Meira's knife was spinning through the air and sank in the man's shoulder. Pox dropped to the deck with a scream.

Barbar and Reji rounded on Meira as she whirled her sword.

Two dark shadows filled the sky and the thieves froze.

Barbar wheeled about at the sound of two low grunts and the beating of furious wings. His face paled as he realized his mistake.

"Are those dragons friends of yours?" he stammered, eyeing the water as an escape route.

The boat sank dangerous inches in the water as Silver Eye and Typhoon thudded onto the deck. The entire craft began to rock from side to side. Silver Eye gave a low warning growl. Vex leaped over the gunwales—not as stupid as he looked.

Reji tried to sink his weapon into Meira, but Typhoon shot forward, battering the man with her snout and sending him careening into the water. Pox dropped his weapon while Barbar slowly backed away with his hands in the air. The ferryman blinked, looking as though he was unwilling to abandon his craft but afraid to face the two dragons. His lower lip quivered.

"Let's negotiate a new deal," growled Darek. "Since you didn't take us all the way across the bay, there will be no charge. In exchange, we won't sink your boat."

Barbar's white hand clutched the railing.

Typhoon opened his jaws wide and let loose a mighty roar that had the rogue's stringy hair blowing back behind his ears. The man sank to his knees, cowering in defeat.

Darek and Meira mounted their dragons and sprang off the deck, leaving the white-faced man blubbering about the greed of Dragon Riders.

"I would have seen through that rat's plan soon enough," Darek growled.

"So you say," said Meira. "We both took the bait."

Darek scowled, not wanting to admit it.

Meira reined in close and raised her voice over the wind. "Can you ride? You look kind of pale."

Darek waved her on. "I'll be ok. Go ahead. I'll follow." He did feel somewhat sick from the drink Barbar had given them.

Meira turned her dragon to face the lush green forest that blossomed along the bay's shoreline. Both headed toward the metallic sheen of the roof where the fish-oil vendor had mentioned Jace lived.

THE DRAGON SEA CHRONICLES: THREE BOOK SERIES

Chapter 12.

JACE

The pair passed over a forest pocked with groves of coconut and stickypalm farms. Darek saw tiny figures milling about, some pushing barrows, others driving beasts of burden to till the land or draw water. The wind, steady from the east, had the dragons beating their wings hard and starting to tire from the long voyage across the Dragon Sea to Manatee Island.

Unlike Swordfish Island, Manatee was flat and less rocky, with natural glades as if the beach had once extended many miles inland. A low ridge peeked up from the south. At its foot wound a calm river of sparkling water.

Rocking with the air currents, they flew on and Darek grew excited at the sight of several dark specks which could only be dragons. He spurred Silver Eye on with greater speed.

"Darek, wait!" Meira called.

But the words were lost to him. He was amazed to see nearly two dozen dragons and their riders in the air. They maneuvered in close quarters, dodging each other, diving and scrapping like kites. Several flew in loose formations like warriors of old.

Two dragons flew in perilous reach of each other, both jostling for position as they hurtled forward. A husky man in leather armor straddled an amber-scaled dragon with a greenish head. The rider and dragon nudged a smaller, blue-tailed beast ridden by a slender woman.

Despite the smaller size, the blue-tailed dragon pushed back, gaining some space and pulling ahead. The man harried her left and right, prodding her with a staff and jostling her mount with his own dragon's flank.

The female rider spun about, blocking a sudden strike with her double-length bow staff, only to catch a sneak jab in the ribs. The attacking green-headed dragon took a swipe with its claws at her mount's plated hide near the harness.

Darek's muscles stiffened; a low growl rumbled in his throat. The blue-tailed dragon faltered and the woman slid out of her harness, grabbing at the stirrup just in time. If he didn't help her she was going to fall! On instinct, he urged Silver Eye forward on a swooping dive.

Silver Eye was only too ready to obey his mental commands. She crashed into the amber dragon, sending it banking right with a raucous cry.

"I'll distract him!" Darek called to the woman as she struggled to regain her seat.

The male rider choked out a furious cry as he whirled his beast to face Darek. "What in Kraton's knuckles do you think you are doing?" He spurred his green-headed mount toward Silver Eye. The two dragons hissed and roared at each other and Silver Eye reared with talons raised, before Darek pulled her back and angled away from the attacking dragon. The woman had re-strapped herself in and turned her dragon and sped off toward a stone archway on the ground.

"How dare you interfere!" the male rider yelled, his face brimming crimson.

The amber dragon thrust out, gashing Silver Eye's back flank with piercing teeth. Silver Eye loosed a howl and snapped her front fangs along the aggressor's flank, but didn't penetrate the thick-armored hide. Darek fought the reins and pulled Silver Eye away from the gnashing teeth and sharp claws. He suddenly regretted his hasty decision to interfere. The assaults had him rocking on Silver Eye's back and almost slipping to his doom. The male rider refused to break off his attack. He pulled something from a bag strapped to his harness, a dart of some kind, and threw it straight at Silver Eye. The projectile caught the thin, gray membrane of her back-left wing. She yelped and fluttered. The muscles relaxed on her wing and the dragon lost altitude, corkscrewing down toward the ground. Darek guided Silver Eye in to land as best he could with an anxious look. *Was it poison the man had fired?*

A lizard-like, yellow dragon squatted in the center of the field—one without a rider. Darek hoped it would be safe to land here.

He and Silver Eye hit hard in a clump of shrubs and his pursuer landed a stone's throw away. The man leaped from his dragon. Somewhere along the way he had lost his staff but stomped over, white-knuckled fists raised and curses on his lips.

The woman Darek had helped also landed nearby but was unwilling to intervene.

Darek ignored the challenge and hurried to examine Silver Eye's wing. The joint and fingers of the wing sagged and the dragon folded the wing closed with a bleating cry. Seavenger lay huddled in the basket under the dragon's other wing, shaken but unharmed.

"What did you do to my dragon?" Darek demanded, rounding on the man.

A meaty fist struck his face. Darek staggered back, then swung with a punch of his own. His reach was longer and the man grunted as he connected squarely with his jaw. The man wrestled him to the ground and tried to pummel him with both hands. Darek squirmed out of the hold like an eel and spun away.

The man gave chase and Darek snuck under a wild swing. He rolled away in the sand and sprang back to his feet. Curses erupted from his aggressor's lips as Darek again evaded his grasp. Others had landed their dragons and now encircled them to watch.

Meira's shouts drifted from nearby. Typhoon nudged the other dragons out of the way as she moved to protect Silver Eye. He sniffed her wing with a gentle protectiveness and roared out a challenge.

The large yellow dragon stormed in, its rider now clinging to his back. The beast snorted and reared up to confront Typhoon.

"Enough!" cried the man on the yellow dragon's back. "Tand, release that young man. You know the rules. Anything unexpected can happen in the air. You were supposed to be training the other members of your Wing."

Darek could suddenly breathe again. He shook his head, dazed. He knew that voice.

"*Harbkuk!*" yelled the rider. Obviously he was in charge. At his word, Typhoon backed away and the rider's dragon sank back to the ground. Despite the metal claw-hook forming his right hand, the sunburnt face of his father, Jace, was unmistakable. Broad of shoulder with a blond ruff of hair and sideburns, he had the same rangy build as his son.

"Tand, who are these gadflies?" asked Jace.

"I don't know, Jarle," replied Tand.

"But this fingerling—" Tand motioned at Darek "—interrupted my attack maneuver and could have gotten us all killed."

The claw-handed man stared at Darek. "Well? What have you to say—" His words caught in his throat, as if he was recalling a figure of the past. "Darek? It can't be you! Has Kraton sent me a ghost, risen from the dead?"

Darek beamed ear to ear, enjoying the irony of it all. *So he does recognize me.* "I'm real enough, but this man's nothing but a bully." He jerked a thumb at Tand. "The gull-eater poisoned my dragon. What kind of Dragonmaster allows that?"

"Careful, boy," warned Jace, "that's my best flier you're talking about."

Darek licked his lips and flashed his father an insolent grin. Kraton's beard, it was good to see him. But what had happened to his right arm? The flesh had been replaced with a strange metal claw that bent on a riveted steel hinge. The metal glowed faintly orange, not unlike the stone at the tip of Agrippa's staff.

"The effects of the dragon dart will wear off in a few hours," explained Meira, dismounting and striding forward. "You'll have to forgive Darek. He's still a hatchling when it comes to dragons—that's why we're here."

Jace gaped. "No, can it be? Meira!" He broke out in a laugh. "It's been too long."

"Who else?" She grinned. "You must have heard by now that Darek survived the Rebirth Ritual. He's free and Agrippa's apprentice now." She approached and gave Jace a warm embrace.

Tand's jaw dropped. "I'll see if the medicus has an antidote for the dart to administer to your dragon." The man retreated with a glower as if not knowing whether to believe the bold claim to wizardom, but at the same time guarding a fear of what a mage might do.

Tears sprang in Jace's eyes. "No, I hadn't heard—folks on Manatee aren't graced with up-to-date news. I thought you were dead, Darek. Please believe me that I tried to find you. I thought I knew what loss was when your mother Thyphalyne left, but when you disappeared, I lost faith in everything. I had no idea where you were. We sent out ships, scoured the sea from coast to coast. Nothing we could find but wind, rain and serpent bones."

Darek's heart softened as he sensed the truth in his father's words. "Surely you must have heard when I returned?"

Jace came closer and placed his left hand on Darek's shoulder. "It was Meira who finally found out you had been enslaved by the Black Claw Clan. I knew Raithan hated me, but I never thought you would be the one to pay."

Pulling him into an awkward embrace, Jace pounded on Darek's back roughly. "You've filled out."

He looked into Darek's red-rimmed eyes. "I came to buy your freedom a dozen times," he said, "but Raithan always refused and only doubled the price. Finally I decided to steal you back, but by the time I fought my way in, they had already moved you—that's how I lost my arm. They told me you were dead."

"I...understand." Darek blinked, now unsure of himself. The anger he had felt at his father seemed suddenly unfounded. "How did you get that?" he asked, indicating the metal arm.

"Agrippa made it," replied Jace. "After the 'accident', I was unable to ride. Everything I had known was snatched away—your mother, you...I couldn't stand being useless as well. The Mage fused it with a dragon talon and some contraption he invented. It's filled with his magic."

Jace lifted the metal claw in the air and opened the talons. "A reward for years of faithful service. Thing's ugly, but the claw-arm lets me grip a harness again."

Darek sighed and clenched his fists. A flood of memories poured in, of the imprisonment, the abuses, the endless hunger, pirates, and the humiliating stint of slavery under the yoke of the Black Claw Clan.

"It's not your fault, Jace. You couldn't have done anything. I was imprisoned by the pirates in Devil's Lair. Things got only worse from there."

"I want to hear all about it, son," said Jace, "but later, in private."

Darek gazed at the sea of faces around him. More riders had trickled in as they conversed. Decked in their sun-bleached leather and protective padding, some of the men and women wore broadswords at their waists or carried jeweled dirks strapped to their belts. They must be Jace's Dragon Riders.

Jace raised his hands for attention. "Listen, all, here is my son! I thought he was lost at sea for years. 'Tis a miracle! His name is Darek." He motioned to Meira. "And this is my lovely stepdaughter, Meira, a Dragon Rider whom some of you know, from Sandfish Bay on Swordfish Island."

Murmurs of surprise rose from the gathering. "You are welcome here," the woman with the blue-tailed dragon said. The silver streak in her auburn hair made her look like a cedar waxwing as she came forward to take Meira's hands in greeting.

Jace looked up at the gathering clouds and the fading light. "We've had enough training for today. Tonight we feast!"

A cheer rose among them and they remounted their dragons and kicked off.

Jace turned back to Darek. "Tonight I want to hear how you survived and escaped the pirates." He approached Silver Eye and extended his hand with care as she took in his scent. "Who is this beauty and what happened to her eye?"

"That's Silver Eye," Darek said. "I found her egg in a chamber below the volcano's crater. She lost the eye saving me from the fire of the Rebirth Ritual."

"That can't be," said Jace, placing an admiring hand on her leg. "She's much too large to have just been born. What have you been feeding her?"

Darek's eyes widened as he took in the size of his dragon. Silver Eye had nearly tripled in size since hatching. *Was that unusual?* He shrugged. "Well, she hunts on her own mostly."

Meira lowered her voice as the rest of the Dragon Riders dispersed. "It was Agrippa who sent us. He's been attacked."

"Who would be foolish enough to attack Agrippa?" demanded Jace.

Darek stiffened. "His Apprentice Mage, Cyrus, ensnared him in some kind of magical prism."

Jace scowled. "Prism? Why would he do that?"

Meira's tone became deadly serious. "Let's just say we don't know where the old man is, or whether he is dead or alive."

"He must be still alive," said Jace. "The fact that Cyrus has not slaughtered us all proves that. But we have to save him." Jace looked around with wild eyes. "If Agrippa dies before another Sea Dragon Mage takes control, the dragons would go wild—"

"I thought the amulets he forged gave each Dragon Rider control?" asked Darek, his eyes widening in shock.

Jace shook his head. "They allow a rider to direct his mount. But it's Agrippa's will that keeps them docile. We have to stop that snake, Cyrus."

"It's Cyrus who's responsible for all the recent sea serpent attacks," Meira spat.

"How do you know?" demanded Jace.

"There's no doubt," she replied. "We heard it with our own ears from the mage's mouth."

Jace cursed. "It's our sacred duty to guard everything west of the Three Sisters' Isles. If Cyrus is using those vile serpents, then he's forsaken all his oaths. Kraton's pits! Without Agrippa there's nothing to stop them.

Darek muttered, "As Meira said, you can blame Cyrus for it. If only I'd made sense of things two years ago when I was on Windbit Isle. I caught Cyrus summoning serpents and sacrificing innocent people to them. I could have warned you, if I hadn't been taken by pirates and then the Black Claws."

Jace shuddered. "We need to tell the Clutch. The Council will know what to do. We must go there—to Aster Island, and petition help from all the clans. I'll send a rider out to set up a meeting in a week. Hopefully chief Lared, and Solene from the Blue Claws can attend. If Cyrus has sea serpents, we'll need every fighting dragon possible."

A distant look entered Jace's eyes as if wheels were spinning in his head of a possible battle strategy. "Until then we'll train like never before. Come!" he said, putting an arm around Darek's shoulder. "Let's join the celebratory feast." He beckoned for Meira to accompany them.

The medicus had covered Silver Eye's wing in a paste that soon returned feeling to her. Before long she was sniffing and play-fighting with the new dragons. With a few coins from Meira, the medicus had taken the wounded Seavenger away and promised to see the bird back to full health.

Jace addressed the group. "Cyrus has betrayed the Dragonclaw Islands. This is no time for petty squabbles—" he leveled a disapproving glare at the grimacing Tand who pulled at his long, dirty blond beard. "We must prepare for war!"

The warriors grunted their enthusiasm, showing their eagerness for battle.

"Come, on Darek," said Jace, smiling, as he pulled Darek along, "let me show you around."

Darek nodded and followed his father's lead toward the far end of the practice yard. They walked along an uneven trail that cut through the hills and ended in a protected bay.

At the waterline, a series of partially submerged, roofed pens stood, filled with dragons. A large wooden longhouse, crafted of thick, old sea firs sat farther up the beach. Behind that stood a low, wooden barracks at the tree line. Through the line of sea firs and stickypalms, Darek saw three docks trailing out into the water. Several fishing sloops berthed, along with some beat-up rowboats.

Jace saw where his son was looking and pointed with his claw hand. "The young dragons we keep in those pens for breaking in, the rest live in their deep sea caves a league past Gullmon, a fishing village."

Darek rubbed at his chin. "Not a bad setup, Jace. Why don't you just let them run free, like Agrippa does?"

"They're *Attakan*, more feral and wild, and if we did, there'd be a lot more accidental deaths than there are now. This way we can control their diet. A wandering tinker told me that the dragons of Manatee Island once fed upon the sea scorpions off the shoals. The venom made them crazy, uncontrollable. You never knew when the unexpected would happen." He held up his gleaming, taloned hand.

"I moved the school from Swordfish Isle. Right after your mother took up with that Black Claw scum." He gave a heavy sigh.

Darek nodded, his mind flitting from one harsh memory to another. "Give me your finest riders, Jace. Let me search out this weasel Cyrus and kill him! If Raithan is with him, then he will fall as well."

Jace stared at his son in mounting pride. "You've got pluck, son, I'll give you that. But if Cyrus took down Agrippa and controls the sea serpents, he'll eat you for breakfast. Raithan will likewise not be defeated easily. You're not ready to face either—not yet."

"Then train me!" cried Darek. "I've already learned so much from Meira."

"You haven't even started," scoffed Meira who appeared next to them.

"There's no time," Jace growled at Darek. "I'll teach you what I can, but at the turn of the new moon we must go to war. Listen to me. Learn from your sister and the other Dragon Riders and you might survive this."

Darek gritted his teeth. He knew Jace was right, but he was too proud to admit it, especially in front of those two.

THE DRAGON SEA CHRONICLES: THREE BOOK SERIES

Chapter 13.

THE DRAGON PENS

They came before the communal lodge, a rambling wooden longhouse made of thick, old sea firs. Set back from the common ground at the fringe of the forest, it sported a rounded roof with sandy-colored sea moss growing from its sides. An overhang provided shade and small thick-glassed windows allowed light; heavy wooden doors with large brass knobs stood dead center. Darek could still hear the faint roar of the ocean through the nearby trees.

Jace thrust the doors open with his claw hand, and he and his riders piled in with Tand leading the banter. Some members hauled fish in wicker baskets; others dumped bags of sea vegetables into the large cauldron at the front. Fires were stoked under the stew pot and fresh filets were put on the braziers.

Darek looked in awe at the immense size of the place and its hardwood table running the length of the hall with enough seating for hundreds to feast.

"We're a dwindling breed, Darek," Jace said. "I hope to recruit enough to fill these halls to celebrate our conquests."

The air lay heavy with smoke from fat torches flickering like small dragon fires. Roasted snapper and sea eel began to sizzle, sending tantalizing odors wafting over the fire and into Darek's nostrils. He looked up, impressed by the thick black columns rising up into the dimness that gave sturdy support for the massive structure.

Jace sat at the head of the table; Darek and Meira to either side. Tand and others sat farther down, as echoes of blustery talk and backslapping filled the hall with the clink of dishes and cutlery. A large, bearded man with a curved hook dangling from his left ear filled mugs of ale and passed them around to hearty drinkers. Jace seemed better able to maneuver with his taloned hand than Darek might have guessed. He skewered fish on his plate and even used it to scratch an itch on his neck.

The other thirty riders, nine of them women, did not bat an eye. Which led Darek to believe Jace had earned their respect despite any physical disability. They looked a grizzled but hardened bunch dedicated to their work despite their small numbers.

Darek turned to his father. "Where do your riders go after you've trained them?"

Jace sighed. "Brave souls, these men and women. Not much to draw us, though. It's a dangerous life, battling sea serpents, Black Claws and pirates, dying at sea with no headstone to mark our resting places. We contract out to the highest bidders much more these days, like common mercenaries. Without a breed like us, I fear the Red Claw way of life will die out. It used to be that we could defend ourselves with ships and schooners, but now?"

"When was that, Jace?" piped up a lean man with a mouthful of snapper. "About 150 years ago?"

Jace snickered as did others. "Not far-off, Mell. You know as well as I, the Black Claws, Free Band pirates and serpents encroach on our territory more every day."

Grumbles attested to the fact. "I don't know which tastes worse." Tand snorted. "Pirate or sea serpent flesh." The remark earned a few guffaws.

Meira turned to her stepfather. "Seems you've forged a decent name for yourself here, but don't you miss Swordfish Island?" Her voice betrayed a hint of resentment.

Jace gave a carefree shrug. "A man always looks fondly on the days of his youth. After I lost my arm, I could feel the contempt in the other Dragonmasters' looks. Here we've formed something of a guild over the years. We own the land, and we have free rein over our training. Nobody can tell us what to do."

"As long as one of the locals doesn't accidentally get eaten," said a mullet-haired rider with braids and beads in his hair.

"An easy thing to have happen," said another, "seeing how nosy the Caermurle folk are. A bit touchy too."

Jace waved a hand. "Vimere speaks the truth. We've had a few unruly young dragons escape their stalls. They got loose, terrorized a citizen or two, before we got them under control."

Darek took a deep pull of frothy ale in his mug. It was a little warmer than he liked, but had a thick, nutty flavor that reminded him of the drinks he and Jace used to share together over a warm fire. "I imagine that must be quite a fright, staring down a hungry dragon in the eye."

Jace smiled. "Aye, most townsfolk don't know that a sea dragon prefers fish above all else."

While they ate, Meira and Darek told Jace about their run-in with the thieving ferryman.

Jace frowned. "Things are getting bad if ferrymen are turning to banditry and slaving."

Darek's face clouded. A sudden pang reminded him of his degrading experience as a slave.

"You handled yourselves well, but you were lucky," said Jace. "Caermurle is a rough place, no less Gullmon a league or two west of here. Rebel pirates have broken away from the main band and there's talk of a pirate civil-war brewing. Those men were likely in league with them."

"Shame they didn't try to con me," said Tand. "I'd have taught those thugs a thing or two about trespassing on Red Claw turf." He unsheathed his blade and gave it a suggestive twirl.

Jace nodded slowly but gave a dark laugh. "You and Darek here should get along well."

Darek grimaced. What was he thinking? He didn't relish flying alongside Tand. He looked over at the hulking man and wasn't surprised to see him casting a steely glare back. Like Jace he was blond-bearded, but the similarity ended there. He sported a roguish, foxish-looking face with red, angular cheeks, thick lips, and a harsh smile.

The big man wiped the sweat from his brow and thumbed his nose at Darek—a gesture that hinted of settling the score between them when Jace wasn't around.

Darek looked away with a scowl.

"Here's to Dragon Day!" Jace cried and raised his mug in a toast.

"Dragon Day!" they all cheered.

Additional kegs were rolled out from the storeroom.

Darek nudged the man beside him. "What's so special about this Dragon Day?"

The leather-capped man grinned. "Oh, some ancient legend. It says four generations ago, there was a time when dragons killed any men they found on the islands to protect their queen. Then Agrippa killed the queen and became their master."

"Wouldn't that make Agrippa kinda old?" asked Darek. "Like two hundred years."

The man laughed. "It's rubbish, if you ask me, but a good excuse to drink!"

Darek couldn't argue with that logic.

In short order, their bellies were filled with roast oxen and enough ale to put a dragon to sleep. Darek and Jace traded tales of the last few years of their lives, their bond steadily on the way to healing. Meira had been silent during most of the meal, and now sat brooding over her ale.

Benches were pulled aside and room made for musicians. Dancing was in order, as two men began tuning stringed instruments and a third began banging on a whale-hide drum with a wooden mallet. Jace rose to beckon a slim, flush-faced woman to the dance floor. Others joined. Riders clapped their hands and stomped their feet in rhythm with the drum as a fife and castanets were fetched from the back room.

The few women present twirled from partner to partner, with a dozen of the men clasping shoulders and forming a ring around them. Some of the men twirled in solo, dancing with imaginary partners with their drinks raised high in the air.

Several of the younger men tried to snag Meira into a dance, but she pushed them away, pleading fatigue. It took an invitation from Jace for her to finally consent. Her hair fell loose as she clacked her heels in time to the music. Jace twirled her around the floor and she began to laugh in a melodious voice. Her eyes sparkled as she launched into a high-kicking dance that Darek had no idea she even knew. Meira's sun-tanned face shone and her dark hair whipped back with a liveliness under the flickering torches that warmed Darek's heart, seeing his sister in such high spirits.

While he stared glaze-eyed at the flickering flame past the dancers, the woman he had tried to help strolled over unnoticed on shy feet. He jumped out of his seat as she touched him on the shoulder.

"My name's Bree," she said. "Grateful for your help, though I didn't really need it. Wasn't the first time Tand has knocked me out of the harness—says it toughens me up."

Darek had recovered his seat, pretending now to yawn and stretch. "Yeah, he must be a real delight to fly with. Well, It's a curse of mine, sticking my nose where it doesn't belong."

She smiled. "You're different, that's for sure. Something to be grateful for."

Darek managed a grin. "What about you? Have you been riding long?"

"About five years now." She flicked back her hair. "It's a tough skill to learn, even harder to maintain. I grew up on the streets of Caermurle, an orphan. Jace took me in when I had nowhere to go. He thought I had the balance for riding and sponsored me himself. I had no idea it would be this exhausting. I'm no fragile flower by any means, but all this training is starting to wear on me."

Darek made no comment. He thought back to his own childhood which was anything but rosy.

"I heard you were a slave to the Black Claws?" Bree asked. "How was that? How'd you get away?"

"It's a long story," Darek said, gazing at his empty mug. "If you don't mind, I'd rather not talk about it, at least not sober."

She noticed his frown and took a sharp breath. "No problem. How are you at dancing?

"It's been years since I tried."

She giggled and held out her arm. "Well, come on then. It's about time you had some fun."

"After you." He bowed. "My name's Darek, but I guess you already know that."

She grabbed his hand, and pulled him out to the floor. Darek had trouble keeping up, but she was skilled at covering up his missteps. After two songs, Darek was only lagging a half-step behind. He followed the swaying rhythm of Bree's hips with his eyes, her body warm against his. She was a nimble dancer and he admired her lively moves and trim waist and wiry but feminine body. They began to move closer together and Darek, loosened by drink, thought of leaning in for a kiss before shouts rose from the far corner of the table.

Two groups had switched from ale to the stronger arrack liquor and were guzzling down cups in a contest of sorts.

"Let's see how well you hold your drink," Bree teased and she ran over to join them. Darek followed, unwilling to be shown up and joined the ranks against Tand and Jace, the two resident champions. Bree set herself against him and matched him drink for drink. They were nearly eight cups in when the room started to spin. The riders' homebrew made the stickypalm ale he and his friends chugged on Cape Spear Bay seem like dishwater.

Darek held up a hand, admitting defeat.

"You're still a boy," cried Tand, slapping his mug down on the hardwood with a clatter to raise the dead. "Not a man yet."

Darek bristled at that.

"Better stick to taking cheap shots and attacking from the rear." The others laughed and Tand gloated, smiling at the sight of Darek green about the gills.

He thought about punching Tand in the face, but the roil in his stomach and the blurry look of concern on Bree's face made him change his mind. He eased himself up from the table and staggered outside to find some secluded place to throw up. He could hear Tand's drunken boasts and laughter from the open door as he saw him pour another round for Bree.

* * *

Darek awoke sprawled in a graceless heap beside an empty barrel of ale. Two other riders snored nearby. At least he wasn't the only one to overdo it last night. He scrambled to his knees, instantly regretting it, and he fell back down, eyes rolling, afflicted with a splitting headache and foggy brain. He uttered a groan, unable to recall how many cups of the sweet arrack he had swallowed.

Silver Eye came nosing by a few moments later, sniffing him, wrinkling up her nose at the smell of ale and vomit. The dragon licked his face and tried to rouse him. Her warm tongue slapped on his temple like thunder.

"Leave off, girl!" Darek struggled to push her wet tongue away. "I'm fine, I just need to rest."

She gave a perturbed cry and settled down next to him. Soon, her stomach started to growl, though she refused to leave his side.

"Go get something to eat," Darek mumbled. "I just need a little more sleep."

That must have satisfied her for the dragon bounded off to fish. It felt like only a moment later when he was roused once more.

"Up, you drunken cuttlefish," laughed a sour-smelling rider. "There's work to be done."

"What work?" croaked Darek.

"Did you forget? Jace ordered your training schedule last night? You're on stall duty today." He prodded Darek with his toe, turning him over like a beached haddock. "Your sister had the good sense to sleep in the barn in the straw, not face first on the lodge floor like some others I know."

Darek closed his eyes against the splitting pain the light caused. "Let the dragons clean their own stalls."

"Better not let Jace hear you say that," said the man as he walked around the corner to relieve himself.

Sometime later, Darek stirred, taking groggy steps out in the sunlight to the practice yard. Riders were already in the air. Several were sparring on the sand with their long staves.

Jace arrived with a frown on his face. "I thought you'd have all the stalls cleaned by now."

"I've just now been able to stand."

"Not an early riser then?" Jace asked wryly. "Around here, we rise with the sun, no matter how much drink we've quaffed."

"That'll take some getting used to." Darek squinted into the sun. "When do we get to ride?"

Jace stared at him as if he were a sea pike. "No riding for you today, boy, as I told you. Did you forget? You were supposed to clean the south stalls. Meira's already finished the northern ones."

"Why should I?" Darek croaked. "My dragon doesn't even sleep in a stall."

Jace cut him off with a sharp claw sweep. "We fly as a team and share the responsibilities of the entire squad. I'll cut you some slack this time since it's your first day, but every rider has to pull his own weight around here." He nodded to Meira who was walking back with a large shovel in her hand.

"I'm going back to bed," she said, handing the shovel to Darek.

"That's not fair—"

"Fair?" Jace barked with disbelief. "Meira's already done her work while you've been lounging around. Now, go shovel dung."

Darek groaned.

Jace's eyes flashed in irritation. "You're full of piss and vinegar, aren't you? No different than I was. I can see it in your eyes." He flexed his good hand. "At least Meira has a streak of her mother in her. But all that time spent as a slave has done little to improve your attitude." He lifted his claw hand. "I lost this limb because I was impulsive. Don't make the same mistake."

Darek frowned. "You said you lost it while trying to free me. What happened anyway?"

Jace lowered his gaze. "Someday I'll tell you. But for now, let's just say it was the biggest mistake of my life, outside of losing Thyphalyne." He gazed out to the rising sun with a dark look. "I still hope there's time to correct it."

Darek remained silent. There was an ominous tone in his father's words. He could not quite put his finger on it, but he sensed the oppressive weight his father must bear.

Darek trudged off toward the south stalls. Two hours passed shoveling massive mounds of fishy, dragon dung. He glanced up with envy at the practice formations and maneuvers in the clear skies above. How he longed to be back in the air practicing dives and rolls. He drew in a frustrated breath, immediately regretting it as the overpowering smell filled his lungs.

He filled another bucket and washed away the last remnants of green slime from a long water trough.

A barrel-shaped figure approached and interrupted his wistful thoughts. *Tand*. Likely come to gloat some more.

"Here's a bucket of fish heads to feed your dragon. Extra rations for the 'Dragon Day' celebration." He gave a great belly laugh and shook out his greasy curls. Then he peered critically through the open stall door. "Not the best cleaning, but it'll have to do. Take ten more buckets of this slop to the far pens when you're done."

Darek thought about arguing, but his curiosity got the better of him. "What's in the far pens?"

"The young and uncooperative dragons. We'll be breaking some in this afternoon." He cocked his head to the side. "Beware young Jispir, that orange scaled dragon yonder. He's a biter and will steal the others food if he can. Isn't that right, Jispir?"

The dragon in the pen jerked its leathery head up at the sound of its name, uttering a low growl.

"Try not to get killed feeding him," said Tand.

"I'll be fine," muttered Darek. Curses wafted under his breath.

"What's that?" growled Tand. "Just because you're your daddy's boy doesn't give you any privileges around here. If it was me, I'd have set you on your heels yesterday. But since Jace says you stay, that means you start at the bottom like everyone else."

Darek took the bucket and started walking toward the pen, but paused and called behind him. "If you were in charge, all your riders would be smashed on the ground by now."

Tand clenched his jaw. "What did you say? You good for nothing mouthpiece—"

Darek was about to tell Tand to shove off, but Bree walked up, leading her blue-tailed dragon behind her. Her warning look made him hold his tongue.

"Jace needs your help in the armory, Tand," she said.

"Aye, a task for a real Dragon Rider." Tand left whistling and Bree gave Darek a consoling look.

"Don't mind him," she said. "He's still sore at you for making him look like a whale's behind the other day."

A thin smile broke out on Darek's face. "The oaf deserved it, beating on you when he didn't need to."

Bree rolled her eyes. "All of the veterans do it. They're hard on us, but for good reason."

Darek continued to drag the reeking fish guts toward Jispir's pen. "Don't they prefer fresh fish? These seem to have gone bad."

Bree wrinkled her nose at the smell. "They don't mind it. A dragon has two stomachs built like steel. They could probably eat stones if they wanted—some of the fire breathers do."

Darek shook his head. Dumping the bucket into Jispir's feed trough, he turned his head away. He hadn't expected the dragon to charge the metal wall, but he had barely time to pull his hand back and only fell flat as he jumped backward, sprawling in a pile of dung...meanwhile flipping the remains of the bucket onto himself. "You rotten ungrateful whelp!"

Darek's curses rolled out of his mouth at the dragon and Bree tried in vain to hide her laughter. "He likes to do that, only Jace can get near him."

Darek shook his head and struggled to stand. "I can see why."

"I see you've found your next task," said Jace, pushing his head in. "You can help me get Jispir here used to his harness. Maybe some of your Dragon Mage Apprentice skills might come in handy."

CHAPTER 14.

DRAGON BREAKING

Jace led Jispir in a slow walk by a long trailing lead rein into a circular, high-walled arena. The dragon's eyes opened wide in panic as the beast snorted through its flared nostrils. "Easy does it, boy," Jace coaxed in a reassuring voice. "Follow me."

Darek walked inside and with nimble fingers Bree bolted the gate behind them.

"I thought a Dragon Rider used a Mage's amulet to control his dragon?" asked Darek.

"When money is flowing, yes." Jace stroked the dragon's orange flank in wide circles. "We all have one for our main mount, but we've lost a few riders recently. The amulets have become rarer and more expensive. Until we land a few more contracts, we'll have to get by the old-fashioned way."

Jispir stomped the ground with his fore-paw and shook his tapered head. Jace slipped a shark leather strap over the dragon's snout. "I'm getting Jispir here used to a bit and bridle, but he won't tolerate so much as a blanket, let alone a saddle on his back."

"What good's an arena?" Darek squinted around the yard. "Can't Jispir just fly out?"

Jace shook his head. "His wings are pinned together with a metal band so he can't fly out, but getting an untamed dragon to accept the harness and reins is still no easy task."

Bree tossed a thin, rope harness and metal bit into the arena. Jispir shied away from them as if it were a sea serpent. Now that the young dragon was free of his pen, Darek became studiously aware of the powerful creature before him. He flashed a wary glance at the long talons and sharp teeth capable of rending a person ear to ear. "How are you going to get that on him?"

Jace released the dragon. It ran in a wide circle around the perimeter of the arena, dragging behind him the trailing reins.

"That's what you're here for," said Jace. He unbolted the gate and stepped outside of the arena, swinging the gate closed and trapping Darek inside with the agitated dragon.

Darek's mouth dropped. "Wouldn't a more experienced trainer be a better choice?

"They're busy readying the other dragons for battle," said Jace. "Besides, how else are you supposed to learn?"

"You can do it Darek," said Bree. "Here, I'll give you a hand," she called, opening the gate and slipping inside the arena.

Darek picked up the harness and turned to consider Jispir who was trying without success to climb over the wall of the arena. Riders had covered it with a slimy stickypalm paste to deter uncooperative dragons from scaling it.

She walked along the inside of the circular wall, waving her arms in an attempt to coax the dragon closer to Darek.

Darek closed his eyes and reached out with his mind. He tried to remember what Agrippa had taught him. The large orange swirl of mist that was Jispir was hard to miss. The mass floated and jumped about the ethers with capricious energy. Darek willed his thoughts to connect with those of the beast, like a mutant jellyfish extending its streamers and merging with anything it contacted.

Jispir was hungry, and very angry and—frightened. He didn't like being in the arena, and hated any constraints.

Darek summoned him as he opened his eyes. *Jispir, Come!*

The dragon's head snapped up and his eyes locked on Darek. With a snarl, the dragon charged him.

"Darek, watch out!" yelled Bree. She lunged for the reins. Jispir knocked her aside, and she fell in an untidy sprawl to the ground.

Jace snatched a spiked whip from a hook on the wall and cracked it over his head. "Bree, get out of there!"

The sound had Jispir flinching, but the dragon didn't slow.

With nearly two tons of scaly death hurtling at him, Darek thought to summon Silver Eye, but by then it would be too late. In a reflex, he lifted his hands and willed the connection to the orange dragon's mind once more. *Stop!*

In a cloud of dust, Jispir skidded to a halt. The dragon sniffed Darek's outstretched hand and gave him a questioning rumble. Darek moved his hand toward the dragon's neck, and Jispir bared its teeth. *At least he was standing still.*

Jace hurried in through the gate and rushed to Bree's side. "Are you injured, girl?"

She rubbed her elbow and dusted off her leathers. "Just my pride." Bree's eyes wandered to Darek who was soothing the dragon's snout with a gentle hand. He murmured calming words while he buckled the strap that held the bridle in place.

"How'd you do that?"

Darek ignored the question, focusing instead on keeping the dragon calm. Spit lathered the bit stuck in the creature's mouth. Judging from the way Jispir chewed it, it was clear the young brute still wasn't completely accepting of the hard metal.

The dragon was unused to mental commands, so Darek tried another approach. *Fish! I gave you fish. More are coming soon.*

That got the dragon's attention. The slavering jaws at last closed, hiding the gleaming teeth. Darek placed his hand on the orange snout. Jispir let him run his fingers across the hard-plated bridge area, up the scaly neck and secured the bridle, and tightening it on a pair of jagged horns.

Darek smiled. "I told him I'd give him more fish." He led the dragon around the arena like a docile cow.

"Maybe you can try and teach me that trick sometime," Bree said with a smile.

"I don't think it's something that can be taught," Jace grunted. "Why don't you try the harness?"

Darek prompted the dragon to turn his head, and they began walking to the edge of the arena. At the sight of the saddle, the dragon froze, nostrils flared.

"It's okay, boy, it won't hurt you," Darek murmured.

The dragon's eyes swung between Darek and the harness. Then Jispir began backing up.

"Hold on!" Darek pulled hard on the bridle. The dragon gave a powerful flick of the head. In a flash of motion, Darek was sailing through the air. He landed in a heap of dust on the arena floor.

"Try again," prodded Jace. The hint of a grin creased his face.

Each time Darek urged the dragon toward the saddle, Jispir refused, squatting like a mule on his hindquarters and uttering an obstinate growl.

"Maybe if I bring it over to you?" Darek lifted the shark leather seat but it only sent the dragon fleeing to the other side of the arena like a squid that jets a cloud of ink cover to evade a predator.

"If we can't get him saddled," muttered Jace, "he'll be useless to us." He frowned at the unruly dragon. "So much for the Dragon Mage."

Darek threw the saddle carelessly over the other side of the wall. "We'll see about that."

Taking cautious steps forward, he coaxed the dragon forward. Jispir approached on heavy, hesitant feet.

"I don't blame you for hating that *contraption*," Darek said. "Why don't we forget about it?" *No harness.*

The dragon settled down on all fours, breathing evenly, his eyes glued to Darek's face. He walked behind the dragon, his hand soothing the leathery wings folded back. "Why don't we get this off you?"

Jace's jaw dropped. "What are you doing?"

Darek slid off the metal bands that pinned the dragon's wings closed. With a roar, Jispir unfurled his wings and beat them experimentally, sending dust whirling across the arena.

"He'll fly away!" Jace flung open the gate and ran up with his whip raised above his head.

"If you let me ride you," whispered Darek, "I'll show you where the fish are." *Ride—Fish.*

The dragon lowered his neck and Darek hopped on his back.

Darek felt a flutter of movement at his back. Bree was scrambling up the dragon's flanks, staring down Jispir without fear.

"I'm coming with you," she panted.

Darek blinked. No sooner had he grabbed her hand and pulled her up on Jispir's shoulders than the creature was vaulting toward the arena's wall. With a mighty leap, it cleared the barrier, beating his wings with a loud thrum that sent Darek and Bree shooting into the air. Bree slid behind Darek and wrapped her arms tightly around his chest. Darek felt a warm rush.

"Watch out for my son!" Jace yelled. His face was red as they took to the skies, leaving the Dragonmaster below holding a limp whip.

Over the pens they flew, skimming the sparkling waters of the bay. Darek ignored a faint, yelled challenge from a rider who might have been Tand, now lost in the wind, and willed Jispir to greater speed.

"Fly him faster," Bree whispered in his ear.

He guided the dragon into a shallow dive toward the water. A quiver of excitement ran through Jispir's back—the young dragon had been cooped up in the pens too long. Bree tightened her grip around Darek's waist and laughed as he spun the dragon into a roll.

They flew onward, with Darek carefree and enjoying the press of Bree's body behind him. Jispir's gut gave a great growl and he was reminded of his part of the bargain. Several patches of water looked promising, but where would he find a school of fish? Silver Eye would certainly know...closing his eyes, Darek spotted a bright swirl of silver near the water's surface.

With a quick tug on the reins, he steered Jispir downward at what looked like a dark circle of fish. Before he knew what was happening, Jispir swooped in a swan dive. "Wait, not yet!"

A wall of water hit them like a stone hammer. Bree and Darek were thrown free as the dragon plunged underwater in chase of the fish he craved. Darek surfaced, spewing sea water and massaging a reddened shoulder. He looked around for Bree.

"Hey, where'd you go?"

Something nibbled at his leg. He gasped. *Sharks?*

Bree's head rose above the waterline, laughing at the prank she had pulled.

"Don't tell me that was you?" Darek splashed her in the face.

"Oh, it's a water fight you want?" She returned a volley of splashes and then dove down, swimming behind Darek and clinging to his back. Darek didn't fight it. He sank like a stone and escaped her grasp. He spun in the water, kicking free of her grasping hands. Doubling back, he enfolded her in a watery hug and brought her to the surface. As his face came closer, she spit water into his mouth and he coughed out the seawater he'd almost swallowed. He held up his hands in defeat. When he regained his breath, Bree swam up in front of him with a mischievous smile on her face.

"There might be hope for you yet."

They treaded water, moving in closer until their faces were almost touching. Bree was a little older than he, an experienced dragon rider, and beautiful—why then was she giving him that look as if he should kiss her?

A shadow glided below in the water—Jispir eating his fill of fish below.

"We'll be here all day while that dragon hunts for fish," muttered Darek.

"Maybe we should go back," said Bree.

"Jace will probably be waiting." He summoned Silver Eye, concentrating his thoughts.

A short time later, a silver spine surfaced in the water followed by a sleek head and single blinking eye. "Ah, there you are, girl." Darek climbed onto Silver Eye's back.

"She's beautiful." Bree smiled, admiring the four folded wings and shimmery hide. "Is it okay if I ride you?"

Darek translated the message through his mind. Silver Eye snorted in response.

"That's a yes." Pulling her up, Darek gave Bree the reins and wrapped his arms around her.

Bree leaned back into him with a sigh of contentment.

Jispir swam over to greet the new arrival, his hunger sated now that a female dragon had appeared. "Silver Eye, meet Jispir." The two dragons sniffed each other and Jispir growled in displeasure when Darek hopped on the other's back. Silver Eye answered with a protective roar.

Jispir was jealous, and the corners of Darek's mouth rose in a wry smile. *Friends. Follow. I will still ride you and bring you fish.*

That seemed to placate Jispir, and the friendly beast swam behind them as Silver Eye headed into the mouth of the bay and on toward the beach where the pens lay. The sun sank low in the sky as they at last flopped on the shore.

Back at the pens, Jace greeted them with a frown. "If you've had enough frolicking about in the sea, then return Jispir to his stall and make sure his scales get a good scrubbing. We don't want barnacles to form."

Darek sighed. The magic of the moments swimming with Bree was lost. He turned back to the south pens, leading Jispir.

Jace stopped him as he passed by. He placed his good hand on Darek's shoulder. "You did well today, son. Get some rest. We'll start aerial combat training at first light tomorrow."

Darek hurried to return Jispir to his pen, a bright smile on his face. Bree showed him the finer points of grooming a dragon, which included cleaning the claws and removing debris from the narrow cracks in the armored hindquarters and underbelly. Jispir made no fuss. Once the dragon was clean, Darek found Silver Eye hovering with an expectant look at the entrance to the pens. She refused to move until Darek had groomed her as well. By the time they had done that, both he and Bree were exhausted. Bree departed with a yawn and a wave, heading straight to the barracks to get a meal and some sleep. Darek was too tired for even that and found a comfortable spot on the beach where he and Silver Eye bedded down for the night.

"Did you hear that, girl?" Darek asked as the dragon curled her warm tail around him. "Aerial combat training...just what we've been waiting for."

CHAPTER 15.

WINGED COMBAT

The next morning, Darek saddled Silver Eye with a heavier, chainmail harness of war. He fitted an armored headpiece along with several large metal plates to protect the dragon's vulnerable areas. At first, Silver Eye shuffled in awkward hops under the added weight, shaking her back and biting at it.

"I know it's uncomfortable," said Darek, "but it'll protect you in a fight."

Several other Dragon Riders were preparing as well. A few strides away, Meira saddled Typhoon favoring lighter, boiled leather armor. Bree covered her blue-tailed dragon Shimmer with an expensive harness crafted from hundreds of interwoven steel links. Bree smiled in Darek's direction.

Tand fitted his orange-scaled dragon Hagar with a heavy-plated harness with spikes at the neck and shoulder.

Jace walked through the wing, checking equipment and the health of the dragons. "Tighten your flank cinch, Darek," he advised. "Ricnad, I thought I told you to patch those holes in this wing membrane."

"I thought this was going to be a race?" complained Darek. "Why do we need all this heavy armor?"

"We're training for war," replied Jace. "You'll need to know your dragon's limits when carrying full armor."

Tand made a quick series of hand gestures and Ricnad laughed.

"What's that supposed to mean?" asked Darek.

"Dragon Rider hand signals," called Tand. "Only the *real* riders know how to communicate with them when the wind drowns out your voice."

"What did he say?" Darek asked Meira in lowered tones.

Meira rolled her eyes. "He's betting Ricnad that your dragon will fall out of the sky."

Darek bristled. "Silver Eye will go claw-to-claw with Hagar any day."

Silver Eye seemed to sense the insult and growled in Tand's direction.

Meira sat atop Typhoon, her white dragon stamping the ground with impatience. "I'm glad you boys will be keeping each other company while I win the race."

"Silver Eye is just as fast as your dragon," said Darek.

"Ha! You'll be lucky to catch a glimpse of my backside after the start," Meira teased.

"I wouldn't mind that." Tand pinched the air in front of him with a grin.

Meira turned bright red as Bree threw a rock Tand's way.

"Save it for the air." Jace raised his hands for quiet. "Let us see how the newer recruits perform. The course will be limited to Crabback Bay. The goal is to round the black buoy and the stone pillars by the pens three times. We want to simulate a combat situation. That means, your dragons must be protected by their armor against attack."

Tand glanced sidelong at Darek with a meaningful look in his eye. He smirked and went back to tending to his dragon.

"We need every dragon in the coming fight, so I don't want to see any permanent injuries—and no fire breathing!" Jace lanced a glare in Tand's direction.

Darek sized up Hagar with a newfound respect. He hadn't realized the large dragon was also a fire-breather. *So, Tand had actually shown some restraint when flying against Bree in the last race by crashing into her...*

Jace produced a silver set of pipes. "Mount up! We start on my signal."

Darek crawled up Silver Eye's leg and vaulted onto her outstretched wing. She lifted it and he slid onto her back, gaining his position in the harness and sliding his legs into the stirrups. Unlike the other Dragon Riders, Darek chose to give his dragon free rein. The reins hung loosely at her neck and he concentrated on sending her mental commands. The reins were only a backup. He patted her neck and transmitted encouraging thoughts about winning the race.

Shimmer snapped her jaws with a warning snuffle as Typhoon moved a bit too close.

"Keep control of your dragon," Meira huffed.

"Stay out of our way when we hit the air," Bree warned. "Shimmer is the fastest flyer in the wing and I don't intend to lose that spot. Not even to the Dragonmaster's daughter."

At a slight tug of the reins, Typhoon rounded on them and Meira glared. "What is that supposed to mean? I earned this just as much as you."

Darek urged Silver Eye in-between the two. "May the best dragon win."

"Shut it, eel-brain," Meira snapped, turning her dragon back around.

Bree frowned in Meira's direction before turning her gaze toward Darek. "Try not to fall out of your saddle during the race."

"I—" Darek cut off as a shrill whistle sounded and the other dragons leapt into the air. *Kraton's beard, we're already behind. Go, Silver Eye!*

Silver Eye's muscles tensed as she jumped into the air, beating her wings in a thunderous storm. She arched herself skyward and they steadily gained altitude.

The other dragons had a huge lead, but Darek flattened his body in the harness, pressing his face against Silver Eye's neck, urging her on to greater speed. The teal water of Crabback Bay soon passed below. They gained on the slowest racer, a thickly-muscled dragon with curved horns. Crusher was one of the larger males, green-scaled, deadly in a fight, but a slower flyer.

Crusher gave a low, reverberating growl as they swept by. Djin, the dragon's rider, stared with eyes glowing like daggers as Darek spurred Silver Eye on toward a cluster of dragons. They jostled for position as their riders sought any possible advantage while going into the first turn.

Meira and Bree rounded the buoy then headed back toward the stone pillars.

"Sea snail!" Meira called as Typhoon passed near Darek in a swirl of white wings. Bree only gritted her teeth, her mind focused on shortening the gap between her and first place.

"Look out!" Djin yelled from behind.

Darek swung about—saw the gangly, dark-bearded rider pointing animatedly—then swung his gaze ahead of him. Tand and Hagar, rounding the buoy, were flying straight at him, headed on a collision course. They would have collided mid-air had not Silver Eye slipped sideways and edged with daring between them.

"Watch where you are going, you drunken albatross!" yelled Darek.

Tand only laughed as Silver Eye struggled to keep up.

You okay, girl? Darek asked with a mental reassurance. Silver Eye growled in fury and dove down toward the black buoy in the water below. *Sharp turn left!* Her wings crested the water as they completed the first turn.

They had lost ground.

Catching up to the tail of the group ahead, Silver Eye rose in the air currents above them, then dove down through their midst.

A brown dragon with a wicked scar running along its side wasn't so easily overtaken and the male's talons struck out to swipe at Silver Eye's flanks—but Silver Eye deflected the bulk of the attack with her hind leg. The plate mail had saved her from the worst of the claw rakes. *Do anything you must to protect yourself!* She dropped her head, slamming into the brown dragon's ribs, to cut a new gash across the male's rump. The other rider spurred his dragon aside and Silver Eye advanced with an over-the-shoulder snarl.

As a group they soared back across the bay and over the pens. Rounding the stone pillars, Silver Eye closed the gap on the few riders ahead.

Tand, Bree, and Meira raced neck to neck toward the buoy and the third turn. Silver Eye would move into fourth place. Darek felt a whoosh of air at his ear as two Dragon Riders crowded him from either side. Brothers by the look of them. They signaled each other with wiggling fingers. Darek yelped as they smashed in unison into Silver Eye's flanks, pinning her in place.

Silver Eye's wings were stuck in a glide as the brothers' dragons bumped up beside her. They dropped several feet as the three riders grappled together in close combat, plummeting toward the water.

The more experienced brother smashed a willow staff over Darek's left shoulder with a loud crack, while the younger one lunged for Silver Eye's reins. Pain blossomed in Darek's back. He slapped the grasping hands away and grabbed the reins. *They were going to crash into the water.* With his other hand, he swung his stave and struck the older brother across the thigh with enough force to leave an angry welt.

Silver Eye swung her horned head and stunned the crimson dragon with a hard knock to the skull. Now she had the room she needed to turn on the older brother's tan dragon. Snatching at the winged forearm with her claws, she bent it back. The tan dragon yelped and dropped from the sky—either that or risk having his wing torn off.

Swooping low, Silver Eye burst ahead, nosing toward the leaders.

They had only to round the buoy once more, then the first to return to the stone pillars would win the race. *Was there enough time to catch them?*

Darek reached the last turn around the pillars, cutting in as tight as Silver Eye was able. "We have to catch them!" he yelled to her. Flapping in a frenzy, she used the straightaway to cut the gap between her and the two leaders. Soon she would be nipping at the heels of those in front.

Darek continued to gain on Bree as they reached the final turn. Meira swung round first, ahead by three dragon-lengths. Darek passed inside of Bree on the turn and drew even with her as they hurtled toward the finish. Bree cursed and urged Shimmer to fly faster, but her dragon had been pushed to her limits, her speed fading.

With the stone pillars in sight, Silver Eye inched forward—first taking a swipe at Typhoon's white tail, then drawing even with her hindquarters. Meira spurred to the right.

Silver Eye had almost edged her out when Typhoon corkscrewed upside down and above them. Darek squawked as Meira straddled Typhoon's neck, cutting her saddle free and throwing it onto Darek's harness. Whether from the extra weight or the surprise maneuver, the distraction was all she needed to push ahead and cross the finish line.

Silver Eye gusted steam from her nostrils as they landed beside the winner. "I thought you never flew bareback!" taunted Darek.

Meira was smiling from ear to ear as the other riders crossed the line. Bree's face drooped.

"Congratulations to the winner!" boomed Jace. "You proved yourself the fastest, and in a battle—leaving your wing behind means you're all dead."

Her smile fading, realization dawned on Meira. "It was a lesson in cooperation?"

"One that you failed," Jace said, nodding, "except for maybe Djin for warning Darek, or the Plith brothers for a coordinated attack."

"This was a test?" asked Darek, dumbfounded. "But you said, we don protected armor to simulate a real combat situation."

"I never said you needed to fight each other."

Others besides Darek groaned.

"Now that you've had a warmup, the entire wing is going sea serpent hunting," Jace said with a grin. "This time we'll work together to track, corner, and kill one—while looking out for our fellow wing mates."

BORMOTH

Agrippa plummeted down in a swirling void. His staff was gone. Cold blue water roiled about him, sweeping him deeper into the murk. All appeared allied against him. His breath caught in his lungs and he held it, allowing his body to roll with the endless eddies churned by the monsters of the deeps. To struggle was suicide. His life was in the hands of the gods now.

He had experienced this feeling before as a younger mage in his journeys to the east across Serpent's Deep. While looking for new islands, his skiff had been caught between two raging serpents. All the magic at his disposal had barely been enough to fend them off. In the end, his power had nearly failed him.

Though his lungs were at the edge of bursting, the old mage remained motionless as strange and frightening things swam in that underwater gloom—half-concealed at the edges of his vision. The light failed to penetrate this place, where fin and fang merged into a scaly nightmare.

So, this is how I will die, Agrippa thought.

A gnawing anguish bit at his heart. The long years of his life passed before him in a chill blur and remorseless fever. He was old, and his life was near the end. But he hoped the young riders, Darek and Meira, had managed to escape—otherwise all was for naught, and the free peoples of the Dragon Sea were lost.

He brought his mind back to the present.

Just when he thought he could no longer hold his breath, a horrendous tail, all slimy and seaweedy, wrapped about his middle. It whipped him up from his aquatic hell and dragged him spinning upward. The creature released him as he broke the surface, sucking air into his lungs, only to fall whistling back into the sea.

The tail grabbed him again, and he bobbed among the waves like a fisherman's lure, his head in stubborn resistance staying above water. Two serpents rode the waves like moray eels ahead of him. On the back of one sat a menacing figure, a sane man's nightmare, guiding serpents with staff upraised—where, to a place Agrippa guessed held untold agonies.

He was too exhausted to mark the passage of time and must have passed out. He awoke, waterlogged, to find himself sprawled on his side in a gloomy chamber set in damp rock. The natural cavern loomed high above him, a dome pocked with crumbling stalactites, a place carved by the endless tide and dripping from the rocks above over untold years. Stone fangs drooped from the ceiling to bite at a dark pool, still as death. The dusky glow of lanterns bathed the chamber in a sickly amber glow.

Agrippa ached all over with a sorrow he had never experienced before. He had failed. *Why was he still alive? Shouldn't Cyrus have killed him?* His body felt hollowed out like a petrified drum, ancient and unearthed, as if part of his magic had been stripped away from him. His lips worked in an angry grimace and his jaw clenched. Cyrus had him deeply ensorcelled.

The harsh reality set in with chilling weight. He was a prisoner. Cyrus would use him like a grimoire, extracting knowledge and incantations to meet his fiendish goals.

Agrippa examined his glowing jail with weary resignation. That damnable prism again, surrounding him like the translucent body of a jellyfish. It shimmered with a baleful energy, pulsing in a low hum that mocked Kraton and the Elder Gods. It was really a marvelous piece of work, completely impermeable, yet sound traveled through it, along with air and fresh water.

"*Agra sinur!*" he called in a croaking voice, hoarse now from the salt water. Though the words sent out vibrating energy, the sound-bubble only bounced back at him with tangible force and prompted him to utter a choked cry. No magic could pass through. It cut him off from summoning any dragons. Cyrus had built the cage well. *Where was the villain now?*

A slithering echoed in the shadows by the far wall. In the gloom, he perceived lateral caves running to other subterranean burrows. Cyrus's lair was as chilling as the bowels of a sunken shipwreck.

Time passed and Agrippa sat with his chin in hands in brooding contemplation. His muscles spasmed in a new wave of sorrow and rage as he recalled the image of Cender's death. He had raised that dragon from a hatchling—loved him as a close friend. There would be retribution. He would find a way, even if it was to be his last act. Cyrus was living on borrowed time.

One means might exist that his captor hadn't considered. He directed his attention to his astral powers. Closing his eyes, he tried to project his will six feet out from the edge of the prism. Nothing. *"Kratonire morvis actum!"* he cursed. The burrow was protected with rune-magic, he could not extend his astral self anywhere in the midst of these caves. *Kraton!* Heavy Magus power lurked here. This was something new.

Almost on cue, the sinister sound of scales scraping against rock drifted from the dark peripheries of the tunnel. A gaunt form ducked under the mantle of rock. Not Cyrus, but a scarred, reddish-gold dragon with long tail and piercing yellow eyes.

"Ah, one of Cyrus's minions," he murmured.

The dragon only growled from an upturned maw and lifted its ugly snout in appraisal.

"A pretty one too, I see. Well, I don't suppose a dog like Cyrus treats you very well?"

The dragon, almost in understanding, curled its lip and crept closer to drip saliva from slavering teeth on the surface of Agrippa's prismatic cage. The rank liquid sizzled, turning into a foul smoke which rose from the surface to the ceiling. Agrippa leaned back and sneered. "Aye, you'd better crawl back to your hole."

A familiar voice jeered out at him, "Agrippa, I thought you loved all dragons?"

Agrippa whipped about to see through the filmy layers of magical glass a dark-cowled figure with a grinning face. The form ducked from a side chamber. In his hands he carried an urn and vase along with several thaumaturgical instruments. The old mage scowled at such devices, wondering what tortures his evil apprentice had for him. "Where are we?" Agrippa demanded.

"Somewhere safe," responded Cyrus, setting down his instruments on the nearby table. "Where prying eyes may not find us." The mage smoothed back his lank black hair in a way that gave him a whimsical look. His greasy hair was plastered high to his forehead like kelp and a feverish light shone in his bloodshot eyes.

The mage stepped out of the shadows and spoke in a more cheerful tone. "For a second there, Agrippa, I feared you were dead. What a shame that would have been, old friend, if the ride behind my lead serpent had been your end—for you and I have much to discuss."

Agrippa croaked out a grunt, his sluggish faculties struggling to keep pace.

"I hope you like your new quarters. It would be remiss of me not to ensure you are comfortable."

"I'll manage—though some clean water and food would be nice."

"Excellent, excellent. I will see to it. I merely sought assurance that you were safe and secured—and of course, you are. You cannot blow your bubbles of death at me from within there. Neither can your dragons win past the magic portal with my warding spells in place." He clapped his hands in a jovial affirmation. "I will call on my assistant to tend to your needs. We can't have Agrippa the Great dying from lack of food."

The old mage gave a low, barking laugh. "You're insane."

"Hardly. Don't think for a moment that I have forgotten how dangerous you are. My faithful servant will care for your wants and safeguard your health. I call him Flamebiter." The dark form waddled closer, eerie in the shadows.

THE DRAGON SEA CHRONICLES: THREE BOOK SERIES

Agrippa looked with sullen appraisal upon the hulking dragon with red and gold alternating scaled flanks. It had an enormous head with gleaming yellow horns, and curious curled tusks, razor-sharp, filed-down—unique for its kind.

"I go now to prepare for a siege of the Red Claw Islands. It won't be long now."

"Oh," said Agrippa, "where do you plan to start your campaign? Bethreny or Wisselgard? The defenses of those towns are perhaps weakest of all the Red Claw Islands."

Cyrus fluted out a high laugh. "As if I would reveal that. Despite your weakened state, I can hardly have you warning my enemies should you manage to penetrate my defenses." His face twisted into a cryptic leer. "What do you think of Bormoth, my laboratory? It's not quite as lofty as your stronghold, but quite impenetrable. You always said—a Dragon Mage must have a quiet place to work."

Agrippa considered the many tables full of magical curios and the pentagrammic symbols that hung from the stalactites. He glanced around at the pagan inscriptions and symbols scrawled into rock and dragon tooth. The skulls, polished and affixed with ornamental eyes, femurs and ribs set in intricate patterns... Shelves carved out of the rock walls held strange and magical curios to assist the mage—in what, Agrippa dared not imagine.

Despite his impressive knowledge, Agrippa did not comprehend all that met his eye: a bone gourd growing from the wall here, a glass vase suspended upside-down there, glittering tubes covered in strange skin, smoking bottles filled with bubbling elixirs... Curious, half crafted experiment no doubt. He shivered anew.

"Controlling serpents is a perversion of your power."

Cyrus gave a chuckle. "You sound like one of those ridiculous priests."

It appeared the dark sorcerer now paid homage to barbarous gods of his own making...the same from which he derived his powers.

"I see you have become more obsessed with the macabre," said Agrippa. "This seems more a warlock's den than the workplace of a mage." It did not surprise him that his former pupil dabbled in dark blood magic.

"Impressions can be deceiving," remarked Cyrus. "I have succeeded where you have failed, finding not one, but three fossilized dragon eggs."

"*Three?*" Agrippa's face twisted in a grimace.

"I have yet to find a way to hatch them. Perhaps you will assist me?"

Recalling Darek's similar discovery under Kraton, Agrippa stirred. He could never allow Cyrus to birth one of the ancients.

"No? I thought so," Cyrus said with a sigh. "A pity."

Agrippa gave a curt grunt. "Yes, I suppose you are in need of dragons now that so many of your serpents have been killed."

Cyrus shrugged. "I have others, but dragons are needed to strike deeper inland. For example, Flamebiter here is from a new, feral breed I call the 'Mymores'. They are fiercely loyal and relentless in a fight. What do you think of his tusks?"

The curls of hard bone were large enough to impale a man. Agrippa stiffened. "A capable, if not savage choice."

A tinkling bell rang from deep in the cavern. Cyrus turned and cocked his head like a hound. "Duty calls, Agrippa. I will leave you to your confinement." He bowed and left the old mage staring into the gloom.

"*Ede Furcifer*," Agrippa swore.

These new revelations made Darek's training more important than ever. Most types of magic were denied to him, but Cyrus did not know that he had confirmed Darek as his apprentice. The bonding process formed a strong mental link... If only he could use it to contact the Mage Reborn.

Closing his eyes, he sucked in a breath, and visualized the form of Darek's body somewhere in time and space, floating, drifting like a cloud, a bird in a windless sky... He couldn't project his physical body past the barrier, but his astral form could rove far.

There! Far away, his young apprentice sat atop a dragon—the silver one missing an eye. *Where was he? Ah, there, on Manatee Island. Good*! He had followed his command. That outspoken sister of his was at his heels, riding beside him. Through the link he heard a harsh, mocking laugh—a thrown spear—a Dragon Rider with a claw hand and red face...Jace was with him.

"Darek!"

"What? Agrippa! I knew you were alive!" came the boy's thoughts.

The old man's voice tolled in his mind. "Darek, I feel you are somewhere safe. That is good. Are you with Jace?"

"Yes! Where are you?"

"Never mind where I am. I'm in a dark place that you cannot reach."

"I will come, get you—"

"No! You cannot. Stay where you are."

He heard the boy choke back his frustration. "Why did you contact me then?"

Agrippa chewed his lip. "To give you guidance—on what you must do next..."

* * *

Darek awoke in the dark before dawn, flushed and bathed in sweat. He could still hear the whispering voice in his head—or was it his ear? Something like the murmur of distant surf against the shore—Agrippa.

Then the old man was gone like a cloud on the wind.

Was it a dream? Likely not.

He lay back in the hay in the spare stable. Already, riders were rustling about in the yard. He could hear voices and the crack of a whip, followed by laughter.

CHAPTER 17.

A MAGE'S PRISON

Agrippa stared at his surroundings for the hundredth time. The clammy chill made him sneeze, likewise the heavy musk thick in the lair. It was dank here, with an oppressive weight that hovered throughout the cavern. Strange objects and magical devices lay scattered around the rock benches and tables that served as Cyrus's work area. A diurnal clock with baby squid tentacles for hands and conch shells for numbers ticked on the wall. At least he knew that two days had passed. The thought gave him little solace.

Sinister runestones glowed throughout the room, powering an assortment of whirring machines. A misshapen shark's head, remarkably preserved, sat on the edge of the far table staring at him with glassy eyes. Agrippa frowned. *What a fool I've been.* His former pupil must have spent years creating this chamber of twisted experiments.

He went back to looking for weaknesses in his prison, probing the luminous surface with filthy fingers. A sullen amber prism surrounded him, twelve feet at its base, buzzing with a low, barely-perceptible hum—just audible enough to drive one mad. A small hole no bigger than a fist glared up from a corner, a peculiar compartment where he could defecate when the need arose. No escape there. It was a double sealing compartment, shut tight on one side while it was emptied on the other. Where in Kraton was he? Some nameless grotto? Deep underground on one of the windswept isles in Dragon Sea? He worked out the different possibilities as he sat slumped in a heap, head in his hand. It was then that a familiar figure came to call on him.

"Lost a beloved dragon, did you, Agrippa? Bormoth provides a peaceful environment for mourning." The figure nodded in feigned sympathy. Cyrus had always excelled in pretending to lend a sympathetic ear to the leaders of the Council that strove to keep peace among the islands.

Agrippa made no comment. Cender was dead, and he was powerless inside a prism he had taught his apprentice how to build. Yet the fate of the Red Claw Clan weighed on his soul. His wistful gaze stared past the dark-robed figure to the shadowy cave tunnels beyond. He counted no less than four passages etched in the hard, porous rock and contemplated what lay beyond. How would he win his freedom? He must find a way!

"Are you thirsty?" asked Cyrus. "I see you have not yet been fed or watered this morning. Boy!" he cried, snapping his fingers. "Bring us food and water!"

In no time, a young man entered bearing a tray of cold fish and a jug of tepid water. With a vacant look on his face, he presented the tray and paused before Cyrus, shifting from one leg to another. He was haggard and withdrawn, his skin as white as the belly of a silver-backed crab—much like his cruel master.

Cyrus gave a gruff nod. "You'll have to forgive Briad. He has proved somewhat...resistant to the harsh reality of being a slave. Once branded, no escape, eh, Briad?"

Agrippa stirred, recalling Darek mention a similar name of a youth who was with him when he was first captured by pirates.

Briad blinked in slow acknowledgment.

"I may have disciplined him with too firm a hand and addled his brain." Cyrus grabbed the slave's wrist, rattling the dishes so they almost fell to the floor. The young man shook with terror.

The mage exposed the star-claw brand of the Black Claw Clan burned into Briad's flesh. "You must remember to bring food and water for the prisoner every morning. Under no circumstances should you feed him without me present."

"He serves his master," continued the mage, "in utter obedience. Flamebiter sees to it."

He snatched the tray from the youth's shaking hands and placed it at the foot of the prism. Pausing to cast a spell over the area, he took up a peculiar, open-faced scoop from the table and inserted it into the side of the prism. Immediately, a gap appeared near the floor, and Cyrus slid the tray in so that Agrippa could grab it before it fell, then he retracted the tube before Agrippa could capitalize on this small window of escape.

Agrippa nibbled at the food and sipped the water. He suspected both were laced with Balwerian seaweed to further dull his mind and weaken his magic. Keeping a sharp watch on the mage and his assistant, he thanked Briad for preparing the food.

If only he could reach a few of Cyrus's instruments!...but they might as well have been a world away, as they sat inaccessible on the worktable.

Agrippa motioned with an elbow at the gloomy confines as he chewed the raw haddock. "This place suits you well, Cyrus."

"Too much comfort dulls the senses. I cannot work under lax conditions, so I keep it dark and damp."

Agrippa gestured to the starfish-shaped device that the young mage's twitching fingers clutched. "How many magic items did you manage to steal from me over the years?"

Cyrus shrugged. "Enough. Why reinvent the wheel?"

"Indeed." Agrippa frowned. "That ornament at your elbow, it intrigues me. What does it do?"

Cyrus turned with curiosity and lifted the shrunken hammerhead shark skull at his side. "This? Oh, just something new I've been working on—not fully tested but potent. Would you like a demonstration?" He lifted the object and touched a blazing crimson jewel, shaped like a carbuncle, to the back of the skull. Upon a waggle of his pinky finger, the lifeless jaws began to work, snapping with a vicious, bright energy.

"Necromancy," Agrippa grunted. He did not flinch, but Briad backed away in dread. "Such a grisly imagination you have. I've seen worse things."

"'Tis nothing, compared to this dragon horn." He held up a gnarled grey cone. "I carved it from a mutant dragon's tusk. With an application of starfish dust, I can summon all sorts of strange creatures."

"Ingenious!" cried Agrippa, clapping his hands. Cyrus was showing off. Best to humor him with some praise from an old master. "But is it reliable? I would love to see a demonstration of your toy."

"No," grumbled Cyrus, "the results are unpredictable. Last time it brought up a giant squid that killed two of my sea serpents. It still needs some refining."

"Understandable. There can be many pitfalls in delving into fringe magic beyond one's grasp."

Cyrus paused, miffed at the condescending remark. His face knitted with a dark frown.

Agrippa flashed him a knowing smile. "Don't you find such dark arts bring on nightmares? They can cause a strain on the mind, you know."

"You underestimate me still," said Cyrus. "The magic you forbid has become second nature now. But enough talk, Agrippa. I have several pressing tasks that await above. Let us continue this intriguing conversation later." He swept off in a swirl of robes.

After the footsteps had died off, Agrippa wasted no time in establishing a link with Darek once more. Closing his eyes, he let his mind drift across the leagues and the chasms of space to find his new apprentice.

There! Darek was kneeling beside his dragon, attempting to conjure fire as Agrippa had shown him. The edge of the practice yard was bathed in the plum glow of sunset, without so much as a wisp of smoke. He called out the boy's name in a commanding voice. "Darek! Not like that."

"What—? Oh, it's you," Darek turned to face the ghostly gray form of the wizard. He assumed it was only a projection created by the old man's mind. "I have to get used to you appearing out of nowhere."

"Never mind that. We might not have much time. The fire is already inside you—you have only to call it forth."

"I've been trying," muttered Darek.

Agrippa sighed. "Focus on the warmth of your body. Sink below your skin to the hot river of blood flowing in your veins."

Darek concentrated; he closed his eyes. His face pinched in a pained grimace. "I...I feel it," said Darek. "But...only barely."

"Good. Now remember a time when you were wronged and your blood boiled."

Darek remembered the Slavemaster's laugh as the tyrant ripped strips of skin out with every stroke of his barbed whip. Darek's lips curled in a snarl. As he unfurled his fist, his skin grew warm with inner heat. Smoke began to stream from his fingers.

"Go deeper!" rumbled Agrippa.

Darek summoned his rage and Silver Eye took to the air in surprise as a small tendril of flame shot out from Darek's right hand, scorching a nearby tree to ash.

"Such power—" Agrippa's eyes widened at the sight "—but wild and uncontrollable. Try again. This time focus your anger into a small ball of fire. Let happier memories cool the flame, then let the two emotions combine and the fire burn white hot."

Darek conjured a larger orange ball of flame, but a moment later it shrunk and winked out.

"I can't do this, Agrippa," he sighed. He slumped down in a frustrated heap. "It burns. The fire pulls at my guts. I feel like it's drawing my insides out."

Agrippa shook his head and pursed his lips. "We have no time for grousing. I can't coddle you like a mother hen, Darek. Jace hid his head in the sand when things got tough. He could have become the greatest Dragon Rider the clans have ever seen. Then he lost his arm and was dismissed by the Council. I failed him—I won't do the same with you."

Darek growled. "Don't talk about him like that."

"I'll talk as I please," snapped the mage. "The truth hurts, doesn't it, boy? Raithan was a stronger man than your father. Thyphalyne knew it and ran off with him. I can hardly blame her for loving two men at once."

Spitting in blind passion, Darek grabbed his staff, and swung. It passed through the apparition like air. "You've no right to talk about my parents like that!" His limbs bristled with surprising power.

Agrippa's ghostly form stood there as before, gazing at him with a trace of sadness. "I'm not your enemy—it's the doubt and fear within you."

Darek muttered a curse. "Enough of your riddles, old man. Go away, leave me alone."

"Don't turn away from me, boy! You're a spoiled stripling, sulking in the grass because life has been hard. You hear one petty slur against your name, or the ones you love and you lose sight of what is at stake."

Darek hung his head. It was true. He slumped in a crouch, realizing in an instant that the old man had been baiting him. Agrippa was right, and the pain was overwhelming.

The phantom of the mage floated closer. "A mage must control his emotions, let his passions work for him rather than against him. I struck this nerve to show you where your weakness lies. I do it because I care. You're the hope of the Red Claws, and all the clans."

Darek wiped away a tear. He nodded, pulling himself back together.

"Now try once more!" urged Agrippa.

He rose, his mouth set in a grim line.

"Visualize the size and shape before you create it. Think about how the fire should act, then deny it that. Form it to your will instead. Think of it like caring for a clutch of dragons."

Darek scoffed. "What does slopping stalls and slugging rotting fish have to do with conjuring fire?"

"Everything. Discipline and rigor are the lifeblood of good technique. Jace works you hard to sharpen your body and your mind. It goes hand-in-hand with our training. An adept mage must master all of it in concert, or he'll always have a weakness."

Darek's shoulders tightened. Deep down he knew the old man was right, but he struggled to accept the concept. He had survived this long on reflexes alone and by trusting his gut. "I play it by ear and do what feels right."

"No longer. Those instincts may serve you well in combat, but a Dragon Mage must see the entire battle and control it like a game of chess." The old man grunted and closed his eyes. "When the time comes, your mind will be distracted by several dragons at once. Your wingmates will look to you to keep them safe—and deal with Cyrus."

"I can barely keep control over two dragons at once, Agrippa." The frustration built up in Darek's face. "When I try to conjure something, the power starts in my stomach and burns up before I can grab it. Sometimes it crashes into my chest and I can barely breathe until I release it."

Agrippa could see the youth's suffering reflected in his sweating brow and quaking arms. "I know, boy. The Dragon Mage force grows in you. It is because you survived Kraton. Now a part of the god lives in your body."

"I thought you didn't believe in such things?"

"I've come to appreciate the subtle irony that only a god could create. You must give in to the power. Do not resist it. If you fight it, it'll crack you open like an egg. Let the knots of fire flow through you! They'll burn themselves out."

As Darek clutched at his hair, Agrippa could see he was struggling, but could do little more than advise him. Still, he dared not be too easy on the boy.

Aye, he knew well the pain that unchanneled power could cause. He felt a growing pride as he watched Darek grow in skill, even using a small bit of power. He could sense the stream of energy coursing through Darek's hands as the boy released only a trickle into his staff.

A 'mage push' it was called. A subtle jab of inner power that could knock an opponent flying. The boy had a natural talent for it. He shook his head. Learning to use such powers was hardly straightforward. All this Agrippa saw through his mind's eye.

"The power can heal as easily as harm," he told him. "One day I'll teach you to be a healer."

After their training, he watched Darek in secret as he sparred with the other Dragon Riders.

A quick flourish with a thrust of his staff, a jab and strike later... The first time Agrippa had shown him the mage push, Darek gasped as a sharp electrical heat ran up his spine and his heart beat like a dragon's wings. He had stared at him with impish amusement. "Smarts, doesn't it?"

The next training sequence was even more intense. Agrippa had made himself invisible and Darek was relegated to listening to his disembodied voice in his head.

"Be patient, boy. Do you expect to master it overnight? By Kraton! Do you think I did?" His voice became softer, less stern. "As a mage, you must bend to the power like a sapling. Guide it to your goal as the wind might. Let it be your ally, not your enemy."

In his mind's ear, Agrippa heard the soft rustling of fabric and the tread of echoing steps. "I must go!" Muttering a hasty farewell, he cut the connection, and shimmered out of existence. .

"Lazy snail!" A stocky figure lumbered over, squinting and cursing at Darek. "What are you lounging around for, and who's that you were talking to?"

"No one." Darek cast his eyes down at the ground, moving to distract Tand, lest he see Agrippa. But the old mage was already gone.

Tand glared around. "What are you playing at? Or are you crying to your imaginary friend?"

Darek gave a noncommittal shrug. "I'm not the one hearing things, Tand. Maybe the hot sun has baked your brain. That, or all the ale you drank last night."

Tand veered in to shove him, but Darek twisted aside, laughing. A backhand caught him on the mouth and stopped his mirth quickly enough.

Darek looked up at him in sullen resentment, wiping his split lip. "I've taken worse from a Slavemaster's daughter." That made Tand pause.

"Get to sparring, you sea slug. There's more than enough work to be done cleaning the stalls and pens. Best finish before dinner at dusk. After that, Mras the cook closes the kitchen and you'll go hungry..."

Darek shrugged, then followed Tand on dragging feet. No more training today with Agrippa. Still, he had learned much already from the wizened mage.

* * *

Slumped on his haunches, Agrippa wiped the excess sweat off his brow. He took a deep breath. He was deathly exhausted from the last mental projection. Just being there with the boy had cost him. The exertion left him easy prey to Cyrus's spells and in no shape to formulate an escape. Yet, it was more important to see the boy through on his training during this difficult time.

A mocking voice interrupted his musings. "Who was that you were talking to? Or has imprisonment finally made you lose your mind?"

Agrippa gave a weary sigh. "I was merely meditating on the *Song of Kraton's Rising*. Back so soon, Cyrus?" His ex-apprentice was wet and gleaming as if he had been wading in a deep pool. "I fear I talk to myself as the days grow lonely in this murk with only your skulking dragon about. The beast has only belligerent grunts to offer."

"Yes, Flamebiter is a sullen sort."

"What are your plans for me?" demanded Agrippa.

Cyrus only returned him an impassive stare.

"Surely I can be of more use than a caged bird to gloat over while building your serpent empire? How long do you think it will be until your sea serpents turn against their master?"

"My serpents are loyal," Cyrus said. "Speak not of them, for they are not your concern."

Agrippa raised an eyebrow. He seemed to have struck a nerve in his nemesis. His lips twisted in a thoughtful smile.

"There is still a gulf between us," said Cyrus. "Why do you still protect the Islanders? Flamebiter, come here!" The dragon stalked forward, drool spilling from its open-fanged jowl. "Help me to hatch my dragon eggs, or I will seal you in the next chamber with Flamebiter until you learn more respect."

Agrippa set his jaw against the threat. "The Islanders might squabble amongst themselves, but I will not help you in destroying them."

"And why not? You could have ruled them with an iron fist as their king."

"You do not deserve your power," the old man barked. "It is our sacred duty to protect those weaker than us."

"Sacred duty!" Cyrus spat the words. "Your newfound piety amuses me. As mages, we are destined to control the universe, not be nursemaids to it. You are a coward, old conjuror, too afraid to seize power."

"Your magic has corrupted you, Cyrus."

The young mage's face purpled. "My experiments cross into uncharted terrain. They surpass the boundaries of good and evil."

"Eloquent words," said Agrippa, yawning, "but your logic is flawed. Kill me if you must, but do it quickly, for I grow tired of this."

With a choked cry, Cyrus threw a thunderbolt of power into the wall. Bright green light dripped down the damp stone like water. "You will stay here and do as I say. Tomorrow we will delve into the Myxolian Magic of Orders."

"The Myxolian realm is forbidden," said Agrippa in a scornful voice. "And for a good reason. All of the mages throughout history who have tried to harness it, have perished."

"They were weaklings."

"And if I refuse?"

Cyrus fluttered his fingers. He turned an amused glance upon Flamebiter. Then his head jolted around and his eyes seared into Agrippa.

Agrippa arched his back. Burning fire surged up his spine and his voice rose in a panged cry. "Stop, I say! Stop!"

"That's better." Cyrus's mouth hooked in a smile. "One way or another you will give in to my demands." He lifted a hand and the prisoner rose in his prism like a balloon. Cyrus lifted them up, cage and all, and the mage's evil smirk glowed like a sinister lantern.

The old man cast Cyrus a withering glare. "I am ashamed to have called you Apprentice," he spat down from his prison.

The young mage pinched his eyes closed in mirth. "I must thank you for your instruction. It has taught me not to become a powerless fool as you are."

"Better to be powerless than consumed by it," Agrippa said.

"I will crush the Red Claws and use the Black Claws as a wedge to rule all of the Dragon Sea. That is my destiny."

"There is still time to turn from this path," Agrippa warned.

Cyrus snuffled out a laugh. "My serpents will lay waste to Swordfish Island and all their towns until the Red Claws bow to my command." He let his hand drop and the cage clattered to the dank stone, jarring Agrippa from tooth to toe.

Agrippa croaked, "I remember a student who used to absorb my teachings with an innocent mind and proud eagerness. Now I see a misfit—a bitter, twisted shell of a man who is only concerned with ruling the world."

"You waste your power healing the sick and coddling the Council. I will channel my energy for my own ends."

Agrippa shook his head. "At what price?"

"There's always a price, old fool—I will pay it gladly..."

The old mage cast his former apprentice a curious glare. His psychic power stretched far enough for him to gain an understanding of the past events that had made Cyrus what he was today. "I see something was done to you in the past... That incident with Margor... a dreadful business, you didn't deserve that shame. I never realized the impact it had on you."

Cyrus's face turned a shade darker at the mention of that name. His fingers curled in anger.

"What do you know, old man?" Cyrus sneered. "You think you are so clever? Ever since that business with the town chief, this Margor, I have hated the Red Claws, and all their kind."

"It left you scarred." Agrippa's brows rose. "From what I remember, several strange canvas balloons floated over the town during the fall fair. You created a nasty mess by exploding them."

"I didn't burst them, the townsfolk did. My experiments floated too high out of my reach. How was I to know the town archers would shoot them down with arrows?"

"You put a hornet's nest in three balloons and fermented whale oil in the others."

"It was supposed to be a joke."

"Many were stung so badly they couldn't work the fields for weeks. It took months for the smell of putrid oil to fade."

Cyrus gave an indifferent wave. "So? Call it a macabre sense of humor."

"Not so funny for you when they found you busting your gut hiding in the bushes. It didn't take long to put two and two together and have you put in the stocks. The priests stripped you of your powers. You were a sorry mess for that week, stoned and tomatoed. I was blamed for your prankstering and told to keep you on a short leash."

"Ha ha, little good did that plan do you."

Agrippa sighed. "I warned you, but instead of being a deterrent, it only encouraged you to dabble deeper in the black arts." He chewed his lip. "My folly for not seeing it earlier."

"We can't always be perfect, Agrippa, or have the hindsight of an oracle."

"How does that explain—"

"Enough of your questions, old codger! Margor was a weed in the flowerbed, one needing to be cut."

Agrippa paused, sensing a chilling revelation in those words. "You were but ten years old. I'm surprised you could even remember that, let alone be capable—"

"I never forget. No, that day has been burned into my memory."

Agrippa's gray eyes grew slitted as he witnessed a lifetime of bitter memories reflected in those of his apprentice. "So... it was you who killed Margor... You left a town without a leader and Lared without a father. Why did I not see it before? You pushed him down that well and left a tankard of ale in the grass to make it look as if he was drunk and fell in while hoisting up a bucket."

"It was easy, the first time I used the *mage-push* you taught me."

Agrippa shook his head in anger. "You have many lessons yet to learn, Cyrus."

"As do we all, old man." Cyrus's voice became harsh. "Now clam up and reflect on yours while you rot in your cage."

Chapter 18.

Escape

Agrippa passed through periods of groggy stupor during the long days and nights that passed. At last he had the chance to be alone with the meek servant who lingered near the entrance snatching glances at the old man.

"Pst. Over here, Briad." He waved the figure closer.

Briad glanced left and right before he scuttled forward, as if undecided whether Cyrus was not still around watching him. The young man's pale brow was beaded with sweat; his fingers still fidgeted like an old maid's.

"Don't be nervous. How long have you been here?" Agrippa asked in a gentle voice.

Briad looked away, as if warring with internal demons. For several long moments he did not speak. "Since Darek and I were captured by Raithan. I've been in this gloom ever since. Feels like an eternity."

"Darek?—" Agrippa's eyes misted. "What do you know of him?"

"I know that he saved my life—from a serpent, and I owe him mine."

Could it have been longer than two years? "What if I were to help you escape?" asked the old man.

Briad gave a vigorous nod.

"Then you must follow my orders," he whispered. "There will come a time when you must help sneak one of my dragons into this black burrow. In the meantime—" the old man peered to either side with sharp eyes "—try to use my feeding scoop to enlarge the opening. Quickly!"

Briad grabbed the eldritch scoop, his lips pinched in a frown at its touch. His dislike for all things magical was mirrored in his expression and body language. With frantic fingers he pushed the device against Agrippa's prism's wall, but it failed to find an opening. The feeding section was a thin band at waist height about an inch wide, pulsing with a peculiar energy. Briad tried again, managing only to scrape the surface and rouse a din of sparks. He jumped back, dropping the scoop and wringing his wrists, as if his fingertips had been scorched with an invisible shield. Agrippa slumped; defeat ran in his face. Only a sorcerer could wield the scoop.

Footsteps. Agrippa turned. "Make yourself scarce, boy. Trouble approaches!"

Sure enough, the dark mage Cyrus returned to investigate. He raised his sinister, serpent-headed staff and shouted at his cowering servant. "Begone! Do not trouble our houseguest anymore. He still has much penance to serve."

Briad scurried away, unwilling to defy his master. Cyrus gave a satisfied nod then returned to his work on the petrified dragon eggs. A tinny hammering once again echoed up the passage.

Agrippa frowned. Somehow he would have to figure a way out of this pen on his own. The only way he could work his word magic was if the prism barrier was let down. Which meant... A cunning smile curled his hollow-cheeked face as he thought about the next time his enemy came to feed him fish and drugged wine.

Unhooking his belt, Agrippa sawed off a thin strand of leather with his teeth. He stuffed it in his pocket for later use.

Another dim holler echoed off the cavern walls, resounding though the ruddy murk of the connecting passage. "Fetch my mallets, boy!" came Cyrus's command.

The pad of hurried feet echoed up the tunnel as Briad snatched a metal tool from Cyrus's workbench. He ran back.

"Not that one!" cried the mage. "I want a straight-backed ball-peen hammer. This one's useless. Are you deaf?"

A sharp rap had Briad hurrying back again.

Cyrus returned, wearing a scowl. His hair was tousled and his face beaded in sweat.

"Any luck with your egg-cracking?" Agrippa asked.

The young mage refused to answer, pouring a cup of wine and flinging some gruel onto a plate. He passed it through the feeding gate with ill grace and turned away, leaving the opening unclosed.

Seizing the rare moment, Agrippa reached out with his mind and hurled his thoughts to Valkyrie Island. He visualized the sandy beach and the crashing surf, and his astral body passed over the silver crabs crawling across the red sands. Many faithful dragons sunned themselves among the rocks and slept in the seaside caves.

He summoned Tarnblower, his eldest and wisest dragon. "Come, you lank-toothed idler! Your master needs saving." The horny snout lifted and the dragon unfurled his leathery wings. Agrippa gave a triumphant smile as the great scaled beast took to the sky.

He masked his delight as Cyrus came marching back and re-sealed the opening, only to stalk off again.

* * *

At his next feeding the following day, Agrippa leaned forward to feign an itch while he inserted the thin leather strand at the edge of the scooping hole.

Cyrus narrowed his eyes. "Farewell, Agrippa, I must leave you for a time—battle and glory awaits. I promise to return in swift order and with good news. 'Tis time for the Red Claw Islands to fall!"

Agrippa's heart grew cold. "And if you do not return?"

The wizard shrugged. "Then you will starve here."

With that he strode off, whistling a happy tune and unaware of the small change that had made Agrippa two steps closer to freedom.

Agrippa shot an invisible bubble of power through the pinhole gap with his word magic. A distant stalactite shivered as beads of water dripped down to plink on the floor. A moment later, the stone cracked to fall and break into a dozen pieces.

"Excellent, excellent," mumbled Agrippa, satisfied with the progress.

The tiny opening created by the fabric had freed his magic, but he must not alert any of Cyrus's minions.

The hours dragged by and Agrippa's eyelids began to droop...until he roused himself. Precious time was wasting. Flamebiter came to check on him at last.

At first the lumbering beast sniffed the air with caution, as if suspicious of Agrippa. The sudden scuttle of a foraging rodent caused him to turn his head and Agrippa loosed soft words from his lips in the form of a powerful spell.

The creature blinked and loosed a guttural snort, then swiped a heavy paw at its snout, as if to ward off a pesky fly. Agrippa concealed a grin. He spoke a single word and the dragon flinched, retreating as it scratched with a fury at the scales on his back. The dragon turned, swatting at the air behind him as if stung over and over again by a persistent wasp.

Agrippa's lip turned in an impish smile. He built an illusion of a swarm of insects covering the apex of the prism around him. A determined attack on that focal point from outside might cause the prism to collapse.

The dragon hesitated, taking a step forward before shaking its head in confusion. Cyrus's hold on the beast was strong. The dragon paused, the thousand red and gold scales of its hide vibrating.

"You are loyal to him," barked Agrippa, "but not so loyal that you won't kneel to my commands. Bend to my will."

Agrippa taunted the beast with fiery pricks against the sensitive areas of his armpits and ears. He licked his lips in glee. "It seems like some pest has burrowed under your skin." There was a method to the madness. Agrippa knew he had no direct control over this dragon. Cyrus had conditioned it too well. He could only encourage it.

At first, the dragon crabbed back, but then it charged straight at him, smashing into Agrippa's prism and sending him reeling. *Not exactly what I wanted.*

The dragon snorted, raking its claws against its scales in an attempt to rid itself of the stinging.

"That's right," laughed Agrippa. "I'm the one creating your pain. What are you going to do about it?"

The dragon rammed his hard snout against the outer wall of the prism, raking the magical glass and sending Agrippa to his knees. The burning beneath the dragon's skin drove it to senseless rage. In one fell charge, the guardian smashed its repulsive snout against the barrier. The enchanted projection exploded and sent Agrippa rolling free with it. A wave of destruction flowed through the cavern, tossing Agrippa aside. Flamebiter's paw struck out, grazing the old mage's flesh, leaving a red strip on his right thigh. Agrippa's spell was broken.

The wrathful dragon was ready to rend him limb from limb, then Agrippa began his word magic again. The vocables streamed like enchanted darts to fling the dragon into a table of Cyrus's talismans. A magic staff and other curios rolled clattering to the floor. Agrippa rose to his feet—free.

A flash of movement at the far entrance marked Briad's presence, a pale figure cowering in confusion.

"Now is the time to seize your freedom!" cried Agrippa. "Take up Cyrus's reserve staff and strike it against the entrance portal. Let my dragon in!"

Briad trembled in the shadow of the rousing dragon. But he snatched up the glowing talisman, grimacing as if it would burn his skin. Off he scrambled to the exit to carry out the old man's bidding in the lower tunnels. Agrippa turned to face down his scaly enemy, murmuring barely audible words while giant claws arched for his flesh.

CHAPTER 19.

ALLIANCE

Cyrus left Agrippa, caught up in the spiderweb of plans in his mind. After a brief walk through the cavern's lowest tunnel, he came upon a wall of porous rock. Unlocking the spell, he revealed a swirling portal of strange filmy substance that loomed before him.

The enchanted mesh shimmered in a milky haze and dissolved. Filling his lungs with air, Cyrus dove through the opening and into dark water. Kicking out with his feet, he breast-stroked his way through the murk, through the secret tunnel of gnarled stone. At times, strange creatures came out to eye him: red-eyed viperfish, squid with blue bodies and numerous jellyfish streamers, but he paid these no heed. It was a journey he and his dragons had taken many times.

Breaking the surface, he drew a deep breath and shook out his lank hair, peering around the small bay. A mottled head rose next to him. One of his serpents guarding the entrance. It came to greet him like a faithful pet. The beast bobbed closer, two large rubbery frog-like eyelids blinked as webbed fins brought the creature forward.

He withdrew the runestones from his sopping robe. Rattling them in his right palm, he gave an eerie call from the back of his throat. The water rippled and several monstrous shapes emerged from the waves. A vast green leviathan rose a little farther away, a hideous monster that dwarfed the rest.

"The time has come," he crooned to his serpents. "Show me your power, attack the ports of men and destroy them." Cyrus muttered to himself, a harsh, cynical sound. He would show Agrippa his mastery of the serpents.

Cyrus scaled the hide of Fercifor, his newest and largest beast, and commanded him across the blue waves to seek out Raithan, the Black Claw captain. The others he sent to attack the Red Claw port of Cape Spear. Such a boon, this secret base on Curakee Island to train and tame the vicious sea serpents. No one knew of his army here, halfway between Red Claw and Black Claw Islands, not even Agrippa. He must keep it that way.

Raithan's schooner anchored somewhere off Seaguard Island, waiting to meet him. The cool glow of dawn burnished the waves a shiny copper, mesmerizing his eyes. It was a great distance to this most southerly of Black Claw Islands, but Fercifor could cover the distance effortlessly with his powerful body. The fiend was tireless. Black fins drove the great beast across the brine and Cyrus clung to the scale-glistening neck with a contented smile as it wormed its way over the shallow crests and troughs. Too long had he waited for this.

Raithan's black-hulled schooner appeared on the horizon, growing in size as they approached. At half mast, with tall spires, *The Soaring Cutlass* was a fast ship, the fastest of the Black Claw fleet, and Raithan had fought his way to become the most powerful captain.

Cyrus's serpent rushed toward the ship like a tidal wave. Coiling to a stop, the creature loomed over the foredeck and the quaking crew, before the mage floated down to the deck with fluttering robes.

The crew stared at the massive serpent and its master.

Cyrus called out a warm greeting. "Raithan, my favorite captain! I trust our plans are moving forward?"

The captain grunted. "The fish grow scarcer and the slave market has all but dried up, Cyrus. While we struggle, the Red Claws continue to breed their dragons and have signed a new trade agreement with the farmers of the Blue Claw Islands."

"I would not put too much stock in this year's crop. My serpents will see to that!" Cyrus laughed. "Listen, friend, I have words to share with you."

"Then speak them and be gone. The concerns of my own people weigh heavy on my shoulders."

The sailors reeled back as Cyrus's serpent sent a flickering tongue raking across the gunwales.

Cyrus approached the captain, throwing his arm around his shoulder and walking with him toward his cabin.

Raithan's quarters were small, but well adorned with thick carpets and trophies from his many victories. Several sea serpent teeth hung on the wall, along with the tail of a young dragon. The table was littered with charts and maps.

Raithan poured Cyrus a strong cup of rum as the two discussed the plan to lay siege to Cape Spear, the stronghold of the Red Claw Clan.

"You are to be my sole ally," said Cyrus. "Together we will destroy your enemies, but stealth will be of the utmost importance."

Raithan exhaled a drawn-out breath. His seaworn face scowled at the part he was to play, as if every fiber in his being sensed the evil in this course of action.

Cyrus's lip curled. "Are you getting soft-hearted? Now is not the time for second-guessing our alliance."

"I had thought to raid along the Red Claw coast," Raithan muttered. "Are such extremes really necessary?" His hand traveled to his sword.

Cyrus glared at him. "You and your fleet are to circle the Red Claws in the harbor. They will try to escape. But you trap them in your net and I will gut them like common flounder. Take as many Dragon Riders as you can muster, I may have need of them."

Raithan seethed, his muscles rippling. "There is much to risk in this plan of yours, Cyrus. If the Red Claws see your approach, they will launch all of their dragon wings and shred my ships' sails before we come into range."

"They have never faced so many serpents before at once," said Cyrus. "They will be overrun. Leave all to me."

Raithan drew his sword and drove it deep into the wooden table. "There will come a day, wizard, when you will not come to me asking such dangerous favors."

Cyrus raised his staff, and the runestone glowed brightly. "You'll do as I bid, or I'll break open the hull of every ship in your fleet like a soft-shelled turtle. Do not forget who brought you your many victories at sea. The plunder of the Red Claw ships, your many conquests, all your wealth—it was I who delivered it into your eager hands. It can all vanish in a moment." Cyrus exhaled a dark warning.

The veins on Raithan's brow bulged. "I wish I had never sworn loyalty to you." He gave his head a spiteful shake. "The greed of inexperience led me down this path. I was too easily enticed to eat the fruit of your dark arts."

Cyrus shrugged. "We all have regrets, Raithan. Be that as it may, you know what I will do to you if you revoke our pact."

Raithan let out a gruff sigh of defeat. "This deed I will do, Cyrus—but this fulfills my oath to you. Afterward, our alliance is done."

"I will release you when I deem the debt repaid, and not a moment before. We meet at dusk at Cape Spear."

With that, Cyrus strode from the cabin, beckoning with a hooked finger at his serpent. It bent its ugly head dripping slime on the rail. The wizard clambered on its back and swept off to the east—toward his unsuspecting prey on Swordfish Island.

* * *

Briad stumbled on through Cyrus's gloomy lair, his heart a-patter like a rabbit's. Cyrus had affixed more of the barbarous lamps with curlicue iron fixtures in the walls. By what sinister means of sorcery they were powered, Briad did not know.

He shook off his unease and made his way down the creepy passage, toward the enchanted portal that separated Bormoth from the sea. His sweating fingers clutched Cyrus's staff but he could not stop their quivering. Dampness curled from all corners of this dank, oppressive place. Hollow echoes sounded, of distant beastly things, crawling nightmares, much older than the dragons themselves that lurked about these forsaken passages.

Cyrus had warned Briad never to broach this secret barrier of his far out from his laboratory, speaking in tones that would hint of dire consequences should he disobey. Nevertheless, Briad struggled on with his jaw set firm. Never had he wanted more to be free, than now, and the old man, his last savior, had given him hope.

Carved in the bare wall loomed a massive oval of glass bounded by a ring of corroded iron. Briad could only stare aghast at the dragon that lurked past that filmy barrier. It was huge. There was water behind that portal, a green murky submarine brine now roiled by powerful forelimbs. This monster of an older generation wore a thick coat of smalt-blue scales and dragged its slavering teeth across the magical surface. Should the creature break through that and come at him... Briad shivered. The old man had hinted the dragon wouldn't harm him. But what if it did, and what if the old wizard were dead and not able to direct the dragon's aggressions elsewhere? He couldn't quite commit to the act he had promised Agrippa.

Briad whistled air through his teeth. He peeled back his lips and firmed his resolve. A risk—one he would have to take in stride if he wanted to escape this prison. He thrust the idea of being mauled by a sea dragon out of his mind and took up the staff.

Curses, but this wand magic was frightening! He was no wizard. On the thing's tip leered a sinister serpent's head, chased in gold. Serpentish runes twined around its stem.

Briad tried swinging it hard against the portal, but no luck. The filmy barrier showed only the dragon's face as a distorted monster of nevermore and a sparking shimmer as the staff bounced off harmlessly where it had raked the surface. Briad smote again, to no different result, and the dragon beyond mouthed a silent roar. Briad shuddered.

On a sudden impulse, he struck at the same time the dragon raked its glistening teeth.

Bazam. A red flare hit him full in the face, knocked him backward, almost blinding him. A rush of water flooded in and he recoiled, wiping at his stinging eyes as he was washed away.

The slave was almost trampled by the rampaging dragon as it sloshed out in a mad rush and broke through the barrier.

The dragon was through and it rose to its full height, head scraping the ceiling, saucer eyes glaring at the young man who quailed before it in the rising water. Briad shrank back in a ball, afraid of what the beast might do to him. The dragon had no interest in him though, and shambled to the end of the chamber, as if guided by a magical signal from the old man.

Briad scrambled after, slogging up the tunnel.

* * *

Under the pall of the dragon's shadow, Agrippa's fingers rounded on the first thing they touched: the hideous shark head that had rolled under the table. His fingers naturally depressed the red jewel, which now flared and the talisman's eyes came to life.

The shark head attacked the first thing it saw—the tusked dragon bearing down on him. Sinking its teeth deep into a left forepaw, the head clamped down, then released its vice-like grip to take another chomping bite out of the dragon.

The dragon howled, swatting the shark head away with its other paw. The dragon sank its own fangs into the rubbery head and shook it like a dog.

Agrippa struggled to escape, but cried out at the gash on his leg. A thin line of crimson welled on his thigh, courtesy of Flamebiter's last claw swipe. Flamebiter swatted the shark's head away and came forward snarling.

A blue-scaled dragon smashed into the chamber, springing on the one attacking Agrippa. The two creatures grappled, biting at each other. *Tarnblower!* Agrippa could have leapt for joy. Tarnblower threw off the younger dragon, slashing across the flank and legs of his opponent. Flamebiter roared, and Tarnblower answered.

Another roar reverberated in the tunnel. A new dragon stormed the chamber, this one with a white back and dirty yellow hide.

Not one, but two of Agrippa's dragons had come! Scarbait was lithe and fast, smaller than Tarnblower, but no less deadly.

Flamebiter was not so easily cowed. The beast charged Tarnblower, then lashed out with its talons, snapping needle-like teeth as the second invading dragon hooked claws into Flamebiter's flanks.

Agrippa staggered forward to send commands to his dragons. Experienced fighters, the two dragons worked in concert, striking at the same time and at alternating angles. Together they hewed with claws and gored with teeth, tearing scales and flaps of flesh from Flamebiter's hide.

The enemy dragon began to weaken. Scarbait got behind him, pouncing to sink its fangs into the vulnerable neck. Flamebiter died in a wash of crimson as the other two dragons rent it limb from limb.

Agrippa scrambled away from the pooling blood, sickened. He wiped his blood-streaked hair, panting, as Briad rushed over to his side.

Agrippa shook his head. "A waste of a dragon, no matter how twisted. Come Scarbait, Tarnblower, to Valkyrie. We will gather your brothers and sisters and fly in force to Cape Spear!" He paused, his eyes grown wide from a sudden thought received from Scarbait. "What's that? They are already gone? Of course,...I should have known!"

"Are you well enough to fly?" asked Briad, pressing a bit of cloth to the old man's wound. He frowned at the mage's babbling. Water dripped from the youth's rank garment but the tattered fabric of Agrippa's sea island cloak was stained red.

"I'll live," muttered Agrippa. "I can't say the same for Cyrus." His left eye was blackening and his voice was hoarse. He clenched and unclenched his fist which throbbed as though he had raked it across fire coral.

"We don't have much time," Agrippa said, turning to Briad. "Are there any other slaves besides you?"

"No." Briad bit his lip, a pained look in his eye. "There used to be six of us. Cyrus killed one after another—until only I was left."

Agrippa took the staff from the cringing boy's hands and patted his back with a shaky palm. "Come, boy, you've done well."

Pausing, Agrippa studied the mage's weapon in his hand. His fingers trembled at its cool, polished feel, the scrollwork gleaming to perfection. A magnificent staff, exuding a rare magic potency.

Tarnblower, eager to quit this gloomy place, loped back down the tunnel from where they had come. Briad pointed out a cavity dug into the cave wall where a discarded harness lay. They quickly fastened it to Scarbait, though Briad shrank back at the flash of the dragon's fangs.

Likewise, Tarnblower had come to stare with a set of bare bloody teeth.

With the portal broken, the cave began to fill with water. Securing the last of the straps, they mounted and mage and slave rode together down the watery tunnel.

"Hold your breath, boy! This is going to be a watery ride."

Seawater sloshed around the dragon's ankles as they approached the broken portal, gushing water at its base.

Briad clung to the harness and gulped down his last lungful of air as the dragon plunged snout-first through the watery channel. At first darkness prevailed, then the tunnel widened and Briad saw a greenish gloom ahead. Scarbait paddled his way upward with powerful forepaws to surface just before Briad's lungs were ready to burst. Tarnblower's head poked up beside them a moment later.

Greeting the sunny sky with wonder, Briad sank back in relief. The chattering seabirds were a welcome sound. He never thought to see or hear those things again.

Then the water around them began to ripple. The guardian sea serpent struck from below, its dark skullish head crowned with seaweed rising from the water to snatch Tarnblower. The dragon struck back, but the larger sea serpent tore Tarnblower's head off.

"Fly, Scarbait, fly!" thundered Agrippa. With a guttural shriek the dragon pushed its hind legs from the water as the serpent dropped Tarnblower's carcass and lunged at them. The massive jaws closed around the end of the dragon's tail as they lifted from the water. Scarbait screamed but flapped forward, ripping off the tip of his tail.

"*Carmina Ignis!*" Agrippa hurled a fiery thunderbolt down at the sea serpent, singeing its head and driving the creature back below the water.

Scarbait faltered, blood pouring out of the wound. Agrippa placed his hand on the dragon and closed his eyes. After a moment, the blood stopped and the wound sealed itself. "That's the best I can do right now, my friend. We must fly with all speed to Cape Spear."

The faithful dragon lifted his wings higher and higher still and they rose above the gathering thunderheads that floated like great warships. Briad clung like a frightened child to the harness as the crescent-shaped island of Curakee dwindled below them. How glad he was to be gone from Cyrus's oppressive domain. Yet he could not help but wonder how many more of the sea serpents Cyrus had taken with him.

Chapter 20.

THE CLUTCH

Members of the High Clutch Council gathered in the great hall at Wisselgard. Among those present were Lared, chief of the Red Claws and many of his lords, then Solene, First Lady Chancellor of the Blue Claws from Aster Island, beautiful in her yellow silk brocade and seashell jewelry. Her weaselly-looking High Minister accompanied her, awash in heavy rings and gold chains. Darek was not surprised at the lack of Black Claw representation. Jace and his unshaven riders milled about, uncomfortable in the formal settings, but Jace strode forth with a determined gleam in his eye, introducing Darek and Meira and urging them to carry forward their message.

Lared frowned. Disbelief reflected in his fiery green eyes that Darek was the same sailor who had nearly won the Cape Spear race two years ago, only to disappear from the islands without a trace.

"Mage Reborn?" came murmurs from the gathered members.

Darek stood shifting from foot to foot, stroking his bristly chin with apprehension.

"If what you say is true, we must attack Cyrus at once," muttered Lared.

"We should confirm this before acting," said Solene.

"I trust Meira's word," said Lared. He patted his muscular thighs. "Darek is beyond doubt Agrippa's apprentice. Is there nothing you can do to free Agrippa from Cyrus's spells?"

"No, I have no idea where he is." Darek loosed a quiet breath. "Agrippa warns of an impending attack from Cyrus. That's all I know. Jace and his Dragon Riders are here, ready to face him." His eyes burned with a fierce light.

Lared bristled at the suggestion. "We don't need his lot to repel a sea serpent. My riders stand ready."

Darek shook his head. "You don't understand. You won't be facing one serpent, you'll be facing a whole army of them. We'll need all the Dragon Riders we can muster."

"An army! That's impossible," Solene said.

"They've never attacked in a group like that before," said Lared. He rubbed his short red beard.

"We'll send our Dragon Riders as well," offered Solene.

Lared laughed. "Even with the few you have, the Blue Claws are more farmers than warriors. What are they going to do, take up hoes against Cyrus's serpents?"

Lared's riders chuckled at that. Solene held up her hand. "Control your tongue! Or have you forgotten that it is our food stores that feed your people through the winter?"

The two leaders glared at each other.

Meira stepped forward. "We've faced a half-dozen sea serpents and lost—and that was with Agrippa fighting at our side." She turned to Solene. "Any dragons you bring to the fight will be welcome."

"I'll send out a message to Bilsbrun town," said Solene. She gave a brisk wave.

A messenger burst in through the double doors, flush-faced and panting. His hands were trembling as he bowed to his lords.

"What is it, Esagard?" snapped the High Minister.

"Cyrus…he is launching an attack on Cape Spear. As we speak, serpents and dragons are heading with speed toward Swordfish Island. They are led by a serpent rider in a black cowl. A fishing vessel sighted them and reported them to a Red Claw scout. Black Claw schooners are ranging this minute on the port."

Lared swung around to face the messenger with a wrathful look. "Those Black Claw vermin!"

Pandemonium struck the hall. Heated words flew from all corners of the gathering.

Solene raised her arms for silence. "How many?"

The messenger gulped. "No less than two dozen serpents."

"That's enough to kill us all," wailed the High Minister.

Lared spat. "Cyrus will try to crush Cape Spear with that many hellspawn at his back. I want all dragons in the air now! Jace, come with us—we'll need everything you've got."

Solene turned to the assembly. "My personal Dragon Guard is here. They number only forty, but I would have Darek lead them. I trust Lared and Jace's confidence in the boy. Captain Salspear, you will follow Darek's orders as my own."

Darek gave a grim affirmation. There was much to be done.

Lared swore. "Half of my Dragon Riders are at Lighthouse Bay guarding the old port. Send word for them to join us—and pray that they make it in time."

"There will be plenty of time to settle old scores," said Jace. "If we can launch coordinated attacks, we can keep the sea serpents at bay long enough for reinforcements to arrive."

Lared gave a short cough. "And the Black Claw ships?"

Darek hardened his jaw. "Leave them to me." He made for the double doors, murmuring back at Meira. "I must try to summon Agrippa's dragons."

Meira hissed, springing after him. "You'll need my help. I'm coming with you."

"It's too dangerous—" Darek shook his head, but saw it was no use arguing with her.

Jace reached out a claw hand. "Take Tand and Bree as your wing support."

Darek shook his head. "They'll only distract me. I must summon Agrippa's dragons." He twisted away and scrambled with Meira out the door toward their dragons.

Jace locked eyes with Tand. "Watch his back."

Tand bared his teeth. "I'll make sure to point him downwind if he starts to piss himself." Tand uttered a harsh command and Bree scuttled after him.

Jace threw his hands in the air. Everything in Tand's facial expression told him that he would follow his command, despite the two's rivalry. He stalked off with his riders and began to mount up.

Darek raced through the overgrown grasses to the dragon pens with Meira close on his heels. There was no time to waste. They harnessed their dragons, vaulted on their backs, and headed east for Valkyrie Island.

* * *

In the deepening dusk as the skies swelled with clouds, Agrippa flew his gray, wind-beaten dragon over a small fleet of black-masted schooners en route to Cape Spear. He gave a short, wet cough under his breath.

With Briad clinging at his back, he zeroed in on the largest ship at the head. *The Soaring Cutlass* was a tangle of masts, shadowy shrouds, twisted ropes and glowering men bustling about the polished gumwood deck.

"You scavenging traitor," thundered Agrippa as he banked low, "selling out to that low-bred cuttlefish, Cyrus! You're a disgrace to the clans." The wizard spat, shaking a fist at the captain with Cyrus's staff clutched tight in white fingers.

"Beware the wizard!" yelled Raithan, "Archers take aim. Ready the harpoon!"

"I've not time to waste on lowlifes like you," Agrippa called down." For now, eat fire—*Agrunk Morir!*" With a stab of fury, Agrippa loosed a bolt of mage fire from his staff, barely missing the belligerent captain who dodged nimbly out of the way. A smoking hole sizzled in the foredeck, catching it alight.

Raithan swore and launched his sword spinning end over end in Agrippa's direction. But Scarbait knocked the weapon aside with his wing and roared. Agrippa turned his dragon away as arrows filled the air, pleased to see that one of the masts had caught fire. That might slow them down.

Agrippa streaked toward the harbor. Even his aged eyes could see Cape Spear was in trouble. The harbor was awash with serpents and destruction. Smoke rose from sinking ships. Necks of serpents strained from the dark waters.

Kraton! More time wasted. He deviated from his course and flew high above the water, heading east away from the battle to drop Briad to safety.

* * *

The warning gong echoed over the peaceful town of Cape Spear. The attack had come with unexpected swiftness. Twenty sea serpents surged forward as one, sending a tidal wave crashing into the harbor, turning over fishing boats and washing away dozens of the townsfolk. Terror spread among the townspeople in the shadow of the coming darkness.

Cyrus loomed on his monstrous serpent Fercifor—a fierce, feral shape with a slime-crusted hide gleaming in the failing twilight. A small squadron of dragons met him, but he scorched their wings with fire, forcing them into the water below where his sea serpents killed and ate them. The handful of chosen dragons that hovered behind him had not even begun to fight.

Red Claw ships drove out in the harbor to form a defensive ring. Steam-powered harpoons whooshed and cannons roared. Two sea serpents lay skewered in the water with steel tips in their necks, and another racked with cannon shot before other serpents, hissing in rage, wrapped the defending ships in their coils and dragged them down to their watery graves.

Cyrus laughed, his face dyed a hideous red as if he were the volcano God himself. With a rattle of the runestones in his palm, he urged his sea serpents forward into the unprotected harbor. Massive waves spilled over the cobbled courts and into the alleys. The locals with their militia raced about, cordoning off the town, and firing cannons from the wall.

Twelve serpents lurched onto the beach and surrounded the town, slithering. Spurred on by Cyrus's command, they craned their necks like agile storks, eager to devour the now fleeing militia.

Raithan's black-masted ships appeared in the distance and the townsfolk gave a cheer—until they saw the Black Claw ships take position to guard the mouth of the harbor. They choked on their tongues as the marauders waited at a distance, cutting off any escape. None lent aid, only bided their time as Cyrus's serpents wreaked havoc. The trap was sprung.

Cyrus leaped from his giant serpent to the back of one of the dragons he'd brought with him. There he hovered like the very specter of death above the gathered armies, clutching a sable staff crowned with a mermaid's skull. He would strike from a convenient distance with a sly grin on his twisted face—saving the slaughter for his minions.

The proud seaside towers of Cape Spear crumbled under his mage fire and the lash of mighty serpent tails as Cyrus laughed and lifted his staff. He would finally have his revenge on the townsfolk. His cruel expression mirrored the memory of the town's chief, plunging down the well so long ago.

Jace's riders appeared from the east, swooping over Raithan's powerful fleet of eleven schooners. His dragons were armored from neck to tail.

"Bank left!" Jace cried over the waves and the hissing wind. Cape Spear's eleven remaining Dragon Riders had taken wing and engaged the rampaging sea serpents in a desperate bid to give the townsfolk time to escape. The poisonous tails of the serpents beat them back, but they held their position, even as one dragon after another fell from the sky.

Jace's left wing formation engaged Raithan's ships, despite Darek's absence. Raithan was prepared, releasing a squadron of his Dragon Riders from the decks of his ships. The two dragon clans dove and clawed at each other.

Jace gripped his spear and bellowed commands as he led the rest of his Dragon Riders to aid the overridden Cape Spear defenses. A golden-scaled dragon—the largest of the Cape Spear defenders—dove into a sea serpent, disemboweling it even as a wicked barb punctured its chest.

The wing under Jace's command rode in tight formation dodging sea serpents' fangs and whistling harpoons. Three of them banked low to separate a sea serpent from the others, disabling its poisonous tail by baiting the beast and carving pieces of its hide out with coordinated blade attacks from multiple directions. One rider fell with a shriek to the sea, scraped with deadly poison. His dragon tumbled after him. A fire-breathing dragon sprayed a serpent's hide with devastating flame, before a second serpent leapt up from the waves and snatched him with its bared fangs from behind.

Lared and his three wings of Dragon Riders joined the fray, turning the tide of the battle as they attacked from the west. The well-trained warriors swooped on Raithan's dragons with claw and talon.

"We have them on the run!" called Lared, earning a salute from Jace.

New dismay gripped the riders as the mighty sea serpent Fercifor surged in with a mighty roar. Not one of them failed to shudder at the wedge-headed thing, twice the size of the others. The creature sported ropy whiskers and flared flabs of flesh trailing from its cheeks that made it look like some catfish-headed underwater demon.

The Dragon Riders divided their numbers. Half maintained the defense against the persistent sea serpents, the others charged toward Fercifor. The sea serpent struggled to raise its heavy bulk from the water, as if to leap up like a flying fish and snatch them in mid-air. Fangs snapped and a startled rider was ripped from his harness; three others were torn from the sky by an arcing bolt of lightning thrown from Cyrus's staff. The remaining dragons in Lared and Jace's wings banked toward Fercifor, but the creature slithered forth like an eel and its tail shot up, licking out at unwary riders.

Jace and Lared ducked the savage sweeps, but two more of their numbers fell to venomous stings and died.

Raithan gave the order for his cannons and harpoons to fire—a ruthless move, cutting down his dragons and Jace's alike. The Black Claw ships invaded the harbor and targeted the remaining dragons, forcing them back.

All seemed lost.

But Darek and Meira flew in from the south, low over the waves with Tand and Bree, and a line of twenty of Agrippa's heaviest dragons. Darek stared at the carnage and wasted ruins before him—he had taken too long to rally reinforcements. Typhoon was clad in dark-dyed leather armor, but Darek's mount and the two dozen of Agrippa's lay unprotected.

Agrippa's dragons swooped in fearless synchrony to savage the serpents that would otherwise be upon the townsfolk in minutes. Bree gave a battle cry as she and Tand moved in to support him.

The sight of Darek's arrival with so many powerful reinforcements prompted a rousing cheer from the ragged defenders. Darek joined the left flank of Jace's company, reeling in place with Bree and Meira at his side. Jace's eyes bulged when he saw them and he shook his head in surprise at their sudden entry. "Take out the other serpents. Lared and I will handle Cyrus's monster!"

Darek closed his eyes. He communed with the horde of dragons surrounding them in the air; Agrippa's vanguard swooped, a fearsome brigade, tearing chunks out of black serpent hide.

Jace's riders dodged steely missiles fired from the ships below, and Darek felt a metal tip flash by his ear. Another caught the flank of one of the nearby rider's dragons and with a bellow from its bull throat, it slewed out of control. A harpoon arched skyward and skewered a dragon through its throat, and it fell, gurgling blood and taking rider with it into the sea. Metal arrows clattered off dragon armor—those that had it. Agrippa's dragons were taking the worst of the flurry of projectiles and Darek turned back to see dozens of quivering shafts lodged in dragon's tough hides. Still they fought on.

Knowing he had to do something to protect them, Darek summoned his mage power and threw a fireball at the nearest ship. The mainsail was ablaze and the crew dove overboard.

Seavenger, fully healed, swooped in, screaming, clawing at a Black Claw rider's eyes, sending the man toppling to his doom in the sea below.

Like a storm, the right wing formation struck at the bobbing serpents. Darek felt a shudder pass through his body as the last hellish serpents formed a cluster in the harbor of his birth.

Jace and Lared flew side by side to harry Fercifor, dodging the monster's fangs and gouging holes in its hide. Rolling out of a dive, they banked to either side, curses spilling from their lips. Maneuvering under the sea serpent's barbed tail, Jace swooped close and reached with a claw hand to cut out a bloody triangle from the creature's glistening hide. Lared attacked from the other side, carving out a wide circle of flesh with his dripping blade.

Fercifor sank with a scream back into the water, but not before smashing the side of its fish-like head into Lared's dragon—Lared fell from his mount, twirling to splash into the dark waves.

Tand and his dragon Hagar guarded Darek's back like possessed wolfhounds. They struck at a sea serpent that ventured too close, slashing at the back of its neck a telling blow that elicited a high-pitched hissing shriek. The thing slid back into the bloody froth of water with gaping wounds from Hagar's claws.

Bree's claw-tipped spear wreaked bloody gashes on serpent flesh on fly-bys as she dove in slashing, then spurred her mount away to avoid the poison-lashing tail. The remaining riders darted in and out of the chaos like wasps, stinging at will whenever possible. Darek cringed as one of Jace's remaining men was knocked flying and tumbled into the jaws of a waiting serpent.

"Get that lead rider!" cried Cyrus, his face a study of fury. Lifting a bony hand, he held his deadly staff aloft and flicked out a blaze of serpentine light to smite Jace, setting fire to his claw arm.

Jace flinched, but did not fall. The beam had singed his claw arm from elbow to claw tip and set it afire, but it was still intact. The magic blurred as a spell of protection on the dragon claw flared to life.

Jace swerved sideways, with a fierce roar on his lips. He dove at the resurfacing head of Fercifor. Astride his dragon, he struck out with his claw arm and slashed the scaly flesh, then gouged out a huge red eye in a dark spray of ichor.

Meira was everywhere at once, her hair flying in the wind as Typhoon cut down every enemy in their path. A hissing serpent twined its slime-crusted body around a civilian Red Claw schooner caught trying to escape. The timbers cracked as the hull split in two and women and children plunged into the unforgiving sea. Meira swung in to help, facing the sea serpent alone. The serpent reared before her. She dodged its snapping teeth and cracked its snout with her bow staff. A curse wheezed from her throat as a surviving Black Claw dragon nipped at her mount's tail.

While harpoons sang around them, Darek gasped. Meira was fighting off the menace until a harpoon lodged in Typhoon's right side, causing the dragon to scream and dive.

The enemy rider was almost on her. Darek winced. He could do nothing, engaged as he was in combat with Black Claw ships and controlling Agrippa's dragons.

Bree, who was closest to the harpooned Typhoon, gave a wild yell and launched a spear. It struck the Black Claw rider and sent him flying. Yet she was turned away and did not see the other enemy rider who veered in, axe raised, to take off her head.

Tand bellowed an oath and struck after them to knock the new Black Claw rider flying with the end of his iron-tipped bow staff. At the same time, a hooked harpoon shot up and skewered Tand's dragon between the armored headpiece and throat gorget. The dragon dropped.

"No!" Bree shrieked as Tand's dragon was snatched in midair by snapping teeth. Tand was sent reeling into the waves and set upon by a waiting serpent. With a mad howl, Bree dove in to attack the serpent that was seconds from gobbling both dragon and the struggling Tand. She plunged after him down into the purple waves, tears streaming from her eyes.

Breaking off his attack on the ships, Darek swooped down to bunt her off her suicide mission but Jace flew up, edging Darek's mount aside.

"Get back!" Jace commanded. "Don't be stupid. Sacrificing yourself isn't going to bring Bree back if she dies. This battle is far from won, concentrate on the dragons!" With a twirl of his spear, he spurred off toward Meira who with characteristic stubbornness, had refused to retreat.

With a yell of anguish, Darek re-summoned his mage power. He threw larger fireballs at the Black Claw ships while the remaining dragons under his control ripped at their decks and sails. Half of the enemy ships wallowed aflame, then a bolt of lightning shot out of the sky and killed one of Jace's largest dragons. Two more fell in the blink of an eye.

Cyrus, sweeping in on the back of his dragon, called down in a mocking voice. "Come, boy, let us see what Agrippa has taught you."

Darek turned in dismay. He had come far with his power, but Cyrus had beaten Agrippa—how could he hope to defeat this twisted sorcerer hovering before him?

Leave him to me.

Darek whirled. The voice in his head was unmistakable.

Seavenger dove in for Cyrus's eyes, but Cyrus swatted it aside with a blast of power and the bird spun wide in a dizzy loop. "Silly beast," grunted Cyrus. "How many times must I kill you?"

Darek gave a grievous yell. *How could the eagle survive that blast?* He raised his hand and blinked against a blinding light heading their way. A gray shape riding upon a magnificent dragon. *Agrippa!*

Rider and dragon circled around Cyrus's deadly serpent. Darek could have leapt for joy. He thrust his staff out with a fierce roar and spurred Silver Eye toward his lost mentor whom he never thought to see alive again.

Meira struck the metal tip of her staff into the mouth of the serpent harrying her. She spurred the wounded Typhoon away and on toward Raithan's ship with a sharp cry—the thrum of unsettled business raging in her heart. With erratic beats of wings and screaming from her harpoon strike, Typhoon raged on.

The sight of her father leading the treacherous fleet had awoken a swirl of emotions in her. She urged Typhoon into a wobbly dive, and the Harpoon Master dared not shoot down his captain's daughter. Down she swooped, leaping from her dragon's back upon the deck to swing her staff at her father's skull.

But he raised his sword at the last moment, blocking the blow.

"How could you, Father?" cried Meira. "You've betrayed your own kind and sided with that madman."

Typhoon snapped her fangs and Raithan rolled to the side, ducking under the dragon's clawed swipe and leering at the fiery woman before him. "You're just like your mother, too much of a dreamer to see the reality of the world."

She pushed forward to strike her father again, but Barnabas the Bosun and other of the crew turned their weapons on her and her snarling dragon.

"Ease off!" Raithan yelled. "I'll not have you spitting my own daughter on my decks. Besides, it would be a bloody mess to clean up with all the dragon blood spilt." He laughed at his own jest, flashing a toothy grin that Meira did not find amusing at all. In a more sober tone, he grunted, "You think you've won—that this is the end of it?"

"I don't know what hold that lunatic has on you," Meira said, her staff hanging loose, "but let it go, before it consumes you."

"I've come too far to turn back now," growled Raithan. A visible shudder passed through his shoulders. "Fly away, daughter, while you still have a chance. Forget me. After this battle, I am done."

Meira saw the struggle in her father's eyes and with a pained grimace, she gave a choked cry. "It doesn't have to be like this, Father. Call off your fleet. Let Cyrus and his serpents burn." The two stared at each other for a frozen moment, remembering a time when they had played together in the waves. Meira shook her head. She saw that her words were having little effect. "Fool! One of those serpents will come knocking at your door. What then?"

Raithan stayed his tongue. Something of a white wall of shame passed over his face. Maybe it was the sight of his lovely daughter standing here against all the odds that moved him, but he at last gave in. "Bosun, attack those damn serpents!" he snarled.

Barnabas blinked. "Captain?"

"I said tell the lads to hold off on the Red Claws! Steer clear of Cape Spear. Harpoon that cursed worm."

"But—"

"No buts, Bosun, move!"

Tripping over his heels, the bosun sped midships to give the order. The man in the crow's nest relayed a message by flag to the other Black Claw ships. Meira's eyes lit up.

"Now get away from here!" Raithan thundered at her. "We'll talk when this battle is over!"

With grateful tears, Meira slashed off the harpoon's shaft from her dragon's forepaw, then leaped atop her dragon and spurred Typhoon into a running leap off the deck.

Raithan fell silent as he watched his daughter fly away. He had never been so proud. Wiping his brow, he felt the weight of a thousand ingots on his soul. With a heavy heart and hollow pit in his gut, he knew his end was fast approaching.

Chapter 21.

APPROACHING DOOM

Five Black Claw schooners lurched ahead upon Raithan's command to attack the serpents.

Atop his dragon, Cyrus gave an angry shout as he saw Raithan's ships move forward. He did not consider they had changed sides, only that they had aided his enemy by relinquishing control of the harbor. Hurling his magic, he set the aft mast of *The Soaring Cutlass* bursting into flaming shards.

Raithan's ship shuddered with the force and slewed sideways, the crew reeling from the impact while the other Black Claw ships surged ahead to attack the largest of the sea serpents.

Fercifor, a giant compared to the other serpents, ducked under the waves as the ships approached. The creature swam beneath them, rising up in their midst and ramming its plated skull against one of the hulls. Timbers cracked and water flooded into her holds as the ship wallowed and the crew jumped overboard. Cyrus gloated, circling closer on the back of a green-eyed dragon to attack the traitor's ship.

The last Black Claw ships fired their harpoons as other serpents attacked them from the sides. Cannons boomed and one of the smaller sea serpents sank in a swirling pool of red. Jace and his riders sensed their opportunity and dove in to jab spears and swords at the serpents' flanks.

Agrippa circled a black-hided sea serpent, avoiding the glinting fangs. The creature's eyes glowed a soft, lurid yellow and its body undulated as if to strike. His challenge rang out over the sea. "Cyrus! You have lost. One or both of us die here and now!"

Cyrus gave a rude, maniacal laugh. "Then it will be you, old man. For too long you have been the pesky eel with teeth in my side. Die!" And with a bellow, he lifted his rune-crusted staff and a malignant green ray shot out to smite the old man.

Agrippa grit his teeth. He winced as the ray smote him but he did not waver. His word magic protected him—for the moment. With terrible sadness, he swung Scarbait about. Tears fell from his eyes as he realized what he must do. He had loved Cyrus as a son. Killing him would be the hardest task of his life.

"So it must be... *Aeger Shukr!* The ocean itself will bring your demise. *Fugis Saeper!*" In the last syllable of that incantation, the wind began to scream as whitecaps formed across the waves. The sky darkened and heavy rain began to fall. Lightning lashed down, giving the remaining sea serpents pause.

With his last wizardly strength, Agrippa called down a great funnel of air and water. The ocean below seethed, as a mighty waterspout grew. It shot up a half a mile high, nearly carrying Scarbait with it. Deep green and blue, the water funnel glowed with sullen wrath from its central eye.

Cyrus's lips sagged in disbelief. Again he fired; this time the green ray caught Agrippa full in the chest. Agrippa fell back on his dragon, releasing a sad bellow from his racked throat. "I'm sorry, my old friend." He rasped his last breath. "For the greater good...we must go...now."

As Agrippa's heart stopped, the eye of the funnel spun with even more fury and caught up Cyrus, tearing him from the back of his dragon.

The sea worm Fercifor was strong enough to rip itself from the vortex and flee, floundering in the sea, yet the vortex turned and scooped Cyrus up—as if with a mind of its own.

Cyrus spun through the air, uttering a spell. Torn, battered, every fiber of his being shouted at him that he had miscalculated.

Yet he was not the only one in the funnel's path. Two of Raithan's schooners, including *The Soaring Cutlass*, were caught up in the funnel's eye. Their bows crumpled and lifted up in the whirlwind's fury. The boats whipped around and around the outer edge of the funnel, before ripping apart from the inside out, boards, bodies, debris flung every which way.

Darek felt the tug of cyclonic winds dragging him into oblivion. "Get back!" he yelped and spurred Silver Eye away, his long hair trailing behind him.

Darek cried out in dismay. He glimpsed Agrippa's body as it was swept away in the raging funnel, Scarbait tumbling end over end—ripped apart by the raging forces. His breath caught in his throat and his spirit sagged.

"You think a little wind can stop me?" thundered Cyrus from below. "Striptooth! Longfang! Kill them all!" Cyrus raised his runestones to the sky and from them came another terrible viridian beam lancing down into the frothing sea. The otherworldly magic galvanized the two serpents that lurked below to action. They shimmered with a baleful glow that sent them rearing up on their tails in defiance. With a howling roar they sprang up out of the water as if swimming on the wind.

Darek swung Silver Eye wide, barely avoiding the fangs of serpents thrice his height. *I must do something!*

But the sudden burning pain inside him refused to cooperate. *Not this time, not now!*

Silver Eye gave a mournful wail as they were sucked into the pull of the whirlwind. Cyrus's raging green serpents came to snap him in their jaws, but then Agrippa's words came back to Darek in a wild rush:

Do not fight the dragon power, Darek, or it will crack you like an egg. Let it flow...

The fingers of doom fluttered at the edges of his vision. He lifted a hand to strike down the dark mage and his vile serpents with this reckless power of his: an impulse born of vengeance and fury. But he froze. Agrippa's words echoed in his brain, as if speaking from the ethers of the spirit world. "I am not your enemy—it is the doubt and fear within you."

Darek surrendered to the raw force of the power. The Mage Reborn channeled everything he had through his body, his very veins—heart, mind and soul.

A flood of fire flowed through his limbs. In one sweeping rush he let it flow. By Kraton, he let it flow!

Straight at Cyrus.

The black-robed wizard was thrown off his guard. He howled and jerked back, dancing like a marionette.

With a twisted grin, Darek raised staff and focused the fire to a searing hot white as Agrippa had taught him.

Cyrus hurled a blazing pulse of energy at him, but it vanished under the gathering power of Darek's staff. A green ghoulish serpent tried to attack from below, snapping out with dripping fangs.

Darek brandished his staff and vaporized the serpent with a blue blast of flame.

Bree shouted from somewhere distant. "Darek, get away from there! The ocean is boiling!" She must have broken off from the serpent attack and reined her beast in.

Darek was beyond hearing.

In a dreamlike trance, time stopped. All sound dimmed in his ears against the roar of Kraton's fury.

Darek caught a kaleidoscopic glimpse of all that had passed: Agrippa dead, Jace fighting for his life, serpent heads and fangs rearing and snapping, Tand spinning out of control to his grave, Meira nowhere to be found. Darek felt his heart quail.

In his mind's eye, he saw the funnel spinning in place, knew it was stuck there, caught in stasis at the moment of Agrippa's death.

Raw power shot through Darek's body. He stood tall in his stirrups and raised his staff. Beckoning to the stationary funnel, he sent it hurtling toward Cyrus.

The spinning tower of wind began to move.

Cyrus blanched in horror. Tail and snout of his closest serpents snagged the outer edge of the vortex. Neck and heads twisted and snapped off and slimy scaly bodies compacted and broke. Others slithered away from Darek's white flame, rearing back into the waterspout, fearing fire more than water, and were instantly consumed.

Darek, reveling over the liquid fire filling his veins, glowed like some sorcerous sea king invested with the power to control the world—then suddenly he was hit with the enormity of the destruction he had caused.

He let his hands down and the funnel ceased its forward motion. With a hiss of rage, he set it swirling below the waves where it dwindled and died. The fire winked out and he came out of his trance, feeling hollow and spent.

Meira hunched over Typhoon's back as her dragon fell back to the water exhausted. She had been a safe distance away when the funnel had hit. After a moment of rest, she urged Typhoon to swim in a wide, circular path to scan for survivors.

Reduced to a fraction of their numbers, the surviving Dragon Riders clumped together in the water, assessing their losses. Together they swam to the ruins of Cape Spear. Silver Eye and Typhoon were the strongest amongst them and began searching for the other dragons. Ten of Agrippa's beasts had perished; none of the Cape Spear dragon guards had survived. Many of the townsfolk were clearing rubble and fallen masonry from the square, rounding up missing loved ones and mourning the dead.

Meira walked around in a stupor, helping where she could and Darek found her as she was, slumped on a chunk of the clock tower.

"Raithan repented before the end," she murmured. Her voice cracked and her head hung low. "So many words are left unsaid between us." A tear came to her eye and she sniffed in grief. "I only wish I had gone to him sooner."

Darek started to say something, but then stopped, and put his arm around her shoulder as she cried.

Jace stood awkwardly before them, flexing his damaged claw. It had turned black and was bent out of shape from Cyrus's blast.

"If I'd only trained harder," Bree said with tearful remorse, "Tand would still be alive. He was the bravest—the bravest—"

"There was nothing you could have done," Jace consoled.

Darek also dipped his head with regret. "Don't blame yourself, Bree—I should have been stronger, then maybe I could have saved him."

"Tand was a hero," said Jace. "He'll be remembered for many years. Many good men and women died here today. But let us honor them, Bree, in spirit and memory."

She stood up and swallowed hard, holding her chin up and nodding. Meira placed a hand on her shoulder.

A thin but vaguely familiar figure walked over with a determined look and Darek squinted in surprise.

"Briad! Is that you? After all these years! How did you end up here?" Darek slapped him on the back and shook his hand with hearty zeal. So many conflicting emotions had his brain reeling.

"Agrippa saved me from Cyrus's lair. Jace, I would join your cause. My life has been nothing but trawling the sea for fish, assuming the dull life of my father's. Now that I've been saved twice from slavery, I have a debt to pay."

Jace's expression crinkled into a grin. "Good show, lad!" He slapped the fisherman on the back. "The riders of Manatee will rebuild themselves. There's a spot open for you in my school any time. Though, I warn you, it'll not be easy."

"That goes without saying," laughed Briad with a smile. He turned to Darek, stammering, "How did that funnel?...I saw you—"

"Agrippa—he channeled the funnel," Darek spoke quickly. "I distracted Cyrus, enough for Agrippa in his last moments to move the thing forward. Through dumbness or anger—whatever, I managed to get away. Cyrus didn't—nor Agrippa."

"We have much to thank you both for," grumbled Jace. He reached out a hand. "I'm sorry for my harsh words earlier, son. Without you and Meira bringing Agrippa's dragons and you standing up to Cyrus, we would have been lost."

Darek nodded, the memory of the burning heat flowing through his limbs making him shiver, and not a memory he was willing to share.

Meira flashed Darek a questioning glance. "What will you do now?"

Darek looked away, his gaze traveling off across the water of the Dragon Sea as the sunlight faded to dusk. "I'll stay here, Meira, and become the greatest Dragon Rider there ever was."

"You'll be in tough company," joked Jace. He cast a suggestive glance at Darek's sister.

Once more Darek thought of Agrippa and the sacrifice the old mage had made and his heart pulsed with a fierce determination. There was sadness there too. He spoke in a lower tone. "I'll also become the greatest Dragon Mage this world has ever seen."

Bree sucked in a breath. A curious look washed over her pretty features, as if recalling the sea boiling and the serpent turning to ash. "That's a tall order, sailor boy. You're going to be the best at *both*?"

Darek laughed. "Well, maybe the *second* best Dragon Rider." He grabbed her hand, pulling her close. "But don't think I'll make it easy on you." He kissed her long and deep, hoping to end any more talk of his mage power.

Meira snorted. "The two of you will be so distracted with each other, you'll be lucky to be second and third best after me."

"That's the camaraderie I like to hear!" exclaimed Jace. "Let's find a strong drink, there're celebrations in order..."

Epilogue

A splash in the nearby water alerted Raithan of imminent peril. He kicked away from the spreading pool of crimson, stifling his horror, as a ghastly harvest of bodies and wreckage bobbed not a stone's throw away. He swam toward a twisted section of deck, clung there, his breath coming in a ragged gasp. He closed his eyes and tried to make as little noise as possible.

The mutilated body of a dead dragon floated next to him, its bloated belly splayed. He recoiled from the thing and dogpaddled away, toward the shadow of another carcass that didn't smell quite as bad as the last. He grabbed onto it, nearly retching as he felt the crimson scales and the sting of salt water on his cuts and bruises.

Sharks would arrive in moments to feast on the corpses. He must get away from this cursed patch of sea if he were to survive.

The waterspout had turned out to sea, receding until it looked no larger than a spray from a whale's blowhole. He ground his teeth. That old, meddling mage had loosed the devilish cyclone on them and swallowed his ship in the blink of an eye. But it was the evil apprentice Cyrus who had killed his crew. No matter. He had seen both Agrippa and Cyrus consumed by the waterspout along with others. He was not sad to see them go.

Vague memories flashed in Raithan's head—of his yelling useless orders to his crew before abandoning ship and diving into the dark waves. The cries of the dying still rang in his ears, their tortured screams as the wind lashed at them like hornets. He alone had managed to dive deep enough and avoid the raging froth that had consumed his ship.

The bodies of his crew floated around him on the choppy surface. Raithan swam past the purple face of his Harpoon Master, the man's leg dipping below the water as the fin of a shark appeared. He angled away from the destruction, careful to avoid the undulating shape of a sea serpent swimming in the near distance. This was his reward for defying Cyrus—no, for his idiocy in involving himself with the black sorcerer in the first place.

Was Meira still alive? He hadn't seen any dragons in the air. Then again, the currents and wind had carried him far away from shore. Perhaps there was still hope.

Another splash nearby chilled him to the bone. There were things other than sharks and sea serpents in these waters. Was that Barnabas's body he saw ringed by fins? He clawed his way past, the chunky crunch of flesh loud behind him. Better not to think of it and focus on the long swim ahead.

Sea birds swirled in the air above. *So, not too far from land then.* A loud splash disturbed the water ahead. He paused to tread water.

A scaled carcass began to move—a yellow-green dragon struggling in the waves. *Clawreaver!* Red gashes in his side spoke of an encounter with a sea serpent. The blunt-snouted face roared a warning as a pair of hammerhead sharks circled him. *Could he reach the dragon?*

One of the sharks lunged for the dragon's hind legs. The dragon snapped its neck around and bit into the side of the shark's head in a spurt of blood. The second shark attacked, ripping off a chunk of flesh from the dragon's wing. With dark tail flashing, Clawreaver smacked the predator away with his foreleg. The shark fled with a flash of tail as Clawreaver consumed its companion.

Raithan made shaky strokes forward. "Clawreaver, it's me."

The dragon snarled, then let the half-consumed shark sink below the water. A look of recognition flickered in Clawreaver's eyes. Raithan swam alongside him and gently stroked the dragon's neck.

"It's alright, boy. You remember my scent." Raithan grabbed at the dragon's slick hide and clambered up on its back. He was no dragon rider, but made it his business to know every creature under his command. He cursed himself for not learning the art, and clung to the dragon's back like a soggy monkey. He turned the scaly neck toward the faint outline of an island in the distance. A trail of blood formed in the water behind them.

Sharks trailed close behind as the injured dragon weaved an erratic path into the chop. Raithan closed his eyes; he doubted Clawreaver would survive his wounds. He prayed they at least made it to the shallows.

* * *

Down through the brackish water Cyrus plunged and rolled. He couldn't fathom what had happened. *How had he failed?* For an instant his life flashed before his eyes, nothing more than a passing landmark on a cosmic map, then his survival instincts kicked in. Staff and runestones were gone, and his enemies thought him dead, but at the last instant before the tidal forces ripped his body apart, he called out the Myxolian Order spell of protection. The necromantic arts paused his need for air or blood. He lived on with full use of his faculties, but without the physical burden of supporting them. He passed unharmed deep under the deadly funnel that still churned victims in its wake.

Surrendering to the powers beyond death was a curious thing. It was like a lotus dream; the haze of hallucination and blurry sense of time made little sense... The mind played strange tricks on those who dared cross into the altered realms.

All sensation faded from his muscles; there was no pain, no emotion as his body sank lower in the cold gloom. When he reached the ocean floor, he began walking in a direction he thought might be the shore. All manner of sea creatures, spider crabs and squid stared at him in curiosity as he crossed their watery domain.

Cyrus did not know how long he traveled. Only that time passed without meaning, until his body finally washed up on a shoreline. Gasping breath forced the water out from his tortured lungs. Pain blossomed once again as he restarted his blood pumping and regained full sensation in his body.

Cold moonlight shone down on his pale limbs. His brain registered the soft surf lapping at his toes and the realization that he might be somewhere west of Cape Spear. Judging from the ghostly bluffs and trees silhouetted up the beach, maybe Whale Island. He summoned his serpent with familiar ease.

Fercifor, his faithful servant, wallowed on the surface beside him, still alive but scored and oozing fluids from various wounds. It was foolish to not have killed that mage boy while on Raithan's ship! Sentencing him to the fire of Kraton had been an even worse mistake. There would be no more errors. Like a half-dead suckerfish, Cyrus clung to the fin of his last surviving beast, and with his failing magic he sent the injured serpent back to his lair on Curakee Island. They slithered away in the murk, leaving the death and destruction behind.

THE DRAGON SEA CHRONICLES: THREE BOOK SERIES

Dragon Mage: Uprising

Chapter 1.

A Pirate Raid

Livis stared with cool resentment at her father as he slammed his looking glass shut, cracking the lens in the process. Captain Serle gave a blustery sigh as he rubbed his square jaw, peering out through black, slitted eyes from the foredeck of *The Singing Gull*. "I'm done arguing with you, Livis. You've come a long way, but you're not ready to raid a Black Claw ship."

"I'm ready, Father!" One look back at the crew under her command made her regret the choice of words. "I thought you said it was an easy target."

Her bear of a father grumbled. "There's treachery about, Liv, I can feel it. That clipper out there is a trading vessel to be sure, but seizing cargo from the Black Claws is never easy. Just pray the report we received is true and they have no dragon riders aboard."

"Don't underestimate the power of our sea dragons," Livis replied. She stroked her curly russet-dark hair trailing down her back, her heart beating with fierce emotion.

Captain Serle glanced over the railing at the mounted creatures swimming below. They circled the rowboat her father had used to cross over from his own ship. The silver-green pair, sisters, sported shimmering petal-shaped scales on their muscular torsos with sharp fangs protruding from long snouts. Black claws descended from lizard-like feet. Fierce hunters they were, deadlier than any shark. The pirates who rode them were either very brave, or insane.

"When that clipper turns in to the reef, my ship and dragons will attack." He glared at her. "Stay out of range until they surrender." He turned and stared down the rest of her crew who stood fingering their weapons aboard the one-masted schooner. "Don't engage. If anything goes wrong, you're to sail straight back to Pirate Cove. Do you understand?"

"Aye, Captain." Livis gave a sloppy salute. She turned away and brooded as her father returned to his rowboat. She gave instructions to her crew to be on the ready for an attack while she moved about the decks, checking the harpoons and cannons for smooth operation.

"But mistress," Skarlee, the quartermaster, protested, "your father expressly forbade us to—"

Livis shrugged. "He also said a good captain should never be caught unprepared."

Serle boarded his much larger flagship, *The Longrunner*. Within moments, the barbaric schooner with its garland of skulls latched to her gunwales was moving into position to attack as she and her crew looked on.

Livis reflected on the past year spent studying her father's trade. The other pirate schooners were on the prowl, chasing down other quarry leagues away. It was just her ship and his...and it gave her a peculiar thrill. Neither had expected to stumble across a lone Black Claw cargo ship. She was at last on a raid with the infamous Captain Serle, only to be left out of the action.

The prey, the three-masted clipper, approached the reef, her white flag and three black streaks clearly visible. As they entered the narrow channel, Captain Serle's ship rounded a small island on an intercept course.

Serle's cannons roared to life, sending a warning shot across the clipper's bow. The two dragons shot through the water, moving to flank the ship. The Black Claw vessel had little room to maneuver. This should be where the enemy captain saw reason and surrendered—only he didn't. The clipper turned just enough to fire broadside at Serle's ship, their guns loaded in anticipation of an attack.

"No!" Livis yelled as the cannonballs ripped through the deck and sails of *The Longrunner*. Captain Serle's men returned fire, but several of the gunners were writhing in pain on the deck, struck with flying shards. The pirate dragons raised their heads and roared, closing in on the Black Claw ship to lay waste to the cannons.

The unthinkable happened. An answering roar sounded from the hold of the clipper, as a massive brown-scaled dragon launched into the air. Its outstretched wings cast an arching shadow over the sea: a fire-breather, one of the rare ones, with a Black Claw dragon rider astride its back. The pirate ship fired a steam-powered harpoon into the air, but the creature ducked under it. In seconds, Captain Serle's sails were aflame. The Black Claw guns swiveled, firing at the first pirate dragon hurtling through the water in an explosion of water and blood. Her sister-dragon gave a keening cry of agony and rage. What should have been a simple raid was now a desperate fight for survival—one that her father would lose without her help.

"Full sail!" Livis commanded. "Give me ramming speed."

The captain of the Black Claw ship saw their approach and ordered his guns to fire, but the second silver-green dragon had clawed its way aboard her decks and was tearing through the Black Claw gunners in a swirling mass of death.

While the hulking brown dragon swooped low over *The Longrunner*, Livis's ship surged ahead. The spiral metal horn mounted to the prow of *The Singing Gull* aimed directly at the wooden heart of the enemy ship. "Brace for impact!" Livis yelled. The two vessels collided with a terrible, echoing crash.

"Follow my lead! Maquia! Skarlee!" Drawing the cutlass strapped to her side, Livis led the charge as her crewmates leapt aboard the clipper, cutting through the dazed Black Claw sailors. Most vicious of all was her harpoon master, Maquia. The scarred and bald-headed man wielded a black-steel cutlass in each hand, using his muscled arms to dispatch any who dared challenge him. Throwing one of his curved swords into the chest of a sailor in the rigging above, Maquia used the other to deflect a blow and cut the throat of another. Few were as battle hardened or skilled with a blade. He'd come to see Livis as a daughter of sorts, with the instinct to protect her at all costs, and she'd earned his respect through fair treatment of the crew. He snatched up his weapon from the fallen man's chest, wiping the blood from his twirled mustache.

Swords flailing, chunking into flesh and sliding off cutlasses, the invaders cut a deadly swath through the Black Claw sailors and forced them back. Dozens of their deck mates lay in bloody heaps. Soon sailors lay down their curved blades and surrendered. The crew's effectiveness at keeping Livis alive was a testament to her father's careful selections—Maquia's lips drooped in disappointment that there would be no fight to the death.

Sensing victory close at hand, Livis stormed toward the Black Claw captain: a lean man, with a coarse beard and broad shoulders. The Black Claw captain laughed through his teeth as she lunged in with a reckless flurry of steel. She parried the deadliest of his strokes and earned cuts in the meantime, yet held her ground against the more experienced fighter. Headstrong, yes...rash, yes, she knew it, but her anger only escalated at his gross taunting, that of a man confident he would win.

His beady eyes tracked a glint of movement: the merciless pirate dragon hunting his men and a red-faced Maquia slinking toward them with a trail of bodies in his wake. Too far away to help, the Black Claw dragon shrieked and dove over *The Longrunner*, harrying her with fury. He roared out an oath and held up a hand. "Hold! I'm a reckless sea dog, but not stupid." He dropped to one knee, offering his sword to Livis in surrender.

Maquia snatched up the blade and tossed it with approval to his captain. "A day well served, Mistress! No more rogues to kill. The day is ours."

"We're not out of this yet!" Livis cried, shaking the blood splatter out of her hair. "We need to help my father! Quick! Turn this ship's harpoons on the Black Claw dragon. It flies still!"

Maquia and her crewmates hurried to obey.

Caught in a crossfire, the Black Claw dragon beat at the air and banked left and right, dodging missiles, but Captain Serle's harpoon master scored a hit that shredded its wing. The creature crashed into the water in a spray of blood and cartilage. The impact rocked the boats as it thrashed about before sinking beneath the waves. Damage to *The Longrunner* was extensive: a gaping hole in her forward bow and her main mast leaning on a drunken angle.

The crew formed a bucket brigade and managed to douse the fires. *The Singing Gull,* entangled with the Black Claw clipper, creaked to the slap of waves at bow and stern. Forced to use winches and dragon power, members of Serle's crew separated the two entwined ships only with much painstaking effort. As they toiled, others patched the defeated clipper's hull. Livis ordered her own crew to tend to minor repairs on deck. Out of the corner of her eye, she watched her father finish directing the repairs before going to his cabin to down several tankards of ale as was his habit. When her deck work was done, she spoke to her mates about the battle and how it might have gone differently. The captain emerged with a lean to his step and a frown on his face. He now set out to look for her.

At last he stumbled to the stern where she gathered about a keg, grumbling with her mates who were quaffing rum like fish.

"I thought I told you to not engage," he said in a dangerous voice, breath sour with grog.

"You expected me to let you die?" Livis demanded.

"While I appreciate your bravery, Livy, I expected you to follow my orders!"

"Well, maybe you shouldn't give such stupid orders."

"That's mutiny," her father rasped. "You're stripped of rank and back on deckhand duty until I decide otherwise."

Her mouth hung open. "You can't do that."

"I just did." The captain marched over to a group of men by the midships cannons. He sated his wrath by berating the man who had sold him the course of the Black Claw Ship—along with the bad information about her defenses that had caused the death of so many men.

The messenger piped back, "If you can't handle one Black Claw ship against two of your own, then you're not fit to be captain."

Captain Serle turned red in the face. Wits already impaired, and at the limit of his tolerance, the man would not stand to lose face in front of his crew. He grabbed the offender by the ears and dragged him to the bow where he ordered the bosun to tie him up. He threw him overboard, then dragged the line under the bow and ordered two men to pull, keel-hauling him. The man survived the first trip, his cries shrill as the scavenging gulls swooped over the chop. A third trip proved unnecessary.

"'Tisn't right to punish the messenger like that," Maquia muttered. Several others nodded their agreement, but kept silent. No one else was willing to defy the ruthless Serle.

The ships dropped anchor for the night and Serle drank himself into a stupor. Yet, Livis did not go to her bunk. Soft words and silent action filled her evening. She recalled how the distance had grown between her and her father, ever since she had freed the slave, Darek, from the prison pens. Life had changed for her from that moment on, her parents treating her with more harshness and mistrust. Just before dawn, she cracked a smile, knowing that in the morning, her overbearing father would awake to find the sails of his new Black Claw prize slashed and his daughter and her crew vanished along with *The Singing Gull.*

Chapter 2.

CAPE SPEAR

The first chalky bluffs came into view as the dark mage Cyrus, once Agrippa's apprentice, circled around the shallow, wooded valley east of Cape Spear. He flew astride Valoré, his young red-scaled dragon. Stone buildings surrounded by coconut groves dotted the area. Cyrus squinted. A large crowd had gathered in the cobbled square of the town, he guessed to elect a new leader after the demise of chief Lared. The air teemed with dragon riders coming from every island to cast their vote. It was a perfect distraction for him to avoid notice.

Cyrus could sense the presence of his target, Darek, amongst the crowd. The divinatory magic never failed. He landed his dragon within a stretch of turquoise sea firs, bent by the wind and scarred with age. He commanded Valoré to stay hidden on the windswept hill overlooking the sea and slowly walked down the hill path, slouching like an old man. To disguise himself, he wore the tattered garb of a beggar and tucked his cowl around his cheeks and brow. The unthreatening appearance should serve to disarm any prying eyes.

A few hundred townsfolk gathered to hear the petitioning speeches of the two candidates. A dais raised on planks stood before the new clock tower, a work still in progress, blocks piled high to the sides.

The townsfolk muttered to each other in quiet voices, still uneasy that their town had been so easily destroyed while under the protection of their previous leaders. The square seethed with angry looks and a rising tide of complaints.

Three figures stood behind the podium, a grey-haired town elder who acted as arbitrator of the debate, and the two contenders, looking as different as night and day.

Cyrus's mouth hooked in a grin. The dragonmaster Jace stood to the left, a surprising candidate in the upcoming elections with his hooked claw of a prosthetic arm and hawk-eyed, stoic sandy-haired face. No doubt he was seen by the townsfolk as a savior, swooping in with his dragon riders in their time of need. Darek, a handsome, well-built youth with a mane of dark hair, stood at his father's side, lending a significant endorsement as the islands' new Dragon Mage.

Cyrus's fingers itched to pull out the runestones and hurl a burning spell of Myxolian magic at them.

Cyrus's hatred for Darek and the Red Claw Clan ran deep.

He resisted that urge. The moment was not ripe.

Looking on with interest, he gazed at the dark-haired woman at the young man's side. She seemed more than a casual acquaintance. *A lover perhaps?* Cyrus bared his teeth in a malicious leer. If he could take her unawares, she could be used to lure the boy away from his place of power. If not, the wench would burn along with him.

Cyrus regarded the other man on the stage opposite from Jace. This was a tall, russet-haired man, who cast a serene gaze over the crowd as he wrapped up his speech:

"—and that is what I promise, good citizens of Cape Spear, peaceful trade and the promise to build a new sea wall that will protect our harbor once and for all from sea serpents."

The crowd cheered.

Jace stepped forward, nodding to the arbitrator. Cyrus watched the figure with bitter resentment, remembering how that claw-handed man had led the counterattack against his serpents not long ago. Not only a daring strategist, the man was a formidable dragon rider.

"Friends, citizens," the speaker intoned in a deep resonant voice, "I am pleased to be amongst you again after a long stint at Manatee Island. Evren, my adversary, has spoken well. I have the utmost respect for him as leader of our merchant guild, but he is short-sighted on many points. Mostly in the area of defense. Our losses have been considerable. Simply rebuilding a wall will not be enough."

He swept a claw arm across the square, a once proud coastal town now nearly reduced to rubble. "The demon Cyrus is no more and his serpents slain with him. Yes, we will restore the town to its former glory, but there are many other threats that a wall will not protect against. Evren suggests trade with the Black Claws is the answer, but we have seen their honor is easily sold."

"Down with the Black Claws," yelled a distraught villager.

"Down with the whole stinking lot!" came more mutters and boos.

Jace raised his hands for silence. "The pirates grow ever bolder and continue to raid. What few ships we've left, must be protected. If we show even the slightest bit of weakness, they'll attack. We must begin recruiting and training a new army of dragon riders."

Evren scowled as the crowd began to cheer noticeably louder for Jace's plan. His wife raised her voice, "The dragon riders failed to protect us once, why would the next time be any different?"

Several bystanders grumbled in agreement.

Jace spoke up again. "I will direct the training myself, with help from my most experienced dragon riders. We'll return the Rookery to its former glory, and bolster our ranks with riders from across the Dragonclaw Islands."

Evren was losing the crowd.

Jace turned to Darek. "Our new dragon mage has pledged Agrippa's dragons. Together with his magic, we'll create a strong enough force that no one will dare touch us."

Cyrus bridled at the remark.

A thrum of mixed reactions rustled through the crowd.

One of the fishermen whose boat had been destroyed raised his voice. "It was Agrippa's apprentice who brought this scourge upon! Now we are supposed to trust another? Never trust a mage, I say!"

Evren saw his opportunity. "Good Wrislin, your voice is heard. I praise the efforts of you and others who have struggled to feed our town without your boats. We all remember how the dragon mage Cyrus made similar promises. We all know that Jace was Agrippa's man and know of his checkered past. I do not trust their kind to have our best interests at heart, let alone keep you all fed or rebuild our trade and industry. How will we pay for this new army?"

Jace snarled. "And how will filling your own coffers protect the Red Claw Islands? You'd rob the people through taxation and fees just as quickly as any pirate."

"We have need of ships and the Black Claws have them," replied Evren.

Darek growled in frustration, but wisely held his tongue.

Jace threw up his hands. "—and have us become a puppet slaver colony to the Black Claws in return?"

Evren shrugged. "We have both made our case, let the people decide which plan is best."

The arbitrator stepped in. "Gentlemen, you have both had your say. Voting will take place three days hence." The debate was over.

Cyrus moved from foot to foot as he eyed Jace's dragon riders at the edge of the crowd. He'd heard enough, and yet his impatience gnawed at him like a hungry serpent. To strike the mage boy down here would be a senseless risk.

Looking around, he saw a hulking youth with the insignia of the city guard standing at the side entrance to the plaza. A captain, judging by the badges on his uniform. Instead of watching the crowd, his eyes were locked on Darek with a look of hate. Cyrus smirked. Another potential pawn to be used in the days ahead.

He shuffled over to him. "Ah, brave captain—my hearing is not what it once was—would you be so kind as to tell me which candidate is better? Seems a hard choice to make."

"No hard choice, beggar," grunted the captain. He wrinkled his nose at the fishy stench, moving back a step.

"Is that so?" Cyrus smiled, recalling the fish guts he had smeared on his cloak to heighten the illusion.

"My father will win. That cripple has no chance. Father to the Mage Reborn—" the guard spat "—what a farce."

Cyrus's eyes sparkled. "You don't trust the mage? He has an honest face…"

The captain grew angry at that, his face turning red. "Begone, before I have you thrown in the stocks. The public square's no place for begging for scraps." With a disinterested wave he turned his back.

Cyrus smiled and selected a green-spotted runestone from his collection. Just as the young man turned, he clenched his hand around the gem and muttered a spell. A strange change came over the captain and he froze. Cyrus's eyes darted left and right, but no one seemed to notice with their rapt attention still on the speakers. He infiltrated the weak mind easily, then moved closer, holding out his hand as if to ask for a few coins. The captain turned to face him, his eyes heavy and unfocused.

Cyrus whispered in his ear. "Follow my commands and together we'll destroy the dragon mage and his father. When it's done, you will earn glory and praise. Is that something you want?"

The captain blinked. "More than anything."

"Good." Cyrus slipped a necklace of shells around the captain's neck. "What's your name?"

"Bralig."

"Be ready, Bralig," Cyrus said, "I will give you instructions soon."

Bralig smiled, nodding.

Not only a captain, but Evren's son. If he could ensure that the father won the election, he could seize control from within.

Cyrus sent a silent thought to the runestone hidden among the shell necklace. *Watch Jace and his riders closely. Report all that you see. I'll hear your thoughts through the necklace you wear.*

Bralig gripped his sword. An ambitious gleam shone in his eye.

Cyrus grunted. This minion would serve his needs well. Then he vanished into the crowd.

He had climbed halfway up the low-shrubbed hill back to his dragon when Cyrus turned. Unwrapping his staff from its hiding place among his rags, he rubbed the glittering end until the white runestone glowed like a pearl. Thrusting the staff into the air, he pointed at the townsfolk and gave a ferocious snarl. *"Curlesfunx ruit!"*

A green blast licked out from the tip and rained down like a flaring snake on the crowd below. The mage boy's eyes lit. As if by some uncanny intuition, he turned about, ducking the blast at the last minute. A man fell dead behind him. Darek held up his forearms like a shield. A glowing sphere of power appeared around him and his father.

By Kraton, where did the boy learn that? Cyrus cursed and ran to his dragon.

* * *

The town square erupted in panic. People fled to all corners—Darek tried to push his way forward and discover the source of the blast. He ran through the crowd, darting several wild glances left and right. "Where did it come from?" he cried.

A woman selling apples to the crowd from her cart pointed a quivering finger up the hill. Darek's eyes squinted to the rustling shrubs.

A ragged-garbed figure had climbed onto a grey-green dragon and the two vaulted into the air. The beast spread its iridescent wings wide and sailed out toward the ocean.

Darek summoned his dragon with a thought. A silver shape materialized and swooped down, plucking him from the ground and soaring back up like a sea eagle grabbing a fish. The chase was on.

* * *

Valoré flew off across the bay like a streak of mage fire, but the silver dragon somehow kept pace. Cyrus sneered. Darek's dragon was a competent flier, but the two could not match Valoré under water. Cyrus took his dragon into a steep dive and they plunged under the waves. He called upon his necromancy and allowed the water to enter his lungs. Without the need to breathe, they could swim faster and deeper and deeper than any dragon rider could hope to match.

The dragon's forelimbs and hind legs propelled them deeper to the bottom, and Valoré swiftly lost their pursuers amongst the many underwater formations and caves below.

The silver-headed dragon soon lost trace of them and bobbed to the surface. Cyrus grinned, imagining a red-faced Darek gasping for air. The day had been a loss, but he still had the advantage. They didn't know who their enemy was.

Chapter 3.

Rebirth

With bitter heart, Cyrus flew back to his sanctuary on Curakee island. He had failed again, but at least he had gained valuable information. His loyal sea serpent, Fercifor, a long, sinuous beast with black fins and massive greenish-black body, guarded the bay as he gathered what few dragons were left to him. He could hardly look at the creature's one eye without seeing the mirrored face of Silver Eye, the dragon of Agrippa's new apprentice, Darek, who he had failed to kill.

How he longed to summon more serpents and watch as they ripped the upstart dragon mage apart. The boy had become too powerful, too well protected. Cyrus's heart writhed in knots and a cold lump frogged his throat. A subtler plan was required to exact his revenge.

He sent Valoré into a deep dive, splashing into the bay and swimming down to the underwater portal hidden under the complex coral shelf along the shore. He held his breath and began chanting a spell to unlock the heavy chain that sealed off the entrance. The iron and wooden portal shimmered as the metal links fell away and he guided Valoré through the magical barrier, sealing it behind him and replacing the chain with a hasty counter spell.

He would not make the same mistake of dropping his guard and allowing intruders in again. Looking to his left, he frowned. The old portal to the outside world had been shattered with his own staff by Briad the traitor. The crack had flooded the lower levels of his sanctuary with seawater. An ugly mess. A veritable battleground of soggy dampness and mold that he could do without. Stripping down to bare skin and ringing his sopping robe of its water, he donned a dry garment pinned to the wall and bid Valoré return to the beast's chamber while he marched up the wide, torch-lit tunnel to his workroom.

It had taken many painstaking days to repair the portal. Windbiter, his eldest dragon, had hauled the stones and provided the fire for re-forging the metal binding along its seams. He was glad to have left the old dragon behind where the others had died in the battle at Cape Spear. Too many of his sea serpents had been slaughtered.

His lost mage staff would have been a problem, had he not thought to create a spare—this one well-concealed from the fugitives, Agrippa and Briad. The loss of the runestones was a bigger problem. He had imbued too much of his power in them. Yes, he had others, less powerful, but functional, and for this, he thanked his luck to have hidden them amongst his collection of curios. Time passed as he brooded, staring at them now, unsure of the best way to make use of the twinkling gems.

For the past two moons, he had remained in hiding in his network of caves, eating fish that his dragon would catch for him, smoked by the dragon's fiery breath, but wracked by his own frustration and anger. He hadn't always been this miserable.

Cyrus remembered a time when the title of Dragon Mage had been his. Now the feckless upstart mage had stolen his place as Agrippa's successor. Fools! He, Cyrus, should have been next in line, and if Agrippa, curse his hide, hadn't denounced him publicly before he died, he would be the *Dragon Mage*.

He had sacrificed everything to ensure no other would challenge him—done so many terrible things... He flashed back to how the Red Claw chief Margar had him lashed and thrown in the stocks over a few mischievous spells when he was but a child of nine. Days passed while urchins threw stones and rotten apples at him. Agrippa, the spineless jellyfish, had gone along with the townsfolk's punishment, only arranging for his release after several weeks. The memory still burned his heart.

It was nearly a year later when a tragic accident had taken Margar's life. The man's wife had suspected Cyrus, but had no proof. When she petitioned the elders, they were too afraid to do anything.

Now the dark arts offered him a chance at revenge, and unlimited power. His path had been chosen for him long ago by Agrippa's callousness. It was too late to turn from this path…

Cyrus cleared his mind, exhaling deeply. The old Cyrus was dead, ripped away after his desperate walk across the bottom of the ocean as he fled from the magical waterspout raised by Agrippa. He could still remember the sight of it tearing apart dragons and ships, a deadly funnel raised from the ocean, destroying everything in its path. An ugly sneer flashed across his haggard face and touched his lips in a curl of hate. His pale fist smashed down on the table, upsetting the magic items.

Never again would he let fickle fate touch him. He must shuck this old skin as the sea serpent did, growing stronger and deadlier. He would become a new version of himself, one his enemies would not recognize. Then he would find a way to crush this unworthy dragon mage and his followers. Let them think he had perished. They would grow fat and complacent, at that moment he would strike. In the meantime, he would prepare the necessary ingredients for the *Tangenesis.*

Back again in his secret workroom, Cyrus consulted his tomes and drew the hammerhead shark head to his side. He had recovered the talisman from its place wedged between the claws of a rotting dragon corpse. He lifted it with macabre anticipation. An instrument of woe, it also served as a divining source, gleaming with an eerie quality under the sallow lamps affixed to the stalagmites. Something about the animus of the undead shark soul trapped inside it had given it power. The Myxolian realms of magic offered untold possibilities to a fearless mage.

He set up a projection spell, firing a green bolt from his staff into a six-sided star chalked on the ground. The light flared; his lips curled in triumph. He knelt, placing the shark's head in the center, its dead grey-black skin gleaming, still moist from necromantic power.

"*Hgraen! Fulgis sorit.*" The words spilled from his mouth like packets of power and the light began to pulse as he chanted in bold tones.

"Tell me what I need to know to rule the Dragonclaw Islands, oracle," he crooned in an otherworldly voice. He stabbed down with his staff and the light flared as the jaws of the shark head snapped shut with a crunch. Cyrus saw a filmy bubble of colored gas rise from the shark head. Dark masses like smoke curled across its surface, forming vague figures. In the swirling haze, a bright blue sky emerged. It revealed a band of roving pirates attacking a Black Claw ship near the Serpent Deeps.

He snorted, nursing a scowl of impatience. "Why would I care about such grubby cutthroats?" But then he paused, his eyes narrowing. "If the Black Claws are weak enough to fall prey to the pirates, perhaps the rogues are more powerful than they seem. They might make a useful ally with the teeth to do what must be done. You are wise, dark oracle, wise..."

He chuckled for a moment, rubbing his chin, as a plan brewed in his mind. Passing his hand over the ghostly cloud, Cyrus searched for the answers to more questions that might aid him. "Show me the mage."

The image shifted to reveal Darek, riding above an open plain on his silver-headed dragon. Others rode with him on green and orange dragons, all laughing in good humor. They wore the same red uniform of the Red Claw Dragon School. The Rookery they called it.

Cyrus spat. How he detested the dragon riders and their infernal school. With fingertip extended, he moved the view down to settle upon the ground where Cyrus recognized the rugged face of Jace, the dragon master, the young mage's father. He would pay this 'rookery' a visit and make time to deal with the overweening pup and his arrogant father once and for all.

The image changed to another scene, one which caused Cyrus equal dismay. A black ship at anchor in a harbor near Rivenclaw Island, captained by a familiar figure.

"No, it can't be!" He swallowed hard. How had the Black Claw traitor, Raithan, survived? His thin jaw dropped and he clawed at his lank black hair, grown rank over weeks of neglect. He had seen the man's ship caught up in the waterspout and torn to bits like the rest of his fleet.

He bounded to his feet. The treachery of his former ally could not go unpunished! Harpooning his sea serpents behind his back. Chin in hand, Cyrus mused. How to dispose of the captain? The man was wealthy and powerful. He would be on his guard. Perhaps an unexpected visit from a different type of sea monster would be best. One the captain would not expect. His mind drifted to a recent memory.

The ancient squid *Archituthis* still haunted the seashore. He had glimpsed its giant tentacles as the creature lurked in the underwater grottos in the bay. It had been a mistake, summoning the leviathan in his first experiments with the shark head...but it might still serve some purpose.

The creature had pursued him with relentless persistence. Even with all his power, the sea monster would kill him, if given the chance. He was forced to travel to and from his underground haven under the guard of a sea serpent. Several times he had been forced to fire a warning blast of green magic when the horned creature had fluttered too close. Cyrus glowered. Perhaps he could lure the beast to the Black Claw Islands and unleash it upon them.

He took his makeshift runestones, gleaming with a sullen amber glow and laid them in a pattern around the shark head. Muttering an incantation, he raised his hands high and uttered some sinister words: "*Agrak Kanrok Fugis Archituthis! Menustris, Flacci Venwn...*" Arcane phrases sprayed from his lips, ones he had learned from Agrippa, but combined with the forbidden Myxolian spells he had gleaned, or rather, stolen from the old man's lair. Agrippa had been foolish enough to leave such knowledge unguarded. To his detriment. Now he lay in a watery grave with crabs and snakes crawling through his eye sockets.

With the spell of confusion woven, the squid would think that Raithan was him and seek the man out. It swam with ponderous thrusts, but should reach Ravenstoke by the new moon. Cyrus chuckled in triumph. Until then, he would focus his attentions on the mage boy.

He scowled anew. He needed a strong beast to defeat the silver dragon the youth rode. It was one of the old ones, the most powerful, birthed from an elder egg, laid in a time before humankind. The elder dragons, larger than most, were naturally stronger with sharper claws and fangs; ancient lore spoke of them once rivaling the size of the sea serpents.

Cyrus had failed to hatch one of his own, but perhaps he had merely been unwilling to do what was necessary. He lit a torch and strode on nimble legs from his cavernous workroom. Windbiter dragged his gray bulk down the corridor after him, with a rasping croak gurgling from his thick, wattled throat. "Come, Windbiter—" Cyrus waved a pale hand back. "We must first see to the egg. I will need your dragon fire."

Stepping into a cavern filled with crystalline stalactites, the mage paused, eyeing the fixtures that hung like serpent fangs. He had suspended long, slow-burning lamps from them some time ago. He lit more now with his burning torch. His eyes gleamed like feral pinpricks in the cavernous light. A dull, oval shape met his eye, a stone egg, long petrified, with color like a great robin's egg. He strode over and patted the cool surface with a distant smirk. The egg towered as high as him and ranged twice as long.

"Yes, pretty egg with a hidden prize. One still living within. But how to awaken you?"

Not an easy task. He recalled the Ritual of Rebirth that had first revealed his power. He had survived then by summoning a sea dragon. Closing his eyes, Cyrus tried to contact the creature within—and was rebuffed for the hundredth time.

With a growl of rage, Cyrus commanded Windbiter by mental suggestion to nudge the egg out into the corridor. The dragon used his wide snout to roll it down the dank passage into a small workroom carved from the cave itself.

Cyrus blinked. Warming to his task, he gathered the required tools from his main workroom: hammers, chisels, volcanic rocks, picks, brimstone, fire sticks, bead-restraints, suppressors, stimulants. Surrounding the egg with volcanic rocks, he coated them with a layer of brimstone. The egg would need extreme heat to hatch. At his command, Windbiter's fiery breath ignited the area around the egg. *Keep the fire hot until the egg begins to move.*

He stroked the curved, robin-egg blue surface with anticipation. It was getting warmer, but not warm enough.

Cyrus had installed a boiler in the chamber for magical experiments. He now filled it with a mixture of fuel and dragon eggshells. He lit it and opened the steam and safety valves, allowing hot vapor to pour into the room. Closing the door, he sealed the dragon inside. If the steam and heat didn't kill Windbiter, the brimstone fumes eventually would—but a price had to be paid if he were to hatch the egg.

Now to wait.

For two days as the new moon drew near, the temperature in the sealed workroom rose until the door radiated heat. Cyrus could feel Windbiter's thoughts grow sluggish as the dragon continued to heat the egg with his dragon fire.

It was a powerful time in the realm, with the conjunctions of stars and planets of magic, as far as mage spells went. Cyrus smiled. *Patience.* He knew the price of impatience. And he wished no more errors in the course of important events to come.

On the eve of the new moon, he pried open the door with a long metal tool and jumped aside as steam and smoke billowed out. Windbiter lay on the floor of the room, unconscious but still alive.

He waited for the room to cool. He walked over to the egg which glowed from within, the surface too hot to touch. Cyrus moved his ear closer, a smile curling on his gaunt face. He could hear the hollow stir of life within. The egg jiggled, quivering to the new thrusts of life. A few test taps with hammer revealed more. Yes, the petrified shell seemed to be thinning. Like a blacksmith striking his anvil, he swung the hammer against the shell.

The sharp blow incited the egg to quiver. He struck again, and again, raining blows on the egg like a madman frenzied on drugs. He conjured forth green fire from his mage staff, covering the surface with sparks and flames. The egg jerked and the shell at last cracked. A wet, gleaming shape slithered out of the broken pieces. The gelatinous mass, sluggish and alien, struggled to rise.

Cyrus gazed in awe. The newborn uncoiled to twice its size, stretching limbs that had been curled in its shell for untold ages.

Magnificent, the creature was magnificent!

His eyes brimmed. The dragon staggered to its four clawed feet, light blue with greenish tufts on its horned head and its splayed-back ears. Cyrus grinned.

A tusked beak parted in a gurgling croak as the dragon sank to the floor. *Something was wrong.* The young scales had a dry and duller cast than normal. The creature's eyes seemed sickly and white fluid leaked from its nose. The dragon's thin limbs appeared underdeveloped. A runt of the litter? Its right leg appeared deformed and unable to support its full weight.

Doubt plagued Cyrus that the hatchling would survive without his help. He retrieved a *dragon amulet*: an instrument crafted of amber crystal, the size of his fist. It had tamed the newborn dragons for centuries in the island kingdoms. He reached out a probing finger. The young dragon snapped at it.

Cyrus jerked his hand back.

"A wounded and pathetic specimen." The mage's grin remained sour. Had he gambled Windbiter for naught? The grey dragon was reviving in its huddled stupor. His eyes settled back on the hatchling. "Though you do have some fight in you. A quality to be admired. No one wants to be ruled by a master. Especially one like me. But ruled you shall be." Cyrus laughed again. "Not to worry, *Dendrok*—that is your name from now on—the *Defiant One* in the old tongue of the warrior mages. With my magic you will grow strong and powerful." He let the words echo off the dank rock. The dragon's eyes wheeled in their horned skull; its ears seemed to perk, as if hearing its destiny in that rough, harsh sound emanating from Cyrus's mouth.

He would make his dragon more powerful than any that had ever lived. With Raithan and Darek out of his way, nothing would stop him from ruling the Dragon Claw Islands. Once he had taken care of the last two gnats in his side, he would start training his serpents to crush the coast and all who opposed him.

The hatchling he would leave here in this secret chamber. Let Windbiter care for it in the meantime. It couldn't fly with its thin, premature wings. With nowhere to run, it could roam free and hunt fish in the grotto's pools. No escape routes existed in the connecting tunnels and side caverns. That he had ensured.

Cyrus flew west on the back of his sea dragon Valoré, the fastest of his remaining minions. On toward the Black Claw port of Ravenstoke he rode, drawing the monstrous squid after him with a familiar fluting call in the back of his throat. He gave a grunt of satisfaction as the water churned behind him as those powerful tentacles slapped the rising waves, propelling its slimy yellow bulk forth with enormous speed.

An instrument of destruction... Cyrus squinted in the sunlight, nursing pleasant thoughts. No need to accompany his servant for the rest of the long journey. The creature was the harbinger of death. It would ravage everything in its path. He imagined it tearing Raithan apart and when it failed to find him among the wreckage, it would return to his lair. The spell could be repeated, possibly even to kill the mage boy himself. He sent the final instructions out to his leviathan while he returned to Curakee on his dragon.

CHAPTER 4.

THE ROOKERY

Jace relaxed on returning to the large training field inside the Rookery. Overlooking the sea, the school's high walls seemed to block out the strange events of the day and the angry mutters of more foul magic at work as he put a wing of new recruits through their practice drills. It was an unrelenting but rewarding task. Thirty-seven new riders had joined the school in the last moon. He walked beside Meira who was straddling her white dragon, Typhoon. Her hair was dark like her half-brother Darek's, complementing the lighter hue of Typhoon's scales. She took after her mother in this regard. The young, athletic woman had always been like a daughter to him and his chest swelled with pride at her assistance in training so many new recruits. Though Raithan was her father, it seemed she was destined to follow in his footsteps instead. Jace looked out with satisfaction over the impressive scene.

The training ground was nearly as large as the nearby town itself, divided into three distinct areas. Curved arches and large stone hoops surrounded the perimeter that formed an elaborate obstacle course where dragons honed their acrobatic flying abilities and raced for rank and position among the trainees.

The first section in the center of the course was a field crowded with riders and dragons in combat training. Several ranges allowed riders to practice with projectile weapons of every kind, from throwing spears to nets and cross-bows. Alongside that three large fighting pits ranged: one for dragon-against-dragon sparring, one for rider-versus-rider, and one where both faced off together. Groups of recruits practiced sword strokes and parries in close-combat, while fire-breathing dragons hurled searing red blasts down-range at stone targets.

The second section was a giant trench filled with sea water. The artificial lagoon held a second underwater course filled with obstacles like stinging fire coral and a submerged network of caves. Riders used the deep pools to extend their ability to hold their breath and practice free-diving.

The third area rose amongst the low-hanging clouds that rolled off the sea and covered the green valley. It had been designed by Agrippa himself for groups of dragons to practice coordinated aerial maneuvers. The section appeared mostly empty, save for dozens of light metal, rope-like columns piking high up in the air, and pulled taut by balloons.

Tethered to each of these columns floated the huge balloon made from dozens of canvas sails sewn together and sealed with gum sap. The sap was sticky enough for dragon and rider to want to avoid, while also providing an air-tight seal. Each was filled with a mixture of gas called "Dragon's Breath", a substance lighter-than-air and self-contained for days at a time.

Large groups of dragons flew above and below the inflated orbs as they refined their precision and perfected their teamwork. Mock battles along with a kind of real-life dragon chess reigned amongst the most popular war games. To touch the balloon meant a deduction of points or they lost the race, depending on the training exercise in effect.

Darek and Bree, his wiry female companion, flew in the middle of the riders, jousting with staves while Briad, the castaway from Curakee, looked on in wonder, taking in what pointers he could.

Jace mounted his big tan-scaled dragon and flew across the different training areas, barking instruction and tips to his trainees. As the newly-appointed Rookery dragonmaster, he used a series of one-handed signals to others too far away to hear his booming voice.

At midday a bronze bell gonged from the clubhouse, calling a halt to the activities. Sweaty riders streamed toward the tall towers of the school buildings. The trainees ate meals and attended night classes within the compound, studying the complicated hand signals and battle formations and mastering the various levels of skill tests to graduate to full-fledged dragon riders.

Novices attended demonstrations of the making and maintenance of the shark-skin harnesses, basic care for a sea dragon and its treatment in the field, plus lectures on dragon breeding. Late each night, the students collapsed exhausted in the west wing dormitory, only to repeat the regimen over again the next morning.

Rider and dragon needed the best possible food as they went through the rigorous training, and today's midday meal was no exception. Rookery staff rolled large troughs of raw meat and fish outside for the dragons, while riders entered through the double-wide doors to the vaulted-ceilinged dining hall. Large sideboards stood everywhere piled high with the full bounty of the sea along with savory mutton and braised shanks of glistening lamb and beef. A team of cooks and workers serviced the school and grounds, all provided for by a generous endowment from Agrippa's wealth and taxes collected from the Red Claw Islands. The ceiling, painted in great detail with the scenes of famous dragon battles, depicted the colorful history of the Rookery.

"A good session out there today. Be proud and fill your bellies!" called Jace. The veteran dragon riders and students ate together and took hearty helpings. Good cheer and raucous laughter filled the air.

Jace had just bit into a steaming meat-filled pastry, when through the wide bay windows, he saw a messenger dragon dropping into the grassy yard. The newcomers angled from the west and landing beside Meira and her dragon. As usual, the young rider was ministering to her mount's needs before her own.

The dragonmaster cleared his throat, his brows peaked in curiosity. He left his meal half eaten and strode out to investigate. The flush-faced scout had a wild look in his eye, his dragon trembling from the exertion of flying hard. It rasped out a guttural roar, teeth gnawing on the bit.

"Festlex, what news?" Jace asked, hailing him and patting the gusting beast's snout.

"Black Claws, Jace. Mobilization of their paddlewheel war schooners. They seem to be moving in force."

"Against who?"

"Pirates from Devil's Isle. But that's not the strangest thing. I swear I spotted Raithan aboard a Black Claw clipper nigh of Ravenstoke. Or his ghost prowling the decks."

Meira uttered a strangled gasp. "My father? Alive?" Her eyes lit up like fire.

Jace shook his head. "Can't be. I saw the destruction of *The Soaring Cutlass* with my own eyes along with the other Black Claw schooners. He went down with his ship."

"Or so we thought," muttered the scout. "Word amongst the Black Claws says he's returned in time to lead the attack. He's been given command of their remaining ships."

Meira closed her eyes, as if in a silent prayer of thanks.

"I was in Ravenstoke earlier, carrying a message to a merchant in the markets," continued Festlex, "I kept my ear out for anything of interest, as you instructed me, Jace. Raithan has apparently bought his way out of the accusations against him and jumped at the chance to redeem his name. He claims he was deceived by Cyrus and was only protecting Black Claw interests. Once he saw Cyrus's dark plan, he made efforts to put him down."

"He left a few things out," grumbled Meira, "but his heart is in the right place."

Jace's lips curled. "Raithan's always sought profit. This ploy to erase his misdeeds sounds just like him."

"I must ride to him. Let me go find out the truth of it," said Meira.

Jace wrinkled his nose, shaking his shaggy head. "I don't like the idea, but I know you'll do it anyway. Take Festlex or Girar with you."

"No," argued Meira. "This is something I must do alone."

"I can't let you do that," croaked Jace. "You'll be in enemy territory."

"He's my father!" Meira's eyes swam with defiance. "He's not going to do anything to hurt me."

Jace rubbed his chin, sucking in a long breath. "Take Briad with you, then. He could use the flying experience. They're less likely to target two young riders who look to be training."

Darek and Bree returned from some private corner where they had been sharing their meal, trading moony looks. Darek's ears perked up at the news.

"You think that's a good idea, Jace? Briad's inexperienced. Maybe I should go, or Bree."

Jace pulled Darek aside, his eyes darting from side to side. "Let me speak plainly, Darek. Before you and Silver Eye arrived, the riders were having trouble controlling their dragons."

"What do you mean?" Darek asked.

Jace gave a heavy sigh, stroking his blackened dragon-claw hand. "The dragon amulets seem less effective than before. Agrippa's influence over them has waned ever since he died."

"What? Is this happening everywhere?" Darek looked around to see who might be listening.

"I've had reports of widespread disobedience and defiance on the rise," Jace said. "But that's all changed here since you two arrived. No, I need you to stay at the Rookery. I can't spare anyone else to go. We've absorbed the Cape Spear disaster well here, but I don't want to leave the central port undefended again. We've added to our ranks, and are swelling in numbers. Give us some time to get up to fighting caliber and I'll start sending out patrols to Drist and Valast up the coast."

Darek nodded and turned to his sister. "Promise me you'll be careful. A high flyby reconnaissance only. If your father is alive, use the white flag of parley. Find out what is happening and then report back."

Clapping Meira on the shoulder, Jace nodded his agreement. "If anything looks wrong, you wing it out of there! He might've turned sides after the Cape Spear siege, but we can't take any chances."

Meira shrugged with a happiness that denied any such betrayal. Hope shone in her eyes and Darek saw there would be no dampening her resolve.

Jace summoned Briad and filled him in on the mission. Darek blinked as Meira flew off into the shimmering sunlight with Briad struggling to keep pace on his grey-snouted dragon.

He was unable to get the crawling spider feeling out of his stomach. He peered over at Silver Eye, his silver-headed dragon stretched in a lazy sprawl on the grass. Why did he sense something unpleasant was going to happen?

Resisting the urge to fly after Meira, Darek shook his head and tried to focus on the larger issue. If Agrippa's death had weakened the riders' control over the dragons, it fell to him to restore order and forge new dragon amulets.

Bree came up to Darek and laced her fingers into his. "It's okay. I know you worry about her, Darek. She can take care of herself, and Briad too."

Darek nodded. He forced a smile and put his other arm around Bree's waist. She had been a wealth of comfort these last few months.

He watched her as she brushed back an auburn curl, tinted a sun-kissed red-gold. She looked beautiful in the warm sunlight, her riding leathers snug about the contours of her hips and chest. Too long had his life been consumed with suffering and violence. Spending time in her arms had helped to fade some of his memories enslaved to the Black Claws and other misfortunes.

It seemed that dropping his guard had been an invitation for catastrophe. Who had been the mysterious attacker in the town square? The figure had flung a mage blast at him. This was nothing ordinary. Something Cyrus would do, but Cyrus was dead, consumed in the waterspout, and he hadn't been seen since. There was something familiar about that evil aura—something cold and diabolical. The situation demanded more thought and he could not ignore the sinking feeling in his gut.

Chapter 5.

Archituthis

After nearly an hour of flying over endless blue water, Meira sighted a cluster of black sailship steamers in tight formation. She veered in, signaling Briad to follow. The dragons swooped down with powerful wings beating a steady rhythm. Briad was handling himself well, considering he had only had eight weeks of lessons on one of Agrippa's dragons. The youth's determination to help their cause had accelerated his progress.

A flurry of activity sprang from the Black Claw decks as harpoons and cannons sighted on them. A sleepy dragon rider roused his dragon to attention and they sprang up to challenge them from the lead ship, its paddlewheels churning.

"Stand down!" came a booming voice from the foredeck. The harpoons and cannons paused in mid-swing. "Any man who fires on my daughter will be used as serpent bait!"

Meira reined in, guiding Typhoon in a perfect circle to land on the lead ship's foredeck with effortless ease. Her eyes searched the face of the rangy captain who approached her, heedless of the dragon's claws clacking on the polished deck. "Father!" She leaped from her mount, ignoring the looks of astonishment on the faces of the deckhands around her. "I knew you'd survive!"

Raithan wiped his brow, a pride shining in his eyes for his daughter who was as fierce as any dragon rider. "I lived, Meira. Bailed ship at the last moment before that wind funnel tore her guts out—but your words about the truth of Cyrus's serpents was what actually saved me."

"It's a miracle," said Meira running forward and embracing him. "I'm just glad you're alive."

Raithan held her for a few moments. "I lost many good ships and men that day."

She stepped back and smacked his chest. "Why didn't you send for me or at least give me word by messenger?"

"No time," Raithan muttered. "I hope you can understand. The wretched pirates have been raiding our ships without mercy, growing bolder by the day. I thought it was best to put a stop to it rather than—"

"Face charges for treason?" Meira quipped.

"Yes." Raithan rubbed the back of his neck. "I'm afraid I spent half of my fortune buying my way back into the Islanders' good graces. It seemed like a good way for me to cement my relations with the Clan." He jerked a thumb at the circling rider. "Who's that with you?"

Meira looked up with narrowed brows at Briad's dragon wobbling in the air currents. "Briad. A new recruit of Jace's."

"Is he going to be able to stay aloft?"

"He should be able to." Meira frowned.

"Well, if Jace trained him, I won't worry." Raithan gestured to his crew to give them some privacy. "Building a dragon corps, is he, the old goat? Well, I can hardly blame him. He's going to need it. The tide of power is shifting, I barely recognize the players anymore."

Meira gave a grim nod.

Raithan's exclamation became more an expression of displeasure at the changing times than anything else. "You must be tired after your flight. Would you care to join me for a meal? We can hole up on the midships deck for a while. I've wasted enough years and this visit is a happy surprise. I thought I'd never see you again."

Meira looked around with a wan smile. "You have any rum to drink on this ugly sea-cow of yours?"

Raithan gave a sheepish laugh. "Old chief Tengra demoted me after learning about the cockup at Cape Spear. After losing most of our warships, I'm lucky to have any command at all. But no one could ever part me from my rum."

Meira saw that the fleet consisted of short-range reconnaissance craft equipped with a mishmash of cannons and harpoons. *Had the Black Claw power really fallen so far?*

They strode to Raithan's cabin and sat together at a low, wooden table. He uncorked a cask of rum and poured two glasses.

Clearing his throat, he cast her a sharp glance. "Are there any young suitors in your life?"

Meira froze in mid-drink. "What?"

"Never mind. As long as you're happy, so am I. Darek is a true Dragon Mage now?" he asked.

Meira's expression soured. "No thanks to you."

"Right, right...give the boy my apologies." Raithan swallowed hard on his drink and poured another. "Darek didn't deserve the way I treated him. I shudder to think what your mother would have done to me if she were to catch wind of it. Fool woman has taken up with some religious cult in Ravenstoke, so is only half there most of the time."

Meira couldn't help but scoff. "You really don't have a clue what you're doing, do you?"

A sudden thud under the hull sent the cask of rum rolling to the deck and Raithan's ship lurching. Meira gasped. She staggered sideways as her eyes caught a glimpse out the porthole: a gray-horned tentacle lifting from the water to smash into the starboard rigging.

Raithan was on his feet and out on deck, bawling orders every which way. "Man the harpoons! Bosun, turn us about! There's squid to starboard!" He stared at the size of the sucker-studded tentacle. "A monster one. Hurry, you stinking laggards!"

Meira ran across the deck, lunging for Typhoon. The dragon edged backward from the huge tentacle and eyed the sky. Briad croaked out some unintelligible words from above and spurred his dragon into a dive.

The crew hastened to obey. Everyone ran in a mad scramble. More thuds now battered the hull and the bow listed sideways on a thirty-degree angle. The deckhands slid to port as the ship lifted out of the water, grasping with desperation at the rail as several slid into the frothing water below. One of the harpooners screamed as another glistening tentacle rose from the water, raking across the harpooner's arm and chest, sending him spinning away in a bloody heap. The crack of timbers filled the air as the forward strakes crumbled, sending bilge oil spilling across the deck and into the sea.

"Move, you slack-witted gulls! Get those boilers pumping double-time." Raithan staggered to his feet while the master engineer and his mate clawed their way below decks to man the boilers and get the paddlewheels turning.

Meira clambered onto Typhoon's back. The two leaped into the air as the hull continued to bend—this time in the opposite direction, as if drawn by a supernatural force.

Urging Typhoon higher, Meira got a full look at the terrible creature below. A horrifying black beak emerged from the water, snapping a swimming sailor in half. Eight wriggling tentacles began to wrap around the ship. A giant eye peered from beneath the surface as the tentacles ripped through the stern castle and pulled the vessel lower in the water.

One of the Black Claw dragon riders responded to the attack. Raising his long spear, he dove his yellow and green-breasted dragon straight at the monster. Throwing the weapon, he struck one of the tentacles, sending spurts of milky-white fluid splattering across the deck. Little did he know that upon returning from his long-range scouting mission he would face such horror.

A second rider rose from the decks of another ship. His blue and white dragon swooped low, teeth snapping at the tentacle wrapped around the bow in an attempt to free the boat. Another thick-horned limb swatted the dragon away as a tail might a mosquito. The last of the Black Claw dragon riders surged from the farthest ship, circling with caution on a brown and black diamond-patterned dragon.

Doubly enraged at the assaults, the squid sent multiple tentacles writhing high into the air. The first dragon rider underestimated their reach and a whipping tentacle grabbed the yellow and green dragon by the leg and dragged both the creature and its rider below the waves.

The sea monster hissed out a spray of water and pulled the clipper farther out to open water.

Meira dove in, signaling with thumbs pressed together that Briad and the closest dragon rider should attack with her. Briad careened in behind her left wing and the brown and black dragon skimmed the surface of the water to her right as they made their attack run.

They hacked at the rubbery flesh in concert, earning hissing shrieks from the monster's gullet. Dodging its whipping tentacles, Meira baited the creature, goading its bulbous head out of the water whose tooth snapped with fury as she flew by. The Black Claw rider flanked the squid and drove his steel deep into the back of the monster's head. Typhoon struck at a tentacle reaching out for Briad. The dragon's fangs snapped as her claws ripped wads of flesh from the squid's hide.

A harpoon shot out from below and sank into the creature's back near the bobbing crown. But to this monstrous beast from the black depths, one harpoon seemed like only a needle plunged into a pin cushion.

"Briad, stay high above its reach!" Meira cried. "Don't swing too close, whatever happens."

The young man, clutching his staff, needed no urging, his eyes wide with fear. Meira grimaced as she flew higher and up over the clipper's masts. Their attack had done little to deter the giant creature. If she didn't act, her father was dead.

Meira surged in for another strike.

Raithan gained his feet. With curses on his lips, he drew his curved cutlass and hacked at the ropy streamers of flesh slowly crushing his ship.

The squid had dragged them away from the other ships. The thing would have drowned them had it not been distracted by the dragons. Its barnacle-covered head rose above the water like a mutant toad. One glossy staring eye blinked, squinting at the sun. A single hoary tooth flashed from its black maw. A tiny island of some nameless archipelago drew near. Mostly rock and some twisted sea firs on its inhospitable shore.

Meira thought of landing on the deck to save her father. When she approached, he screamed at her to get back. "Let it die with my ship," came his hoarse gasp.

The ship began to crumble—the main mast broke in half and the hull splintered as water flooded the deck. The crew were doomed.

Deckhands spilled overboard and three disappeared down the monster's maw. Raithan struggled in the water, a madman fighting for his life. He clung to a wooden crate. Meira landed Typhoon in the water with a splash, reaching an outstretched hand toward her father.

A tentacle looped out and forced Typhoon to dive under it, sending Meira spinning into the water.

She surfaced, gurgling an oath, spewing out brine.

Briad gave a sharp cry and spurred his dragon down in reckless despair. "Faster, Smeald. Faster!" he croaked. The sea monster caught the movement out of the corner of its bulging eye and lanced out a gray tentacle rippling with enormous strength. It curled around the dragon's neck and smashed it into the water. The dragon twisted sideways and Briad was thrown clear. The tentacle pulled the quivering beast into its maw with a bloody crunch. The squid seemed to relish the taste of sea dragon, its eye twitching with excitement at the leathery flesh.

The thing now rose out of the water, towering like an avatar over the last struggling castaways. Panic-stricken, they dog-paddled to the promise of safety on the island's shore in the wake of wreckage and broken bodies. The squid's champing tooth gnawed everything in its path, mouth slobbering, eager to taste every last morsel and fulfil its master's wish.

No beach graced the shore, only bare rock, grey and cold. The fugitives thrashed toward the bluff against the crashing waves. Typhoon scrambled out of the water, took one look at Meira in its path and dove at the rampaging beast.

A cage of pillar-like rock fanned the cliff face like serpent fangs. Just possible to slip past those broken teeth if they swam fast. The fluted rock forms looked to be carved by ages of erosion. Meira pushed through the gap first where she saw caves sheltered in the dimness behind. She stood knee-deep in water, grabbing at Briad who struggled in the backwash.

With a stab of hope, she pulled him in and Raithan somehow managed to claw his bulk up on the rocks. After his mad paddle, he was coughing up water and had a severed whitish-gray piece of tentacle still wrapped around his leg. The grizzled flesh was still moving, squeezing tighter as the suckers cut deeper into his flesh. Raithan kicked at it in wild fury, but Meira drew her knife and hacked at the member, releasing its stranglehold. Raithan crawled forward with heartfelt thanks, his breath heaving in ragged gasps.

Briad gulped lungfuls of air, white-faced with horror. He shook like an old man with a fever, spitting out seawater from his trembling mouth. He pointed at the approaching squid. It would be upon them in moments.

Typhoon bellowed a roar as she surfaced for air, attacked a tentacle and then darted away like a seal. The dragon circled in, harrying the monster beneath the waves and striking at its domed head. The squid released an ear-piercing hiss into the air.

Meira cried, "Stay away! Avoid its beak!" She whimpered in distress, the memory of Briad's tentacle-twined dragon imprinted in her mind. Briad watched aghast as Meira's dragon swam close to the monster's one watery eye, feigning an attack only to spin wide and strike at another tentacle. The dragon clawed and snapped at squid flesh, deaf to Meira's pleas. Buffeted sideways at times, the dragon roared, barely able to stay ahead of the squid's counterattack.

Meira choked with anxiety. The thought that her dragon would end up in the squid's belly terrified her.

Her eyes flicked to the dark inlets that led back to the damp rock. Possible escape routes, she reasoned, but the monster was guarding these with three of its deadly tentacles. Raithan dodged a flicking member and squeezed himself beyond the first protective row of pillars. Gasping, he ran forward and threw a sharp stone at one of the tentacles. Meira realized with horror that Raithan was luring the monster away from them. "Father, no!" she cried, confusion swarming over her features.

"Go! Find a way out the back of this hellhole," he rasped. "I'll lure it away. Run, I say! One death is enough."

Stalactite had joined stalagmite over the years to create a calcified cage which the squid battered its tentacles against. The openings, too small for anything to squeeze through but the tip of the monster's tentacles, afforded a temporary respite.

Raithan's echoes were lost in the steady smash of the waves and the monster's angry hiss. Meira winced and tried to squirm after.

"Go now!" he thundered.

She clambered back, tears in her eyes as she pulled Briad away toward the hidden caves that sank deeper into the grotto's network.

Briad stumbled after Meira in the plum-colored gloom while the sounds of slapping tentacles on wet stone resounded behind. Meira heard grunts of anger and pain echoed in those folds of dimness. They tripped through a cramped back cavern with jumbled stones and dripping moss. Briad gasped as he scraped his knee and staggered on.

We must get to open air above! Meira could sense fresher air and it drove her to speed. Briad winced as his hand slid over wet rock, and he jarred himself with another quick tumble. Stubborn as a crab, he was back on his feet again and scuttled on, every weary bone in his body aching and trembling. The passage narrowed as they moved through a thin wedge of rock. Meira slipped and toppled forward with a grunt, but she paused, squatting on her haunches and wiping her dirty hands.

Not for the first time did she wish she had the power to summon dragons. Where was Darek when she needed him? She must make do with what she had: strength and wits. These passages were too narrow for Typhoon to navigate anyway. She wondered if Raithan still lived. Her heart beat in her throat, imagining the worst that might happen to him.

They scaled some steep natural rock ladders where a patch of light shone above. Meira gasped in triumph. She reached the top and scrambled down the thicket-strewn rock, putting two fingers to her lips to loose a shrill whistle. "Typhoon! Come. Where are you?"

"What if she's dead?" whimpered Briad.

"Don't say that. She'll come, I know it!"

Soon enough, a flapping of wings beat at the air. The exhausted and bloodied dragon landed at her side, talons clacking on the bare rock. Meira inspected her dragon's wounds. Many of the cuts and bruises were superficial, but a gash bled above the dragon's eye and her left ear was torn.

"You beautiful, precious dear," she soothed. "Headstrong and stupid, taking on that beast alone. Quickly, we must move!"

Typhoon gave a mournful snort. She coughed out a wad of sticky phlegm, her red tongue flickering out.

Meira and Briad clambered on her back, Briad swinging in behind, clutching at her waist.

The hill loomed between them and the sea. They had come a long way through the dark. *Now time to double back to the squid and save Raithan—if he's still alive.*

Meira drew a curved spear from her harness; she handed Briad a small tulwar of plain bronze which he gripped fiercely in his fist.

The squid still raged before the grey rock, probing for fresh meat. With little urging, Typhoon arrowed toward the repulsive creature and vented a rumbling roar. Typhoon wove in and out, dodging the tentacles as Meira brought them in closer.

"Stay here!" she commanded Briad. She leaped from Typhoon's back in a downward fall straight at the squid's bullet-shaped head. Landing feet planted wide apart, she plunged her spear deep into the rock-hard flesh, releasing a gush of mucus and milky-white ichor. The creature lurched about, its tentacles knocking the weapon free from her hands and Meira into the water.

"Why won't you just die?" she screamed, thrashing in the water.

"Meira!" Briad cried. He slashed at a tentacle and half torn from the saddle himself. He clung to Typhoon's back like a lamprey, his face white with fear while he swatted out with his blade.

The squid's beak arched toward Meira. Death was there, and waiting for her.

In a sudden inexplicable moment, the squid's body writhed in agony. The monster's head swiveled about. Back toward the cliff face it raged, lashing tentacles at the fang-toothed stone. Raithan managed to loop and loosely knot one of its appendages around the stone cage and was hacking away at it like a madman with a broken sword.

In an insane rush, the massive body crashed against the stones, crumbling the small cave shelter as Raithan disappeared under the rubble.

Briad spurred Typhoon down, plucking a struggling Meira from the water. With a cry of triumph, he returned to the air.

"Meira, he's gone!" he screamed over the roiling water and wind.

The young novice had to hold her back as Typhoon retreated in the direction of the Red Claw Islands.

"No, no!" she wailed. "We must try!"

Briad shivered behind her, his breath fighting the wind. "Typhoon is exhausted. If we go back, the squid'll kill us! We need to get Darek and Jace!"

She bowed her head, mumbling her grief, but knew Briad was right.

Off they flew and Meira stole a glance back over her shoulder where the squid continued to pound against the rock and sinking island. Maybe the creature would bleed out from its wounds? She didn't know. If only Darek were here to blast the monstrosity with his powers! Curse him! Curse her! Why did she insist on making this trek alone? Their only chance was to fetch Darek and return with help. Kraton help Raithan now…

* * *

It was only a matter of time. A lashing tentacle curled around Raithan's waist and pulled him out of his sanctuary beneath the hard pillars. So this is the end, Raithan thought. Cyrus's curse had caught up to him in the form of this demon. At least he had saved Meira. Crushing force laid into his chest as the slimy loops tightened. He closed his eyes, wishing for a quick end.

But the squid's grip suddenly loosened and the tentacle fell into a limp heap. Its rubbery head drooped and its one eye fluttered in a rictus of death. The sea monster gave a great unearthly moan that rocked the stone and what was left of the cliff shore. He looked down to see a jagged pillar of stone embedded deep in the creature's center mass. The squid had impaled itself down to the heart. Its mammoth bulk slid into the water like a dying whale. It twitched once, twice, then wheezed out a throaty gasp and lay still.

Raithan recoiled from the blood and stench drifting all around. Coughing and sputtering, he kicked out his feet and paddled for safety. It took everything he had to stay above the water. He couldn't remain here. Only death and horror lingered. His strength was ebbing fast. A chilling numbness spread up his right arm and his left hip felt wrenched. He lost track of how many aching strokes he plied in the cold water, until at last he spotted a patch of shore glinting off to his left. He struggled toward it and half collapsed in the surf.

Chapter 6.

Dendrok

Cyrus scanned the blue-green waters of the silent inlet. Not a ripple touched the surface. Then Fercifor, his faithful serpent, poked his mottled head above the water at the far end. Returning to his workshop, he took up his instruments and continued dissecting a giant sea salamander. Magical spells required some odd ingredients at times.

Lip curled, he flung the scalpel down in dissatisfaction, unable to concentrate. Could the squid have failed? A day and a half had passed since its mission and still it had not returned. Maybe it had eaten the captain and swam off? Or had it been drawn away by a passing humpback whale? Too many possibilities. The oracle? No, he had consulted it a half-dozen times already. He summoned Valoré while gathering his runestones and staff.

On his journey north toward Ravenstoke, he discovered scattered bits of wreckage and floating bodies in the cresting waves. His breath quickened. No ships. A nagging feeling tugged at his belly. Something was off. No sign of Archituthis. Where in Kraton was the ancient squid? He called out to the creature with his mind. No response. Odd. Was it toying with him? He turned his dragon into the setting sun and followed the trail of wreckage out to sea.

The mage grew more perplexed. Here a floating boot, there a barrel and wooden crate bobbing in the waves. Had the ship been gobbled whole by the giant squid?

He flew like a gale on Valoré, suspicion and annoyance warring with each other. He did not relish mysteries.

The barren island came into view and Cyrus banked toward it with impatience. *What's this?* One of the bodies twitched with life—the traitor Raithan, washed up on a patch of windswept shore. He looked ragged, tattered, a figure moaning and groaning and clawing feebly at the sand like a helpless starfish.

Impossible! Half coiled on the small beach, the other half submerged in sea brine, lay the lifeless husk of Archituthis. The terrifying body sprawled maimed, two of its eight tentacles broken and still oozing white fluid. It had pulled itself along the thin stretch of pebbly beach seeking a place of refuge before the tide had washed it up on shore amongst the rocks and shells. *How had the rogue managed to kill it?*

Cyrus loosed a screaming curse. He hopped off Valoré and stormed over to investigate. Raithan's eyes gazed up at him in surprise and agony as if at an apparition. Cyrus lifted a hand; the mage staff streamed out power.

"You've ruined my plans for the last time, Raithan. A quick death is too good for you." The beam of green mage light levitated the exhausted captain like a slab of whale blubber.

Raithan had barely the energy to resist as his body drifted to the back of Cyrus's dragon. The mage strapped him into the harness with cruel efficiency. The captain would make a good sacrifice for Dendrok when the time came…

The squid was dead, but Cyrus would not allow something as trivial as death to stop him. He placed his staff against the rubbery hide, injecting a blast of energy from its enchanted tip. The corpse trembled. It would take much of his power, but he would not be thwarted. Calling upon the Myxolian Spell of the Undead, he unleashed an invasive jolt of necromantic energy. Like a titanic marionette, the thing jerked upright and shuddered to life. A large eye sprang open, mouth gaping slime. Cyrus withdrew the staff, re-animating the corpse.

"Rise, you broken doll! Your work is not done." Quivering with triumph, he took to the air on Valoré. The broken squid floundered in the water below with an odd squeal, but then managed to follow in unsteady spurts as the grim-lipped mage rode west to Curakee Island.

* * *

Cyrus slapped the dazed Raithan into his fabricated prison: a pyramid of light, twelve feet long at each side, glowing with a sullen amber heat. Grunting and cursing, Raithan struck at the outer film, but Cyrus paid no heed. The captain could thrash to his heart's content. No living person, even that mage boy, could penetrate the enchanted barrier.

He strode from his cavern of a workshop down the dank corridor to examine the newborn dragon. The adjoining grotto with its scattered pools was dim and gloomy. A cool waft tickled his nostrils. The chamber was silent, save for the drips of cold water trickling down the spiked stalactites to lie like large teardrops upon the ancient stone floor below. He heard a quiet splash and walked to the edge of the pooling water. There he found his new dragon wading in the crystal clear water.

Windbiter followed at his heels and gave a wary sniff at this strange new hatchling. The beast seemed resentful at the amount of attention his master afforded it. Dendrok let out a whimpering croak and steam puffed from its nostrils.

"Mind your manners, Windbiter. I haven't forgotten you."

He stroked the young dragon's head. "Dendrok. I see you have grown much in my absence—a curious trait of one born from an Elder egg." His hand tightened around his mage staff and he smiled, wondering if he might cure the creature of its sickness using the same magic he had used on the squid not long ago.

"You will be strong. I will name you my champion in future days fast approaching." His grating echo rumbled with ominous suggestion off the damp stone.

Cyrus's grin faded as a disturbing image came to mind: the mage boy's power at Cape Spear. With the amount of energy he needed to apply to his new dragon, Darek might yet challenge him. Agrippa had trained the boy well. More cunning spells would be required to defeat the fledgling mage.

A daring plan began to brew in Cyrus's mind, which would stretch the limits of the Myxolian spells.

Gathering the old serpent tooth he kept in a cobwebbed corner of his workshop, he flipped through the pages of the *Necromastus*, the dragon-scaled tome he had stolen long ago from the unsuspecting Agrippa. With great relish, he read from the forbidden pages of faded vellum:

Prick the Serpent's Tooth deep,
Doused with the blood that the living shun,
The price of flesh in agony comes...

Cyrus read further. He selected a dark runestone and smeared it in serpent's blood. He mixed dragon's blood with carmegedon, mistrel, argest, and noxious herbs. He beckoned to Windbiter to heat the foul mixture. Smoke rose from the brew that stung his eyes and made his stomach churn.

"Dendrok, you are in for a fine treat," Cyrus croaked with mirth.

He stoked the fire again, and set stone bowls under the stalactites to collect the tears of the dormant volcano. He coaxed the young dragon toward the flames. The creature looked at the fire with an innate curiosity, licking its lips at the warmth radiating from the flickering fire.

"Soon you will taste the flesh of man and become more than just dragon or serpent."

The dragon's jowl parted, showing glinting teeth.

An ancient, forbidden spell that not even Agrippa knew shivered from his lips. Cyrus invoked the magic from the ashes of the dark god Oprisx, whom he had long worshipped while attaining his dark powers:

"*Agris Serpentium Dracium Amun.* FERUS NAUR!" The last words he spat with venomous triumph. The flames rose high and the dragon's breath hissed, his eyes growing wide as never before. Windbiter dropped his head and slid backward away from the sorcery.

The smoke rose to the ceiling and touched the hanging stalactites. The pure liquid running down the shapes changed—corrupted by the smoke. It dripped from the cone-shaped rock and ran into the stone bowls. The splatter sizzled with promise.

He dipped a rag and laced the gleaming serpent tooth's end with the thick, amber liquid, then moved toward the young dragon.

Cyrus recalled the old Xeban scrolls warning against the creation of unholy monsters. They had been feared and worshipped, their dark masters all-powerful until their bloody end. Many said such mages met their doom at the hands of their own creations.

Cyrus gave a harsh bray of laughter. He would prove that theory wrong. He held up the stone vial and fluted a soft whistle between his teeth.

He would rise above such snares designed to catch the feebleminded. Weaklings—too cowardly to explore beyond the basic precepts and master the dark entities they once worshipped.

On soft feet Cyrus approached the unsuspecting dragon, clutching the serpent tooth laced with the foul brew behind his back. Close enough to smell the subtle tang of the creature's scales, he slammed the tooth hard just above the creature's flanks. The tooth struck home, burrowing between the soft scales and lodging underneath the ribs. The dragon recoiled from the pain, but Cyrus whipped out his staff and loosed a dazzling ray. He cauterized the wound, keeping the poison contained to ensure it would enter the bloodstream and merge with the creature's essence.

Dendrok raised its snout and uttered a scream of terror. The young wings flapped at the air, but could not bring it airborne. The creature thrust itself at Cyrus, eyes shining with betrayal, enlarged pupils that traveled backward in its skull, no longer a soft yellow, but pulsing a glaring crimson—wild and dangerous.

Cyrus turned to direct a gloating chuckle at Windbiter who had ducked behind a row of stalagmites, ears flattened on his grey-green head. As he looked back, Cyrus gave a sudden cry of agony. A rustle of movement had preceded a stinging torment as caustic liquid burned his flesh. A gummy wad of the newborn's phlegm hit him on one side of the face, splattering his cheek. The dragon's spit burned like acid. The pain was excruciating and he clawed at the ruined flesh on his face with one hand, shrieking as splotches of poison dug ever deeper into his pores.

Gathering his wits, he wiped his stinging eyes, cloudy with the steam coming from his skin. His nostrils rejected the nauseating reek of his own burning flesh. Even as he called forth the order for protection, Windbiter came lumbering on all fours to shield his master as Dendrok once more attacked. The young dragon's claws came at its master with all-out fury, teeth snapping, while it bit and spat with vicious contempt at the older dragon's hide.

Windbiter fended the mad creature off with a mighty flick of his tail that sent Dendrok tumbling back.

Cyrus stumbled to his work area, cursing as he struggled to apply a healing balm. Not enough to arrest the scarring, but at least to ease the pain. The creature would pay dearly for its insolence. He would punish it with lashes of chain, fire and hot oil until the hatchling bent entirely to his will.

This shrew of a dragon would need a more powerful nursemaid to care for it—some caretaker impervious to its outbursts. Stumbling through the halls, blinking his stinging eyes, he mumbled an incantation, and summoned an elder serpent to the nearby caves.

No longer would he keep Dendrok in his cave. The creature was too dangerous. This transformation would incite it to turn on him again one day, if not sooner. The juvenile would become something new, neither dragon nor serpent and it would dwell in the caves outside the bay with the other serpents. There it could grow and become more ferocious every day as he trained it to become his ultimate weapon.

He returned to the chamber of pools where Windbiter held the fuming dragon at bay. Already, its head had elongated like Fercifor's and its yellow fangs had grown longer like a viper's. Dendrok's legs seemed smaller, like the clawed stubs of a sea serpent. With a grimacing curse, Cyrus cast a spell of binding that would prevent it from swimming too far without excruciating pain. He could not have his prize running from its birthing father and gaining its freedom.

The scum, Raithan, he would move too, in preparation for the man's ultimate fate. With a sweep of his mage staff, he transported prison and traitor out of his cavern to a nearby grotto off the island shore.

The captain would look out from his new cave upon the breaking waves, shivering and gnashing his teeth.

The serpent-dragon that was Dendrok swam in the water below the traitor's glowing prison, staring at him with its blazing crimson eyes, licking from time to time at the magical barrier. The captain, even in his current delirium, would learn that serpents' blood was not meant to be twined with that of other creatures.

The act had surely driven the creature mad. Raithan's shoulders slumped into the depths of despair; he knew his destiny was inescapable, that he would be consumed sooner or later by this hideous reptile.

Chapter 7.

Pacts With the Wolf

Other concerns weighed upon Cyrus's mind, distracting him from the thought of sacrifice. He could not ignore what the dark oracle had revealed; the Black Claws were useless to him now with Raithan turning traitor. His strategy could only succeed if he conspired with a more powerful force, the pirate horde.

United they could stand against many threats. If he could somehow drive a wedge between the different factions, he could seek an alliance with both while pitting them against each other. Such a plan would require skill and stealth.

Cyrus consulted his shark head. He lit a roaring fire in a hearth carved out from a sperm whale's skull and fueled it with the creature's blubber. This wasn't the first time he had placed the shark head into the flames, but it still surprised him that the totem was unharmed by the heat. In no time, the oily puffs of smoke began to coalesce into twisted shapes and glowing figures.

He leaned in as the fire flared behind the grinning head. The cloud billowed up catching him full in his half-scarred face while the fumes made his head giddy. Yellow-green swirls danced at the corners of his vision. Was he truly seeing this, or did the image only form in his mind? *No matter.* A surly figure appeared on the deck of a pirate warship somewhere in the emerald seas. A familiar place appeared, somewhere between Windbit Isle and Seaguard Isle. *Planning their next raid. Perfect.*

The arrogant captain prowled the deck of his ship like a sea lion. A rough, uncouth man whose volatile and simple emotion would be easy enough to manipulate. What better way to tempt the rogue than with riches beyond his dreams and the power to conquer all his enemies?

What's this? On another pirate vessel only a few leagues away, a young woman was forming an alliance of her own with a second pirate ship's captain. Out of nowhere, three Black Claw warships appeared on the horizon, cutting the meeting short. The two ships turned to run and the warships gave chase.

Cyrus wondered if he could turn this escapade to his favor. He could see ambition burning bright in the young woman's heart. With a little help, she would become a pirate queen. But first, she would have to out distance the three Black Claw warships that had caught her scent. The woman's ship was at full sail, but still the black-masted hunters were closing in and Cyrus curled lips in a sneer. She was vulnerable and would be grateful for any aid he provided. A debt that could be leveraged later.

With a pleased grunt, he summoned Valoré and sped off in good spirits, leaving Windbiter to keep watch.

Cyrus's keen eyes narrowed to the south. The light was beginning to fade as the seas calmed. Burnt ochre ripples stretched across the sea of wavelets as the sun continued to sink. Against the orange horizon five dots grew. Valoré's mighty wings brought them in close in a matter of minutes.

Ah, there was the girl. Just as he had witnessed in his vision—a beautiful, raven-haired reaver with three Black Claw ships on her tail.

But here was a new development. The Black Claw vessels were nearly upon her. She had led them on a merry chase—into the undertow of a whirlpool. Clever, but foolish. Now they all struggled to escape its unforgiving grip—and soon would be dead if he didn't intervene.

Cyrus pulled out the runestones from his cloak; he whispered an arcane incantation. Clasping the glowing pebbles in his palm, he felt the stones grow hot to his touch. A strange, cold blustery wind began to blow from the east across the Serpents' Deep. Cyrus grinned in anticipation. From what foul places it came, not even he knew. This was the magic of the dark gods—a boon which he planned never to repay.

The pirate vessel's black sails filled with the wind and a cheer rose from the mates on her decks. At snail speed, she broke from the grip of the whirlpool, leaving the other ships swirling to their doom—into that wide, ringed mouth of death. The Black Claw ships floundered, sucked into the maelstrom and disappeared in a crunch of timbers and many a wail of sailors over the wind and crying gulls.

Cyrus cocked his head and closed his eyes. He rubbed the runestones over his ears, using his mage power to listen in on the conversation on deck.

"Skarlee, I thought you said we were too light to be caught in the whirlpool?"

The quartermaster shrugged. "They move around, Livis. No charts can predict them. Kraton's breath was what saved us—you must be favored by him. The whirlpool did its job no doubt, pulling your enemies down like anchors. Even Captain Serle has never defeated three Black Claw ships at once."

Others of the crew cheered. "Captain Livis, Plague of the Black Claws!"

Farnoss, helmsman and navigator, returned to his work, shaking his mop of shaggy black hair. "The Serpents' Deep is evil, Skarlee, unpredictable as a moray eel."

Skarlee frowned, his hazel eyes thoughtful, rubbing first at his scalp's bare dome then the tufts of greyish-brown hair flanking his ears. "Best be away from these waters—sea serpents, monsters, whirlpools; we should return to the Pirate Isles."

"It's a risk to stay out here, Skarlee." Livis's smile faded. "We must find some safe harbor, but we're not going back."

A dark shadow loomed over the deck. "What in Kraton is that?"

All whirled, weapons gripped in knuckled fists as a red dragon with a black robed rider came bounding down on them. The figure on its back gripped a short mage staff of gray witchwood. "Not Kraton, but I, Cyrus, the Dragon Mage," he thundered. "The one who saved you from that whirlpool." His dragon landed on the deck, the crew reeling back as it snapped and roared.

Livis sucked in a breath. "A mage? But you let the Black Claws die." Her hand gripped the cutlass at her leathered side, frowning in suspicion. "Why would you help us, wizard?"

"A thousand-shell question." Cyrus calmed his dragon to stillness with a hand laid on its neck. "Let's just say I have a vested interest in you. Your father, Captain Serle, has grown very powerful. Some would say to oppose his will means death." He looked at her askance. "So you've finally earned command of your own ship? How does it feel to step out of his shadow?"

Livis barked out a laugh, her eyes widening in contempt. "Many a captain's suffered under my father's lash for too long. I'll forge them into a fleet and offer them all equal shares in a new enterprise. Enough will jump at the chance." With a nod to her left, Maquia the harpooner rotated his weapon on the foredeck in the wizard's direction. "But that is no concern of yours. Best be on your way."

Cyrus's eyes narrowed in amusement. "Why would they believe an unproven corsair such as you—and a woman at that—" he reared back on Valoré with a mocking snarl "—unless you had command of a dragon and the coin needed to build new ships and outfit them for battle?" Four heavy purses filled with gold dropped to the deck.

"What do you ask in return?" growled Skarlee. The man stepped up, waving his cutlass before the dragon. "I don't like this one's smell, Livis, nor the way he keeps his face covered."

All the same, Livis seemed to consider the offer. She'd need a great deal of wealth to entice other captains to join her. She turned a cold but inquisitive glance up at the wizard. "What do you propose?"

Cyrus's grin returned. "An alliance. Consider my offer and keep the gold as a gesture of goodwill."

With a sneering grimace, the mage signaled his dragon and Valoré leapt back into the air. As Livis bent to pick up his coin, Cyrus knew she was his. Now to see about the girl's father.

* * *

The mage watched with curiosity as he neared Serle's schooner. The captain's face creased in a grin as he joined the four other pirate schooners bearing down on the lone Black Claw clipper. Heavily outnumbered, their prey was attempting to escape under full sails.

"Look to starboard! A Black Claw scout!" wheezed the lookout in the crow's-nest.

"Send out a dragon rider!" Serle called.

Cyrus reined his dragon down over the deck and the shouting figures. "Hold!" he cried. "I come in peace."

"There's no peace in our world," bawled a barrel-shaped rogue. He took aim with a harpoon even as he smoothed his beard.

Unperturbed, Cyrus dropped Valoré to hover a dozen feet over the deck. "You'll never catch that clipper. She's too fast—even your dragon riders would fall short."

"She can't escape us," cried Serle. "We'll catch her in time. Now, state your business or we feather you with harpoons."

Cyrus shook his head in annoyance, as if he were talking to a large-mouthed sandfish. The man was bold but stupid. Powerful yes, with muscular upper body, dirty blond beard, and mallet fists with thick short brown fingers, but did he have the guile to do what was required?

"I've a proposition for you," he said.

Serle laughed. "What can you offer me, who has taken more gold, dragons and ships than any other alive?"

Cyrus smiled. "Much, if you'd care to listen." The mage and his dragon landed lightly on the deck.

The pirate frowned, tugged at his beard. "I'm listening. But be quick about it."

Cyrus gave a crisp nod. "Black Claws make tasty morsels. But before you waste your ships on a long chase, why not end it now and look for more profitable quarry?"

The barrel-shaped harpoon master snorted. "Eh? Speak sense, not riddles."

Cyrus inclined his head and stared with curiosity at the man, as if examining a lower specimen. "That ship is fast, but what if she has no wind?"

Hreg licked his finger and stuck it in the air. "Plenty of wind."

Cyrus clicked his tongue in frustration, wondering how simple minds like these sea rogues could even sail a ship. "*Ventus morteum!*" The wizard raised his staff and the sea went instantly calm.

The crew stared in goggly-eyed wonder. "What the—?"

The bosun slapped the harpoon master's back. "Just a coincidence, Hreg," he muttered. "This man's obviously an imposter. Got a bag of parlor tricks larger than Captain Zared's strongbox. Begone! Even without wind, we would still have to fight that ship tooth and nail. Unless there's something else that funny little walking stick of yours can do."

Cyrus shot him a crafty smile. "And what if your harpoons burned with an unquenchable fire on their ends and could fly even this long distance? Like this..." He lowered his staff, runestones clutched in his palm. A blaze of fire shot out and lit the metal tip of the foremost harpoon. The cannon fired on its own, glowing a faint greenish hue.

Hreg jumped back a step, even as the ropeless harpoon flew thrice its normal range to land on the enemy deck, igniting their mainmast. The pirate crew cheered a round of raucous laughter as the enemy crew raced about to douse the flames. Cyrus lit another harpoon, this time motioning Hreg to do the honors. Hreg pulled the lever to fire and watched as the second fiery harpoon crashed into the clipper's sails.

"A clever shot," grunted Serle, "but what do you demand in return?"

Cyrus stared, his yellow teeth glinting. "Consider this a gift, Captain Serle. I'll give you dragons and forge new weapons for you that will guarantee your victories. I merely ask that you make my enemies your own."

Captain Serle's face snarled in suspicion. "What enemies?"

Cyrus dismounted from his dragon, soothing it to stillness. "Surely you have dreamed of raiding the Black Claw and Red Claw islands till they bleed. I will make you the greatest pirate warlord ever, if you swear your allegiance to me!"

"I must reflect on this with my other captains first," muttered Serle.

"Very well, but do not delay too long," Cyrus intoned. "For now, enjoy your spoils. Let us meet at Windbit Isle—say, in three days."

Captain Serle strode over and stabbed his sword into the deck planks before the dragon. "Why not join us in claiming this prize, wizard? I share my spoils and would not have the conspirators who won them leave empty-handed." His mates around him blinked and grumbled.

"Serle, you impulsive fool!" cried the ship's carpenter. "You have no idea what this trickster is about. He could turn us all into blinking toads for all we know."

Captain Serle waved off the drunken carpenter and stared down his other men. "Let me handle this, Yarl."

"You stinking codfish," cried Yarl. "You're a bleeding fool. Been into your cups ever since Livis mutinied and can't think straight."

"Have a care with your words. You're no less into your rum than I." Captain Serle retrieved his sword.

"No! I won't stand idly by while you sell us out to the devil." The carpenter drew his sword and charged the wizard.

Cyrus sat motionless on his dragon. As the pirate approached, he lifted a relaxed hand and a green prism appeared, enclosing the charging man and levitating him in the air. The carpenter cried out, slashing with his sword at the magical barrier. To no effect.

On a word to his dragon, Valoré leapt forward and snatched the man out of the air. The crew watched in stunned silence as rows of serrated teeth devoured the man in snaps and gulps.

"I can make you all rich beyond your wildest dreams," Cyrus said, "but I will tolerate no insolence. Let us turn our efforts to our common enemy." He raised his staff once again and the stranded Black Claw clipper glowed a sickly green. To the crew's astonishment, it began to move—backward. "Does anyone else question my power?"

"Let us kill these wretched Black Claws first," growled Captain Serle.

Hreg laughed. He gave the orders to board the ship that backpedaled in their direction while the crew groused over the death of the ship's carpenter.

The ensorcelled Black Claw ship was within arrow distance now, curses and yells loud on her decks from the astonished crew. Their captain had the fire under control but the gunners couldn't draw their port cannons fast enough, distracted as they were by the flames.

The pirates donned dragon-horned helms and swung across from the rigging as the ship came into range, knocking the defenders back. With cheers and shouts, men clamped grappling hooks down on her gunnels and slid planks across the rails while the rest of them surged aboard the clipper. Two pirate dragon riders swooped in low from the other ships and sprayed the enemy deck with arrows.

The pirates stormed over the gunwales on the makeshift gangplanks, slashing with curved blades, intent on making a quick end of things.

Cyrus watched the battle with a catlike grin.

Captain Serle and Hreg were amongst the fiercest fighters, swinging blades and rallying their men. They parried Black Claw short swords and ran steel through the howling clot of defenders in a frenzied free-for-all.

Many of the Black Claws fell in seconds with steel in their bellies. Blood trailed down their whale hide leathers. The lookout tumbled from the crow's nest, a hurled knife sticking out of his windpipe.

Serle ducked a high swipe and whirled to dodge a pair of knives flying through the air. Chopping under a flashing blade, he sliced open a man's gut from navel to armpit. In his other hand flashed a long knife which he slashed across a knife-wielding man's face. He bulled into his chest with a head-butt and one-handedly took him on his shoulders, swinging him out over the rail to the sharks below.

Hreg whirled and parried a death-giving blade then kicked a man back into the rail. Soon all the Black Claws lay slaughtered or cowed. Bodies of the dead were thrown overboard. The pirates shuttled the survivors, wrists tied at the back, to *The Persephone's* hold to be taken back to Pirates' Cove as slaves to work the mines.

The reavers swaggered in with savage glee to loot the hold. Several hairy-armed invaders pulled up barrels of mead, bales of fabric, and crates of salted fish. They stripped the captain's room bare, taking anything of value: spyglasses, charts, maps, heirlooms, and gold coins. Others took some finely woven rope, halyards, a pair of cleats, and all of the weapons of choice. The ship was still seaworthy, so the marauders assigned a skeleton crew to man it and add to their convoy.

Cyrus watched with lips compressed, analyzing the fighting skill of the men, nodding from time to time at certain brutal displays. A rare sport watching these seamen carry out their business. A good pick, Captain Serle and his band of reavers.

With tempers cooled by spilt blood, the men broke open kegs of rum while Cyrus turned and mounted his dragon. An oral agreement would serve, an alliance to which he would hold them.

With a brief laugh, he vaulted off.

Serle shouted after him. "Have a care, wizard! See that you keep your promises. I'm not a man to cross."

Cyrus tipped his head in a mocking salute. "We meet at Windbit Isle in three days, Captain. From there we plan our first attack and the spoils they will bring—if you are man enough!"

* * *

The pirates on *The Singing Gull* gathered about Livis on the foredeck. "Well, at least, we'll have some plunder to cap off this day," Farnoss muttered. "That merchant ship was easy pickings."

Livis wrinkled her nose and waved a hand at her navigator. "We've lingered long enough, pull the men back from looting."

"But mistress—"

"No buts. You too, Skarlee. Get us out of here. A curse lies on these waters. I can feel it in my bones. We'll take this wizard's gold and be done with it. Let's quit this wretched patch of sea. Only death awaits us here."

"Storm gulls and blood," grumbled the quartermaster "—thrice and tenfold, an ill omen for any sailor, no matter how you look at it."

Chapter 8.

VALKYRIE ISLAND

Darek awoke in a cold sweat, with dawn's dim glower creeping over his private room in the Rookery barracks. The grumbling of the other trainees had set him off, after trying to explain to them that he expected to be treated like one of the regular recruits. He'd vowed to pass the same tests they had and earn their respect. It seemed that being a Dragon Mage meant he would always be set apart.

Now he stretched his arms, breathing in thankful relief for the added privacy. His sleep of late had been plagued by nightmares. Every night the same dream: After clearing out the last of the sea serpents from Serpents' Deep, he rode back with Silver Eye along the arching shadow of the sacred volcano Kraton, only to feel the tug of sinister magic pulling him down into the Devil's whirlpool. The churning water swallowed him whole, separating him from his dragon and dashing him against the rocks. Try as he might, he could not surface and the current pulled him down deeper. As his last breath expired, he saw Cyrus's ugly face. His mouth swirled like the whirlpool, gaping wide to swallow him whole.

He jerked upright in his pallet, wiping the sweat from his brow and shaking off the chilling memory. Cyrus was dead. What did the dream mean?

"What is it?" mumbled Bree, rousing beside him with a yawn.

His lips brushed hers in a slow kiss. *There were advantages to having a private room.*

"Nothing." Darek shrugged. "I just need some air." He threw on some clothes and staggered out to the practice yard where a fine mist spread over the grass. The breeze was just starting to blow off the ocean and the morning sunlight streamed down, erasing the lingering darkness of the dream. The grey fog burned off as he approached the dragon pens. The younger dragons had already left for their morning feeding, while the older ones continued to doze.

Silver Eye loitered by the pens, looking as hungry as ever. Her dominance over the other dragons and her fighting ability had surprised many of the other riders. She'd established her position among the others in short order. Jace had commented several times on the rarity of a dragon with four wings, but other qualities had marked her as special. She'd continued to grow at a rate faster than normal, her impressive wingspan for one, and now she stood eye to eye with the much-older adults. Her claws and horns had hardened and darkened, making her a menacing sight indeed.

"Never seen anything like it," Jace mused after a full examination one day.

With Darek approaching, he received a loving brush of her large head against his chest.

"Morning, girl," he croaked. Then he grinned. "We're going off on a journey today, aren't we?"

The dragon dipped her head, blinking the one good eye. The injury she had taken while saving his life in the crater of the active volcano Kraton during the Rebirth Ritual—it had never fully healed. Protective scaly skin now covered the wound, though clear fluid still sometimes leaked from the eye. A low croak rumbled from the depths of her throat as she looked with concern in the direction of Typhoon's stall. Darek's grin faded.

Three days ago, before his nineteenth birthday, Meira had returned from Ravenstoke harbor. She and Briad had clung to the back of the wounded, half spent dragon. In shambles and trembling in shock, Meira had garbled out a story about a monster squid.

Darek, flying with speed north with Jace and four other riders, had embarked on a frantic search for her father. By the time they arrived, only wreckage and white blood littered the shore. Raithan and the mysterious creature had vanished from the barren island. They could only assume

Raithan had perished on that nameless rock off the coast of Rivenclaw. Upon their return, Meira had been devastated.

Darek shivered, trying to imagine such a grisly death at the hands of the monster she had spoken of so animatedly. Retreating into solitude to mourn, Meira was of no use to anybody. Not that he could blame her. He was sorry for her loss, but he couldn't quite bring himself to grieve Raithan's death—too much had gone unsaid between them.

Bree sidled up to him, dressed in a light-blue robe and her hair tied back with a coral-green cord. "I said I would go with you to Agrippa's island, and the offer still stands."

Darek turned and flashed her a wan smile of gratitude. "Let's go then, Bree. Doing something would take my mind off things and no one will notice if we sneak out now."

She nodded. "What exactly are we looking for?"

"Spells and magic items that can assist us, and instructions on how to make new dragon amulets—hopefully Agrippa bothered to write the formula down. Go and get ready. I'll join you shortly."

Silver Eye flew down to the feeding yard to fill her belly with fish while Darek trudged up the nearby knoll known as *Dragon Watch* and peered over the Rookery wall. Far below, the inhabitants of Cape Spear were just starting to stir by the seaside.

Workers lay hammer and chisel to the gray limestone taken from the hill quarry to rebuild the town hall. They'd already completed the clock tower and a great many put grit and sweat into the older buildings centered around the town square. In a few more months all sign of the destruction Cyrus's serpents had wreaked would vanish.

Would the memories fade as well? Darek did not know. All were still too fresh in his mind. He turned away from the sight with a sigh.

Bree returned from rounding up her gear. Together they made their way back to the pens and worked on loading up Storm, her new dragon, for the flight. Able to fly for hours at full speed without rest, Storm bit at her harness, a feisty blue-gray beast of pure stock, known for her strength and fidelity.

"Did you have to pack so much?" Darek shot the bags a wry glance. Packed within were tent, blankets, assorted fruits, bread fresh from the ovens, dried beef strips, and a cask of wine.

"Better to be prepared," Bree said with a smile. "We don't know the state of Agrippa's larder—one of his dragons might have broken in and eaten everything."

A lone screech echoed down from the branches of an old dogwood tree creaking in the wind to the side of the pens. Seavenger, Agrippa's sea eagle, spread his wings and soared over to land before Darek's feet. Darek held out his hand to stroke the eagle's head. Bree laughed and fed the bird a scrap of meat.

The bird had fully recovered from his injuries and could often be seen flying high above the Rookery. The town medicus had done his work well. Now the eagle seemed to sense they would be returning to his old hunting ground and Darek blinked as the long, black talons gripped the earth, and one reached up to scratch its ear.

"Faithful friend," said Darek, stroking the fuzzy grey-brown feathers along the sleek wing. "It's good to see you strong again. We could use a scout. Want to come?" Darek cocked his head in mimicry of the bird's sharp head movements.

Seavenger focused an intelligent eye on Darek, then spread his wings in agreement.

Silver Eye returned with a full belly, squirming, fixing him with a sulking stare as Darek fitted her with a new, larger harness. Then they set off north over the interior of Swordfish Island. Dense hilly forests of the great sea firs carpeted the inland route. Bree pointed down to green meadows of spring flowers in full bloom. They passed the glades marking the few isolated hamlets of the Red Claw clans and their small houses of murlstone and gumwood. Cool, clear waters of sparkling lakes shimmered in the morning sun.

In happy spirits once again, Silver Eye raised her long snout to the clouds and rumbled with a hint of excitement at having free rein over new territory. Leading the way, she soared under the clouds while Bree and Storm flew close at her side. Darek paused to admire the sight of the wind in Bree's wavy hair, blowing the dark strands back like a rippling mane. Seavenger circled above them, patrolling in wide arcs and screeching in pleasure at the return to his domain.

"Catch me, if you can!" Darek yelled. He spurred Silver Eye on to new speed. Bree, never one to pass up a challenge, vaulted after, with a flick of her fingers in the dragon rider hand signals that meant *Watch out for my dragon's tail.*

Darek let her outpace them for a moment to better admire her fine figure. Bree was as beautiful and fierce as the day they had first met on Manatee Island. He smiled, remembering the fool he had been trying to rush to her aid in what had merely been a training exercise.

As he later discovered, Bree needed no one to save her. They had grown much closer since they first danced at the Dragon Day celebration. *So were they a casual or formal couple?* Darek frowned. He vowed to speak to her about it after they returned.

The north coastline appeared, jigsawed with rocky coves and stray islands. The vast Dragon Sea spread to the north like a blue mantle, as vibrant and expansive as the noonday sky. In the distance he could just make out the hint of islands toward the horizon.

They flew for a time longer, eventually approaching a stark island ringed in volcanic rock. The low cliffs, lined with the porous-gray stone, loomed in mystery, with a small patch of pale beach in the center. Stands of tall sea firs stuck out on their top like parakeet plumes. The twin towers of

Agrippa's stronghold forked up toward the sky. *Valkyrie Island.*

Seavenger cried out a sudden warning. A dark shape swooped upon them, massive wings beating at the air. A hulking, charcoal-grey dragon lurched forward to greet them. A female, by the look of her shrunken face with high peaked ears But her greeting was less than cordial. The creature reared back, talons splayed and a snarl on her lips.

Silver Eye launched forward, baring her teeth. Darek recognized the other dragon—Winguard, Agrippa's loyal protector of his island realm. The dragon roared a challenge.

We are friends. Darek sent the command in silent authority, along with other soothing thoughts. *Peace. Calm down.* The dragon relaxed and yielded to Silver Eye's dominance. But Darek still tensed in disbelief. He had not expected such unruly behavior from dragons that had once fought at his side.

Another roar sounded from below as a firebreather took to the air. The dragon shot straight up at them, in no less disobedient mood. Storm veered sideways in alarm.

"Broodhorn, stay back!" Darek cried. "What's gotten into you two?"

Yet he knew the answer. With the death of Agrippa, the control over the dragons had waned and chaos now infected the link between human and dragon. Too long had he stayed away. Darek gave a silent curse. He must not let this happen again. Shaking his head, he spurred in to bunt the rebellious Broodhorn aside.

After some gentle coaxing, Broodhorn retracted his claws, perhaps recognizing Agrippa's faithful eagle. The two circled each other for a dubious moment taking playful nips at each other's wings. Darek breathed a sigh of relief.

They landed near the brow of a juniper covered hill, not far from where Agrippa kept his stronghold amidst the old ruins of Valkyrie.

Bree vaulted off to stretch her stiff legs. "Where are the rest of the dragons?"

The same question had burned in Darek's mind. "Probably down sunning themselves on the beach." He dismounted, unharnessing Silver Eye, then sent her and the other dragons fishing.

Bree peered around the shrub vegetation. Her eyes followed Darek's gaze to the tangle of rocks and meandering goat paths that comprised Valkyrie. "This place seems deserted."

Darek loosed a breath. "Valkryie has always been a lonely place. It's an island as old as the seas themselves. Agrippa said the first magic of the clans was practiced here, by the ancient *Diori*. This island they called 'Vyre', the place of summoning."

Bree gave a visible shiver. "It does have the feel of ancient magic lingering about."

The top of the old black stone ruins poked over the brow of the hill. "Come on, let's go inside."

Darek gestured for her to follow him.

She grabbed his hand and cooed with excitement. "Let's spend the night in the tower! You're the Dragon Mage now, right?"

Darek winced. *Wait till she gets a look at Agrippa's gloomy abode.*

Clearing his throat, he paused. "Hold up a moment." On a hunch, he swung down the seaside path to the dragon caves. "Let's go see to Agrippa's dragons first. Many of the older dragons I left on the island after the battle of Cape Spear."

"Oh, alright." Her eyes shone as she followed.

"Agrippa never let anyone into his dragon grottos. They're my responsibility now."

The trail, nothing more than a goat path, wandered between a few small trees as they approached the seaside. The aromatic scent of pine and fir filled the air; Bree bent to smell the many small blue flowers. Cool air drifted from the seaside caves where the pounding sound of surf echoed from the entrance.

Three dragons lounged on the sand before the dark opening, poking up their heads at their approach.

"So few dragons," grunted Bree with a frown. "I expected more. I count only eight."

"At least half gave their lives defending the harbor," Darek said in a gloomy voice. Their bones still lay at the bottom of Cape Spear harbor.

"I suspect the others have flown off, now that Agrippa is—" He didn't finish that sentence.

A huge black dragon came hurtling out of the nearest cave.

Whalethorn.

Darek and Bree froze.

"Down!" he commanded, but the dragon continued to rush them. Bree shrieked as he pulled her out of the reach of the arching claws.

Be still. We're friends!

The dragon roared, defiant of the command. The creature clawed at the ground, kicking up clumps of sand and pebbles, as though defending his territory. It drove forward, extending front claws to attack again.

Darek summoned Silver Eye with a shrill mental command. *Danger! We need help!* He stood tall on his toes and raised his arms in a defensive V pattern, fingers curled together as Agrippa had instructed him. He closed his eyes, visualizing a larger teardrop of power. The space between his arms glowed blue and orange. As the dragon circled to strike, he deflected the blow with a protective prism and launched a jet of fire into the air. The dragon shrank back, venting a growl of surprise at the pulsing power.

Whalethorn came blinking back to his senses. He curled up in a heap, wings folded back as he uttered a submissive howl. Silver Eye landed but ten feet away with Storm at her side. Their wings kicked up sand in a swirling vortex. Silver Eye, rearing up, bared her front claws and fangs in a display of power. Her four wings flapped in unison as she hovered in the air, daring any to challenge her. The disobedient dragon only retreated deeper into the cave.

Darek hurried forward, arms raised should he need to disable the black dragon. Bree scrambled to his side, brandishing her sword, regarding Darek with new awe. Silver Eye and Storm advanced on Whalethorn, cornering him between the shrubs and the cave and cutting off any escape.

Puzzled and dismayed, Darek approached on wary feet. "What's gotten into you?" His heart panged, seeing the fear in the black dragon's eyes. "I'm sorry, old fellow. You don't remember me, do you? We fought together at Cape Spear."

The dragon wheezed out a plaintive howl and drooped its ears. Silver Eye loped forward to encircle the dragon's neck with her teeth and Whalethorn allowed it, displaying his underbelly in submission.

"What a mess," Darek sighed, shaking his head. "It's okay, Silver Eye. You can release him." A streak of pride flamed in him, knowing his dragon would fight to the death for him. As would he for her. *Let's hope it never comes to that.*

Bree took a cautious step forward. "What's wrong with Agrippa's dragons, Darek?"

"They've turned feral, Bree, away from humans so long with no amulets to control them. The ones at the Rookery—well, they've shown similar signs as well."

Bree's eyes widened. "Maybe we should go back."

"No, I need to find out how to create new dragon amulets. Otherwise we'll lose control of the dragons forever. Don't worry. Jace can keep them in check. Look, there's Meshoar and Wildfire." He gestured a hand to the purple patched dragon who pawed at the sand. "Wildfire looks like a savage brute with her scarred face and missing fang, but she's really a lamb when you get to know her."

"I bet." Bree frowned. She moved closer to Storm, less trusting after Whalethorn's attack. The two dragons only gathered around them in welcome, grunting and snorting.

"Good to know they haven't all gone wild. The last faithful wards of Valkyrie," he murmured. "I'm sorry for my neglect. I'll take better care next time."

The dragons flattened their ears in acknowledgment.

"I know it may sound selfish, but I'll summon you if the time comes—to fight. I'm sorry to have to drag you into these wasteful wars. Your old master would have wanted you to stay faithful to me. I pledge to look after you, as Agrippa would have done, if you'll have me."

The bond between them strengthened and Darek straightened. His power of communication grew stronger, for the dragons' jaws parted in slow recognition. Meshoar and Wildfire sniffed at Bree then shambled over to get a whiff of Storm's and Silver Eye's hides. Many scars still showed on their flanks from the wounds taken at Cape Spear.

In a final token of recognition, the dragons lumbered forward to inhale Darek's scent, their long red tongues flicking out and tickling his cheeks. Their thoughts reverberated clear as a bell in his mind.

Darek touched each of them on their iridescent heads. "Thank you for your loyalty, friends. I'll need it now more than ever."

Chapter 9.

SOLARICUS

Darek and Bree's dragons soared along the seaside path, following Seavenger's lead from high overhead. Passing the brow of a hill, the shallow valley spread out before them like an enchanted rock garden. Landing at the foot of a broken murlstone wall, they dismounted and gazed at the weathered gate thrust open and guarded by winged iron gargoyles on either side.

They entered the courtyard and moved like puppet figures beyond a cluster of blue-gray slabs now overrun with weeds. At the center rose a rickety windmill, one of Agrippa's now-abandoned innovations. Bree's eyes rounded at its enormity and its unusual, grasshopper-like shape. Ahead, the old ruins towered high with stone arches, broken columns, and weathered bricks withstanding the ravages of time.

An air of solemn grandeur permeated the place. An old rounded keep stood at the fringe of an ancient castle. The overgrown court showed a gallery of broken statues and stones large enough to overwhelm the eye. Darek remembered the last time he and Meira had sparred amongst these thistles and fallen masonry. Everything seemed empty now without the presence of the old man…all too quiet without the wizard's deep rumbling laugh to echo off the cliffs. Darek could almost hear the sound of Agrippa's walking stick clacking on the stones, followed by one of his wintery barbs.

"That's Agrippa's tower there," Darek called in a hoarse voice. The rounded tiers rose one on top of each other. Twin turrets forked up to the sky, one shorter than the other, as if hammered by ballistae or ancient weapons.

"Let's go settle in," said Bree.

"I wouldn't feel right sleeping in Agrippa's chambers, and the other tower has too many rats' nests," Darek murmured. "I suggest we sleep on the beach down by the dragon caves. It's more comfortable down there."

Bree couldn't hide her look of disappointment.

"Well, let's search his laboratory. It used to be his secret hideaway." She brightened at that. Darek motioned to a shoulder-high mound of earth and stones. A wide and heavy gumwood door embedded in its side led underground.

He gripped the iron ring and gave it a sharp tug. The door creaked open with a rush of stale air. "This is where Agrippa spent most of his time."

"Is it booby-trapped?" Bree asked with awe.

"Don't worry." Focusing his power, he ignited a limb of deadwood and held it up with a grin. "Agrippa keyed all of the island's defenses to my presence. I'll light the sconces below. Come on, we've nothing to fear."

He stepped down the crooked stone steps, lighting the cressets along the wall as they descended. Bree followed with mincing steps, snatching a glance or two back at the dragons who looked on with curious wonder.

At the bottom of the landing, the passage turned ninety degrees. They walked thirty feet down a passage and stood in a wide hall. Once well-maintained, it had grown thick with dust. "Agrippa's laboratory," Darek declared. He spoke a word and the torches on the colonnaded wall lit up, transforming the room from its eerie gloom.

"What a creepy place to work," Bree grumbled.

Darek forced back a grimace. "Agrippa was a secretive sort. He never threw anything away. Let's start by looking for things of value."

Lurking to the side loomed a huge engine, a device made of metal and wood with pulleys and crystals to generate power. The wizard had tried to explain to him how the strange machine worked, but it still remained a mystery.

"That was Agrippa's final invention. A generator of *Eel Light*, he called it. Taps the wind power above from the windmill to make light. One day it'll replace oil lamps and torches—or so the old man said."

Bree grunted, clearly doubtful of such a scheme. "I suppose this is all yours now?"

"It seems so," Darek murmured.

"Lucky you." She stared at the cobwebs and the fervid skitter of rodents in the shadowy corners had her shivering.

Darek turned to consider the assortment of wands and tools hanging from nails on the wall. Heaps of magic curios and scrolls littered the tables. All had now passed to him according to final instructions left with the Clutch Council. Darek felt a thrill at the privilege but overwhelmed with the responsibility.

"Help me explore this place," he said. "We need to gather as many amulets as we can. Also, find the instructions for forging new ones, and anything else that might be of use. He made a sweeping gesture of hand. "Better than having all this just sit around collecting dust."

She nodded. Taking slow steps, Bree poked around, but winced, afraid to touch anything. She nosed about like a cautious rodent.

Darek scouted the perimeter of the chamber, feeling pangs of old memories prick his heart while Bree inspected talismans on the low tables and workbenches. She studied them with an inquisitive eye. "He must have been a genius," she said, "a man ahead of his time."

"There'll never be another like him," Darek mumbled. Tapping at the wall near the floor, he began searching with increased fervor for trap doors and secret entrances to a lower level. Having no luck, he rummaged through dusty crates of supplies where all manner of gadgets, tools and raw materials were stored, many of which he could make no sense.

Bree gasped in excitement. "Darek, come look at this."

She pointed to a lower section of the wall that seemed discolored and more uneven than the surrounding area, as if cut out and put in as an afterthought. Darek frowned, kicked it and it gave way.

As he pushed the false section inward, a small rat ran out. Plugging his nose against the stink of rat droppings, he crawled through.

It was a secret chamber all right: an extension of Agrippa's underground laboratory. Mumbling with awe, he stumbled forward in the dark and lit a torch on the wall. The chamber opened up into a rounded alcove. Bookshelves cut into the walls contained dozens of volumes. Tacked to one of them a handwritten letter read:

"Darek, I knew you would one day discover this room upon my death.

If you are reading this, accept these as my parting gift to you. My most precious books, the sum of all my knowledge. I leave them to you. Guard them well, for they are more valuable than all the gold in the world.

Take these treasures and use them for the greater good. Some of the wisdom in the more complicated texts may escape you for now, but you'll learn it in time. Most important are the instructions to create new runestones and the dragon amulets. My magic will fade in time and with it the control of the dragons. You'll find a list of materials and my handwritten notes on how to create your own.

I'm sorry we did not have more time together. Kraton knows I would have enjoyed teaching you everything that I know! There's enough reading material here to keep you busy for a lifetime. I know you'll figure them out, and if you don't, well to Kraton with you!

Take good care of my solaricus. Each of the three weapons of power may help you against the most powerful of enemies.

A final note, beware of the dark arts. Such magic corrupts even the purest of hearts. I have sealed those volumes in wax for a time when you are ready to resist their temptation. Do not break those seals lightly.

Keep longtime foes within arm's reach. Even dead ones have a knack of turning up at the worst of times, through rain, storm and fire. They live on in our hearts and minds. So it has always been.

That is all. Time is running short. Remember what I have taught you and look after my Islanders. They, along with the Council, are like errant children who'll need your guidance.

For now, farewell, my trusted apprentice.

Agrippa, Sea Dragon Mage of the First Order, Protector of the Dragonclaw Islands

Darek's face creased in sorrow and a wracking sob came from his throat. He forced himself to focus on the task at hand.

Bree appeared at his side. "I'm sorry, Darek. I know he meant a lot to you."

"It's just like Agrippa," he said, "to teach me just enough to get myself in trouble and then disappear." He blinked back tears. "What if I can't do it?" Even as he said this, one of Agrippa's lessons came back to him, which he mumbled aloud, as if in a trance:

"When the sea fir was still alive, it was like a willow, surviving for centuries by bending but not breaking. So must a dragon rider meld with his mount, as free as the wind, as *liquid as a waterfall, yet ready to spring back in times of danger...*"

He forced a smile, recalling the wisdom in the words of his master and the crooked grin on the lips that delivered them. Better to remember that valiant mage this way, with his sage advice and inventive spirit, rather than those last tragic moments at sea.

Bree laid a hand on his shoulder. "We all owe him our thanks for what he did."

"I remember him telling me once when I was out training with Meira, *'Don't ride your dragon like a horse! You're too busy fighting like a man—you need to fight like a dragon.'* He laughed. "I didn't even know what he meant at the time."

He shrugged it off. "I sure won't miss his harsh training with the staff, or the bruises. Enough reminiscing. There's work to be done."

"Memories like these keep him with us," Bree said. She gave him a hug.

Darek held her for a long moment, then he gave an absent nod. Passing eyes over the dragon amulet scroll, he grew more absorbed with every word. He didn't realize Bree had left. The merest touch of the parchment transported him back in time, as if Agrippa were here with him. He imagined himself with gray hair, a hundred years old, trying to pass down teachings to a young hooligan like himself. The thought made him laugh—but not for long.

He glanced about. On the wall, under the flickering glow, he discerned what resembled an *astrologia* with vaguely familiar zodiacal symbols. The device sported a giant clock face immersed in a water-filled glass case where small multicolored fish swam as in an aquarium. Had the fish fed off algae? Fed off each other? Arcane symbols were inscribed along all points of the compass. Agrippa must have been able to track the paths of the stars and planets and divine future events.

On a table caked with dust, he noted various polished bones and glass tubes. Here lay the bones of dragons, bleached and sharpened. Several colored flasks, alembics, and vials surrounded a gleaming white dragon skull tilted on its side. Sharp teeth and polished claws, glistening beads, runestones, crystals, wands... all the trappings of thaumaturgical mystery made the eye dizzy with wonder.

To the side loomed a pair of dragon wings, real from what he could see, attached to what resembled a complex engine with wheels. The device seemed to be powered by dragon eggshells. A half-finished flying machine?—Kraton, but the old man had an imagination! A chill fluttered up Darek's spine. Things here had an eerie, almost surreal cast, as if Agrippa had an alter ego, unlike the Agrippa he knew. Then again, Agrippa had been the one to teach Cyrus, though the old mage spoke little of that.

Darek wondered if the only difference between Agrippa and Cyrus was that his master knew when to stop, whereas Cyrus had sought power above all with no conscience. It seemed a thin line to walk between good and evil. He could see where Cyrus had been tempted and he must be wary not to fall into the same trap.

He saw some dried flakes in a covered bowl on the table and dropped a handful through the stoppered top of the *astrologia's* aquarium, figuring the fish would appreciate it. They did, and devoured the sustenance, darting about, casting him grey-eyed stares.

A small dog-eared book with a leather-bound cover caught his eye and he flipped through the pages. The title read *Nemestomis*. His finger rested on a section detailing communing with the mind called, 'Telepathy and Dream Magic'. It was a subject his master had mentioned. He could communicate with his dragons easily enough, but not with people. Agrippa had been the only one able to converse with him by mental link. The dreams he suffered were getting worse, as if an evil presence invaded his mental space. Could someone be using dream magic against him? He needed to protect himself, but his skills in that area were sadly lacking. It was too much to master in a short time. He'd have to save the Telepathy section for later.

He sat down to read ahead, his face lighting up with relief to see a section devoted to runestones. A set of ruby runes glittered on the table beside him and two dragon amulets hung on the wall from a stout cord. He could make use of those. For the little he knew of amulets, they could as well have been rocks from an alien planet. He knew he had to master the skill and learn to forge new ones to control the dragons.

For nearly an hour Darek struggled with the complicated art of runestone transmutation. *Perhaps if he learned some lesser spells first?* He recited several stanzas from Agrippa's old phrasebooks while trying to understand all the nuances of the higher teachings. With sweat breaking on his brow, he bungled his way through old dialects and tongues of the mages in a time before cannons and harpoons existed and when dragons ruled the sky.

His vision began to blur. The strain taxed his brain and he realized there were too many things to absorb in one day. With care, he selected several of the books and wrapped them in sharkskin leather along with the runestones and the dragon amulets. Their secrets would reveal themselves in due time.

Darek's mind drifted back to the stanza, *"Keep longtime foes within arm's reach. Even dead ones have a knack of turning up at the worst of times, through rain, storm and fire...."* Why would Agrippa write that?

He pondered the phrase, wondering anew about the mysterious figure who had assaulted him in the public square. He sat down and meditated on what he had sensed that day. The presence was so familiar—could it be...Cyrus?

He shook off the chilling thought. With his own eyes he had seen the mage consumed by the whirling tower of water. But if the knave had somehow survived—all of Dragon Sea was in terrible danger.

He must make sense of these inventions as soon as possible!—master what spells he could, and take whatever steps necessary to ensure the safety of the Dragonclaw Islands.

A sudden voice called from the gloom. Darek nearly jumped out of his skin. Bree had snuck back down the stairs.

"Don't do that," he hissed.

"Any luck?"

"Made sense of some of this lore. But there's more than a lifetime worth of reading here."

Bree gave a sardonic smile. "Should I start planting a garden then?"

Darek shook his head and laughed. "I might have a few sleepless nights ahead of me, Bree, but I'll uncover what we need to fix all this."

She clicked her tongue. Rubbing her arms to ward off the chill, she shivered. "It's cold as a crypt down here."

Darek looked around, realizing at last what was missing. "The forge is cold." He added fuel to the boiler and squinted in the shadows. His eyes discerned a tiny pipe leading to a burner. He lit it with pieces of tinder, hoping for a flame. His fingers found the pressure valve and gave it a firm twist. The boiler roared to life; with it blossomed a small flame. "It'll take hours to reach full strength—unless..."

He nodded at Bree. He pointed to three waist-high contraptions, squarish in shape. "Agrippa used this solaricus device to help it along. With a spell, of course." A reflective shield of polished silver ran down one side. *Was it silver?* It seemed harder and heavier. The main bulk consisted of a box with tubes and liquids within the tubes. A short black rod stuck out opposite the shield, some kind of firing mechanism and here Darek tugged at his stubbled chin.

"From what I remember, the shield absorbs sunlight and projects a beam from this metal rod. The crafty mage used it like a kind of magnifying glass to heat the forge."

Bree gave a doubtful grunt.

Turning back to the mysterious spell book, Darek held up a page to the flickering light and started to chant some of the arcane phrases. A foul smoke drifted from the nearby candelabra. *That's odd.* He paused and frowned. "Somehow I don't think that's what Agrippa had in mind with this spell." He repeated the last syllable.

Bree wrinkled her nose, waving the brown smoke from her face. "You must have misread. Try again."

As he did, a humming sound grew from the ceiling. His eyes trained upward to the damp, dark stone. *What in Kraton...?* He repeated the words with more energy. *"Annos Furor Marcheat Dracos. Akron, Vekron, Lumis Summaré!"* The torchlight wavered and hissed. A sudden raw spurt of luminosity burst from the nearby *astrologia*—light in the form of a serpent's head—ricocheting off the wall and igniting the forge in an explosion of flame.

Bree cried out, her hands shielding her eyes.

The blast had nearly taken off his head, but he had ducked just in time. "Kraton!" he cursed, feeling his hair singed. An acrid smoke curled in the air. *Why had the spell taken the form of a serpent's head?*

"Are you sure you know what you're doing?" Bree quavered. "Maybe we should take a break."

Darek paled and drew in a sharp breath. She was right. He could have killed himself—or Bree. No wonder Agrippa kept his magic guarded.

He mumbled under his breath, "Help me haul this piece up with us, so we can study it better in the light."

They struggled to roll and half drag the magical device out to the landing. She peered at it with a distrustful eye, as if expecting it to shoot flame as they hauled it up the stairs. At the top, Darek summoned one of the younger dragons to help drag it the rest of the way.

Silver Eye and Winguard reveled in chasing each other around the ruined courtyard, nipping at each other's tails while Seavenger circled in low arcs, admiring the sport. Storm watched from a distance through cautious eyes, not knowing what to make of the other dragons.

Darek turned his attention to the solaricus. In the daylight, the metal gleamed a sullen silver. The shield, if that's what it was, glowed purple around the edges, its arc about two feet in diameter. Exposed to the sunlight, the liquids within the tube bubbled in the device's core and it vibrated with an odd humming sound when he touched it. Darek stood puzzled. Bree drew back, mistrustful of magic items like this.

Darek waved a hand. "Let's find out how this works." He fiddled with the knobs on the side, at last pressing a small, shell-shaped button that seemed important. A greenish-red ray zapped out from the black rod in the center, burning a sizzling hole in an ancient column forty feet away. Seavenger flew higher and Silver Eye lurched back in surprise.

"Whoa, this thing is deadly," Bree yelped.

"But useful," Darek mused.

Bree narrowed her eyes, hands on her hips. "You could have struck one of the dragons. Ever think of that?"

"Sorry," Darek murmured. "If we mounted these on dragons' backs, riders could use them as weapons."

"Or get themselves killed."

Darek's lips pinched in a wry grimace. "Let me see if there are any more down there."

Bree gave a soft sigh. "Call me when you're done playing with your toys. Silver Eye and Storm can round us up some good shoal fish. I've got enough gear on Storm for us to fry them up."

"Good idea." Darek jogged back down the stairs and continued searching through the many mysterious wonders below. He leafed through a dozen books, litanies of ancient spells and a seemingly endless supply of strange devices that tickled his imagination, yet of whose use he still had no inkling.

So engrossed was he that he completely forgot about dinner. He gave a silent curse. Bree would not be happy. He rubbed his eyes, yawning, having made no more progress than he had hours ago.

Darek stumbled out in the open air, too exhausted to absorb any more cryptic spells. A myriad of stars wheeled overhead. A cool sea breeze brushed his skin, forming goosebumps on his bare arms. He held the torch before him and made his way down to the beach, breathing deeply of the pungent smells of juniper and sea lilac. Bree lay curled deep in sleep wrapped in a blanket with Storm by her side.

A half-eaten codfish sat hardened in a skillet above the coals of a smoldering fire. Darek ripped off a small piece and munched on it, lost in thought. At last, he lay down beside her, glad of her warmth. She made small cooing sounds when he pressed his body next to hers and held her tight. Worming her way against him, she snuggled into his warmth. "Took you long enough."

"Thanks for waiting up, Bree."

"As long as you're done for the night," she murmured with a yawn.

Yet she discovered him gone and the pallet empty as dawn's light curled over the sea, the pull of Agrippa's knowledge greater than the promise of breakfast.

* * *

Bree returned to the workshop after the sun had warmed her bones, detesting the journey back down that gloomy passage, only to find Darek nursing a burnt finger and berating one of the smaller solaricus devices smashed on the ground. His red-rimmed eyes fought exhaustion.

She wrinkled her nose at the stench of magic-laced burn marks on the table. "Trying to make a volcano?"

Darek winced at the reference but he couldn't help but chuckle. "All power is fraught with risk, Bree, so Agrippa told me more than once."

She sniffed and laid the rest of last night's fish on the table. "Thought you'd be hungry. Hope you like it cold."

"Thanks." He munched on it as he worked.

"Maybe I should give it a try?" she said with a sarcastic smirk.

"Might as well." He shrugged, picking up a nine-armed sea star. "This starfish is supposed to be some kind of talisman to ward off magic. Perfect for riders to wear around their necks if they ever have to face a mage like Cyrus again.

"According to the *Nemestomis,* it also protects against illness. It's supposed to glow orange, but the invocation doesn't seem to be working. No whistling sound like it says in the book—" he trailed off, holding the crusty shape to his ear. "And this—" He pointed to the smashed shards on the cold stone floor "—is not working either."

She watched him for some time trying his hand at the spell.

"You've a good heart, Darek, yet I just hope your curiosity doesn't get you killed."

"What could happen?" He laughed, his face breaking out in a cheeky grin. "Magic, serpents, dragons, barracudas. Bring them all on."

She turned to him with a look of frustration. "It's not a joke, Darek, you know I worry."

"All of the Dragonclaw Islands are depending on me. I can't let them down because you are worried."

Bree wrinkled her nose. "I'm no help to you here."

"Jace said we have to stay together. No solo flights, remember?"

"Then come with me!"

Darek set his jaw. "I can't. You know I have to go through Agrippa's inventions here and see what can be used and what can't."

Bree struggled with her patience. "I hate being of no use."

Darek looked away, as if guessing as much. "One more day, Bree, I promise. Then we'll start back."

She shook her head and turned away. "If you're going to just spend every day with your nose in a book then maybe I should just leave."

"Don't you realize how important this is?" Darek cried, unable to conceal the impatience in his voice.

"Of course. Are you calling me stupid?"

Darek felt his temper rising. *Why was she being so difficult?* "That's not what I meant."

"All I know is we're wasting time here instead of doing something worthwhile at the Rookery. You said yourself that the solaricus engines could help protect the Red Claw Islands. We should have taken them back already."

"There's more at stake here than that, Bree!"

"Fine!" she yelled. "I'll leave you too it. Meshoar can help me haul the solaricus engines out, then he, Storm and I will take them back to the Rookery."

Darek shook his head. "It's not safe, Bree. I can't let you do it."

"Let me do it?" Her voice took on a dangerous tone. "I don't need you to tell me what I can or can't do."

"Can't you see reason?"

"Maybe we're not a good match," Bree said coldly.

"What?" Darek was astounded.

She stared at him, daring any contradiction. "I'm going back to Cape Spear. Meira needs someone's support."

What did that mean? "By Kraton, I can't help everyone at once!"

Bree turned away. "No one is asking you to."

Just like that, she wanted to end it? Darek's mouth hung open. *Why couldn't she understand he had more pressing duties?* He didn't like her leaving on her own, but she was already furious. He thrust the thought out of his mind. Negative energy only manifested a negative outcome.

Meshoar was a dependable dragon and would see the task through. Storm would protect her. Her dragon was strong and loyal. He summoned Meshoar. After an hour or so they had dragged all of the devices up to the surface in stony silence. Darek helped lash the last solaricus devices to the dragon's back and gave it a pat on the rump. "Go!... You too Seavenger. Watch over Bree."

The dragons took a hopping run and launched themselves up in a cloud of dust. Seavenger screeched a definitive note in the stiff wind. He watched Bree vault off while a terrible feeling grew in the pit of his stomach.

Chapter 10.

THE COVE

Darek sat in Agrippa's secret study, holding his head in his hands, the frustration mounting in his heart. It had been four days since Bree had left Valkyrie. After several more fire-streak burns, nearly a dozen scrapes, and countless hours spent in study—he decided he had learned enough for now.

He packed up his runestones, spell books and dragon amulets and climbed on the back of his dragon. The sun sank low in the sky as he made his journey back to the Rookery. He swung first north over the island to check on Agrippa's dragons, well, his dragons now. All of them seemed content, basking in the sun like lizards. Let them enjoy their rest, he would call on them soon enough.

Leaving the island far behind, he was struck with the sense of awe and freedom flying above the open seas. It never ceased to exhilarate him. Aquamarine waves stretched for leagues in every direction. For a time, the seas were his.

Banking east, he surged down on a sudden whim. Silver Eye spread her wings and picked up speed. Dropping between clouds, Darek spotted movement below. Seven black specks grew in size, five schooners and two clippers. All flew the skull and crossbones and ploughed through the waves in heavy pursuit of a lone ship displaying no banner. The streamlined schooner had a light brown hull and picked up speed as it caught a gust of wind; a fast runner, one that had managed to outpace her pursuers. Curious, he swooped lower, staying well out of range.

The schooner made for the cover of a nearby horseshoe-shaped island, part of the Black Claw outer archipelago that loomed to the east. It ducked out of sight in a small cove, hiding herself behind a hook of land, evading the hunters. A Red Claw ship? No. He bid Silver Eye to drop closer.

Another pirate vessel! So that explained it. He had no love for pirates or their legacy of blood and slaughter. The suffering he endured while enslaved on Pirate Cove still stung like a scorpion's tail. Escaping only to become indentured to Raithan and the Black Claws had turned into a bittersweet pill. Perhaps he should try out some of his new spells on this lone craft? He dropped down with a wild gleam in his eye. Time for some payback on the rogues.

The schooner was unremarkable: a two-masted jury-rigged whaling craft with no dragon riders that he could see aboard. Though one or more dragon riders could be out scouting. He'd have to be careful. The crew, all eight of them, roamed the gumwood deck. Hardened buccaneers wearing bandannas or eye patches and cutlasses belted at their waists.

A sandy shoal loomed close between ship and shore. It gave him an idea. He summoned his inner energy and invoked the Spell of Mobilization. Closing his eyes, he visualized a strong undertow beneath the ship's hull. Faster and faster he whirled it in his mind until the sea churned in a white froth to the port and starboard of the unsuspecting ship. The mysterious tow drew the ship closer to the sandbar. The crew's curses fell on empty ears as the vessel ground ashore, stern first on the soft sand.

Darek nodded in satisfaction. Probing the vicinity with his mind, he searched for a suitable sea creature. There must be one about. Ah, that would do nicely—a hulking grey whale swimming a few furlongs out. Time to test his skill. Could he summon something besides a sea dragon? Why not? *Come into the bay, big boy. Much krill to eat here.* He reached out with his mental feelers and sent the massive mammal finning in.

Darek gave a hoarse chuckle. The great gray beast drew its blubbery bulk toward the pirate vessel and its tail whipped up and plunged down again while a chute of white water spouted up from its blowhole. *Good work, boy. Let them think you're responsible for their grounding.*

He swung in to get a quick peek at his handiwork. The exasperation on the crew's faces grew. His heart missed a beat when he saw who stood on deck barking orders at the crew.

Livis? Could it be?

The same who had freed him from Pirate Cove?

But a girl no more. She had grown taller, and more alluring. Her auburn curls shimmered in the sunshine and russet ringlets trailed down the middle of her back like strange jewels. Tousled by a sea breeze, her hair was a demiurge's mane. The proud face seemed chiseled from pure, white marble. She had become a rare beauty. *But how had she become a pirate captain?*

The lookout raised a fist. "Ahoy, enemy rider to starboard! Man the harpoons!"

In a trance, Darek eased Silver Eye down closer to the knot of sailors, ignoring the danger.

"State your business, dragon rider! Or we'll shoot you down." A rough-bearded buccaneer with black beady eyes bawled a curse.

"Ask your captain," shouted down Darek. "Long time ago she loaned me her knife—about time I returned it, eh, Captain?"

For a moment Livis's lips parted in astonishment. Then her cheeks burned with a lighter shade of dark auburn. She recovered and called out a sharp word. "Darek!"

"So, you do remember me?" he said with a shark's grin. He hovered a dozen feet above the goggling crew before settling his dragon on the foredeck. "You've come far, Livis—I see you have your own ship now."

"Things have changed for us both it seems. Got yourself a dragon?"

"I have." He vaulted off Silver Eye and strode over to her with ease, his heart hammering, but feeling no fear. He grinned away the flush threatening his cheeks.

"Mistress, surely you'd rather have one less dragon rider in the air?"

"Hush, Maquia," Livis said with a subdued laugh. "You're far too mistrusting. Darek here is a friend of mine. A guest on my ship, for now."

Maquia didn't appear terribly pleased by the remark. "Seems odd that we should run aground just as this dragon rider appears." He peered over the rail at the sand and mud gripping the boat's hull.

Darek nodded his head. "The currents are strong in this part of the sea."

"What would you know of it, dragon boy?" he snapped. His mates grumbled their agreement.

Barely hearing the words, Darek remained mesmerized by the sight of his long-lost love. Those eyes of hers. They could stare right through a man. Swallowing hard, he found his feelings for her growing only more intense after these years. *Did she still think of him in the same way?*

A wave of guilt washed over him at the thought of Bree. *He still had feelings for her, didn't he?*

"I know enough not to run my ship aground," he said. "Looks as if your men will be busy for a few hours."

Livis cracked a smile. "If only there was something to help pass the time." Her voice assumed a husky quality.

Darek's eyes widened. "You wanna go for a ride?"

Maquia bristled. "Mistress, you shouldn't go—"

"Why don't we kill him and take his dragon instead?" barked Skarlee.

Livis scowled at the idea. "Don't be impolite, Skarlee. I know this rider. I'll be safe with him." Livis removed her doublet, revealing a tight, boiled leather bodice below as she tied her hair in a knot.

Darek's jaw dropped as he took in an eyeful of this hot-blooded pirate beauty.

Maquia cleared his throat while Darek turned back to his dragon, regaining his senses. "Come, meet Silver Eye. You can pet her. She doesn't bite, much."

Livis clicked her tongue and Silver Eye raised her head at the sound. Sashaying over with confidence, she raised her hand for the dragon to smell. "I've learned a thing or two about dragons."

Silver Eye didn't seem to mind as Livis stroked the dragon's neck. With a shrug, Darek tightened the harness and helped her up on Silver Eye. His skin tingled as it touched hers. She flashed him a suggestive smile and his heart pounded like a mad drum.

He hopped up beside her and Silver Eye sprang from the deck before Maquia or any others could further object. Up into the sky the trio soared over the shoreline. Livis's lips parted in exhilaration and she voiced a breathless laugh. "Faster, Darek! This is so much more fun than sailing a ship."

"It's a lot more fun," he agreed, "but also more dangerous." He launched into a few deep rolls and dives to impress her. Silver Eye plummeted to the breaking waves and their hair whipped back. Darek felt his stomach move in sync with the motion as his powerful dragon swooped up and buzzed low over the trees on the shoreline.

Livis clung to him ever the tighter with a short gasp. "Where'd you learn to fly like that?"

"Been practicing. I'm in training at the Rookery. Where to next?" he called back at her.

"Fly north," she cried over the wind. "I think I remember seeing a teal lagoon over there."

Darek banked Silver Eye to where a green wooded hill rose high above an inland river. Livis's schooner became a small brown dot in the curved cove behind.

Her warm body clasped to his back like a mat of ivy. A shiver ran up his spine as her sun-browned arms snaked around his waist, a thrill that he couldn't ignore. He looked back at her, his blood quickening, as her bright-green hazel eyes stared back at him with an insistent challenge mixed with admiration. *Try to seduce me if you can,* screamed every pore of her being. She winked and he laughed and leaned back into her.

Darek swooped Silver Eye over the sea-firs blanketing the nameless island. How he wished to land in those meadows of flowering lilacs and take her in his arms. But a pang of guilt assaulted his conscience. Just a few days ago he'd held Bree in his arms. Harsh words had passed between them and she'd flown back to the Rookery by her own choice, but he still didn't feel right.

She seemed to sense his hesitation. "Take us down to that field below. Let's stretch our legs."

He gave a nod; Silver Eye landed on the grass with a thud near a patch of water. The place was silent but for the quiet birdsong and the rustle of a faint breeze through the green leaves.

She shook out her hair, reddish in the late afternoon sun, and stretched her slender legs. She examined Darek's dragon with keen eyes. "I've never seen a dragon with four wings before."

"She's special. Found her in a cave—actually a volcano."

She snorted at the plausibility of that and turned to watch a yellow-winged butterfly fluttering nearby. They walked a short way up a flowery hill.

"There's the lagoon!" she called and ran to get there first.

Darek struggled to catch up with her. Her long legs were as fast as they were shapely. As he chased after her, an image flashed in his mind: how she had set fire to the corral and created the diversion that allowed him to escape her village. Without her, he'd be in shackles, rolling stones in some mine.

Livis reached the water's edge and stopped short, allowing him to catch up.

"I owe you a big favor, Livis," he murmured, "for what you did back at Pirate Cove—"

"That was a lifetime ago," she said. "Back when I was a silly girl who would have married the first boy who looked my way."

She grabbed his arm and pulled him closer to the edge of the lagoon.

Darek looked up at the sky while the sun banked low in the horizon. "Won't your friends be missing you?"

She gave a bawdy laugh. "They're a bit protective."

"Should we head back?"

"No," she chided, clicking her tongue. "Not until we've had a swim, and I learn what has been happening to you."

Flashing him a mischievous grin, she turned her back and pulled her bodice over her shoulder.

Darek couldn't quite look away as she slipped her breeches off and splashed into the water. "Aren't you coming?" she called over her head.

Darek peeled off his shirt and threw his trousers aside, not wishing to look the prude. He caught her quick glance as she turned to give him an appraising look. Taking two steps into the water, he dove into the lagoon and swam out to her.

She smiled and swam a few strokes away. Darek followed, but she was as fast in the water as she was on land. She slowed, either growing tired or allowing him to catch her.

Darek grabbed her shoulders with a laugh. She gave a playful scream and shrugged off his hold on her, only to swim in closer and run her hands across his chest and behind his neck.

She leaned in close. Darek's lips were drawn to hers in a slow, deep kiss that seemed to last for eternity.

"I've been wanting to do that for years now," she murmured. A dreamy look entered her eyes.

Darek struggled to catch his breath. "I never thought I'd feel your lips on mine again."

He smoothed back a lock of hair that had dropped over her cheek. "You're even more beautiful than I remember, Livis."

She gave his muscled bicep a gentle squeeze. "And the boy I remember kissing through the bars has become a man."

"I would have come back for you," Darek said, "but things went from bad to worse. I traded one prison for another, then was swept up in a war."

"You don't have to make excuses," she teased. "I understand."

"What did your father do after I escaped?" Darek asked.

Her face twisted into a scowl. "It took nearly a year till the bastard let me out of his sight. That's the real reason he agreed to take me with him to sea—so he could keep an eye on me."

"So you're a pirate now too?" Darek asked.

"Not like my father," Livis grunted. "He worked me hard as nails, said if I was to sail with him, I'd have to become as hardened and ruthless as he was."

Darek put his hand around her waist. "You don't seem hard."

She splashed water in his face. "He tried to make a man of me. I've spent the last year slogging it out, but I came to see him for the cruel man he was. I've struck out on my own."

"Captain Serle let you go?"

She sniffed. "I stole the ship and the crew. We're on our own now, hunted by my own clan with my father leading the chase."

"I'm sorry, Livis."

She punched him in the shoulder. "Don't be."

"Can I help you in some way?"

"Don't need it," she replied. "I'm allied with four other captains. We got separated in the last raid when Black Claw schooners came out of nowhere after us."

"I saw those ships from the air. That's how I found you."

"Enough about ships." She drew near him and her hot breath tickled his neck. Darek's blood kindled and his eyes traveled over her lean curves, but he pulled back.

"What are you waiting for, Darek? You're getting cold feet now?"

"It's just that—" A pang of guilt assailed him.

"Is there someone else?"

"Yes—I mean no. There was. I mean, it's over now—" He tripped over his words and she gave a throaty laugh, studying his rugged good looks.

Darek looked away.

"I see." Her smile faded. "You still care for her. I should have known a man like you would already have someone in his life. Why were you leading me on like that then?"

"I wasn't—" Darek frowned. He was hardly leading her on. He felt so mixed up now, and it only seemed to be getting worse. "It's getting dark, we should probably go."

"Just like that?"

"I just need time to figure a few things out, but I'd like to see you again."

She shrugged. "Sure, but only if you're serious about it."

He felt suddenly stupid. "Let's meet at the south end of Valkyrie Island in five days."

"For you, dragon boy, I might wait five days. But no more."

"Fair enough." He brightened. They swam back to shore.

As Livis was tying her bodice, she called over her shoulder. "Whatever happened to your young friend who was with you in the pen? The timid one, always scared of something?"

Darek frowned. "You mean Briad. He's part of the dragon riders at Cape Spear under the care of my father who runs the Rookery."

"That's the first time you've ever talked about your family."

"I've a mother, but she left with a Black Claw captain when I was young," said Darek with some heat. "My sister, Meira, she is—well, also at the Rookery with Briad. He escaped from a mad wizard with the help of an old friend."

She blinked, absorbing the information. "Briad got lucky. Mad wizard? Funny, there was a warlock flew in several days ago on a mean-looking dragon wanting to form an alliance. Gave me a couple bags of gold."

Darek's breath caught in his throat. "Warlock? Describe him."

"His face was all pockmarked as if he'd been scalded, maybe burned." She frowned and seemed to shiver. "Caught a glimpse of his face, as his cowl slipped. The rest of him, rake thin, all pale-skinned was covered from neck to toe in a black robe. A strange sight. Spoke elegant words, but I sensed a deep cruelty underneath all that veneer."

Darek's shoulders sagged. "Cyrus!" *No, this couldn't be...the wizard, still alive?*

"You know him?" she asked.

"I should have known. The devil himself. Stay away from him. He communes with sea serpents. So many Red Claws have slipped down their gullets. Feeds them live victims. He nearly destroyed Cape Spear."

She shivered. "My father's already formed an alliance with the rogue, according to what the wizard told me."

"We can't let him!" Darek sprang to his feet.

"Have you seen him? The wizard's magic is powerful enough to pull ships out of whirlpools."

"I can defeat him."

She croaked out a laugh. "Fat chance of that, dragon boy. And forget about talking sense into my father. We're talking about Serle here, right? Better luck convincing an eel to walk on land. You think you're going to tell him to back out of some skullduggerish plan to get rich and bleed his enemies dry?"

Darek lowered his head with a grimace. He rubbed his temples, racking his brains for some inspiration. "I have to think on this more."

"Well, don't think too long—or you'll miss your chance to seize the treasure." She let the seductive hint hang in the air.

She was about to ask more when an eerie horn echoed through the trees from across the bay.

"Serpents' teeth!" She scrambled to her feet. "Serle's horn. We have to get back. Now."

Darek looked around wild-eyed. They raced back to Silver Eye who was napping. He nudged her awake and gave Livis a push up on her back as he as he beetled his way up himself. Dismay hit him that the intimate moment had passed but the thought of Captain Serle and his pirate ships worried him more. A dozen mixed feelings warred in his heart.

Darek guided Silver Eye skyward to pass over the proud, green-boughed sea firs. They plunged down over the shore toward the cove where Livis's ship gleamed, still beached like a shiny whale. The crew worked with minimal success, hauling on lines as several men shoveled away at sand holding the bow in place. No sign yet of other ships. Maybe the horn was a false alarm? The embankment would shield them for a time, but it was scant cover.

Silver Eye landed with a thud on the ship's bow. Livis sprang off to address the struggling crew. "Serle's near! I heard his war horn."

Others raised their heads from their work. When the mournful sound echoed again across the waves, she snapped a command. "Serpents' breath! Shovel faster!" She whirled about as a pair of schooners with skulls on their gunnels edged around the shoals of the island. "That's Serle alright. She flung out a hand at the startled mates. "Farnoss, Pipler, get us off this bar! How could he have found us so soon?"

Maquia gazed with enmity at Darek. "This squeaking porpoise must have brought him straight to us."

"Mistress, I studied the charts and had the lookout keep watch," protested Skarlee. "We've been aground in the lee too long."

"Never mind." She turned to Darek. "You'd better make yourself scarce, Darek. If my father catches you, he'll tear your legs off. Maybe if I offer him the mage's gold, he'll let my crew live—but you?" She winced. "He still thinks it was you who set fire to the village that dark day."

Darek grimaced. "I guess he would never suspect his own daughter of setting fire to her village."

"Never mind. Put your backs into it, you sea dogs! or Serle'll skin us alive!"

Darek's fingers clutched for his knife. Kraton's balls! Maybe beaching the craft hadn't been such a good idea after all.

"My dragon can help!" Darek cried. *Silver Eye, grab that tow line while I help push!*

He readied a small Mobilization spell, something he could use to help move the vessel without attracting attention.

Maquia dragged a heavy hawser from the bow, winding it off the capstan. His mates took hold and wrapped it about Silver Eye's harness. She growled at them, snipping at their hands, but on a word from Darek, allowed them to secure it around her breast. Darek jumped into the waist-high water and took up position with the other men. Maquia and a group of men spread across the sandbar, pulling the ropes taut.

On his signal, Maquia and her men pulled, aided by the mighty tugs of Silver Eye. The boat shuddered, but still refused to move. "Pull, Silver Eye, pull!" Darek called.

He thrust his back against the boat, using one of spells from Agrippa's books to strengthen his body for several seconds. He ignored Maquia's look of doubt and braced himself. Several of the men around him did the same. "Everyone, push!"

"*Motus*," he whispered. A surge of power traveled up his spine, pushing out his back. *The Singing Gull* lurched back into the water—just as the incoming ships veered in like killer barracuda. Shouts grew from the enemy decks, carried over the waves like demon chatter. Harpoons whizzed by, tearing the foresail of Livis's ship. Darek ran to free Silver Eye as Livis's crew took battle positions and swung the ship around.

The foremost ship angled in fast, preparing to ram her. Darek took to the air as Captain Serle's lead ship's prow smashed into the side railing. Horn-helmed men with eye patches and scars dropped from the rigging and streamed over the rails, yelling, wielding cutlass and knife. Livis fought hand to hand with the invaders while Maquia's cutlass cleaved limb and skull and threw men overboard. Skarlee's and Farnoss's blades rose and fell in red.

Captain Serle stood glaring on the foredeck of the second ship, sword gripped in a clenched palm. His brow gleamed with sweat, his voice hoarse from bawling orders at his men and gloating at his moment of triumph. His eyes caught a glimpse of who it was on the dragon. "You!" His jaw dropped in recognition and his face curled into a sneer, of wrath and disbelief.

"*Motus transvenio!*" Darek hissed, sending the full force of the Mobilization spell through the pirate raiders like a wave of air. Several boarders toppled over the rail while the others sank to their knees. The spell filled the sails with a contrary wind and the lead craft began to move backward as if possessed. The crew of *The Singing Gull* threw the last attackers overboard as Livis steered the boat away. She headed around the south end of the island and toward open sea.

"Kill that dragon rider!" Captain Serle ordered, looking up at Darek in rage. "Any man who comes between me and my feckless daughter pays with blood!" He ordered his dragon riders to take to the air.

A harpoon skated up, glinting in the golden light, glancing off Silver Eye's light armor. Darek's dragon gave a throaty rumble as another caught her flesh, spilling out blood. The tip struck below the breastplate where a seam had burst, leaving her vulnerable. Hot blood began to pour from the wound. Darek wheeled her about and spun down, feeling every bit of Silver Eye's sting. The rope had snapped but the harpoon's end still protruded from her chest. *Nobody harmed his dragon!*

With the hawser still tethering them to *The Singing Gull*, Darek drew his knife from his hip and leaned forward to hack at the binding around Silver's chest. The rope frayed then snapped. Silver Eye launched herself away from the ships.

Serle's dragon riders gave chase, leaving only his ships to pursue Livis. Darek hoped he'd given her enough time to escape, but he couldn't be sure. He led the other dragons through a series of low dives and spinning rolls, drawing them farther away. The beasts were no match for Silver Eye, a dragon among dragons. After a time, they circled back to the mother ship.

Darek's mind reeled with the turn of events: the unexpected reappearance of Captain Serle, Cyrus alive, their unholy alliance cemented and the lovely Livis caught in the middle while pirates lurked like crocodiles, waiting to attack.

The game board was a complex mix of pieces. Better to fly back to the Rookery, gather his allies in Jace and the others. Right now, there were too many foes to fight.

Bristling with agitation, he circled high and flew over the water until he found Livis' ship. She had a significant lead on her pursuers and seemed to be outpacing them. Raising his hand, he waved down to her. She stood looking back from the bow of the retreating ship—raised five fingers, meaning five days until they met at Valkyrie Island.

Silver Eye's wings beat the air with irregular rhythm. Her breath came in labored spurts. He placed his palm on her back and sent a pulse of energy down to the wound, gently pushing out the tip of the harpoon. She gave a soft groan as her body healed and the scales knitted closed.

The wavelets sparkled a million shades of scarlet as the ochre sun moved to the west to sink in a wallow of cloud. Despite the victory of the day, Darek's stomach felt like lead.

Chapter 11.

Darkthorn Isle

A black flag with dueling dragons rode high on Serle's lead schooner's mizzen. He commanded *The Persephone* with a stern hand, guiding it through the waves like a fine-honed sailfish. His thieving daughter had evaded capture again, but larger prizes were for the taking.

Twelve schooners trailed in his wake as would a pod of whales. Four were commandeered Black Claw vessels outfitted with pirate crews. Captain Varnet, master of *The Calliope*, had just joined Serle's fleet. A bluff, blond-bearded man, eager for spoils and slaughter, he ruled with hand almost as stern as his own. Fame tempted the man's mind, with a longing to make a name for himself. His three ships sailed in unison, crowded with men bearing gleaming swords at the hip, eager to stretch their limbs across the deck of the next ship they fell upon.

The remainder of the fleet belonged to Serle, bringing the count to thirteen ships. He grinned. *An ominous number.* Unfavorable for his enemies.

The weather stayed fair, a hint of squalls to the south. A steady wind blew from the northeast. Like a flock of snow geese, the rogue ships rode the breeze, tacking back and forth across the blustery reach as they approached Darkthorn, the northernmost and perhaps most unwelcoming isle of the Black Claw territories.

Serle rubbed his leathery cheeks, the skin toughened by decades spent in the sun. If only they could seize enough Black Claw ships in this next raid to cement his power!

Soon enough, he would move against Rivenclaw itself and take the main port. It would cost him in blood and ships, but such a move would yield enough wealth to make up for the losses. Such was the pirate's code and the game he had played all his life.

The fall of the Black Claw Empire was long overdue—the cursed Black Claws, yes, they would tumble, and his armada would be supreme. Skull and crossbones would ride the flags of every ship from Fairweather Town to Xandu, everywhere across the Serpents' Deep. He would have the last laugh.

If this strange wizard, Cybox, or whatever the fool's name was, stayed true to his word, that dream might come true even sooner. Not that he trusted the poisonous sea snake any farther than he could spit. No doubt the man would betray them on the drop of a silver shell. He'd tangled with serpents of his kind before—slimy, slick-tongued and dangerous, with about as much mercy as a striking adder—but this one was an extra special breed.

Perhaps the fool would deliver what he promised and die in the act. With all his heavy black garb and pale, twitchy hands, the wizard had one foot in the grave.

"Sails to starboard, Captain," grunted Myx, his misshapen gunner. "Shall we engage?"

Serle jerked his attention back to the sea.

"No, Myx, let them flee before us. We've bigger fish to skewer. Ahead full sail to Darkthorn Island!"

"Aye, aye, sir." The helmsman Grar grinned.

Serle reached for the horn of grog at his side and grimaced. His mind, already wrapped in a fog, would require a sober cleansing to ensure victory in the days ahead. Like an incoming storm about to break, the mates moved about the decks with restless mutters, ready to revolt. Livis had already mutinied; others would follow. If they didn't respect him, they'd fear him.

Keel-hauling Lebe had been a hard choice to make. The wretched bugger had sold him false information and given him lip. So he had deserved his fate. Made him look bad in front of his crew.

He was a harsh captain, but fair. He'd given fifty lashes to the forward deck archer Kestra yesterday, for spilling oil on the deck and nearly setting the ship on fire. The man's incompetence was astounding and had earned him the flogging as a lesson to everyone.

Serle's fists clenched. He thought of Livis and what he'd do to her when he caught up with her skulking band. She'd regret stealing his ship. The sniggers behind his back made him want to break heads. How she'd played him for the fool! Her cunning still burned his ears and irked him to no end.

Speaking of which, he still had to punish that lout Besgor for his thievery the other day. He reached for the horsehair flail by the midships cannons, but Hreg grabbed his arm. "Leave it, Serle."

Serle flung Hreg's arm off and glared at him. "What's this?"

"Ever since Yip took that poison arrow and you became chief, you've led us into spoils, Serle, I'll grant you that. But you've got to let up on the mates. All that keel-hauling and drunken beating's starting to wear on the lads. Look! Look at you, you're like a bleeding executioner. You're going to have a full-fledged mutiny on your hands before long."

Serle growled in agreement. "Honest words, Hreg." He shook his head with a sigh, and threw aside the whip. "Things used to be different, Hreg, simpler. I used to dream of the day I would give my daughter's hand to some promising captain's son, like your own boy, Nax. A mother of champions, and to bear me grandsons. Now she's a renegade, fighting against my command."

"Livis's a spirited wench, let's give her that."

Serle spat. "Spirited wench? Unruly and defiant is more like it. Taken up with that philandering Red Claw boy again. Serpents' tails!" Spit from his angry lips flecked the deck. "On a dragon, no less! I'd recognized that glib face anywhere."

"Yeah, well, his head'll be pinned to our rails before long."

Serle gave a snort of disgust. "That's not the point, Hreg. Won't change anything. Black Claws're getting smarter, more desperate. Their ships are stacked with more cannons and deadlier harpoons. Their dragons fight like they're half-starved. Maybe they are. The Red Claws are no less easy targets, avoiding pirate territory like the plague and protecting their fleets with scores of dragon riders. They retreat to Cape Spear and other safe harbors rather than risk engagement. Can't say as I blame them."

Hreg gave a careless shrug. "The few we can catch are faster than dolphins, and run double sails with lighter hulls."

"Enough. I feel blood in the air; there's battle in the works."

The afternoon had grown old and the outliers of dusk crept over the moody swells when the first defenders of Missel Town challenged his fleet. They'd seen his vanguard and now poured out from their stark jut of windswept shore clad in gumwoods and seathorn. Eight Black Claw vessels turned to meet them, aiming harpoons and cannons.

521

Captain Serle squared himself at the bow, his hand reaching for the pommel of his sword. A single dragon flew across the sky, then another.

Serle's mouth twisted in challenge as he flung forth a fist to the helmsman. "Engage, Gisor! Show them Kraton's fury!" He had more ships, and more dragon riders. "Send our riders out to soften their resolve."

Almost as he hissed out the commands, a stream of arrows rained down from on high and struck the midships deck, one taking the second gunner in the leg, pitching him to his knees.

The crew sprang for shields. Another deckhand caught a shaft in the throat, gurgling out his last breath. Blood stained the deck.

Pinned behind the bulwark, Captain Serle gave a florid curse. "Turn us hard to port and give them a broadside!"

As the ship turned, the next flight of arrows missed wide. The gunners dropped their shields, running to the cannons and rolling them forward.

"Return fire!" Serle yelled.

Cannons roared and the deck of the closest ship exploded, killing scores of the archers aboard.

The dragons collided in the air above, screeching with rage as they raked their claws across armor. Following his orders, Serle's dragon riders broke after the initial impact and flew in a wide arc around the Black Claw ships. The Black Claw dragon riders gave chase, exposing their flanks.

"Harpoons!" Serle ordered.

Gleaming iron shot up at the beasts, skimming off the closest dragon's protective plate. The beast fled under the onslaught.

Other ships of his brigade drove forward into the center, separating the six defending vessels into two groups. Outnumbered and outgunned, the enemy ships slowed and wallowed.

The battle appeared turning to their favor when all of a sudden the lookout gave a shout from above. "Sails to stern!"

Serle swung his bulk around as two Black Claw man-of-war ships appeared. Kraton's hammers! *How did they get behind us?*

"They must've slipped out of that cove back there," called Hreg. "An advance guard or something."

Serle ran to the wheel and gave it a full turn. "Prepare to fire!"

Captain Varnet sized up the situation and broke off from the fight. His wingman's ship, *Seawrack* veered in after him. *The Calliope's* gunners fired at the enemy lead ship, but the shot flew wide. Serle's men, still reloading from the last round, stared aghast as cannon shot burst from the first man-of-war and raked her starboard bow. A gaping hole smoked in the railing. Two cannons went up in flames, their powder igniting in an explosion of dying men. Varnet's ship took minor cannon shot, but Captain Darnmeyer's *Seawrack* suffered a more serious hit; her forward bow cracked and water spilled in as fire spread across the main deck. The first man-of-war closed in for the kill. The second still barreled toward his ship at full speed. She set in to ram *The Persephone.*

"Kraton's beard!" Serle yelled.

Over his shoulder came a thunder of beating wings. Three dragons, the size of small whales, glided over the choppy waves to strike at the two new Black Claw ships. The first dragon, red-bellied and tinged with wide, grey-tipped wings, swooped down upon the enemy craft and seemed impervious to their harpoons. The lead beast ripped claws through the main sail, dropping low to rake men with claw-tips. The black-robed wizard riding the dragon clutched glowing stones in his palm and chanted some dire words.

The bow of the first man-of-war tilted and Black Claw sailors slid to one side, mouths agape. A half score fell overboard in waters swirling with sharks gathered at the scent of the blood already spilled.

The second sea dragon, riderless with gray-wings, wheeled in fury to harry the second craft. The beast plunged into the water, dove down, slamming against the hull. It kicked up a small tidal wave that sent the boat rocking to near oblivion. Up it burst from underwater, cracking its snout on the keel while the hull splintered and began to take on water.

The last Black Claw rider took wing and flew a wide ring about the red-bellied dragon, yet he turned a shivering glance at his adversary, not relishing a fight with that behemoth. The moment of hesitation cost him. A green fireball sailed through the air. The dragon rider dodged, only to have Valoré veer in like a falcon and dig eight-inch talons into the dragon's chest. The claws bit between breastplate and belly, prompting a shriek of agony, sending its rider to the sea. Like a leopard shark, Cyrus's mount whipped the smaller dragon back and forth in its teeth, then tossed out the mangled husk as an orca toys with a wounded seal. Blood and gore splattered over the crews below, raining Serle's men in a bath of crimson.

Valoré screeched overhead like a banshee from the grave. Cyrus's yellow eyes gleamed. A wingless, headless dragon torso struck the deck, nearly crushing Serle and Hreg.

Serle shrank back from the violence of such a beast. He stroked his beard. Such powerhouses, these dragons of the wizard. They had saved his growing fleet from a surprise attack—that he could not deny. Another lapse of judgment on his part. He sent a fist crashing down on what was left of the railing. To the deeps with his ineffectual dragon riders! Those of the wizard's made his riders look like flying fish.

Not for the first time, Serle felt a tickle of dismay creeping in his innards. What had he gotten himself into, joining with this ruthless maniac? Men, dragons, ships, whole islands were nothing more to him than jellyfish waiting to be crushed.

The sounds of destruction, splintering wood and cannon shot, drifted over the water alongside anguished cries.

The Black Claw ships were either smashed or cowed, and the remaining pirate vessels swarmed in like seasoned vultures to loot the ships and give death to all who resisted. The battle was won, but at high cost. Like it or not, Serle had to admit the balance could have gone either way. While his men saw to repairs, *Seawrack* floundered on her side, sinking in red foam. Angry curses filled the air as men abandoned ship, taking to rowboats to join Captain Varnet on *The Calliope*.

Hreg gripped his captain's arm and showed a yellow row of teeth. "Shall we join the mates and loot the town? They're defenseless now. Her navy's crushed and ripe plunder awaits."

Serle gave a careless nod. "Go to it, Hreg. They'll have land forces waiting, but nothing we can't handle. Can't have that greedy Drakus and his cutthroats taking more than their share."

True, the lads were ready to pillage and take slaves to bolster their wealth. Serle ordered the dead crewmen dragged to stern and thrown overboard.

Cyrus's red-bellied dragon glided over to hover above him and his crew. The enormous beast had the mates on edge.

"Feasting on your spoils, my seacrows?" cried Cyrus. "This is only a sampling of the power I give you, Serle." He flung out a sprinkling of runestones down on the deck at the captain's feet. Green and red they glowered with a baleful shimmer to their edges—twelve misshapen beads, strung in a ring of corded leather. "Twelve, one for each of your ships. Take this talisman, the ring of Behydra, and it will generate a circle of protection for you and give your mates an advantage over your enemies."

He motioned to the tan-scaled dragon at his side. "I give you my third dragon, Forgefighter, who will aid your cause. I stole him from a wounded clipper not a few days back. I've already penetrated his mind. He'll follow your commands. See," he clucked in amusement at their ogling looks, "he has the dark dragon amulet wrapped about his neck—a secret crystal forged from Windbiter's dragon fire. The dragon is still too young to breathe flames himself, but he's eager and cunning.

With my magic he can scorch the masts of your enemy and burn the sails of those who refuse to bend to your will. A caution though. Should the amulet break, or the binding snap, the dragon will turn on you and kill you all. The same if you should think about deserting me."

Serle examined the beast with a grimacing stare. "Just like you, wizard. Gift us a weapon more likely to kill us than be of use."

Cyrus grinned. "Don't lose your nerve, Serle. Without my help you'd have fared poorly in this battle. Gather your ships and celebrate your victory. Your power grows with each passing day. Soon we'll be strong enough to attack Ravenstoke and Cape Spear."

Serle hitched forward and snatched up the garland of glimmering stones. His eyes glowed, mesmerized by their witchling light. "How do I use these evil pearls?"

"Rub them in your palms till they are warm. Hold them up to your brow. Give the silent command, *Verbestul!* One chance will they give you to conjure some weak magic, if the dark gods favor you. They'll grant the first wish on your mind."

"Weak magic," spat Serle, "or a spell-ridden way to control us further?"

Cyrus's lips quivered in anger. "Don't think I dish out my magic lightly, knave! Be careful what you say and be grateful that I give you anything. This is a rare opportunity for a man such as yourself."

Serle grunted. Myx and Hreg stared with suspicion at the stones and muttered under their breaths. Others flashed the wizard sullen looks.

"All well and good," growled Hreg, "but after that, wizard, what's the plan? You'll have the Dragonclaw islands under your heel. And then what use will we be to you?"

Cyrus cackled out a laugh. "You've a strong sense of self-preservation, sailor. I commend you for it. Prove yourselves to be loyal then the seas shall be yours."

"We already have—"

"Do you think Kraton and the islands are the only ones in this great sea?" he boomed. "There are coasts and lands undreamed of in the endless leagues that lie beyond the Serpents' Deeps."

A chill tickled up Serle's spine. He'd only envisaged a Dragonclaw empire, not a seawide one. Such a prize was worth the sacrifice. "What is your will?" he grunted.

Cyrus's flourish brought the third, younger dragon down with a roar. The beast landed with a thud on all fours on the midships deck, eyeing the pirates with peculiar dispassion.

"We'll strike Three Sisters' Isle in the next week. Just to keep the Red Claws on their toes and show them they're not immune to my power. From there, on to Cape Spear."

"As you wish, wizard." Serle thumbed the end of his blade. "I gave those Red Claws a chance long ago and they spurned my offer to join me, laughing in my face. Now they'll pay for their insolence."

"All in good time," croaked Cyrus. "Fate plays odd tricks on prideful men. I have my own score to settle with both clans. The Black Claws will pay dearly for their betrayal at Cape Spear. Casks of blood will flow. Groans of despair'll fill the skies as their fleet dwindles to nothing." With that, the wizard summoned Windbiter and flew off on Valoré, his billowing black robe trailing behind him like a dark flag of doom.

Chapter 12.

A Bold Plan

Livis's quest for allies had taken her far and wide. A newfound independence had stirred fresh confidence and strength, and somewhat more appreciation of the work needed to manage a fighting crew as large as her own.

"Ak!" She caught Maquias's blade on her cutlass as they sparred in the bright sunlight. Her long hair whipped back in the breeze and her stun-tanned body gleamed with sweat, showing new muscles and bruises earned from long hours training with a man whose skill at the blade knew no equal.

She danced back and forth, swinging her blade, goading the master swordsman into a mistake or hoping to catch him in an awkward position. With a quick flick of blade he deflected her ripostes and stepped in to attack. In a sudden lunge of impatience, she turned his sword, edging in sideways to stab at his ribs, a dangerous move which Maquia caught on the haft of his blade with a laugh. "Not bad, Livis, but risky. You left your weakest side exposed."

She stored the instruction in her mind and drove in for another strike in a whirl of steel difficult for any eye to follow. Maquia let each blow slide off his long blade, smiling through his teeth as the crew, backed to the rails or hanging from the rigging, watched with silent appreciation. The clank of steel rang high, echoing across the white waves.

He growled, "Take the parry early on the downswing. Catch my blade closer to the tip. It could spare you a bloodletting in a real fight."

Livis acknowledged the advice with a grunt. Her bare arms and legs shone with exertion, and she kicked at his leg, earning a sharp exclamation and another grin, this one less jaunty. "Fighting dirty, are you? You're worse than Serle." He stabbed in with a flourish and this time it was Livis who crabbed back on defense.

Backpedaling, she felt her shoulders brush the captain's cabin. Maquia had that look in his eye and she was cornered. "Enough!" She held up a hand in surrender. Her breath came in gusts and she sheathed her sword. Even the swordmaster's sweat beaded on his brow in the noonday sun. His chest heaved, rising up and down, a rare occurrence for him.

Skarlee came up behind them, cutlass gripped in the other fist. "Kraton's tears! Good show, Livis."

He pulled off his gull-feathered cap and wiped his gleaming head with a sigh. "You swordfish are going to cut each other to pieces along with the ship if you don't take care. Though I don't mind seeing Maquias have to work hard for his keep."

Maquias bowed. Livis sheathed her blade and gave a throaty laugh. "Unfurl the gib, Skarlee. We're nearing port and I see Rarl still hasn't changed out the slatting sheets—curse his lazy bones. I won't have my sails blowing in that state, peppered with cannon shot. Check in the forward hatch. There might be some spare canvas there."

"We'll be vulnerable. You sure you want to do it now?" Skarlee asked.

"Do you see any enemies in sight?" Livis smirked.

Life at sea was a battle of wills—one every captain worth his salt realized sooner or later. So did the thought brush her mind as she stretched her sore limbs, feeling a new sense of surety. A swift ship, a hardworking crew... the beginnings of a new life, free from the shackles of her father. Not a shred of guilt stirred in her breast for stealing *The Singing Gull*. Taking what one wanted, after all, ran in her blood.

Huffing up the rope ladder, Skarlee halted midway up the foremast. He wheezed out a tired breath and set to uncleating the sail. "We can expect your crotchety father to drive us on like a gale after that last bout. Sharks take the man! He and his mates'll will never let us be."

"Then we'll just have to stay two leagues ahead of them, won't we?" Livis moved panther-like forward and grabbed strips of torn sail as Skarlee cut them away.

Skarlee looked to the sky and shrugged. "Easier said than done."

"We raid and keep growing our forces," she said, tossing the rags aside. "Eventually we'll be strong enough to make my father pause before he bothers us again. Not so complicated, is it?"

Grins came from the mates.

"I like the sound of plunder," growled Kisten, the master gunner. "But Serle's raiding the Black Claws. He'll hardly appreciate the competition."

"Then we'll raid the Red Claws whenever opportunity knocks," rasped Maquia.

"That'll land us a net full of more enemies than friends," croaked Farnoss.

Livis unsheathed her sword and spun it with a flourish. "They've always been our enemies." The stories she'd heard of her clans people hanged by the Red Claws in their public squares still rankled. The only good thing that had ever come out of the Red Claw Isles was Darek. The lithe islander and his dragon rode at the edge of her imagination; her heart quickened at the merest thought of him.

Eight men on her own ship, and twenty more she'd recruited from Bonzai island and the Gull bluffs—lean, hardened seadogs to the last man, each as disenchanted as the next with Serle's drunken rule. Three ships she'd added to their brigade. Krag's, Drass's and Numestis's, all capable captains. For that she was proud.

Mutiny and uprising was a stale crust to swallow, but she'd treated her crew with fairness, unlike the harsh justice of her father. For this reason alone, she hoped to forge a different path.

Other ways existed to win the loyalty of the crew. Being the pirate chief's daughter carried some authority and earned her a measure of automatic respect. She'd built on that through a series of sound judgments and by allowing each man a fair say and equal share.

"Before we try the same tricks on the Black Claws, better call a war council," muttered Maquia. "Kraton has blessed us so far, but we need to be ready when his favor shifts."

Livis sent the call to the captains and they rowed over to her ship with their quartermasters and immediate officers. Numestis, thin and wiry, rose a head taller than his crew with black eye patch and spiky ear bangles to go with it, dangling from both lobes. Drass smiled through his bad teeth, dressed in his ragged seaman's smock, bagged at the knees and a black hat tipped on an angle. Krag lanced them all piercing glares, as if divining the purpose of the parley. The gray-maned ruffian had terrible scars on his left cheek. Black boots rose to his knees and a red sash curled at his waist; twined tattoos of anchors and exotic ships rode on his bare shoulders and forearms.

"Gentlemen, I welcome you," said Livis with a sober salute. She thrust jacks of ale in their hands and they gave gruff mutters at the offering. With a grand sweep of arm, she ushered them to the bow and seated them about an old, scarred table that had seen many games of dice and bloodier games still. Skarlee cracked out a keg of rum from her personal stock.

Livis took a generous swig before she began. "We need more men—and more ships."

The men's eyes followed her gaze as she peered out over the rail at the captured Black Claw ship rocking in the waves, hard at anchor. Only three men walked her decks: not enough fighting men to outfit her.

"Where can we find loyal crew, experienced sailors who hate the Black Claws and my father's rule as much as we do?" she mused aloud.

Drass clenched a fist. "We sent the word out to the clans back on the islands. There's unrest while Serle's yet away. More ships and mutineers will join our cause."

"Not enough and too slow," growled Maquia, quaffing his drink.

"We could look for hired mercenaries," offered Krag. "Let them share in the spoils."

"But where?" demanded Skarlee. "Black Claws will not fight Black Claws."

"With enough gold they might," growled Krag. "Why not break into that pretty stash of gold the wizard gave you—"

"No, I don't like it. The wizard's not to be trusted," said Livis.

"What? You're just going to sit on a goldmine and let it rot—"

Livis slammed her dagger point into the keg and hissed Krag to silence. "I said, no!"

Skarlee gave a solemn mutter. "Shanghaiing men's not as easy as trapping crabs."

The word 'trapping' gave her an idea. "Then why not recruit from the prisons? A man grateful for his freedom and given a chance at gold would be ready to fight."

"Eh?" grunted Skarlee.

"The prison," Livis repeated with impatience. "We raid the Black Claw town jails and collect dissenters, smugglers, thieves. None of those scum would think twice about slitting Black Claw throats."

Skarlee stroked his beard. "Not a bad idea."

"And not a good one either. They keep condemned men like that at Pearl Bay on Mee peninsula," said Farnoss with a frown. "Off Serpent's Isle. I know because my grandpappy was thrown in there years ago. He never made it out. It's guarded night and day with only one approach during high tide. I've heard the inside is like a labyrinth that you'd be lost in, even if you did escape. They call it *Deadman's Hold*."

"That's an old wives' tale," snorted Skarlee.

"How close is this prison?" asked Captain Numestis.

"About twenty leagues."

"Then let's heave ho," he grunted. "A night raid. We could be there in an afternoon and out again as swiftly."

All but Krag seemed on board with the plan.

Maquia fingered the edge of his sword with a sinister grin. "My blade is thirsty."

"You're incorrigible," said Skarlee. "Only thing you ever think about is a chance at splitting more Black Claw skulls."

Livis grinned. "You got that right." But her smile faded. Darek's warning quivered in the back of her mind. Foolish to risk using the wizard's cursed gold. She thrust it and Darek's strong, sun-browned calves out of her mind with an angry sniff. On their rendezvous in three days, what if he refused her?... what if he already dallied with another? *Well, too bad for him.*

Chapter 13.

Sabotage

Cyrus gazed upon the burning wreckage of Bimsbrun Town with satisfaction. The Blue Claws would remember this day for many years to come: the ruined buildings, the floating corpses, the broken ships, and flaming piers. Flames licked unchecked through the town, courtesy of Windbiter's breath. Their few ships would soon lie as sunken wrecks at the bottom of the shallow harbor.

The simple farmers who lived here were no threat to him, but they provided the source of the supplies for his enemies. The peaceful seaside haven had minimal defense, making it an ideal first-strike for Dendrok. The mutated dragon had performed admirably during the raid. Coupled with Fercifor's savagery and Valoré's power, the three creatures had lain waste to the town.

The dolphins and young whales he had sacrificed to the hatchling had filled Dendrok out, nourished his young body, which was sickly no more and growing at a startling rate. In time, the drago-serpent would come into his full power with the ritual human sacrifice he had planned on the upcoming moon.

The merchant-chief Evren had proven useful in keeping the Red Claws distracted. The longer he prevented them from moving against the pirates, the more chance his plan of conquering the islands had of succeeding. Cyrus had only to whisper a suggestion into Bralig's ear and the lad parroted it back to his father.

Likewise, the doubt and fear he had instilled through dream images into Darek's mind had done their work. Summoning the oracle's divinatory cloud, Cyrus looked within its enigmatic swirls and saw how the boy woke in a sweat every morning, gasping, with wide, staring eyes, looking for ghouls hiding in the shadows. Poor fool! Cyrus's lips curled in a grin. So much could be done from the safety of one's cave.

A loud, mournful roar played across the crimson waters. Cyrus blinked, his concentration broken. Dendrok seemed to be growing impatient at the late hour as the sun set over the waves. He called off his winged horrors. Enough havoc had been wrought for one day. Valoré had tasted his fill of blood and licked his teeth with a rattling purr of relish. Cyrus turned his dragon around. He summoned Fercifor and Dendrok and Samon and Windbiter, fierce dragons in all, who served as Dendrok's nursemaids.

Fercifor resisted the command, toying with a still-breathing farmer like a rag doll.

Insolent creature. "You mustn't kill them all, Fercifor," Cyrus teased. He gestured a hand. "Windbiter, fetch me three live sacrifices! They will feed new serpents' bellies before the moon wanes."

While Windbiter flew off to the town to search for survivors, Dendrok's fangs glinted in the sallow, late afternoon light. The half dragon hovered before his master, teeth flecked with bits of fabric and bone, his blue snout dripping with slime and blood.

At last, Fercifor bit into his kill. Dendrok flew over to investigate and Fercifor snapped at his tail, a show of playful rivalry, or was it more? Dendrok gave a low, warning snarl.

Cyrus scolded his serpent with a jaunty laugh. "Fercifor, don't be jealous!" But then his expression blackened.

"Where is Samon, my serpent?" he bellowed. His eyes strayed to the surf, where a coiled form lay washed up, half concealed in the wreckage-strewn waves. A large chunk of flesh had been gouged out of the serpent's back and claw marks raked its broken body. *Killed by a dragon.*

"What have you done?" he yelled at Dendrok. "She was my pet. A faithful servant of mine and the first to raise you from a hatchling—"

Cyrus realized all in a split of a second. The feral creature was not to be trusted. Perhaps the old fool Agrippa was right. Anything with serpent blood would bite the hand that fed it. Most of his serpents followed his commands, but infusing serpent blood into the dragon and treating it with such cruelty had made it rebellious.

He discarded the thought. The voice of a weakling. He mustn't let such doubts influence him. He straightened his back and spoke in stern tones. "I see I will have to discipline you more harshly, Dendrok! Even if it means I must keep you under tighter leash next time. Come, you ghoulish wights! Let us away to Curakee!"

The grisly troupe prepared for the long journey back, Windbiter, gripping the end of a cart of wailing citizens in his teeth, while the ashes of the town cooled and the cries of despair echoed over the smoldering buildings.

* * *

Two days later, Cyrus touched his dragon down in an area well back from the Rookery. He crouched in the trees atop the hill, looking out from between a twisted pair of tall dogwoods. The position offered him a fine bird's eye view of the training grounds. Such a quaint little place! Too bad it would have to burn.

He considered his options. A mage blast from his vantage would draw quite a stir and likely provoke a counterattack. No, it would not do to draw attention to himself or have that mage boy and his infernal rider friends come charging after him. Something subtler was in order—but with equal devastation. Of course!

Squinting in the bright light, he studied the layout of the Rookery, rubbing his chin from time to time with the beginnings of a plan. The riders passed inches from those large floating balloons on their route through the obstacle course. A tempting target to plant an explosive there. It would be quite the tragedy if the mage boy happened to be near one when it went up in flames... Nighttime would be best for setting the trap, but he needed a distraction.

Sending a mental command, he called for aid. He cached his dragon higher up in the woods and donned his beggar's garb. Then he limped down to the town square where he met with Bralig, the young town guard, his accomplice. Cyrus favored the curt youth with a conspiratorial wink. "Hoy there, Bralig, what are you doing so far from your post?"

Bralig grimaced. "You again. Begone, beggar. I'm searching for a thief who came this way."

Cyrus scowled. It was curious the way his commands caused Bralig to delude himself. The mage lifted a palm. A scarlet gleam radiated from the runestone clutched in his hand and made the young man stare.

"I require a task of you, Bralig. Lure away the night guard from the Rookery this evening. He sits on Dragon Watch hill atop his dragon with a lantern."

"Why? What do you plan to do?" Bralig's eyes continued to stare as if caught in the grip of a hex.

"Never mind the reason, just heed my words."

Bralig's frown deepened. "It sounds dangerous."

Cyrus waved a hand. "It is." His lips curled in a trace of irritation. He was losing the young guard. "Think of the rewards." He opened his palms and the ruddy shine of the runestones caught the young man's attention once again. Bralig's eyes gleamed in response.

"Remember your enemy, Bralig—the mage boy who rides the silver dragon. Remember how he humiliated you at the sailing races long ago."

Bralig gave a slow nod. "I remember." His teeth clenched. "I'll do as you say." His face clouded in a vindictive grin.

"Very good." Cyrus threw him the runestone. "Now go."

Bralig turned to leave but hesitated. "How will I lure the guard?"

Cyrus's eyes flashed. "Use your imagination." He clawed at his brow but his cowl slipped.

Bralig gaped, peering at the scorched face. "What's wrong with your face?"

Cyrus pulled the cowl back over his cheeks. "At midnight I expect *Dragon Watch* to be clear."

Bralig gave a nod and shambled off. Cyrus shook his head—the young guard may fail him; he may need a backup plan.

***

Darek was dreaming of flying… the wind whipped through his hair and the spray of the water cooled his skin. Silver Eye carried him far and wide across the Serpents' Deep. The water below boiled with dozens of serpents. Kraton! Had they been breeding unchecked? Vile serpents spread across the ocean, bobbing, hissing, tongues flicking from wedge-shaped heads like nightmare ghouls.

A monster dragon, half serpent, all blue green and fiery scales, presided over the army of sea worms. The beast flew with wings spread, never moving. On its back perched a black-robed grinning figure, harboring a skull face, piking magic staff held high in the air. The figure lifted a pair of red stones in a bony hand that shone with a putrid gleam.

The swimming serpents fled from the piercing light, bowing in obedience, moving as one writhing mass to overrun the coasts of the free islands to the west. Darek tried to fight, to fly down and strike the black-robed figure, but the mysterious rider lifted his white fingers and projected a green ray that struck Silver Eye between the eyes and killed her. With a groan of anguish, he toppled into the sea toward the horde of serpents below.

As he fell, he strove to unleash his magic to scorch the waiting fiends below, but his power failed him. Just as the grotesque fangs, dripping with slime, snapped at his flesh, he awoke in a cold sweat...

Darek jerked upright, his fingers clenched. He cried out, a choked gasp sticking in his throat. The nightmares had gotten worse. Something was wrong... and yet, these nightmares ranked amongst the least of his problems. All the dragons but Silver Eye had grown unrulier and harder to control by the day. Just yesterday, one of the juveniles had snapped at its young rider, nearly taking off his arm. Then Winguard, whom he thought he had tamed back on Valkryie Island, bucked a veteran rider causing a broken rib and sprained wrist. Thankfully they had been flying low and no more damage had been done.

The entire Rookery grumbled about the dragons' disobedience. Bree always seemed to have a sarcastic remark for him, and he found himself suddenly impatient with her sulking. Meira's temper had reached an all-time high and Jace shook his head at the many mistakes Darek had made during his training maneuvers.

He could make no more progress with the dragon amulets. The bad dreams had shattered his concentration and the proportions of ingredients always seemed to be wrong. The dragons guarded their eggs with a vengeance and obtaining the egg white needed for the amulets' magic became a dangerous chore. Somewhere he felt Cyrus's hand in this. If only he could locate Cyrus and deal with him once and for all!

On an impulse he raced to the common area to seek out Briad and see what details the young rider could remember regarding the location of the mage's hideaway. Unfortunately, he could only give him conflicting reports. Was it east, or west? Briad shook his head, unable to remember much. Darek threw up his hands in exasperation.

That day he flew the obstacle course, his turns sloppy in his full armor as his mind wandered. Perhaps it hadn't been a good idea to agree to the race. The wind whistled in his ears as a dozen dragons flapped behind him, vying for position. He was just veering around the last floating balloon, his ten-foot spear clutched in hand, when a hidden rider came jolting out of nowhere, striking Silver Eye hard in the flanks. The sudden impact sent him spinning away and he grunted, realizing that the tough leather of the harness was the only thing that had saved him from falling.

A nearby flash of light blinded his eye. He gasped, remembering only a red-hot fire singeing his back, then Silver Eye howling as both nearly erupted in flames. Her back arched and Darek roared in pain. Palms held up, he sent a cooling shield around his own body then an icy cloud of energy over his dragon's back. Blue smoke rose from her scales.

As the smoke cleared, he looked back over his shoulder. The other rider was gone—incinerated on the spot. A cold lump formed in Darek's throat. The explosion had ripped several other dragons out of the air. Scraps of the large balloon rained down, ablaze with fire. Riders came from all corners of the Rookery to help the injured dragons and their riders.

Silver Eye flew in erratic circles, dazed and in shock, not quite knowing what to do. Darek guided her down to a grinding halt in the yard, breathing in hoarse gasps. He slid to the ground, feeling the stinging pain in his back starting to lessen. They'd been lucky. If the other racer hadn't knocked them clear, they'd have been killed. It had all been a blur. *What exactly had happened?*

Darek's mind worked with unusual clarity. Other balloons crackled with flame but didn't explode. Agrippa would never have used combustible gas around fire breathing dragons. Two trainees were badly singed and a third had been incinerated on spot. This didn't seem like an accident, they'd been targeted. *Cyrus*!

Who else could it be? His stinging eyes roved about the grounds. The mage was nowhere in sight. The louse could be hiding anywhere, disguised as some beggar, or maybe turned himself into a bird or something—Darek still didn't know the depth of the mage's power.

He and the others grieved the loss of Frun, the young rider who had been roasted alive. Many of his own wounds he'd managed to heal with his mage power, but Silver Eye'd been badly burned. As he passed hands over her blackened scales, they turned a softer shade of silver and her low whimpers faded. The techniques Agrippa had taught him regarding visualization and applying healing touch had made a difference. Meira took the poor creature to the medicus and Jace ordered the Rookery to high alert.

The events of the day gave Darek an idea. He closeted himself in an unused wing, still under construction. For a day and half he set to his task with grim purpose. The details of his dark dream remained fresh in memory. With him he brought only some cold bread, a jug of water, and Agrippa's spellbook, the *Nemestomis*. Away from Jace, Bree and the others, he could concentrate.

Times were desperate. Cyrus was willing to destroy everything they had worked for. Despite Agrippa's warning, Darek broke the seal on the wax binding. His eyes roved over the faded script, seeking the dark gospel of the forbidden sections, his heart beating with a quiver of temptation. Much was here that described powers not meant for mortal eyes, much that he didn't understand and which brought chills up his spine. *The Spell of the Black Plague, Charms to Ensorcel the Innocent Heart, The Chant of Past Weaving, The Spell of Unbinding, Nexorius Avant, Crippling Mage Fire, The Spider Curse...* In several places Agrippa's hasty scrawl had been half blotted out, scorched by flame or hidden by dripping wax. But still Darek's eyes deciphered certain passages: *...to thrust a person or violent animal back in time... to strip a warrior of his physical abilities... revoke a wizard's otherworldly powers... counter the hexes of witch or warlock... commune with the dead...*

conjure the living undead... raise a trapped soul from the grave... and on and on.

He swallowed hard and sat up. His eyes rested on a particular stanza, *The Spell of Unbinding.* Spellbound, he read but not without trickling fear. As his eyes traveled further down the page, his guts tightened, and he knew, even as he recalled the warnings of Agrippa on the temptation of dark spells, that he had found what he was looking for...

Several hours later, he emerged with a new understanding of Agrippa's need for seclusion and his dire warnings. Being a mage was not what it was cut out to be; it required difficult choices and mental labor that tore apart the spirit. He still knew too little. With a grim exhalation, he announced he would be returning to Valkyrie for further study.

Bree came to his room not long after. She clicked her tongue and muttered. "Don't you think you're of more use here, Darek? What if we're under attack?"

Darek shook his head. "The fire was meant for me. The best thing I can do is to lure the threat away. I might find what I need studying Agrippa's spells." He looked away with a downcast sigh. It was only half truth, but somewhere he knew Bree was not ready to hear about Livis. She turned on her heel and strode off while he finished packing up his gear. A short time later, he flew north on his dragon, hoping to draw Cyrus away from his friends and family.

Chapter 14.

Deadman's Hold

Serpent Isle was a mysterious place, even more so at night. The sinuous coves that wove along the shore gave it a shape like the body of a snake. By day, the brooding, crow-haunted cliffs frowned down over the pounding surf. It was one of oldest Black Claw islands, at least from what Livis knew. The local clans still shunned the cliffs, ghostly now in the moonshine, and wore their black blood stripes on their arms to show their lineage and creed.

"Who will join Skarlee and me?" Livis asked.

"I will." Numestis stabbed his dagger in the deck rail.

"Can't do it without me," grunted Farnoss. Maquia, of course, would be Livis's shadow.

Krag and Drass elected to stay back should things go sour and defend their escape by sea. While their schooners lay at anchor at a safe distance, Livis and the others shipped four rowboats and took up oars in silent determination toward the beach.

The prison, looming on the bluff above, was a grey cinderblock, whose rough stone was studded with twin turrets at either end. Two gates stood connected by a high wall. A dusty trail wound up to the jailhouse, nothing more than a goat path. A torch flickered on the mantle over the scarred and weather-beaten door.

The boats ground ashore and Livis and Numestis and their respective parties beached them out of sight behind a rounded outcropping of boulders. Farnoss lifted a hand. "There. See the north end on the bluff. That's where the side entrance lies."

"Still think we should have brought in the dragons as backup," muttered Numestis.

Skarlee slapped the captain's shoulder and hissed for silence. "We've been through this before, Numy. We need to get in and out quietly without any guards raising the alarm."

Up the thistle-shrubbed slope the group snuck like thieves: Livis, Farnoss, Skarlee, Maquia and four others. All were seasoned fighters, with weapons and cutlasses gripped in hand. Their booted feet made with no more noise than the pads of ferrets.

At the gate stood a lone guard, his chin drooping, a yawn heavy on his lips. Livis gave a sharp gesture for silence. Maquia darted forward and snapped the man's neck. Fishing out the man's keys, he and Skarlee put shoulder to the prison door. Two horn-helmed men looked up in surprise from their game of dice. Maquia and Skarlee's swords arched a path of crimson ruin. The sentries died hunched over their rickety table, the dice still clutched in their hands.

A third man in the hallway reached for a dangling rope to sound the alarm bell—but Skarlee surged forward, hurling his knife to take the man in the neck.

A burly guard with a beard emerged from an inner room, steel sliding from his scabbard, Surprise and terror glinted in his eyes. Skarlee knocked him sideways and the sword clattered to the stone. Maquia pounced on him with his longsword, leaving the man writhing in a pool of his own blood.

Livis gave a curt grimace. "Stay together, we need to find our way to the cells fast."

Farnoss fiddled with the dead man's cloak and pulled out a heavy key on an iron ring. He fitted it in the locked door at the end of the guardhouse. They continued down a flight of steps to the main cells.

They moved through the torch-lit passages on swift feet, avoiding any patrols. Reaching the main floor of the prison, Livis discerned a dozen separate cells, with a large one in the center. Her crew spread out, cutting the throats of any guards they encountered. Livis put her hand on the iron bars of the center cell. Nearly twenty figures stretched in the moldy hay. Each wallowed in reeking, tattered garments, with long ragged hair and defiant faces covered in dirt.

"What a foul reek," Farnoss cried, plugging his nose.

Livis put her finger to her lips, urging silence.

Skarlee motioned the prisoners to stand with his sword. Unlocking the gate, he turned to Livis to whisper. "Are you sure this rag-eared lot can fight?"

"A few square meals will set them right," Livis said.

A rough-bearded convict stepped forward, clearly their leader. "I'm called Strut. What be the price of freedom?"

Maquia flourished his blade. "This is your lucky day, Strut. All we require are your worthless lives."

"You have a ship?" crowed the man.

"Aye, and you're going to sail in it," rasped Maquia with a grin.

There came a spate of grumbles from the ragged group, but they stumbled out of their cell, still amazed at their luck.

"Let's get a move on then," grunted Numestis.

The group hurried back the way they had come until they reached the guardhouse. Livis warned the men to silence. "The moonlight might reveal us," she hissed. "We hold until the clouds can hide us."

An eternity seemed to pass, waiting for safe passage. As the moonlight faded, Livis signaled the others, but their stealth came to naught.

They had not yet reached the bottom of the hill, when one of the prisoners tripped on a root, smashing his nose on a rock and crying out in agony. His mate kicked him in the gut, hissing at him for silence, but a torch on the high wall flared to life.

The gong tolled in loud peals echoing across the moonlit bay.

"Kraton end that stupid fool!" hissed Livis.

Booted feet came echoing down the cobblestones from the garrison then arrows were striking the sand around them.

The raiders raced for the rowboats in a shambling run, many of them stumbling on rubber legs.

"Move your coral-spawned hides!" Livis yelled.

Arrows sang out, whizzing over the convicts' heads, catching one in the back. He fell like a piece of driftwood.

Like beetles they scrambled up the beach, insects escaping the jaws of a predatory bird. With a snarling curse, Farnoss directed them into the boats and they set them rocking in the lapping waves.

Livis turned in dismay as Garvee, the third gunner, crumpled as an arrow took him in the eye. "Hurry!" she croaked.

Into the dark waves they rowed as a cannon atop the wall roared to life. Men ducked low in the boats as a near miss sprayed water into their flat-bottomed sterns.

Livis put fingers to lips and gave a shrill whistle, signaling the ships anchored in the harbor. The first wide-waisted dory thudded against *The Singing Gull's* hull and the light crew dropped ladders for them and reached hands down to haul them aboard one by one.

At that moment, a high-hulled ship drove out of the harbor after them. Then came a second. At that moment, a thick fog drifted in from the sea, veiling the moon in a ghostly wrap of fog.

The shriek of a dragon pierced the air.

"They're risking dragons for some escaped prisoners?" croaked Farnoss.

Livs cried out, "It can't be that. There must be a price on our heads. Defend the ship!"

"Take up weapons, you ragbags!" shouted Skarlee over the mayhem.

The deck shuddered as a ship rammed them. Grappling lines hooked on their rails and horned-helmed Black Claws wielding axes and swords stormed across the gap.

With fierce yells, a score of bearded thugs shambled forth to grip cutlasses, axes and knives, and they fought shoulder to shoulder with the pirates of *The Singing Gull*. The prisoners fought like wild dogs rather than risk capture.

Livis was knee deep in corpses by the time the fog cleared, but more were coming.

Livis jabbed out her sword. "There!" she screamed, pointing to the enemy dragon.

The gunner Kisten's head jerked about. With a mad curse he swiveled the harpoon. The line shot out and a gleam of metal hit under the armored breast of the beast. The dragon shrieked in midair and corkscrewed down toward the sea.

"Good shot, Kisten!" cried Livis. "Let's get out of here."

Kirsten returned a faint grin. "Lucky shot."

Someone threw oil onto the enemy deck and Maquia tossed an accompanying lantern. They cut the grappling lines and the enemy ship floated away in a blaze of fire.

In slow motion, *The Singing Gull* drew away from the burning ship and pulled out to sea with the other vessels of her brigade.

Livis sank in a crouch before ship's wheel with a grunt of exhaustion. "That was too close." She peered from face to face, surrounded by the exhausted members of crew and convict alike.

"All for the sake of a few ruffians," growled Skarlee.

"They fought well." said Maquia. "We can use that kind of mettle."

They anchored in a safe place several leagues off Serpents Isle as the moon faded with a red dawn.

Red morning moon, dead by noon. Livis murmured the proverb, a grim feeling pinching her gut, something of a premonition stirring the fibers of her being. She shrugged it off. Just nonsense. She couldn't afford superstition now.

"Call a meeting with Numestis and the other captains." She looked out to sea and frowned, counting only three ships instead of four.

"Where's Krag?"

"We saw him leave before dawn," said Kisten. "Thought you had put them up to some secret task. Come to think of it, Vray our cargoman's gone too."

Livis's jaw sagged. She ran to her cabin to check on Cyrus's stash. The gold was gone. She drew her cutlass and stabbed at her desk until it collapsed.

Maquia came and stood by her side. "Nice kill, Mistress. Vray has skulked off with the gold. Do we go after them?"

"They'll be long gone by now," said Livis.

With many black thoughts on her mind, she forced her anger aside and turned with resolve to face the prisoners huddled in a knot at midships. She ordered Maquia to break open a keg of her finest spirits and let them drink their fill. She saw them fed and gave them new clothing. With solemn ceremony, she addressed them.

"You're sprung from prison, but you aren't free men—yet. You have a debt to pay and I'll take my payment in the blood of your enemies. From this moment on, the penalty for betrayal is death. Serve me loyally though, and I'll make you all rich with a share of the spoils."

A few low cheers rumbled amongst the ragged group, then came grins and laughs.

The rat-tangle-bearded man who had raised voice in the jail spoke in earnest. "We shall fight for you, pirate. You've treated us fairly, and not set us with ball and chain yet. See that you honor your promise."

Livis acknowledged the remark. It seemed she had won their hearts. "The bulk of you'll outfit the *Crowhaunt* for now. The others I'll scatter amongst Drass's, Numestis's and my own crew."

Strut grinned and drank his rum in a leisurely gulp. "Not to worry, 'Mistress'. As long as you keep the rum flowing and the food in plenty, we'll follow you into Kraton's belly itself."

Chapter 15.

SKULLDUGGERY AT SEA

Satisfied that the convicts had been settled in their places, Livis met with her officers. The sudden strange fog faded to a memory, as she focused on repairs. Two more pirate vessels came to join their cause.

The next day, a ship bearing the flag of the home clans approached, hailing them with a companion flag of truce.

Livis, skeptical at first, watched as a young captain rowing in with his quartermaster and engineer to parley with Livis and the pirate band.

"Name's Bresus," he called up from his rowboat as it brushed the hull. "We sailed from Pirate Cove when my dragon scouted your ship. I hear Serle's own daughter has betrayed him. Never cared for that codfish, we'd like to join you."

"A generous offer," Livis called down to him in an even voice. "As you can see, our forces are small—for now. What news from Pirate Cove, Bresus?"

The blond-bearded man's face grew grave. "Tensions are high. I'm sorry to tell you, your mother's been wounded."

"What?" A choked cry came to Livis's throat. "What do you mean?"

Bresus's eyes dimmed. "She took an arrow in the arm from a Black Claw raid. They took the clan by surprise in the middle of the night. We sunk two of their miserable ships before they could escape. The medicus says she'll live."

"Praise to Kraton then! Those cursed Black Claws'll pay!"

Maquia laid a hand on Livis's shoulder. "Don't fret, Mistress. We'll burn their towns all along the coast. I promise that."

"Return to your ship, Bersus," I'll send for you soon. The captain rowed back to his ship and dropped anchor.

Skarlee scoffed at him. "And can you blame them for retaliating? This is Serle's doing. Ever since he joined with that foul wizard, he's been hitting the Black Claw coasts hard and stoking their wrath. It's gotten out of hand. We've been raping their coasts for years now. This is the last straw."

Livis would hear no reason and gave her head a bitter shake. "No mercy, Skarlee."

"What about the gold?" Skarlee asked. "Won't the wizard think we spent it and took his deal?"

Maquia raked his sword along the rail. "We'll use whatever ships we have against this mage should he try to force his hand upon us."

"You've got spirit, Maquia," said Skarlee with a sardonic laugh, "I'll give you that. But not much brains."

Knife in hand, Maquia drove in with a snarl.

Livis sprang to her feet to catch Maquia's knife on her blade. "Now's not the time to turn on each other. I'll deal with Cyrus if it comes to that. For now, let's concentrate on the Black Claws. Any prisoners we take, we give them a choice—to join us and fight, or it's to the mines."

She thought of her mother Darmestra and raw rage pushed bile up her throat. "We'll build a navy that'll be the envy of the world! We'll restore order, then destroy this evil mage."

There were cheers to the boast, but some doubtful mutters ran amongst the crew.

Skarlee grumbled into his beard. "You saw his magic, Mistress. How are we to defeat such a foe?"

Maquia snorted in disgust. "No man's invincible. I don't care how many dragons or what type of magic tricks he has. One harpoon in the gut, it's over." He ran a finger across his neck. "We'll make short work of our wizard, leave it to me."

"Scour the seas for Krag and the crew. Fate'll catch up with them sooner or later, and we'll slit their throats."

They raided up and down the Black Claw coast as they searched for the thieves. They captured two more schooners and freed another group of prisoners to further bolster their ranks.

On the fourth day of full-out raiding, they caught up with Krag. Livis had doubled the number of ships at her command and they now overflowed with fighting men. Krag wisely raised a white flag and surrendered.

Livis's boat glided alongside his. The captains at their bows shouted over the waters, their gunners near the cannons.

"Krag! We've been missing you and our gold," hollered Livis across the gap.

"Aye, Livis, but can you really blame me?"

"I'm sure you won't blame me for seizing your ship and retaking what's mine."

"I would return it to you, but every last piece has been spent. All captains have equal share in the decision-making, remember?"

"That doesn't give you the right—"

"I have new ships and men to outfit them—all for the cause."

Skarlee quipped, "Mercenaries by the look of them."

"How do you like my new sea villains, Skarlee, fresh from the Isle of Mea? An independent island broke free of the Black Claws generations ago. They feud with their brothers all the time."

"I like them not much more than your own treacherous face. And I see some fine new leathers to line your own pockets."

"And why shouldn't I?" shouted back Krag across the waves. He twirled his sword. "I demand some return for my efforts. Wouldn't you? Do you refuse to make use of the ships and men I've gathered?"

Livis hesitated and her heart quailed with the spending of the Cyrus's money. Frustration grew to sudden anger and her heart raged with the urge to lash out and have Krag whipped. Then she softened, hearing the echo of her father's voice in her bitter tone. She shivered, hating the sound. *I'll not be like Serle!* she vowed. "I treat everyone as equals," she cried, "but I will not stand for mutiny. My men will take command of your ships, and you'll surrender to my judgment."

Krag, eyeing the cannons aimed at him, snarled. "Perhaps it's time for new leadership, 'Mistress'. I challenge you to a duel!"

Livis scowled. Krag was a skilled fighter, but she had been training hard with Maquia. No reason why she couldn't win against this blowhard. "Very well, Krag. Winner take all."

Maquia whirled on her. "Mistress, are you sure? Krag is—"

"—an arrogant oaf who needs to be taught a lesson."

Skarlee grinned as Livis drew her sword and fingered her blade with confidence. "We fight on neutral ground," she shouted across the waves. "On Numestis's ship."

"No quarter," he yelled back. "We fight to the death. If I lose, you get my ships and my men. I win, I become first captain, Agreed?" Livis could see in his sharkish expression, he would not hesitate to kill her and see his fortunes rise even further.

"Agreed. Now are you ready to fight, or do you need to wax that fine new coat of yours first?"

The man cursed and ordered his rowboat dropped in the waves. Livis did the same and soon they were both aboard Numestis's ship.

Numestis's mates cleared an area at the midships deck. The various crews gathered around to watch.

Livis drew her cutlass and beckoned Krag to initiate. The man attacked without preamble, hacking furiously in a bid to end the fight with as little ceremony as possible. Livis parried, then gave ground. Maquia had taught her well...wait for an opportunity to draw out an impatient opponent.

Krag made a quick sally to pin her against the mast, but Livis caught the blade on her own, turning it aside as she spun to his left flank. She blocked his strike, then another, while the man began to tire, raining blow after blow with curses thick on his lips. Men began to jeer as Krag's sour threats grew desperate. He overturned a barrel of grog and threw a coiled rope at her. Livis dodged only to earn a cut on her thigh.

She forced back a yelp but held her cool and wiped away the blood.

Krag laughed at the crimson line on her sleek flank and slashed a murderous loop, surging in for the kill. So...the exact move she had been waiting for. Rolling forward, she ducked under Krag's strike and crashed her shoulder into his chest. Krag fell back, wrenching her blade from her hands while she brought both of them to the deck. In instinctive desperation her fingers snatched for the dagger at her belt.

Snarling, Krag's momentum brought him up again, bounding forward to finish her off. Then he paused, peering down at the dagger protruding from his chest. Livis rose to her feet to cheers as Krag sank against the railing, the whites of his eyes wide in disbelief.

She pulled her blade free as Krag gurgled his last breath. "No one steals from me."

Her command now cemented, the pirates went on to raid prisons up and down the coasts and capture what ships they could. Krag's absence was not missed. Livis set Vray along the shore of the Serpent Island, knowing that such men could not be trusted.

On the sixth blood red morning of their reign of terror, a troop of fifty pirate vessels angled out of the mist and tacked in to intercept them. Livis's heart gave a hollow flutter. She checked that emotion and held her head high, calling orders for her crew to maintain battle positions. She had the crow's nest man signal Drass and others to stay close, keeping cannons and dragons on the ready.

The lead ship came abreast *The Singing Gull*, fluttering the white flag of truce.

"That's Serle's ship, Mistress," gasped Farnoss. "We can't outrun them without leaving our fleet ripe for the taking."

Livis stared at her father's schooner, riding high in the water. Men stood at the rails, training fore-cannons straight at them. "Well, let's hear what the sea-crow has to say."

The Persephone drew nearer, and Serle pushed through the knot of men gathered at the port bow to grip the rail. He ordered his fleet of half a hundred warships to stay well back.

"Livis!" he boomed over the water. "I see you've gathered quite the armada. Bravo. But I could have expected nothing less. You're my flesh and blood after all."

She tilted her head in feigned surprise. "And what do you want of me, father? To take these ships as your own?"

"No, no, nothing like that. I've had a change of heart." He spread his arms to include her ship decked with its retro-fitted cannons and decks full of plunder. Her rigging swung heavy with able-bodied seaman and the new faces of recruits.

She shrugged. "Say what you have to say and begone, Serle." There were mutters of approval from the crew.

Serle's lips curled in anger, but he held his peace. His expression dulled, but she could see the gears turning in his mind.

"Join with me and together we will rule the Dragon Sea!" called Serle. "We will take the coasts, the towns and rule the islands."

"I plan on doing that—without you."

"Listen! The wizard Cyrus—"

"I don't want anything to do with that black-slimed creep," cried Livis. "You can take him and all the gold and dragons and shove—"

Almost as if on cue, a daunting shape swooped down from the sky.

"Ah, you've brought more ships for me!" called Cyrus down from his dragon. "Father and daughter, a team united at last," the mage crowed over the wind, his cackling voice edged with sarcasm.

Serle looked up at him with barely-concealed anger. "You have a gift for bad timing."

"I make it my specialty," asserted Cyrus. He turned to Livis, spurring his dragon closer to her ship and goggling crew. "I see you've made good use of the gold I gave you. As for your part of the bargain, you and your father will meet in three days to attack *Three Sisters' Isle*s with both fleets. *Don't* disappoint me."

Livis stroked her cheek, giving a sullen grunt.

Cyrus spurred his dragon closer, gripped with a sudden angry insight. "You've no intention of meeting me at *Three Sisters' Isle*, do you?" His eyes dimmed to slits. "Do you?" he yelled. "You dare to defy me?" His voice, cold as ice, hissed like the viper's.

Livis said nothing; her mouth twitched and a sudden snarl raged from her lips. "Begone, you serpent-tongued bottom feeder. Sacrifice someone else to your monsters, not us."

"So! You wish to see a sample of my power?" His voice hissed. Cyrus held up his runestones in a pale hand. A cloud of foul smoke appeared behind him, all green and thick with menace as it swirled and swarmed. Fantastic shapes formed in the air before his dragon's snout.

The mysterious smoke whipped out and formed into a giant clamshell. He raised his staff and the clamshell flew over the water and snatched Livis from the deck of her ship, closing like a trap around her.

Maquia and Skarlee hacked at the sinister, glowing shape but their blades found no opening. The smoke-formed sides resisted their strikes. Shell and all lifted off the deck.

Livis beat at the magical barrier with her fists while her crew shouted below.

"Cyrus, let her go!" ordered Serle. Harpoons and cannons turned on the wizard. Cyrus lifted a hand and the pirates' harpoons flew wide; their cannonballs turned into green puffs of smoke.

The mage signaled Valoré and the dragon gripped the clam shell in its claws and soared up into the sky with a cry of triumph.

Cyrus's deep-throated cackle faded to a dull echo, as the seamen from both sides stared. Valoré was too fast for their missiles and evaded the gleaming tips that sought to penetrate the wizard's magecraft.

Serle sank to his knees. No amount of drink would ever save him from the sight of his daughter whisked off by that madman.

* * *

The third day passed with still no sign of Livis. Darek paced the beach on Valkyrie, his hands behind his back. The dragons watched him with confusion. Jace had sent an angry letter by dragon reprimanding him for not returning to Valkyrie and helping train recruits. No matter. He knew something had happened to her; he could feel it in his bones. Now he began to worry. Mounting Silver Eye, he flew over the white-capped swells of Dragon Sea, heading north. Winguard and Broodhorn trailed after him.

Up and down the Black Claw Coasts he scoured, looking for her. Instead he found broken debris, wreckage from ships, and fires burning on island shores. Cyrus and Serle's handiwork. Darek's heart sickened over the destruction. He had been distracted from his duties. When would such destruction reach the Red Claw islands?

With no sign of the small schooner that was Livis's ship, he thought to turn back. Night was coming. There. A glint off a metal harpoon caught his attention. The wind whistled in his ears as he banked Silver Eye in a steep dive.

The pirates aboard *The Singing Gull* trained their harpoons on him as he swooped closer.

"Hold!" cried a voice. Skarlee thrust a finger up at him. "You! I knew you were working with the black-robed wizard. Where has he taken her?"

"Cyrus took Livis?" Darek stared gape-eyed.

The pirates frowned at one another. "You claim not to know?"

"No. I was supposed to meet her. She didn't show."

Skarlee spat out a livid curse. "Then take your dragon and find her!"

"I'll find your Mistress," Darek swore, "but I'll need your help against Cyrus."

"Done! If you can find her, we'll kill whoever needs killing," croaked Skarlee.

"I'll gut the black wizard myself," rumbled Maquia, lancing his sword in the air.

With murder in his heart, Darek spurred Silver Eye back into the sky, back to the Rookery to seek Briad. Only he knew where the magician's lair lay. He would use whatever magic it took to extract the knowledge and find that secret place.

CHAPTER 16.

CURAKEE

The red dragon's wings beat at the air. Livis shrieked as it glided through the opening of a gloomy seaside cave and sent her sprawling on the stone. The glowing clam shimmered then dissolved in bands of pale jade-colored smoke, as if it had never existed.

Her eyes flitted about in bewilderment. A black strand of water stretched from shore to cave mouth, rippling in the gloom. In the middle of the chilling water glowed a strange prism, perched on a gnarled tongue of rock. A man was imprisoned inside.

Cyrus leaped off his dragon and raised his mage staff. Livis struggled to gain her feet, but a beam of energy shot out from the staff and struck her in the chest. She sank in agony. Choking, gasping, she tottered to a crouch but fell back rolling in pain on the damp stone.

Cyrus stepped forward, a grin carved on his face. She tried to crawl away. Cyrus grabbed her arm and threw her back roughly on the cold stone and forced her chin up to look at him. "You take my gold and expect to give nothing in return?"

"I didn't spend your gold, you cretin. Krag and his stupid henchmen did—"

"A leader is responsible for those they lead."

"I'll not grovel like a worm before you," she spat. Her chest heaved. Rolling to her feet, she tried to strike him, but Valoré was faster. He thrust his snout in between her and his master who grinned all the more. The dragon bunted her back and she slid across the stone floor, the wind knocked out her. "I'd rather die," she croaked, massaging her bruises.

Cyrus's mouth curled in mockery. "Be careful what you wish for."

She clenched her fists and looked for an avenue of escape. None presented itself.

"I see you are too unruly to see reason." Cyrus sighed. "A pity." He raised his staff, this time his runestones clutched glowing in the other palm. The green rays reflected in Livis's eyes.

She fell in a deep mesmeric spell as he drew her into a world beyond, casting aside her strength of will and free spirit. Her eyelids drooped and her head hung in a state of deep trance.

Cyrus smiled, the satisfaction stretching from cheek to cheek. This day's catch had been grand. The mage boy's consort—this young beauty… A rising leader amongst the foul pirates, perhaps a queen to replace her drunken father.

The dark oracle would shed light on what should be done with her. Yes, he could use her in his plan...*though sacrifice to Dendrok remained the most practical option.*

"The oracle will decide your fate." He prepared the necessary ingredients and soon a foul smoke rose over the shark head talisman. Dire images swam before his eyes—fire and raging beasts, charging him in a mist of vapor, breathing fire and poison. His own shrieks faded in the mists of illusion, then spouted an image of himself hunched over as an old man. A drawn and thin figure, bony like a skeleton and sitting on a fallen log on a lonely shore. His head lay in his hands...a man lonely, pathetic, and stripped of all magic.

Cyrus shook his head in disbelief. He hurled his mage staff aside and swept the air with his hand.

"Oracle!" he bellowed. "Why show me this? I need to see the truth of this girl and how I might use her, not some fanciful tale."

He conducted the divinatory rite, tossing a pinch of myrtle and the egg sack of a frog, the hind legs of newt, and a serpent's tongue. As the shark head disgorged more smoke, doubts flashed before Cyrus's mind. The images moments ago had been disturbing. Could the Oracle have erred?

He turned his eyes back to the pool of smoke rising about the dead shark's head. This time it showed a woman's belly, bloated and a child within—the mage boy with his hand on her curve of abdomen. The pirate girl—daughter of the drunken corsair—would become mother to the mage boy's child. Lord and queen of the band of reavers. Interesting...very interesting.

"So, they will have a child. A child like no other. I will turn this to my purpose and take the stripling as my apprentice. If the Oracle's vision is true and by some freak turn of fate I am to lose my powers, I will absorb his essence as my own."

He set out to put a taint on the girl's womb. First, he tore aside the leather cloak so her bare belly showed, white and tender. His lips uttered the syllables of a forbidden spell.

"*Agnis Moreunt Vaxetir.* I cast the spell of the Darkling Hour, the *Brioasis*—where a child not yet seeded becomes a dark servant. Your unborn child shall taste the dark edge of the god's nectar."

He mixed the fetid powder of beetlewort and stag worm into a paste, drawing a curved symbol on her belly and pressed his mage staff down upon it. "*Nagastos! Ablastis! FERUS NAUR!*"

There came a fierce flame that licked the stalactites dangling above and nearly singed the black hair on Cyrus's head. It burned an odd star shape in her navel, at which the near naked body flinched, even while ensorcelled in a deep trance.

"Tis done!" Cyrus cackled. "You will be the instrument of my power and the mage boy's doom." He bound her mind to his, concealing from her all memory of what had happened.

* * *

Darek stood before Briad, trying to sort through the young man's garbled thoughts—he saw an image of Cyrus's lair concealed in an underground cave on some deserted island. He grabbed the young man's shoulder and looked into his pale eyes. "Think, Briad!" He breathed an exasperated sigh. "Livis's life may depend on this."

"I don't know, Darek, I don't know!" the dragon rider moaned. "It was months ago and Cyrus never let me out of his cave. When Agrippa and I escaped, the light was fading. It was almost impossible to see anything. We flew south toward Swordfish Island. I remember a hill, a bare outcrop like a great bald eagle's crown overlooking the inlet. The stones were a curious sandstone pink. The cove was shaped like an *S*, like one of those deadly serpents that haunt Cyrus's waters."

Darek chewed his lip. "Time is running out."

"What are you going to do?"

An insight and flicker of hope kindled Darek's spirit. He would just have to hope for some luck. "I'm leaving right away."

Briad winced. "Don't go alone. The harbor is crawling with serpents, or was. Agrippa and I barely made it out with our lives and at the cost of one of Agrippa's dragons torn apart in a serpent's jaws."

Darek shuddered at the image. "I'll do what I must." He put his hand on Briad's shoulder and the young man gave a faint, faltering smile.

"Go with speed, Darek. Kraton protect you."

He paused and studied Briad's face. "Remember, say no word to Jace about our conversation. I don't want to jeopardize any more lives."

He had one final loose end to tie up before he left. Leaving Briad, he caught up with Bree as she was cleaning out the dragon stalls. She was alone—fortunately. He approached on delicate feet.

"Bree. I have to leave for awhile."

"I'm getting used to it. What is it this time?" She halted her shoveling, her face crinkled in irritation.

"Livis is in trouble."

"Who's Livis?"

"Captain Serle's daughter."

Bree's mouth dropped as if she couldn't believe her ears. "The pirate that's been wreaking havoc on the Black Claw coasts? Is this some kind of joke?"

"No joke, Bree, she's innocent of her father's sins, in trouble and needs my help."

"Are you crazy? How do you even know her?"

"She helped me to escape from slavery—"

Bree got very quiet. "I see."

"When I was flying back from Valkryie. I ran into her. She was supposed to meet with me on Valkyrie three days ago, negotiations and all—She never showed up. Her mates told me she'd been kidnapped by Cyrus."

"I thought Cyrus was dead?"

"I—I'm afraid he's alive."

"Go to your pirate wench then, Darek. Seems as if she's more important than defending your own people. You and I are done. I see now where your heart lies." She tossed her dung shovel to the floor with a clatter and stalked off.

Darek winced. He hadn't wanted to hurt her. He nearly went after her, but hung his head in shame. There was no time to try and explain. He couldn't deceive her, nor did he have time to argue over fine points. He'd lost her.

Darek left the dragon pens in a black mood, pausing to gather some dry food and fruit before readying his gear. He hopped on Silver Eye and set out north and west over the lush forests of Swordfish Island toward the no man's land between Red Claw and Black Claw territory. He scoured the islands for Cyrus's secret hiding place.

There must be hundreds or thousands uninhabited islands dotted across the endless seas. When he thought of Livis and her perfect smile and dauntless spirit, his heart leaped. The thought of that madman harming her set his blood on fire.

Darek began probing the surrounding area with his mind, invoking the power of communion he had been learning in Agrippa's secret study.

There! A faint murmur at the edge of his mind, like the flutter of a bird's wing. It was a cry for help. Livis was out there somewhere, west and north of here. He closed his eyes, trusted his instincts and flew on. His eyes searched for anything remotely resembling the strange bay with the salmon pink crown of rock that Briad had described.

For hours he rode, until Silver Eye's wings grew heavy. Could Briad's memory have been mistaken? As he was about to turn away, he saw a cluster of pink between two islands separated by a thin strait. Livis's presence grew stronger in his mind. His heart could have leapt for joy.

The bay glimmered, sheltered behind a rounded hill with a bare top of pink stone. A dormant volcanic peak poked up to the west. Darek paused to scan the surrounding water. Did serpents guard the bay? A stir rippled the placid water at the far end.

Briad had mentioned an underwater portal. He would have to risk entering the water. Giving the ripple a wide berth, he landed Silver Eye on the far shore. His dragon waded into the water with a questioning look just before an eerie, wedge-shaped head took pains to surface. Darek inhaled a deep breath and the two quietly submerged.

Following his instincts, he directed Silver Eye among the fungus-like rock formations. It grew darker by the minute as they dove deeper. A narrow channel reared out of the gloom; on Silver Eye's faithful strokes they followed it to the mouth of a cave, carved into the coral-like rocks. Around him the porous rock glowed with a green, luminous algae.

The strain on his lungs grew. He reached a dead end. *This had to be it.* Tracing frantic fingers along the rock face, he made out the contours of a smooth metal ring. Summoning his inner power, he pressed his palms against the rock and pushed.

A deep rumbling shook the surrounding mantle. The rock fell inward, opening into a shadowy tunnel. Darek swam through the gap, pushing the stone door wider so his dragon could squeeze through.

They surfaced in a rocky chamber and he took greedy gulps of air. Silver Eye had not even been phased. If only he could hold his breath like a sea dragon.

Even as his thoughts traveled to Livis and what the dark mage could be doing to her, he pulled himself onto the stone shore, blinking, allowing his eyes time to adjust to the dimness. Muted light flickered from some crude sconces bracketed along the stone wall. He had found Cyrus's lair.

He drew his sword, sloshing up the watery corridor. Silver Eye padded behind him without fear. Darek shivered. What was this place? He poked his head into a side tunnel, lips parted at the sight of a crude workshop. Tables and benches stood littered with skulls and potions. This could only be Cyrus's handiwork.

Silver Eye rumbled a low growl, sensing danger ahead. Reaching out with his mind, Darek probed for Livis—then flinched at a flash of movement at the end of the tunnel. An old grey dragon lumbered out of the shadows, snapping at him. Darek lurched back, the creature's long yellow teeth dripping slime as it rose on its hind legs in challenge.

Silver Eye crouched, ready to attack, her scales shimmering an odd bluish color.

"Hold up!" Darek called. He sent waves of truce and used his power to soothe the creature. Its mind was a patchwork of terror, shattered and twisted from years of Cyrus's cruelty. The dragon responded only to fear. He revealed a hint of his power, while offering a quick escape. It proved all too easy to cow the dragon, but would it last? It blinked and shuffled away like a dazed auroch.

A distant shriek echoed up the tunnel. Darek crouched on the balls of his feet, his heart jiggling in his throat. *That sounded like Livis.*

He hurried toward the sound, his full attention now on the muted cry, recognizing Livis's singsong voice as he rushed into a large cavern.

A large, red-scaled dragon came lumbering from the shadows and bared fangs and showed claws. Silver Eye sprang to his protection.

THE DRAGON SEA CHRONICLES: THREE BOOK SERIES

Silver Eye! Fend off this dragon! Kill it if you must. I need to find Livis.

Chapter 17.

Sacrifice

Livis jerked awake from her trance, a gasp on her lips. Her belly felt sore and she vomited. Damp stone surrounded her, a clammy chill lingering in the air. Was her memory failing her? The wizard was nowhere to be seen. This place was different. She lay on her side, blinking in a vast cavern with a shaft of pale light shining down from a high slit in the rock above.

Rising to her feet, she traced fingers along the cold, damp wall, then crouched to pick up a handful of pebbly rock. A sickly blackness plagued her mind. She felt as if something had been done to her, or had it all been some fevered dream? She shoved the spidery memories from her head and crept ahead.

Her eyes wheeled to the far wall where a row of rock teeth jutted out. The flash of white fangs disappeared beyond as of a creature struggling to burst through. Echoes of strange murmurs and grunts pierced the gloom, human? Then a slither and a hiss.

She sensed a movement nearby. A white and brown banded serpent darted from a hole, its tongue flickering out at her. She recoiled and kicked at it. The creature hissed at her, raising its wedge-shaped head like a cobra and struck, missing her foot by inches before slithering away to disappear in another dark hole.

Livis shivered. From the ledge above came the thud of heavy paws and an unmistakable gust of a dragon's breath. A pair of shining eyes revealed the hideous red dragon that had carried her to this place. The thing looked hungry.

Cyrus appeared at the dragon's side, stroking its scales with loving tenderness. The man's dark eyes gleamed like a dragon's, his hair matted like a bedraggled rat. Livis stepped back, looking with desperation for an escape.

The mage's cryptic voice rumbled, "You may go, Valoré."

The beast snuffled and turned on its hind legs to disappear back up the passage.

Figure stood staring down at the cavern, at its single occupant. "Welcome to Bergerax. You wonder why I have brought you here?" His echo boomed like a distant evil bell.

"What do you want?" she said, not liking the waver in her voice.

Cyrus grunted and motioned to a sunken pit in the floor. Livis heard a human wail and ran to the edge of the pit. A ragged man clung to the wall, half-starved. "I thought you should see what becomes of those who betray me."

Livis hissed, appalled at the wizard's cruelty; she knelt, better to study the victim, feeling a pang of sympathy for the wounded, trembling man below. She saw a figure who had once been handsome, but now hunched with wild darting eyes and haggard limbs. His limp hair stuck to his scalp like a drowned rat.

"Who are you?" the man called up in a hoarse whisper.

"I'm Livis, and you?"

"Raithan, once captain of the Black Claws," he mumbled. "I've a daughter—much like you. Meira, the same age. If you survive this, tell her my thoughts were, of her until the end." He hung his head and his lips trembled, as if he knew in his bones he would never see his daughter again.

"Meira?" croaked Livis. "I remember that name. Darek, a Red Claw, mentioned a sister by the name of Meira. Do you know him?"

"Aye, the same. Darek and Meira—they're half brother and sister."

Livis's eyes widened in astonishment. She licked her lips. "Then, that means…"

"Enough!" growled Cyrus. "Now that you two have made the proper introductions, let us move on."

Livis recoiled at the fetid reek, of stagnant pools and musky, rotting things.

"It is time you witnessed Raithan's punishment." With a malicious sneer Cyrus flourished a hand to the mesh of rock pillars where Livis had seen some foul beast struggling to gnaw its way through.

"You'll have to forgive Dendrok. He hasn't eaten for several days." The wizard gave a raucous chortle. "He's nearly broken through. When he does, Raithan will receive his trial by combat."

"Let's get it over with," coughed Raithan. Yet Livis thought she saw some fight in the condemned man's eyes.

Cyrus sighed. "Prepare yourself! The trial begins, now!"

Raithan flashed a rude gesture Cyrus's way.

Cyrus rubbed his wrists. "You've a part to play as well, Livis. If you can reach the ledge atop the cavern, you will win your freedom. Fail, and Dendrok will have two sacrifices instead of one." He stared meaningfully at Raithan.

"Let her go, Cyrus," Raithan grunted. "She has nothing to do with this business between you and I."

"She has everything to do with it!" thundered Cyrus. "You've both betrayed me! The pair of you will suffer for it! The question is, which one of you will be the first to enter Dendrok's jaws?"

"You're a madman!" shrieked Livis.

Cyrus crafted a small bow. "Thank you for that wisdom, wench. Dendrok requires a sacrifice—to achieve his birthright. So it is ordained. The dark oracle has spoken."

"What's he talking about?" moaned Livis. She looked up at the ledge, an avenue of safety, circling along the cavern and up to the high slit above.

Raithan shook his head "You want me to explain the musings of a lunatic?"

"Silence!" Cyrus screamed. "Insults will earn you little quarter."

The captain grabbed at a jagged rock. "Find anything you can use as a weapon," he hissed.

Livis nodded and moved to the side to retrieve a broken spear.

Cyrus studied their efforts with some amusement. "Little good that will do you."

The rockface holding Dendrok back had started to crumble. Livis leaned down into the pit and extended a hand to help Raithan out.

A pair of jaws broke a hole in the crust. Long claws reached through to widen the opening.

"Get on my shoulders!" Raithan hissed, crouching down by the wall where the ledge swung lowest. "I'll lift you to the ledge."

"But how will you get up?"

"Do it!"

Shaking her head, Livis climbed on his back. With a grunt, Raithan lurched to his feet, hoisting her up and she shot out a hand to the jagged ledge.

With precarious skill, she teetered in place as her fingers grasped cold damp rock but fell short by several inches. "It's no use," she cried. "I can't reach it."

"You'll have to jump!"

She jumped back down. "I won't make it."

"Then we're both dead," murmured Raithan sadly.

Dendrok had gnawed through the thinnest pillar and spat out the last crumbling bits from its mouth. Like a water snake, it squeezed through the narrow gap and flopped on all stubby fours, moving head from side to side like a gator. Its tongue flickered out and its web-like wings drooped as if numb. The eyes blinked, pinpointing its quarry. It sprang in their direction.

Livis grabbed up the largest rocks and leaped aside as it whistled by her side like a blur of nightmare.

Raithan dodged the white, dripping fangs that came snapping at him. He whirled and tossed his chunk of rock, striking the creature square on the snout. The creature growled and swatted out a clawed foot.

Livis threw her spear, taunting the dragon, "Over here, you ugly beast! Catch me if you can!"

"Beware the tail! It's poison," shouted Raithan.

The creature slavered and lunged at her. Livis rolled back, stumbling as she struggled to get away. Razor-tipped fangs snapped out at her. She howled as it grazed her leg, leaving a thin trace of crimson.

Raithan lifted a heavy rock, smashing it on the spiked tail. Dendrok whirled, giving Livis time to limp away.

Cyrus clicked his tongue. "Is that the best you can do?" he crowed down.

Claws arched out at Raithan, who grunted and sprang sideways, trapped now against wall. He yelled at Livis. The dragon's back arched just under the ledge.

Spying an opportunity, she leaped up on the monster's spine and clambered up to the ledge, her fingers grasping at the crumbling rock. Raithan attacked, striking at the beast's eyes. Her fingers clutched empty air... then three fingers caught at the edge, her legs dangling.

The beast knocked Raithan back and leaped up, snapping at her heels. Livis kicked at its crusty snout. With a hoarse gasp, she pulled herself up.

Squealing in frustration, Dendrok turned to Raithan, who backed away.

"I'll find a weapon!" Livis yelled. Wriggling across the ledge, she hugged the wall and crept inch by inch where another tunnel joined the cavern. Bits of crumbling rock tumbled down.

Cyrus, grinding teeth at her progress, lifted a hand to direct a searing blast. Livis teetered back on her good leg as green fire shattered the rock at her feet. She jumped back with a gasp. Twenty feet of ledge crumbled before her eyes.

"Oops!" called Cyrus. "How careless of me!"

Dendrok's wings fluttered as it closed on Raithan. Cyrus's dark chuckle reverberated through the cavern.

As Livis sank to her knees, she caught a shiver of movement from a tunnel to her side.

A figure with strong young body stormed out and stood on the ledge, chest heaving, sword in hand.

There was a familiarity to the proud stance. Could it be? "*Darek!*" Her breath caught in her throat.

The Dragon Mage ran to the ledge's edge.

"You!" cried Cyrus. "Come and meet your doom."

Darek held up his sword and a green orb of fire grew around it. "We'll see about that, Cyrus." He threw a ball of blistering fire.

* * *

Cyrus deflected the attack and launched a bolt of his own. Darek leaped aside. Flakes of rock peeled off the wall where Darek's head had been.

Livis and Raithan both alive. A miracle! Raithan didn't look though as if he had long.

He instantly sized up the situation, sending a torrent of mental sound to confuse the half dragonish creature hovering in the pit. It turned to face him, pumping its wings with fury, but seemed unable to stay aloft in the cavern. He threw up a shield around himself and Livis.

Darek took a running leap and jumped to the floor. He rolled to his feet to face the drago-serpent. As he hoped, Cyrus paused his attack, not wanting to hit his own creation. Dendrok surged toward him.

"Down, you hellion!" he commanded.

The dragon charged him, bypassing the command, its mind like a serpent. What was it? Some hybrid of serpent and dragon? But neither. The thing was a slithering monstrosity of wild potential, an untamable deformity of this world.

As it winged in, Darek felt a strange fluctuation in his magic. He watched his blast bounce off the drago-serpent's hide like rain off a duck's back.

Cyrus laughed, pleased at his creature's natural resistance to magic. "How do you like my new creation, mage boy? You'll find him a formidable adversary. Dendrok, kill them...now!"

Darek gasped as the dragonish beast lurched at him.

"No!" cried Darek. With a livid curse, he loosed a beam of mage fire that singed the beast's nose with flame before it could devour Livis and Raithan. The creature gave a scream of agony and swatted at its snout in pain. Such assaults, as powerful as they were, did not dent its scaly hide. With a fury of ages it dove at Darek, and launched claws raking the black stone.

Darek spun back in fright, clawing for support on the ledge. Cyrus loosed more magic upon him, green rays slewing sideways in a wild rush. Darek absorbed the first volley with his shield and dodged the follow-up bursts.

"Run!" he yelled to Livis, pointing at a tunnel opening down the ledge from where she stood.

Cyrus's shrill words filled the cavern as summoned a foul wind that knocked Raithan to his knees.

"Go!" Raithan, shouted. "Leave me!"

Livis's eyes grew wide with fright. She reached the tunnel and turned back to look at Raithan.

Dendrok, driven back by the falling rock, loomed like a shadow of death over Raithan and both Darek and Raithan knew the captain had seconds to live.

"Save yourself," Raithan howled. He met Darek's eyes. "I'm sorry."

The monster struck with its barbed tail, impaling Raithan in the stomach.

Raithan grunted in pain.

"Noooo!" Darek cried out in horror. He was too late.

The drago-serpent roared and its jaws descended to devour Raithan. Livis turned her head, choking with grief.

Darek reached out with his mind, drew in the gamut of his mage powers. While one blast arched toward the gorging serpent, Cyrus stared, amazed, as Darek closed his eyes, constructed a shimmering blue ladder-like bridge that folded across the twenty-foot gap.

"Get across!" Darek cried at Livis. "Find higher ground" He pushed the distraught woman forward. Shock had overwhelmed her.

A shriek of ecstasy shrilled from the beast's maw that rocked the roof of the cavern as Raithan's blood fired the Spell of Binding. Cyrus had cast such spell on the dragon from its birth. Its back arched like a bow. From its putrid jowl came an ear-splitting howl that quaked the very rocks to the core. Imbued with a power undreamed of, the beast shot up like a hurricane. Its iridescent wings in full power, it fled past the quaking victims clinging horrified to the ledge and crashed against the thin slit of rock above. Shards crumbled and fell down into the stagnant pools below.

The beast bounced back, shaking its dazed crown. Again it smashed its serpentish skull against the rock, as if impervious to pain. This time, huge chunks of rock fell from on high, while the creature slipped through the opening to raise snout in a final shriek of rapture to the sky.

Fear twisted Cyrus's face. He rumbled dark incantations, letting them gather weight in a whirling ball of power. He launched the Spell of High Binding on the beast. To no avail. The beast tore through the rock, shearing off bits of its wings in the process, as a bird tears through a spider's web in search of the fly. Nothing could stop it as it tore through the last layers of rock and moss and moldering earth and gained its freedom at last.

Darek took the moments to grab up Livis and flee that cavern of madness while the deranged wizard stared, crestfallen.

"How did you—" croaked Livis.

"Never mind. Keep going!" Darek pushed her on, keeping his eyes closed, holding the visualization of the bridge.

The moment his powers of visualization faltered, the emanation shimmered and its blue-glowing outline vanished and he slipped, his leg falling through. With a grimace, he pulled himself up and scurried on. He took a running leap, grabbed for the other side, just as the mirage winked out forever. His fingers clutched the crumbling edge.

"Darek, grab my hand!" She sprang for him, clawing at his arms and pulling him up. Her raven hair was blood- and grime-streaked in the gloom, but her eyes shone with a fierce light.

Cyrus, saw their escape imminent and roared up a challenge and summoned his beastly red-scaled dragon, Valoré.

Cyrus, enraged and thunderstruck, summoned his beastly red-scaled dragon, Valoré. It seemed he didn't control Dendrok after all. Perhaps the Spell of High Binding had failed.

Just at that moment, Silver Eye came flying out of the passage, her claws raking at the dark-robed Cyrus, who ducked back and gave a grunt of roaring surprise and anger.

He flung a bolt of magic which missed her hide by inches and continued on to strike the far wall. A great slab of rock fell into the pool below.

She coursed up the cavern at that place where Darek and Livis stumbled in the murk, a great gash on her side where the red-scaled dragon had clawed her.

As Silver Eye flapped in place beside him, he jumped on her back and drew Livis beside him.

Cyrus mounted Valoré and streamed up after them, the dragon's teeth aching for a piece of Silver Eye, to whom he had lost the last fight.

Darek burst through the gap; Livis clung to him, her heart thumping against his back.

Out from the gaping hole the red dragon burst. Cyrus, at first pursued Darek and the girl with a blistering vengeance as the sun's last rays fled the skies. But he turned on sight of his drago-serpent flapping with mad glee for the shelter of the nearest volcano. "Back, Valoré! Follow Dendrok!'"

Darek spurred Silver Eye away from the wretched place, to the islands that dotted the seas to the east.

Chapter 18.

A Seed is Sown

 Darek and Livis flew on the back of Silver Eye away from the dark loom of Curakee Island. He turned to gaze back as blazing mage fire light the distant volcanic cone and the twilight sky.

 Cracks, bangs of doom...such could only be Cyrus battling his drago-serpent in the dormant cone. Darek shuddered and Livis cringed.

 He felt her quivering body press herself against him. "Take me far from this horror," she murmured.

 "I will Livis, I will." With a wordless grunt, he spurred Silver Eye through the darkening sky. Her flanks were battered and gashed, but his wounded dragon surged tirelessly on.

 For leagues they flew, Livis nursing the slash on her leg as the stars wheeled over them and the sea breezes stilled. A dark blot appeared below and Darek swung Silver Eye down toward the island growing larger and larger.

"I knew there was something special about you," whispered Livis in a husky tone. "I felt it in my bones the moment I saw you."

Darek smiled, his eyes slitted with mischief. "I thought it was my good looks and wit."

"That too," she laughed, batting him with a playful swat on the shoulder.

Guiding them to a place up the shore, Darek dismounted between a grouping of sea furs and a copse of windblown gumwoods. He helped Livis down, his hand lingering on her hip. The tide washed moonlit water up the sparse beach. "This should be a safe place to rest for the night. I'll make a fire."

She gave a wordless murmur but stumbled, clearly exhausted. Darek caught her as she swayed. "Kraton! You're hurt. Here, sit down. Let me see that leg."

She winced as she sat, extending her leg as Darek peeled back the sopping leather. The dark cut ran from ankle to knee, still oozing blood.

"Another inch and that monster would have killed me," she grunted.

"You fought well."

"Your friend, the Captain, I'm so sorry. He seemed like a brave man."

"Raithan!" Darek rasped. A flurry of mixed emotions gripped his heart. Yet in the aftermath he could only feel sadness, despite the grief and slavery the captain had caused him. He spread palms an inch above her wound and moving them in slow circles, visualizing warmth and a rosy good will. A cleansing heat tingled in the wound and the young woman's leg twitched.

"Oooh..oh... What are you doing?"

"Relax." He cauterized the cut, stopping the flow of blood. Then he reached into the wound with rich healing energies and began to mend the tissue that had been damaged. He let out a breath and a shiver ran through his upper body.

"Another of your rare talents?" she gasped.

"Agrippa was trying to teach me the finer points of healing before he died. I'm sorry to say he had not enough time, but I've been practicing. There, that's the best I can do. Silver Eye is next but I have to rest."

Feeling much relieved and lighter of spirit, she gained her feet and limped around, clearly pleased by the lack of pain. "Ok, dragon boy, in the meantime let's get to work on that fire." Darek, shaking his head at her resilience, helped gather up driftwood and fallen dalcus leaves for a camping pallet.

"I don't think your girlfriend is going to like us hunkering down together for the night."

Darek gave a rueful sigh. "That's over now. Bree heard one mention of your name and bailed on me."

She chuckled out a thin laugh. "I have that effect. Not to be known as a man-stealer, Darek, but in your case, I'll make an exception."

Darek looked away, still unsure of his feelings.

Livis shivered. "It's cold Darek. Would you hold me?"

He swallowed hard, but wrapped his arms around her. A rustle of passion like no other stirred in his chest. "You're beautiful beyond words, Livis. I'll never stop thinking of you. I couldn't stand the thought that you were in danger. I'll kill Cyrus for what he did to you."

She shuddered, her shoulders convulsing. "I don't think that's a good idea."

"Why not? I've beaten him before."

A wild fear entered her eyes and passed over her pale face like a cold wind from a storm. She shook her head. "Whatever grave that madman has risen from, he's become more powerful than ever."

Darek scoffed. "No matter. He'll pay for what he's done."

"Stay with me, please." He held her tight, taking in her scent from the top of her hair. Her skin was soft and inviting to his touch. She leaned back into him as his breath fell hot upon her neck. She turned her head and he kissed her. Darek felt her hands search his body, pass over his arms and to his chest and lean stomach. They lay down together by the fire as the waves continued to pound against the surf and the fire flickered with warmth. That night they spent wrapped in each other's arms, passion washing between them like a storm, sharing a moment that would change the world…

Bathed in the afterglow of union, they nodded off to sleep. Neither saw the star-shaped flash of light in Livis's navel Cyrus's dark prophecy began its inevitable journey.

* * *

Cyrus employed the mighty power of Valoré to catch up with his errant servant Dendrok as he hovered before the chalky mouth of the dormant volcano. Aldrax was its name and revered by a distant tribe out of time and mind. The creature let out a hiss of warning as his master approached. More than ever did the hatchling look like a flying serpent in his late stage of development. Cyrus's lips compressed in a roil of mixed pride and anger.

"Aye, you magnificent beast! Why do you threaten me? 'Tis I who birthed you. Have you forgotten? Come and attack me and see what happens!"

The drago-serpent understand some of these words but stared at him with sightless eyes. The creature had been deformed since birth, but with its new powers it no longer needed eyesight. So passed a battle of wills between mage and serpent. The drago-serpent hissed and lashed its growing poisonous tail, now deadlier than ever—but Cyrus dodged the fangs and tail, his malevolence an overpowering force.

He lashed out with a green beam of fire and stung the beast on its left flank. The creature shrieked and its wings folded back, caught by an invisible net that wrapped about it like a fly in a spider's web.

The beast plummeted down the forgotten volcano and landed spine-first, kicking up a cloud of dust at the bottom of the ashy caldera.

Cyrus drifted down after it on Valoré with leisure, gloating like a clucking chicken.

The drago-serpent writhed in pain on the shards and ashes below. Its eel-ish body glistened in the starlight and rising moonlight like something from another world, something undreamed of. Wings like wasp wings, insectoid to the end, made Cyrus reel with pride at his sorcery. Cyrus came to settle beside his errant beast. He chanted the endearment spell and Dendrok was once more his, a thrall under his power. He gave a terrible, grave chuckle.

"Don't be disappointed, my pet. All eventually kneel to my will. Rise and pay obeisance to me, Cyrus, Dragon Mage of Dragon Sea! Endless rewards will be yours for carrying out my will of death and fire. Crush my enemies, Black Claw and Red Claw alike. I have given you life and power—power beyond any creature's measure. Yet you sit there like an angry cat and spit at me. No more!" With a vengeful cry, he reached in his robe and threw a pinch of caustic powder at its snout, igniting it with a spin of his mage staff. The dust flared and scorched the beast's face. Dendrok howled in pain. "Yes! Feel the scars you gave me at your birthing—and as you do, let our shared pain bind us! *FERUS NAUR!*"

The creature's eyes shut; its pale tongue loosed a hiss of torment.

Cyrus patted the creature's head. "A fitting punishment for your disobedience, Dendrok. But so too come the rewards."

He raised his hands and the creature's cloudy eyes cleared. The blindness was lifted and Dendrok could see.

"Challenge me again and your blindness will return."

He mounted Valoré and flew up out of the volcano as the blazing stars burned in their bright profusion. The beast, compelled to obey and overwhelmed with the return of its sight, took wing after him.

Landing in the bay, Cyrus hauled three of the Bimsbrun sacrifices out of the hidden cave where he kept them along the shore. Pale, shivering creatures with haggard faces, whimpering in the night breeze. Cyrus dismounted Valoré and prepared the necessary ingredients. Then he set a fire blazing. Serpents would rise tonight. He raised his arms to the sky, chanted the forgotten words, *"Fastaslix Neros Maunos Fuit!"*

Dendrok cocked his head at the sound, watching closely as a nebular shadow crept over Curakee Island. A dozen grotesque shapes slithered from the waves and onto the moonlight beach like silent wraiths. Lean and sleek they gathered as one, with wedge-shaped heads and pale, green-gleaming saucer eyes. Never blinking, they contemplated the human victims with a hunger unknown to even dragons. The human victims cringed, fought against their bonds, but to no avail, exposed as they were to the serpents' tongues and pointed fangs. Their cries faded. Twelve new beasts, sated with human blood, became new servants under Cyrus's power, ready for the dark deeds ahead.

* * *

Darek awoke before dawn and scouted out a grove of palms, heavy with fresh coconuts. He picked several for Livis, dropping them by her side along with a cache of fish caught by Silver Eye.

Darek conjured a fire and roasted eelfish on gumwood skewers. He and Livis ate in peace, with the silence between lovers stretching for long moments.

Livis gazed into his eyes. Her heart, he saw, filled with pride and appreciation. They kissed for long moments unwilling to let one another go and unsure when they would see each other again. The fragility of life on the Dragon Sea was ever in question, a constant source of worry on any islander's mind.

"If only we could stay here forever, Darek, far from the worries of this mad world."

Darek stroked her arm and ran his fingers through her hair, relishing every moment he had spent with her, and she blinked with appreciation at his tenderness. He smiled but fell silent. Cyrus was a vile menace that must be stopped at all costs. Now that he knew where his hideaway was, there could be no other choice. He would return with Jace and the entire Red Claw clan to crush the mage.

Livis firmed her lip. "Take me back to my crew, Darek. I'll fight this wizard with you and defy my father if I must."

Darek gave a quiet grunt of acceptance. "I thank you for your support. The raiding needs to stop."

She nodded and Darek grew solemn. "I may need to call on you for help soon." He sat up and looked across the water, wondering where Cyrus would strike next.

He helped Livis to her feet and onto Silver Eye's back. He mounted his faithful dragon and guided her airborne to search out *The Singing Gull*, feeling a renewed sense of purpose as never before. At all costs, he would stop Cyrus.

Chapter 19.

Visilee

Life at the Rookery was a welcomed relief. They trainees had settled back into their routine after the recent sabotage, and yet Darek felt something brewing in the air. He knew he should tell Meira what had happened to her father, but he didn't have the heart to spring that news on her now. Let her remember him as he was.

While Jace instructed a group of young riders on storm weather battle tactics, an unknown rider, flying a blue-gray dragon, landed with a heavy thud in the training yard. All eyes turned to her. Darek saw the crest of Three Sisters' Isles on her leather jerkin.

Jace came hurrying over to soothe the panting beast. "What is it, longrider? You have come far."

"Aye, Master Jace!" the woman croaked, breathless. "Terrible news! Serpents and dragons have overrun the Visilee coast and are laying waste to the Port Town. With them are half-a-hundred ships flying the banner of the free band pirates."

Jace cursed. "What? Kraton's devils! This news comes at the worst possible time. We're undermanned and the trainees are not all ready for battle." He turned to those gathered, of which more were arriving. "Darek. Round up the riders, we fly at once to Visilee. Vass! Sound the alarm! Kraton take us. This is Cyrus's work."

"We knew it was coming," muttered Darek.

Jaced ignored the remark. "Meira, fly down to alert the Cape Spear guard." He grunted. "Have the sea guard launch every ship they have. We can reach Visilee within the hour. The schooners will take longer, at least a few hours more, even the fastest runners of our fleet. We will have to hold until they do. Devil strike all serpents!"

Men and women hastened to obey.

"Bree, Briad—you'll fly in my Wing with Meira. Darek, stay with me as well. Make sure you outfit two competent riders with Agrippa's devices."

"Not to worry, Jace. I've already instructed Vesinex and Hasilnor on the use of the solaricus."

Jace nodded. The yard exploded in a flurry of activity. Riders donned padded leathers and outfitted their dragons with protective mail plate from the armory. This would be the first real engagement for many. Tensions were riding high as flushed faces looked on with excitement and fear.

The first veteran riders took to the air with the sounding of a gong, while many geared up in their boiled leather and iron helms. Any skilled marksmen grabbed arrows and darts, strapping quivers, filled with hundreds of projectiles, to their harnesses.

The five starfish talismans from Agrippa's lab Darek distributed amongst the youngest riders. They drew straws and Briad was one of the lucky fighters to gain a protective amulet. Darek placed the amulet in his palm and closed the young man's fingers around it. "Take it, Briad, and may Kraton protect you."

Briad's lip quivered. "I owe you everything, Darek. I won't let you down."

"Good lad," said Darek, slapping him hard on the back. "Now let's get going." A cheer went up amongst the riders.

The army flew south over the moody, grey-waved seas. The attack had come later than he had anticipated, giving them a flood of new recruits. At seventy strong, would it be enough?

Silver Eye, fiercest of all dragons, could out distance any in the pack, so Darek pulled ahead to scout out the terrain. His father's protests died in the wind.

The seas opened up to an endless plain of cresting waves. Aster Island grew in size on the horizon. Skirting the bouldery coast, the wing of riders banked east and on toward Visilee Island. Kraton, the sacred volcano, loomed like an open wound across the sea to the east, its black, stark peak smoldering with flames, and now gray smoke, as if it might erupt any moment. None could guess the will of that mountain. It might belch ash into the air at any time.

Darek did not like what he saw. Visilee island came into view, the most distant of the Three Sister's Islands: a dark green blur of sea firs with wide sandy shores overlooking the Serpents' Deeps to the east. On its beach an unholy legion gathered. Squinting in disbelief, Darek sat up in his harness and his breath drew short.

Cyrus's mutant dragon hovered at the forefront, a bluish-green behemoth, grown fat and huge as from a glut of magic. Cyrus rode behind, leering from the back of his red dragon, runestones glittering in a palm. Three other dragons ranged along the coast, including the old grey dragon Windbiter—but the real threat was on the beach. Nearly thirty serpents slithered on the sand and in the shallows, while a fleet of pirate ships guarded the bay.

Jace and his seventy riders soared in, breaking from formation to meet Cyrus and his army.

In moments, Albatross Cove was awash with foam and bloody water. The wreckage of boats and floating bodies sickened Darek's heart. The serpents had retreated to the water after smashing the town and destroying all the piers. The smaller fishing settlements up the coast lay in shambles. Cyrus had conjured a massive tidal wave that had leveled buildings, boat and human alike.

Yet Cyrus stayed out of the fight. Darek wondered why, then saw a massive squid, some yellow parody of a monster, crawl from the water. The thing's giant tentacles could strike dragons from the sky as easily as a flying fish snatched insects.

Darek saw it all at once. Serle and his growing band would raid on their slow march to Rivenclaw Island. First Manatee, then Sprawlee Island, and finally Swordish Isle—a crushing loss for the Black Claws.

A dozen of Livis's ships broke away from Serle's fleet in a surprise attack on their northern flanks. Darek's heart leapt.

Jace led the charge upon the first serpents on his orange dragon Waxmoon, and Meira and Bree rode their dragons at his side. Briad guarded their rear, no less brave in his battle yell. Darek wheeled in battle to join them. He threw flaming harpoons, engulfing several of Serle's pirate ships in flames.

Jace roared over the wind, "Darek, take Vesinex and Hasilnor with those sun devices and blast the serpents in the first wave. We'll cover you!" His claw hand lashed out to make mincemeat of an enemy pirate rider's arm, shredding leather and biting to the bone. The enemy rider gave a shriek of agony and careened off, clutching at the crimson ruin of his limb.

Darek's two wing warriors, wielding the solaricuses strapped to their dragons' backs, moved forward.

Darek reined in beside Vesinex. "Aim for those serpents below! I'll go after Cyrus's monster myself."

The two riders spurred their mounts down toward the coast where the serpents smashed their tails and ravaged the shore.

Silver Eye roared in, charging Dendrok and ducking a long, whistling orange flare that spewed from the drago-serpent's jaws. Her depth perception was not perfect with her missing eye, but she compensated with her acute hearing. The drago-serpent had become deadlier than ever. A few feet closer and the thing would have roasted him alive.

By Kraton, when had Cyrus added fire breath to his flying serpent's arsenal? The serpentish creature was much larger than before. Darek chewed his lips in grim thought and circled back to charge from behind, aiming the solaricus at the monster's face. As it turned, a red glare lit up from between its teeth. Far away a similar glare flared at Kraton's tip. Was the creature drawing power from the volcano?

Darek slammed a fist into the weapon's firing mechanism as he banked in to engage the flying demon. The solaricus's ray shot out, scorching the area behind Dendrok's neck. The beast writhed in agony. Smoke rose from the bluish-green scales on its back now turned black, but the blast did not penetrate the flesh, not deeply enough.

Darek looked up as the sun dipped behind a bank of dark clouds. Kraton, curse his luck! The devices drew alchemic power from the sun, but the clouds now robbed them of their power. He could see the other dragon riders struggling to flank Dendrok, wary of getting charred by its red-hot breath. Others sought to contain the serpents below in a perimeter. Solaricus blasts had leveled some serpents and they lay in broken bits on the water, but many still slithered through the waves like worms, hunting the few surviving Visilee ships.

Cyrus joined the battle and unleashed a surge of mage fire at riders and Visilee ships alike in a terrifying display of might. Darek's heart sank. Could his magic prevail against such violent darkness? Agrippa's words came back to him in a rush.

"...Keep longtime foes within arm's reach, Darek. Even dead ones have a knack of turning up at the worst of times."

Darek flew in for another strike, though it may cost him everything.

He watched as Vesinex whistled down in fury, his face carved in a grimace of hate. The untold loss of Red Claw clansmen had affected everybody. As the sun peeked through a rent in the clouds, he engaged the button and a saffron beam shot out and took the head off a nearby serpent undulating in the chop. The rider shouted in triumph and banked his dragon in sharp curve. He fired again. A green serpent's neck smoked a foul reeking blue smoke as it thrashed about the water, licking at the burning flesh.

Laughing in wild glee, he dipped down to knock out another beast, but he coursed too low and a prowling serpent with yellow eyes goggling above the waves, piked up fangs like an eel and flashing teeth tore at the underbelly of his dragon. Down went Vesinex to the cresting waves and rider and solaricus were lost from sight.

Dendrok's jaws peeled wide. It spat a tongue of flame which scorched three of Jace's riders. Dragons and riders fell in charred lumps to the waiting serpents below. The demon swooped low and one of Livis's pirate ships went up in flames as it spat fire. Masts crackled like tinder. Livis's band fell back under the onslaught.

A cloud of arrows blotted out the sky from the Cape Spear marksmen, pincushioning several of the serpents, but only seemed to anger Dendrok.

While Meira and Bree struggled to keep the serpents at bay, Briad got separated and caught in the crossfire. He recovered from a swipe by a pirate rider and jabbed his ten foot spear at the grinning's man's chest. Briad ducked and feinted, just as Jace had taught him, his spear tip sinking into the man's ribs as his dragon kicked out, slashing the eyes out of the enemy dragon.

Cyrus rode in on Valoré to finish off Briad.

"Look out!" Darek called.

Briad saw the attack coming and spurred his dragon in a steep dive toward the water. Not fast enough. Cyrus's violent green ray caught him broadside, and the young man glowed in green fire for an instant, the starfish amulet of protection shielding him. Then he simply was gone. A deafening blast turned the air to liquid fire as the protection failed and Braid was incinerated.

Darek gave a wordless scream and dove in to attack. Cyrus raised his staff in time to block, but he and his dragon went spinning in a dizzy loop.

Darek pressed forward, but was pushed back by a stream of Dendrok's fire. He threw up his mage shield, a blue encircling dome, but dozens of other dragon riders were caught in the blaze and fell charred in its wake.

In an instant their numbers were cut in half.

Jace rallied the survivors to him and launched a concerted assault against Dendrok. The pirate riders recognized him as their leader and pounced, swarming him like bees.

Jace banked his orange dragon low, pursued by three relentless pirate riders who forced him low toward the serpents' maws. A green-eyed monster thrust up its snout and smacked one of the pursuing riders and his mount howling into the chop below. Another fanged horror snapped out, shearing off the hind legs of Waxmoon. Jace went spinning down to the water with his maimed dragon, an echoing shriek dying in his throat.

Darek's heart plummeted in dismay. "Jace!" he cried. He turned Silver Eye in his direction, but he was too far away. He couldn't help him. Dragon riders and serpents harried Silver Eye from all sides. Fercifor, the green-and-black bellied beast rose out of the water to face him, as if remembering the power of his mage fire from the battle of Cape Spear.

Jace struggled in the water as three serpents surged his way. The pirate dragon rider struggled nearby and clawed his way toward Jace. Jace kicked him the chest and sunk claw hand into his sea dragon's back, clambering up on its hide as the dragon turned to nip at him. But Jace, ever the dragon whisperer, gained control of the beast and clung to its slippery hide as the serpents lunged in for the kill. On a sharp command, up winged the dragon over the waves before the serpents could tear at him. In a single formation, they lunged in to devour the unfortunate pirate dragon rider and Jace's dying orange dragon, Waxmoon.

"Kraton!" Darek shook his head in a dream daze. What else could go wrong?

He turned as Meira's shriek drew his attention. Breaking free from the Cape Spear formation, she had lured a pair of pirate dragon riders to chase her. Bree gave a wild shout and coursed to her aid.

Two harpoons arched from the pirate ships below, but Bree dodged them. Typhoon swung about with a snarl and Meira leaned over to rake the first pirate's crown with her long-barbed spear. The man fell limp in the saddle, feet dangling from the stirrups. The other shot up to hack at her with his longsword, but Bree smashed Storm's snout into his dragon's flanks and jabbed her spear between the joint of the dragon's armor. Bewildered, the man flew off his saddle and into the waves, his dragon screeching roars of confusion.

Jace, on his new mount, ordered the others spread out into a rotating formation. They swung up and down, repeatedly attacking and retreating, stabbing spear and swords and ploughing arrows at serpent flesh. The Cape

Spear riders tried to unseat Cyrus, but he picked them off one by one with his green fire of death.

Darek readied Silver Eye for a dive straight toward the murderous fiend.

Chapter 20.

Nameless Isle

Darek's reined Silver Eye up short as he saw Livis's boat below bombarded by pirate cannon fire. He faltered, then swung Silver Eye low over her ship. Her forces were in desperate need. Harpoons ripped into her ship's hull from every side. Her dozen ships were beaten back, suffering terrible losses.

Gritting his teeth, Darek crossed his arms in a V and loosed a streak of mage fire against the first of Serle's attacking vessels. He positioned Silver Eye between them. Suddenly, a harpoon flew from the deck of Livis's ship and sank deep into Silver Eye's flank. A gasp died in Darek's throat.

Had that shot come from Livis' s ship? No! He looked back and saw Livis herself behind the harpoon gun. She had fired at him? *Betrayed!* He saw a strange green glow in Livis's eyes. Cyrus must have bewitched her.

It was too late now. His dragon lurched and fell with a screech, twisting in the air and clawing at the harpoon sticking out of her. Livis snapped out of her dark trance and put hands to her mouth in horror as Darek and his dragon fell crashing into the water.

He coughed up brine as his head bobbed to the surface. Silver Eye struggled twenty arms' lengths away. He dogpaddled toward her as she thrashed and writhed in pain. He dove down, trying to remove the harpoon wedged in her side. It had bit deep. He drew himself toward her, bellowing in anguish as she spun in helpless circles, leaking dark blood into the water.

Darek sent his mind out; healing magic poured out upon his dragon as he struggled to save her. The metal had pierced a sensitive organ and Darek now knew there was nothing to be done. His dragon was dying before his eyes. She met his eyes for a last time before wheezing a gust of seawater. Then her once powerful limbs fell still and she sank beneath the waves.

Darek loosed a howl of rage. Disbelief and sorrow warred in his heart as if he must be in some mad dream. "Cyrus!"

As the tears rushed to Darek's eyes, he kicked himself away from the bloodied water. His first meeting with Silver Eye flashed before his eyes.

The black-robed figure drew near, hovering on his red dragon over the grieving Dragon Mage. "Ah, the loss of a dragon. A terrible blow to bear. Now, Mage boy, you will also die." Cyrus raised his hands. "Dendrok comes."

Sharks began to circle in the water below as Darek struggled in the swells.

A shark fin poked nearby. He quailed as it dragged down a dead body. Others looped around, circling for prey, dead or alive and serpents were on the prowl. He could see their ugly, mottled heads and spiked tails plunging them closer as the sharks finned about the water. He swam for some wreckage bobbing in the waves while Cyrus hovered over him like a black ghoul.

As Darek angled toward the bale of cargo, Cyrus raised hands for a crippling strike, giving time for his serpent to finish the job, but Bree came shrieking in on Storm and landed beside him. Darek clawed onto the dragon's back.

Cyrus loosed a cry of rage. "Away, you wench! I'll kill you for that."

"Darek, hold on! Are you alright?" She whisked him off into the air as Cyrus's twisted ray flew aside.

Darek shivered. "I'm not so good, Bree." He clung to her back, quivering.

"I told you not to trust that pirate girl. Now look, your dragon is dead! And you almost with it."

"It wasn't her, Bree. Cyrus's spells. I saw it—"

"How do you know?"

"I know!" Kraton but he wished the Red Claw fleet would get here and cannon and harpoon all these fiends. But they were half an hour away at best. It was him and the riders. No one else.

With red rage, Darek turned about and reached out with his dragon power to summon the nearest Black Claw dragon, riderless, swooping over its mother ship. It turned and dove toward him like a gale. He jumped off Storm's back when it was directly underneath them, ignoring Bree's choked cry. The green-scaled beast flew off as he landed and pulled himself up toward its neck. His face a mask of pure vengeance, he bid the dragon circle back to Cyrus. He would avenge Silver Eye's death and all the Red Claw citizens who had perished today. His thoughts, angry ones but clear, brimmed with power, and the power of anger tolled like a rain of fire in his blood.

Dendrok came hissing in like a plague of death.

"Slay the mage boy!" cried Cyrus, fending off the dragons that attacked him.

The drago-serpent started forward, but hesitated, unsure of the power emanating from Darek. He began to murmur the harshest spells to combat the dragon-serpent's flaming rush, the most destructive emanations committed to memory from Agrippa's spellbooks.

Yet something stayed his tongue, for another power grew inside him to replace the rage in his mind. The power to commune with dragons blotted everything else out. He reached out to Dendrok and spoke to the creature's tortured mind:

It's time for the pain to stop. You're a dragon, aren't you? Not some nasty serpent. Take your freedom. End your slavery to your dark master!

The creature turned toward Cyrus and roared. The mage raised his arms with a snort of disgust and called upon the power of his runestones. The green flare arched out and singed the drago-serpent's snout—but instead of shrinking back, it lost all reason. Dendrok, a rippling mass of muscle, charged his master, sinking its fangs in Valoré's hide and sending Cyrus reeling to the water below.

The runestones fell out of Cyrus's grasp and he plunged into the dark water. He gripped his mage staff, but it was not enough. His serpents turned with a hiss.

Dendrok dove down to finish off his hated master.

Cyrus blinked in utter disbelief, his magic faltering at the worst time and his confidence with it. At the loss of his runestones, his dark arts seemed to desert him. Only Fercifor came to his aid. The other serpents rallied against the cruel mage.

The great black-green worm Fercifor reared out of the waves like a demonic cobra, snapping fangs at the descending drago-serpent. Dendrok reared and flailed front and hind claws ripping out chunks of flesh from Fercifor's tube-like body.

Cape Spear riders surged forth to attack dragons and serpents while Dendrok and Fercifor tore at each other.

Now did Fercifor catch Dendrok at the base of the tail and whip its serpentish neck like an attack hound, flinging the drago-serpent far out in the water.

Cyrus's lips quivered in horror, as if recalling Agrippa's fateful words.

"You see it now, don't you, mage?" boomed Darek down at him. "You can't control these serpents. Agrippa was right. See your own beasts turn on you."

Cyrus howled a miserable cry. "No, you are wrong! Fercifor defends me. Look, he is loyal!"

"Fercifor is not enough and he is lost too. Watch how Jace and his riders slay all your serpents."

Cyrus lanced his staff which he gripped in his fist like a jealous child and flung up a ray. But the ray was nothing that didn't sputter and die against Darek's most basic shield.

The serpents, now masterless and frenzied with blood, sprang upon Dendrok floundering in the water. The serpents tore at its wings and slithered in and about, hissing and biting at each other for spoils. Darek, despite his desire to see the end of this horror, felt sorry that innocent creature.

Jace, Meira, Bree and the others swarmed in on the serpents like spiders amongst a swarm of flies.

Even Windbiter, hovering from afar, did not come to aid Cyrus. Perhaps the mage's spell had been completely broken, for a glimmer of recollection seemed to spark in the old grey dragon's eye with the memory of how Cyrus had let him roast in the cave while it blew hot breath to heat the egg that would become Dendrok.

Cyrus's magic was at an end.

But a strange feeling washed over Darek as the sea churned with blood and he glimpsed a new menace. A yellow-bellied squid speeding with hungry eyes toward its long-awaited prey, tentacles arching and plunging it forth in bursts of speed. It reached a gray tentacle and wrapped it about the flailing mage's waist, pulling him toward its gaping two-toothed.

Two more seconds and the monster would eat him alive.

But a power moved within Darek of which he had no control. He sent a streamer of fire from his hands that shore the tentacle in half. Cyrus fell back in the waves, limp. In dreamlike trance, Darek sent his new dragon swooping down to snatch up a length of rope from the wreckage. He tied an end fast to his dragon's harness and swung over Cyrus who grabbed the moving line in a grateful fist. He pulled the mage up into the air. All the painful deaths the mage had caused swirled in his mind, and all those that he should rightfully instil on the mage, but none of those would come to pass. Out to open water he flew, south and east, while the riders watched in astonishment. He summoned Meshoar and Winguard whose riders had both fallen in battle. He would need those beasts for the task ahead.

Along the way, he ignored Cyrus's yells and insults. Without staff and runestones, the mage seemed powerless.

Also deathly afraid of letting go of the line and dropping in the middle of the ocean. Was he scared of the serpents and squids that haunted the seas? Perhaps cursing himself for the depth of his dependency on his talismans? Darek gave a sinister laugh.

They passed over a lone ship, flying the black skull banner of fleeing pirates. It was Serle's ship tacking along the dim seas, trying to escape the battle now not in his favor.

"A good catch, boy," Serle called up at him, seeing the bedraggled mage. "Give the wizard to me. "I'll have his gizzard for breakfast at what he planned to do with my daughter."

"Be gone, Serle!" snarled Darek. "You're a treacherous rogue, if you're anything. Not a man I'd trust with even such a simple task. Your fate awaits you, I think. Look, the Black Claws still have teeth, and I see the Red Claws have arrived. Think you can outrun two enemies now?"

The captain turned a glance even as Darek spoke. Many enemy schooners pursued him—a fleet of Black Claw and Red Claw ships from both sides, allied for the first time in a hundred years. The pirate captain slammed his fist on the rail. Darek laughed and sped off with wizard dangling like a worm on a hook and Agrippa's dragons trailing far behind.

At last, having thought long and hard, Darek leaned over his saddle and roared down at the mage, "You who has caused so much death, Cyrus, I strip of all power and banish on some nameless isle. To never see a soul again, to live out your life in misery."

Cyrus snarled up at him. "And how are you going to do that, Mage Boy?"

"You'll see."

"Pah, I curse you, mage boy, and all your kin for the end of time. May the hex of the dark dragon strike your scions for the end of time." And he laughed a maniacal sound, for Cyrus had gone completely mad in that moment. But in the tone shivered a hint of truth that he knew something Darek did not.

"I hope you're watching this, Agrippa, wherever you are," Darek whispered, struggling to maintain the higher path. Booming an arcane phrase and with a fling of hand, he smote the wizard with the *Spell of Unbinding*, which he had been practicing for long hours in the secrecy of his room at the Rookery.

A brilliant streak of multicolor hit Cyrus in the heart, lighting him like a rainbow fish. Cyrus howled and arched his back.

"You will wake each day to the memory of your foul deeds, Cyrus, your sacrifices and twisted deeds of outrages upon man and beast, knowing you are powerless to do so again."

Cyrus gave one last screech and flinched in pain and horror as an electric shock sizzled through his body. The mage was unprepared for the eternal transformation that would strip him of his most prized powers.

"Justice is served," growled Darek. "You have life. Now get out of my sight. I never want to see your dirty face again." And he bid Meshoar and Winguard to take the broken mage far away. He cut the line and Cyrus fell into the waves and Meshoar grabbed him by the scruff of the neck and spread wings to fly south and east across the graying seas while the wizard flailed and gnashed. Winguard trailed after, a backup should the mettlesome Meshoar fail in his mission. Far away, a strange, yellow-bodied squid swam after the dragons, following an imperceptible scent that only the undead could track.

Chapter 21.

New Beginnings

Darek, leathers torn, blood-streaked and haggard, made his way back to his scattered forces. A troubling doubt still plagued his mind, that a man as crafty as Cyrus could not be contained so easily, but it did not feel right to kill the man outright. No, too swift and unavailing a punishment for one who deserved to suffer and reflect on his misdeeds. Then he remembered the bloodthirsty squid that guarded the island and a shiver crawled up his back. Cyrus would not be escaping that island too soon.

The Red Claw ships, having at last arrived, cemented their victory. In aftermath of the battle, they gathered up the pieces of the Visilee sea guard and searched for survivors. Any remaining sea serpents had fled to deeper waters. The small Black Claw force that had joined them on their way to the Three Sisters' Isles drew back to their savaged ports.

Darek's new dragon was a dependable mount, one that he'd come to respect, black with yellow stripes. He called it Phaeton for its faithful service. As he flew low over the hodgepodge of ships, his keen eyes caught sight of some commotion on a Black Claw deck. He swooped down to investigate. Two familiar pirates, hands bound behind their backs, crouched in a slave line with other pirates, joined by a common rope. Serle and Hreg. The Black Claw captain stood with his sword raised like an executioner's axe, ready to lop off the head of the first, Serle, who had caused them so much woe.

Darek thought of Livis and he made an instant decision. Urging Phaeton in a dive, he cut the line holding Hreg and Serle, snatching up the end and fastening it tight to his dragon's harness. He ignored the cries of outrage and urged his dragon skyward, the two pirate criminals were pulled from the deck and jerked up in the air by their thumbs.

A grin broke out on Darek's face, even as harpoons missed him by inches. He laughed and saluted the astonished faces of Serle and Hreg as they dangled like fish from a line. There had been too much bloodshed this day.

On sight of *The Singing Gull*, Darek swung low. He dropped his prisoner's to Livis's deck. The pirate queen sported many cuts and scratches, her hair disheveled and blood on her sea leathers, but there was nothing of the mad look he had witnessed before.

He still couldn't meet her eye. "I thought you should be the one to deal with these two," he growled. "A couple of codfish, I rescued from the bait hooks." He cut the line holding the prisoners and the two rogues rolled at Livis's feet.

She stared at her grubby father and nodded. She signaled to her harpoon master, Maquia. "Cut them loose, harpoon master. But beware their teeth, they're sharp."

"Aye, mistress, as are mine."

Serle loosed a fiery curse upon all of them. "You rotten guttersnipe. I surely don't mind my neck being saved from those Black Claw scum, but did it have to be you?"

Darek tipped his head in a grin. "We can't always be choosy about our saviors, can we?"

Darek sent Phaeton onward. "Lots to do, Livis. We will meet up soon." He circled back to Visilee even as an emptiness stole over him. There would never be another dragon like Silver Eye.

Livis waved and a sad quiver touched her lip, at the sight of him no longer riding his silver dragon.

Though heartbroken, his spirit felt lifted of a weight of duty. Phaeton snorted, complaining at last over such exertion following the battle. Darek soothed him with soft words.

Of Cyrus's dragons, only Windbiter had survived and Darek took the trembling beast under his wing to add to the diminishing forces at the Rookery. He hoped in time to heal the damage done to Windbiter's mind. He returned to the

Rookery to find Meira with a great white bandage wrapped around her brow. She had been awarded the title of 'Assistant Combat Instructor' and sworn an oath to protect the Red Claws from further invasion.

Bree was cut and bruised, but still alive. Two of Jace's ribs were cracked and his claw arm wrenched, but he was as stoic as ever. Darek mourned Briad's death along with those of many others.

Darek sighed. At rough count, three quarters of the riders and dragons had died in the battle of Visilee. There would be cries of backlash from Cape Spear.

Evren, the glib, slick-tongued merchant-chief, could maunder on all he wanted about Jace's incompetence and the risk he incurred in taking the Cape Spear forces to their near decimation, but nothing could change the facts—without the Red Claw intervention, Dragon Sea would be under the dominion of Cyrus right now.

"You still have not told us what you did with that madman," grumbled Meira on the Rookery training yard. "He's escaped death before."

Darek shook his head. "No, Meira. Cyrus has his old friend to keep him company—a squid." She wrinkled her nose at the memory of that creature and traded frowns with Bree. Darek gestured. "Somehow I don't think he'll be swimming to safety or building a raft too soon. Last I checked, his undead monster was haunting the shores like a predatory ghoul. One of his zombified experiments, I guess.

The creature'll come to haunt the villain for the rest of his days."

"Good riddance!" Bree shivered.

"Just be sure the blackguard doesn't escape," grunted Jace. "I'd feel better if Cyrus's head were on a pike, or he was locked in one of our jails."

"No, Jace. Cyrus is stripped of his powers. You can rest assured. He'll wake each day of his life to the memory of his foul deeds knowing he'll never be able to wield magic again."

There were grumbles at that, some hear, hears, and nothing more was said. Though many asked which island Cyrus was on, Darek would not tell anyone.

He devoted his energies to regenerating the dragon amulets. After many unsuccessful attempts in his private study, he at last found a successful combination. Even the most stubborn young dragons returned to the stalls. Waving the amulet in front of their feral faces, they became pacified by the crystal glint of the red-gleaming stones and Darek loosed a sigh of relief. It had been a difficult set of magic to get right. Two sets he gave to Jace. One set he kept for himself. For the first time, he could truly call himself a 'Dragon Mage'.

Darek decided to stay on at the Rookery, as both teacher and student. He returned to Valkyrie often as his private retreat. There he set up a shrine for Agrippa and continued his mage studies using Agrippa's extensive collection of books and talismans. A startling realization gripped him one day. He knew he would one day need to find an apprentice to take over his duties when he was gone.

Darek at last returned to Livis's side. She had never forgiven herself for her last act of madness in harpooning Silver Eye, despite Darek's reassurances that it had not been her fault.

She greeted him with a sigh. "What a pawn I've been in this whole game. What a fool."

"We all were," said Darek, stroking her back. With his support, she took over for Serle as resident leader of the decimated pirate bands. They signed a peace treaty with the Dragonclaw Islands, focusing on rebuilding their colony.

"What did you do with Serle?" Darek asked.

"Serle's been relegated to bosun of *The Persephone*," she said. "Skarlee's acting captain so he can keep an eye on him."

"Good to hear. Now let's focus on what matters." He held her tight, placing his hand on the swell of her belly.

"The pirates will never accept me as their chief," he said in a quiet voice.

"In time, they may. Especially if you bring them dragons and gold."

"If they won't accept me, at least they will accept our son—but I want him to become a Dragon Mage, not a pirate."

Livis smirked. "Oh they'll accept *her* alright, but why can't she be both?"

THE DRAGON SEA CHRONICLES: THREE BOOK SERIES

I

EPILOGUE

Some months later, Darek landed in a glade on Valkyrie Island to meet with Livis while her ship anchored in the bay by the dragon caves. Now that she was pirate queen, she commanded a much larger and faster vessel, but still sailed *The Singing Gull* for nostalgic reasons. Her belly had grown to near bursting, already ripe with the child they would have together.

"What shall we call *her*?" asked Livis.

"We should call *him* Grippa" Darek remarked, wide-eyed.

"Or Aggra?"

He shook his head and sighed. "You're something else."

She brushed him a cool glance.

"Okay, Zara then. In the old pirate tongue, Zara means 'warrior'."

"It has a nice ring to it, Livis. Okay, Zara it is."

They both lay on the grass, holding each other in their arms. Darek felt a soothing, pervading warmth; harmony and peace reigned in the island realms. Tracing a finger over Livis's belly, he could not help but recall the bitter curse Cyrus had laid on him and his descendants. Why it flashed in his mind at that moment, he did not know, only that he thrust it aside as quickly as it had come.

"What's wrong?" Livis murmured.

"Nothing. Just a stupid thought."

They watched the clouds pass by, calling out the shapes of each one. So happy, oblivious to the fact that even in defeat, Cyrus's magic had put a spell on the child that would change the course of the Dragonclaw islands forever…

- To subscribe to the authors' newsletters and be the first notified when new books release, please visit www.cavecreekpublishing.com/dragons/

THE DRAGON SEA CHRONICLES: THREE BOOK SERIES

SAMPLE CHAPTERS

BOOK 2: THE WOLF OF DORIAN GRAY SERIES

PURGATORY OF THE WEREWOLF

BRIAN S. FERENCE

THE DRAGON SEA CHRONICLES: THREE BOOK SERIES

Chapter 1.

The Wolf of Dorian Gray: A Fresh Start

Dorian felt uncharacteristically well rested after the night spent in Sage's musty, yet comfortable mahogany four-poster bed. The rusty springs and well-worn frame sagged in all the right places. The several layers of feather mattresses seemed to envelop his body with an inviting embrace. The goose down pillows may have been old and faded, but the feathers inside were still soft and smooth. In a bed like this, it was easy to pretend that the events of the past week were simply part of some nightmare. He shook his head and cleared the thought from his mind.

He closed his eyes with a sigh of contentment. With a flash, there appeared the snarling face and hideous form of the monster. Its bloodshot eyes knew where he was hiding and the long claws extended toward him, dripping with blood. Dorian's eyes shot open. He had lingered here for too long. He needed to formulate a plan to escape before the beast found him again. He would wait until nightfall to leave. Then he would gather some funds and leave London immediately.

Dorian spent that afternoon chopping firewood with the old steel maul that he had found sunken into an oak stump. Once he had sharpened the edges, the ash logs split beneath his swing like butter. The repetition was soothing and he continued for several hours. He felt like each block of wood was a terrible deed from his former life. With each downswing, he smashed the memory into a thousand pieces. He cast his shirt aside, his muscles strained with each rhythmic blow until the hot rays of the sun pulled a sheen of sweat from his skin.

After he was done, he brewed a pot of black tea using an antique Hester Bateman teapot. He had discovered it hanging forlornly above the stove. It was tarnished and dented, but it made the finest pot of tea Dorian had ever tasted. If only he could stay in this simple life forever. But he knew it couldn't last.

Dorian would have to sneak into his own mansion without detection. He remembered his blood staining the hardwood floor. He had been gone long enough that anyone who saw the room would certainly think him dead. He would return to his home and gather any small valuables that had not already been spirited away by the servants upon hearing of his death. But the most important thing was the painting. That wretched painting that had been the source of all his pain and misery. Yet it still held his secret. To leave it behind and unprotected would be unthinkable. He must retrieve the painting and vanish before anyone discovers he is still alive.

Despite Sage's attempts to explain it to him, it was still beyond his understanding of how that painting had linked his soul to the wolf. She had started the process by dabbling in Romani magic and had mentioned something about *The Spell of Making* to increase the realism of her painting. She told Dorian that she had foolishly mixed his blood and the wolf's with her brushes and applied them to the canvas to achieve a deeper color of red. According to Sage, her biggest mistake was combining these two actions with the third Romani art of naming. Sage had named the wolf cub that they had rescued *Little Dorian Grey* and put all of herself into bringing the canvas to life. She had succeeded in the worst possible way and it had cost Sage her life.

Dorian had not even cared about her death at the time. How could he have committed all those terrible deeds? He had killed innocent men, and even burned a man alive. As Dorian embraced his most base desires and set down his destructive path, the once innocent wolf had slowly begun to change. It became more gruesome and violent as if it were the living embodiment of his many sins. Dorian, however, was completely unchanged. He had gained eternal youth. Dorian was beginning to suspect that he might have developed other strange abilities as well.

It was his fault that Sage was dead. He had seen her killed right in front of him and done nothing. Perhaps that was when he had lost his soul. But that was all behind him now. Before he had awakened in the forest, he had been the real beast. Now he could feel the weight of his conscience and the fullness of his soul within his body again. He was a monster no longer.

There was still a very real monster out there somewhere. The werewolf. The sun had finally faded in the sky, casting a reddish light that played off the clouds and the dust of the fields. He slid back his chair and picked up a threadbare coat that he had found forgotten among Sage's other possessions. He walked through to her art studio where he and Sage had spent so many days in innocence and laughter. He remembered with a smile the image of his friend at her easel as he played with the small wolf cub. Dorian and Sage had been best friends once and could have been more. But he had been so selfish and in love with the thrill of bedding as many women as he could. He saw now that she had loved him completely, maybe even more than her art.

His eyes felt moist and blurry as he looked at the empty easel still there in the corner. *She would never paint again.* "I'm sorry Sage. Please forgive me."

Dorian turned and strode from the room. He closed and locked the door tightly behind him. Knowing he could never come back again, he took one more look around in the fading light. Then Dorian walked slowly to the woodpile and lifted the heavy handle of the steel maul. His thoughts went to the werewolf that prowled the night and his hand tucked the weapon into his coat.

Chapter 2.

The Crime Scene

Detective Inspector Gerald Clarke removed his black-wool felt bowler and ran his sweaty palm through the rapidly thinning hair in the center of his head. He inspected the deep slashes in the wood floor that followed no discernible pattern. They were long and numerous, as if made by a deranged lunatic stabbing at the defenseless floor repeatedly. Splintered shards of glass and twisted metal littered the ground. The scene gave voice to the violent struggle that had taken place here. *Fascinating.* There was far too little blood to suggest that the victim had met his demise here as *The Telegraph* and the local constables had reported.

He was at a complete loss as to how Mr. Gray's assailant had entered or exited the second story room. The interviews he had conducted with the servants all told the same story of an eccentric gentleman who regularly locked himself away at night alone. The five-centimeter thick steel bars on the door stood undiminished in a testament to their strength. Two constables had first reported the room soundly locked and completely empty. The Valet eventually turned up completely unaware of what had transpired and smelling of cheap wine from a night spent at a nearby Pub. He swore that only Mr. Gray had the key that unlocked the bars to the room—and he had vanished without a trace. They summoned a locksmith, but the surly man had been unable to bypass the stubborn and expensive mechanisms preventing their entry. This had blocked him from making a more thorough investigation of the scene and limited him to observations made from outside of the room.

With that entrance eliminated, the assailant could have only entered through the large window overlooking the gardens below. The glass to the window was shattered and the metal frame bent and twisted outwards as if from an explosion. The lack of any burn marks made that theory unlikely. So what could have caused that level of damage? He had already examined the peaty soil in the garden below the window and the red clay tile of the roof above. Regrettably, the steady rain that had begun falling two days before his arrival had scrubbed away any clear signs that might be found there.

The only other items of note he observed in the room were a single overturned chair, a faded looking table, and a torn screen on the floor. That and of course the presumed murder weapon. It was a silver Garland knife covered in dried blood. The small blade appeared to have an engraved handle and was the sort of instrument that a nobleman would use for opening his letters.

The inspector reached his stout fingers through the bars. He needed to get through these confounding bars. Squeezing between them certainly wouldn't work. He turned to stare at his reflection in the small mirror hanging in the hallway. He was a short and portly fellow, with long wispy sideburns. He assured his wife he did not grow them out to compensate for his diminishing hairline. No, the additional hair on the sides of his face merely added some warmth during the many cold nights spent in the service of Scotland Yard.

An audible click sounded and a smile came over the locksmith's bearded face. "Ah, that's got it. There you are, Inspector. A fine piece of workmanship this was, but no match for a determined mind."

"A determined mind can overcome any problem, no matter how difficult. Thank you for your service, my good man. One of the constables downstairs will have your fee for you. You have my personal thanks as well as that of Scotland Yard. Constable McDonaugh, please come in here immediately."

CHRIS TURNER AND BRIAN FERENCE

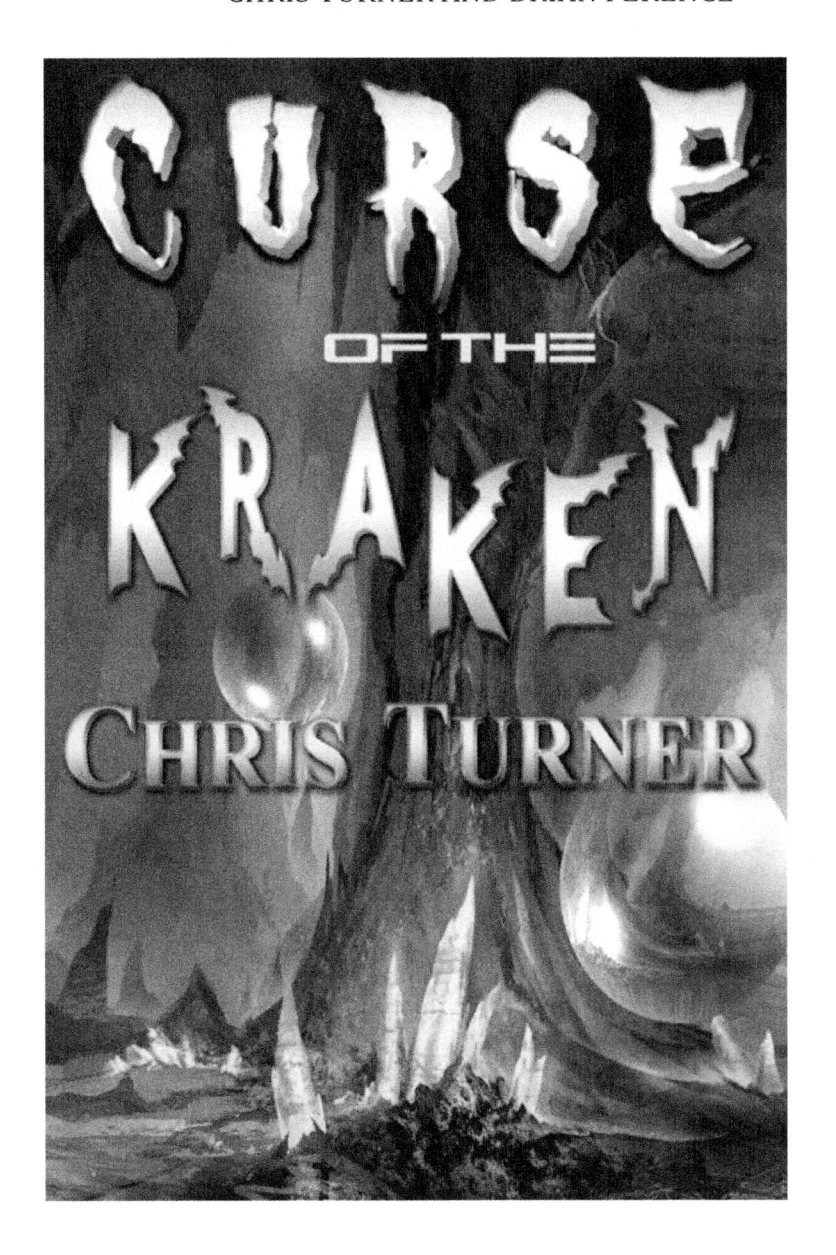

CURSE OF THE KRAKEN

Chris Turner

THE DRAGON SEA CHRONICLES: THREE BOOK SERIES

CURSE OF THE KRAKEN

Chris Turner

I : LORE OF THE ANCIENTS

In the year 712, three shrewd mages, Anamog, Dranmog and Thanmog, became the elite *Magi Consules* to King Pyrmog at Mog palace. Anamog, wise, thoughtful, experienced, was the maven, the unspoken leader, who founded the group, and was wary of the power of the dark arts. Dranmog, edgier, was prone to a degree of risk-taking while Thanmog resided somewhere in the middle. The latter maintained a special skill of the taming of the beasts, this hooded monkish figure. Whereas Animog guarded an aristocratic face, rich with sombre features and a cultured tongue known to articulate wise and careful phrases, Dranmog was wily, with cat eyes of the softest amber, and graced with a darting expression of certain penetrating compass. He was forthright with chuckles that often irked listeners who did not realize what he found so amusing. It was more precise to say that of all in the realm, these three were the intellectual force behind the kingdom's functioning, creating policies that king Pyrmog would be a fool not to heed.

It had been nine hundred years after the third great ice age that the north-dwelling gnomes had migrated down from their blue-glittering ice caves and founded the fortress of Elsmaere on the bleak mound at Mog. They had come to be the forerunners of the Mogel race—a short, burly, dark-complexioned people with skin like leather, wide, tough heads and uncannily deep olive-green eyes. These gnomes were squat, no more than four feet tall, and enjoyed two main loves in life: sacred magic and the crafting of stonework, which included the finely-wrought structures of vaulted archways, adorning pillars, buttressed gothic stairwells, and graceful scrollwork, reminiscent of the Mogel famous palace, which had its beginnings in the earliest of times as a single turreted keep.

One day in the fall of 729 the three mages embarked on a pilgrimage. The 'quest', as it was called—which was surprisingly much against the will of Anamog. He could sense ill coming of the venture, but through one means or another, acceded to the cause anyway. It was Dranmog's idea, the youngest of the three, who with great ardency urged the others to comply and search out the krakens' treasure. It was reckoned past the fabled snow downs into the haunted land of the ice crags. This was the place of their heritage and interested Anamog at least for its mystery. For two moons Dranmog had been digging through mouldering chests in the cellars and crypts filled with tattered remains of the Sisenian Scrolls. Here were writ hints of ancient treasure amongst the lost antiques of the five lands. The Scrolls, whose origin was shrouded in myth, were quilled by the long line of scribes, a doughty folk who had recorded events since the times before the Great Pillaging. Dranmog had read more than most, and one eerie reference to a fabled beast, or beasts—*krakens*, which were reputed to live in holes in the hills in the frosty fastness where the ice gleams an aquamarine blue and the snow sparkles silver. Krakens learned to 'collect' shiny things, so it was told, most beautiful and pleasing to eyes. The beasts flew hither to the southlands to acquire glittering items of beauty and resplendence. Terrible and ferocious was their means of locomotion: forty-foot wings that edged the sky with thorn-tipped spikes, flapping hideously like mechanical crocodiles. Gory-pointed snouts mantled razor-sharp teeth; bony-finned backs glinted gold and hooked claws dangled. With wicked gleaming magenta eyes, the creatures swooped, waving their hammer-pronged tails, and with one fell sweep crumbled the mightiest towers of the Valkorian people along the eastern shores of the Emerald Sea and lay low the strongest outposts of Kusse and Neanz farther away in the realm of the plains where dwelled the giants. Hungrily, the krakens would savour the spoils. The flesh of men and ogres they would eat, but the jewels, shiny and twinkling, they licked up with relish with their horrid black tongues, regardless of the scintillating sword hafts and shining blades clenched between their teeth. The treasure chests piled high with necklaces, diadems, sceptres, pendants and lolled at the back of their throats. The beating of their wings was like the creak of castle gates as they tore across the sundered sky, whilst the denizens of Valkoria and Ogredur, who had been raped of their treasures, would whip out their pikes and curse the krakens while sadly picking up the pieces, repairing the damage wrought upon their citadels.

Dranmog translated a curious riddle from the Scrolls.

"Caves of old where krakens and gold,
Lie in darkness and dream, so it's been told,
In mouldering depths an intrepid one finds,
The unnameable things which always bind,
That which is more precious than treasures bold,
Glinting brighter than silver, brighter than gold,
A vessel guarding secrets never been told—"

"I say there may exist a chance that this enchanted plunder remains," he cried.

"And what of these beasts—these krakens?" argued Thanmog.

"I've heard nothing but similar horror about their lot," attested Anamog.

"How do you propose we contend with the like of these hellions, when and if we find these mythical caves?" demanded Thanmog.

"Do not be pessimistic!" Dranmog muttered. "For long seasons we have fine-tuned our magic. Surely we can make a go of it? No creature is immortal. All the monsters can't have survived."

Thanmog tugged at his beard.

"It has been an age since the beasts have come down to ruin and pillage," Dranmog went on in his conniving voice. "Surely krakens must die sometime? Why do we not investigate the truth of the riddle? The guardians are likely piles of dust now—and yes, Anamog, I agree, the enchanted brooch of Olion may still exist in the plunder."

Dranmog and Thanmog turned to face their leader, awaiting his ruling, for his decision would be final. Eldest of the lot, Anamog stood pensive, frowning, with eyes narrowed and big black brows twitching, the weight of ages on his shoulders.

"We shall go, brother Dranmog," he sighed, "—as you suggest. But I sense no good to come of it." His voice betrayed his qualms. "It is a long and difficult trek to the Fiasma Hills. We will need a few moons to get there and back."

"That we shall," responded Dranmog promptly, and with more enthusiasm than his usual. "But there may be other items of interest for the finding. You heard the riddle: *That which is more precious than gold.* Is this not a glaringly obvious lure worth the chance?"

"Perhaps."

Dranmog scoffed. "What would we be as mages if we did not pursue our dreams?" His voice had gathered an echo of passion in its momentum as he edged closer to the old mage.

Anamog, who had grown wiser and more cautious in his years, demurred. He saw only too well his fellow's flawed plan. "Adventure is all good in moderate doses, Dranmog, but not on ill-planned impulse. In haste, a venture as this could be watchword for disaster." He looked deeply into his fellow mage's eyes; they were so full of hope, and an unbending striving he had seen far too often in others. Anamog hesitated. He saw a miniature version of himself from the past. In distant days he was Dranmog's mentor and had often wondered whether his pupil had chosen the right path . . . Ah, well, so was life. Dranmog, stripling acolyte who had shown great promise in the early thaumaturgical arts, was not grounded in restraint . . .

"Fate be it that your eyes wandered over that excerpt, Dranmog," he acceded wistfully. "Still, after all these seasons, it baffles me what strange paths our deeds lead us on to. The king shall not be pleased with our news."

"Bother the king!" laughed Dranmog. "Our monarch too often depends on us for strength. We are *Mages*—not petty politicians. Is it not time that dear old Pyrmog learned to rule on his own?"

"Calm your tongue," warned Anamog. He paused, considering. Clearly, he was assailed with some doubt. "Yet perhaps . . ." he mused. His mind was wandering in other regions. Why the sudden change in Dranmog? The mage was eager for discovery and plunder, no doubt—but what had infected his already zealous overconfidence these days?

The old mage chose his words with care, "For the nonce, we must help rule Mog—to keep peace and prosperity in the hands of the people. It is our duty—not the royalty's. Without us, the wisest of kings or queens would have turned to mischief and war as we have all seen many times. More than just mages we are—we are statesmen..."

Dranmog stared dumbly at his master. He had spoken with haste—yet he resented Anamog's sanctimony. Ambition was one thing, but he was no fool. Plans for future glory occupied his churning mind. He was a ship caught between two boiling waters. Anamog would be passing into his dotage... *yet he was still young.* And who would supersede the old master?

About The Authors

BRIAN S. FERENCE lives in Cave Creek, Arizona with his wife Rachel and three children Nathan, Lena, and Victoria. He has always had a passion for reading and writing from a young age. Brian loves new experiences, which has included operating his own company, traveling the world, working as a project manager, diving with sharks, and anything creative or fun. He is always up for a new adventure such as writing or other artistic pursuits.

CHRIS TURNER, writer of fantasy, adventure, and science fiction. Visual artist, musician. Chris's books include: The Timelost, The Dim Zone, Avenger : a swords and skulls fantasy, Beastslayer : Rise of the Rgnadon, The Relic Hunter series, Denibus Ar, The Rogues of Bindar series, Fantastic Realms and Future Destinies. And read all of Chris's free books here: www.innersky.ca/booktrack

OTHER BOOKS

The Wolf of Dorian Gray Series:

- Book 1: A Werewolf Spawned by the Evil of Man
- Book 2: Purgatory of the Werewolf
- Book 3: Lupari – Werewolf Hunter

Werewolf M.D. – A Paranormal Romance Series:

- Werewolf MD (pen name Taylor Haiden)
- Werewolf Epidemic
- Coming Soon: Werewolf Pandemic

Dragon Sea Chronicles

- Dragonclaw Dare – Prequel
- Mage Reborn – Dragon Sea Chronicles Book 1
- Dragon Mage – Dragon Sea Chronicles Book 2

Chris Turner

- Dragon Lords
- Dragon of Skar
- Denibus Ar
- The Dim Zone
- The Relic Hunter

THE DRAGON SEA CHRONICLES: THREE BOOK SERIES

Printed in Great Britain
by Amazon